Blue Dragonfly

by Joseph Bingham

ISBN: Paperback 979-8-9892855-0-1
ISBN: Ebook 979-8-9892855-1-8

Design and publishing assistance by The Happy Self-Publisher.

Cover art by Arianna Guirola ariannaguirola.com

This is a work of fiction and takes place in a fantasy world. However, the people, the animals, the plants, and the diseases of this fictional world are similar to ours. The names, characters, places, and incidents are either the products of the author's imagination or used in a fictitious manner. Any resemblance to actual persons, living or dead, or actual events is purely coincidental.

CHAPTER ONE

Shushuhador

Pedí grabbed his collecting bag, doused the lantern, and went out the back of the laboratory. Only his mentor, Doctor Arias, knew of his plan to leave before dawn.

The night sky was not as dark as he had hoped. A waning half-moon shone through wispy clouds, giving the Sanctuary's orchard a dull glow. The air was heavy with moisture, and mists rose from the ground and swirled around the rows of fruit trees. Pedí used the cover of those mists and the shadows of the trees to pass out of the grounds unseen.

He paused to listen when he reached the road between the Sanctuary and the city of New Losobon. The only sound was the incessant chirping of the tree crickets.

No other creature stirred.

He was safe.

The healing mushrooms would not be found and stolen today.

The men who wanted his ancestor's cure should be sleeping, unaware that Pedí was on the way to the secret meadow. Nevertheless, when he walked through the wagon-rutted streets of the town, imaginary assassins hid behind each tree and in every shadow. He jumped when a stray cat streaked across the roadway. The walls of the clay houses that abutted the narrow passages pressed in on him like the sides of a coffin.

Pedí gasped for air before bursting out of the tomblike city and into the woods north of town. Amidst the vegetation, he could breathe again. His racing heart slowed from hummingbird speed to match that of the tree sloths hanging motionless in the forest canopy. This was his haven. The seventeen-year-old grew up in these wild lands with his mama and grandparents. His family was the last of the Idonata people.

Pedí followed a path through the trees and entered a grass and flower-filled meadow. The first gleam of morning reflected across a brook that meandered through the open space. It was similar to the stream by his grandparents' thatched hut—slow, hushed, without ripples. The penetrating odor of the thick grasses along the bank triggered a memory.

The time when he caught his first frog!

He was just five years old. After snatching the spotted amphibian from the water, he spoke to it. Instead of trying to escape, it sat unafraid on his open palm.

"Pedí!" Grandpa had shouted. "You're a Shushuhador!"

Grandpa rejoiced that his grandson was favored with a gift from the Moon Goddess. But despite Grandpa's pride in him, Pedí was nothing but a disappointment, although Grandpa never showed it. Pedí was not at all like the ancient Shushuhadors. He could talk with frogs and an occasional snake but not much else.

From across the meadow, faint footfalls sounded out of the dark forest he had just passed through. Grandpa had taught him to detect the softest sounds, the stirrings of the tiniest of creatures. This wasn't the noise of a wild pig walking, nor that of a red deer, and for certain not a forest cat. Soft, padded feline feet could move through the wilds without crunching even the driest leaves.

It had to be a human.

A low, rattling cough echoed out of the trees. Pedí recognized the sound and shook his head in disbelief.

Dark figures emerged. Hoods hid their faces, but it was the same two. The way they walked and the hunch in the older man's shoulders were unmistakable. He waited for it—the old man coughed again.

Pedí had led the men in circles a week ago, the first time they followed him. Three days ago, he hid from them in a hollow tree. But today, he had left so early that it seemed impossible for them to be here.

A large owl burst out from the forest. Its shape was just visible in the gray dawn as it winged across the glade. Pedí's courage flew away with it. The men were much too close and would soon have him.

He took off running into the trees ahead of him. His pursuer's steps followed close behind and matched each of his own. When the path turned, and he hoped they couldn't see him, Pedí climbed onto a red sandstone outcropping that rose from the ground beside the trail. It was partially hidden amidst the trees. Fifteen feet up was a deep fissure that formed a small cave.

He knew it was there, but Pedí had never entered it.

Today, he had no choice.

Pedí scrambled up the rock and plunged into the cave's shadows. The two men raced by on the trail below, visible through breaks in the trees.

His held breath escaped in relief but then caught in his throat when he glanced at the darkness of the cavity before him. Despite being only two feet in, Pedí was in trouble. Facing the men who wanted the mushrooms might have been a better decision.

He backed against the red sandstone, and his trembling fingers searched the rock's surface at his side. There was an etching in the stone.

Please let it be a depiction of her!

He turned to look. There was just enough light to make out the carved face and the long braid—still distinct despite being there for hundreds of years. Even a trace of silver paint remained on one of the strands of the plaited hair and on the crescent moon mark sculpted on her upper chest.

It was her!

It was his heroine, Adací!

The Idonata wisemen had placed Adací's symbol at the opening of every cave they discovered. Fortunately, they had not missed this one. He would need her protection if he had to go further into the cave.

Pedí startled when a voice sounded from the trail below.

"He must have left the path about here."

The men had doubled back. The older one had spoken, his words punctuated by his cough.

"Damned forest boy," the other man swore. "He tricked us again."

Pedí twisted to look down at the trail and recognized the youngest of his pursuers. He had pulled off his hood, uncovering his round, full face. It was Ivo, the ruffian who used to torment Pedí when he had worked in the sugar cane fields before he had begun his training to become a healer.

Pedí's cheeks throbbed, remembering the many times Ivo had struck him.

The older man he didn't know. That man wheezed and struggled to catch his breath. His gray beard hung several inches below his chin. He put his hand on the large knife strapped to his side as if ready to soon use it.

Ivo had a knife of his own, also in a leather sheaf. "The captain will feed us to the vultures if we don't get the mushrooms this time."

The wheezing man pulled some smoke leaf out of a pouch. "That Idonata boy is like a snake in the grass, but we'll find him. He couldn't have gone far."

"Just let me get my hands on him." Ivo opened both huge palms, then made fists. "I'll make him show us where his special toadstools grow."

The gray-bearded man rolled the dried leaves, then took out his flint and steel. "Go into the forest on that side. I'll explore these rocks."

Ivo went into the trees on the opposite side of the path. The older man pulled some frayed bark off a dead limb, then struck the flint to start a small fire in the middle of the trail. He lit the roll of smoke leaf and began puffing on it. After stamping out the flame on the trail, the man walked into the trees between the path and Pedí's hiding spot. Fragrant smoke swirled and eddied around the trees and circled the vines that hung from the towering hardwoods. Like the tentacles of a sea creature, the sweet yet pungent odor rose up and entered the cave.

Pedí glanced again into the cavern's blackness. Between the knives of his pursuers or the dangers of the cave, which one should he confront?

Caverns and cavities in New Losobon were all dangerous. Most who entered a cave would not come out alive. Many were the lairs of the spotted forest cats. Cornering one of them was suicide. Those not taken over by the giant felines were often inhabited by Wanderer spiders—the deadliest arachnid. These strange and deadly spiders didn't make webs as traps. Instead, they scattered out at night hunting for food. During the day, they sought dark shelters. Caves were their preferred hiding spot, which they adorned with their silken strands.

Pedí had cared for a man at the infirmary who a Wanderer had bitten. The unfortunate fellow had screamed from the pain of the bite despite the potions Pedí and the other healers had used. The man's sweating became profuse, followed by vomiting, and then convulsions. When all his muscles contracted and didn't relax, his breathing ceased.

Pedí shuddered when he imagined what may be waiting for him inside the cave, but also remembered the warning from Doctor Arias. *"Don't let anyone know where the mushrooms grow. You have to keep them a secret."*

Pedí pulled the clay image of Adací out from his pocket. Grandpa had given him the miniature statue. The effigy was age-old and had been endowed with power from his heroine before she had died. Pedí touched the painted mark given to her by the Moon Goddess—the tiny silver crescent on her chest. It matched the engraving on the side wall of the cave. Many centuries ago, Adací saved Pedí's ancestors from the six evil spirits who had escaped from the underworld.

"Please protect me!" he whispered to the little statue and then to the engraving.

He must risk going into the cave if it would save the new cure.

Pedí placed Adací's image back into his pocket, then entered the cavity's darkness.

The ceiling was lower after the first ten feet, and he was forced to kneel. The sandy floor was moist, and there was a musty animal smell—just from a fox, he hoped—one that might have used the hollow to escape from a storm.

Please, not a forest cat!

Spider webs brushed across his face as he crawled.

This cavern was not the home of a cat!

It was the home of spiders!

Most likely, Wanderer spiders!

Yet, other spiders sometimes used caves. Pedí chose to believe that it was not a Wanderer. He knew he was foolish, but what else could he do when forced into the cave?

Pedí froze when a voice from outside reverberated off the cavern's walls. "Do you see it?" the older man called out.

"Now I do." Ivo must have returned from his search in the forest.

"If he's in there, we've got him."

Scraping noises sounded against the sandstone. One of them was climbing up.

Pedí rushed forward on his hands and knees, ignoring the spider webs he passed through. He ran into the rear wall. The cave ended only twenty feet from its opening. He looked for a side tunnel, but there was none. There was no place in this rock cavity to hide.

Except . . .

His eyes had adjusted to the dark, and Pedí could see a ledge or crawlspace along one side of the cave. He lay on his back and slid sideways underneath it. Parts of the crevice were tighter than others. There were two inches or more to spare above his face, but he had to wedge his hips and thighs to get them to fit. Webs clung to Pedí's face as he moved under the overhanging sandstone, but he saw no spiders. He closed his eyes and breathed in and out in relief.

He then realized that his right arm was still sticking out from the shelf. He could only hope the men would not see it.

Something crawled onto his hand—the hand outside the ledge. He couldn't twist to see, but he felt hairs brush across his skin.

Were they spider hairs?

Whatever was there was as big as his hand! Bird spiders can get that big, not just Wanderers. And they would go into caves, sometimes. That's what it is—a bird spider. Their bite would hurt but not kill.

The tickle of the hairs intensified as the creature crawled up Pedí's arm. He tried to stay as motionless as the sandstone. But he couldn't repress a shiver when it reached his shoulder and crossed the curve of his neck.

It continued to move and went onto the side of Pedí's face—right across his frog tattoo—reaching his upper cheek. The creature was too close for Pedí's eyes to create a sharp focus, but he could make out the scarlet bristles around needle-sharp fangs. Only a Wanderer had such coloration.

It wasn't a bird spider!

He was doomed!

He might try to brush it off if he could get his free hand to his face. But if he were unsuccessful and only irritated the creature, he'd be bitten for sure. Pedí would die and follow his grandpa on the deer path that passed through the stars to the other world.

He stifled another shudder when he thought of the stages of suffering he would have to pass through. As these images flashed in his head, the last words his dying grandpa said to him seemed to emanate out of the sandstone as if the kind man were nearby. *"Believe in yourself. You're a Shushuhador."*

I'm not, Grandpa. I'll talk to the spider, but it won't hear me.

Pedí whispered to the creature. "Help me, friend. Don't bite."

Sensing a threat, the Wanderer raised its four front legs in the air—its defense move. Pedí's moving lips had startled it, and it was clear that it didn't understand a word he'd spoken.

The ancient Idonata Shushuhadors possessed a unique gift—the ability to communicate with most of the animals. A few were known to converse with spiders. A true Shushuhador could have ventured into this cave without fear. The last of them had rallied the forest cats and poisonous serpents to aid the Idonata queen in her battle against the foreign soldiers and settlers. When the Blue Dragonfly came to help them, the Shushuhadors could even communicate with wasps and army ants, which they sent against the soldiers. That was two hundred years ago. No new Shushuhador had been born among the scattered remnants of his people.

Until Pedí?

No, not him. Grandpa shouldn't have called him a Shushuhador. Pedí didn't have even a portion of the powers of his ancestors. For certain, he would not be able to talk to any creature living in a cave.

I'm sorry, Grandpa. I'm not a Shushuhador.

The hairy spider on his cheek opened wide its fangs, poised to plunge them into Pedí's soft skin.

CHAPTER TWO

The Baby in a Red Cloth Sling

A tiny baby girl swung back and forth in a red cloth sling. Mama carried her and tried to run, but Mama limped with each step. A broken-off arrow pierced her thigh. Blood dripped down Mama's leg, crossed her bare feet, then went between her toes. Mama left a bloodstained trail on the narrow pathway through the cliffs. Papa followed those marked footprints but struggled to keep up. His injuries were even worse than Mama's. A deep gash split open his arm, another his side.

The baby began crying when Mama stopped and waited for Papa to catch up.

"Hush, little one," Mama whispered, rocking the sling that hung from her shoulder. Mama's breath moved in and out in short gasps, and her body trembled. "They mustn't find us."

Not far behind, a dozen warriors followed, intent on killing them. The evil men wore grotesque masks made from the front half of a human skull. Their eyes looked out of the bony sockets. They inhaled and exhaled through the hideous nose holes. Skeletal teeth hung down from each skull, partially covering their mouths. They carried bows and arrows and clubs studded with razor-sharp obsidian spikes. The black spikes were covered with remnants of torn flesh and dried blood.

Papa staggered out from around a bend in the narrow canyon. He caught up to Mama and the baby and then pushed them forward. "Go! Go without me!"

But Mama wouldn't leave his side. They stumbled together on the path that wandered past rock falls and around the buttress roots of Ceiba trees, which had found a footing in the dark soil of the confined passageway. Black vertical cliffs rose high on each side. A strong wind, wailing like a phantom's scream, blew constantly at their backs.

Mama and Papa shook when an eerie call, like that of a howler monkey, joined with the sound of the wind. They turned to listen and recognized the whoops and yells of their pursuers. The death-headed warriors were closing in.

Mama and Papa tried to run faster.

But Papa fell.

Mama stopped to help him. They both glanced to the side when she pulled him to his feet. A dark cavern opened into the rock. Mama and Papa looked back and forth at each other and then at the baby.

The baby girl wailed but couldn't talk and tell them to stop and not go in.

Something inside the cavern waited for them, something even more frightening than the evil men wearing half skulls across their faces. But Mama and Papa did not sense what the baby did. They stepped inside the cave, oblivious of the danger.

━◆━

The young woman woke with a jerk and realized she'd been screaming.

The nightmare had come again. It always ended the same. She never got to see what lay waiting inside the dark chamber.

Footsteps sounded in the corridor, then a knock at her bedroom door. It would be Marina, her other mother, not the mama from the dream.

The door opened. "You cried out in your sleep again. Did you—"

"Yes, Mother. It was the dream about my other mama and papa."

The recurrent vision came often, even though the young woman had no memory of her birth parents. They died when she was only six months old. Injured and ill, they passed away soon after they handed her over to Marina and Sergol.

"Why do you keep having this nightmare?" Mother shook her head as she said it.

"I always see Mama's long black braid with the silver streak. And her moon tattoo! And the arrow in her! And Papa's injuries! When I first told you about the nightmare, you said what I described was true."

"But it doesn't make sense. You were so little. Your dreams scare me."

"They frighten me too." The young woman hugged herself. She needed and wanted something to bring her peace, to erase the fear associated with the vision. If Mother would tell the story of how she came to be adopted, she could imagine her birth mama and papa in another way—a less frightening way.

"Tell me again what happened when they gave me to you."

"Not now, in the middle of the night! You need your rest. Otherwise, you might do something crazy at the captain's house today."

As usual, Mother found an excuse for telling the story, though her reason was more legitimate this time. Adací knew if she kept asking, Mother would give in. Hearing about the moment her birth parents placed Adací in Marina's arms calmed Adací, though she suspected the tale Mother related was not what actually happened. It was the way Mother looked away from time to time as she told it, the sighs and the occasional tears. They all suggested to Adací that the true story was something else. But if she ever asked, Mother wouldn't admit it, so Adací accepted the version as it was and hoped the true story was at least close to it.

"Please, Mother! It'll help me go to sleep."

"Just the short version, then. When your birth parents brought you to us, they were dying. I don't know how they were still alive; their injuries were so serious. They must have traveled far with little or no food."

Mother took a deep breath and let it out before continuing. "Your father and I had gone to Poor Man's Field to take food to some stranded travelers. We didn't see your mama and papa at first. They were hidden in the trees. But they must have seen what we were doing and chose us to become your parents. They staggered out of their cover, then called for our help."

"And was Mama beautiful?"

"How many times do you have to hear it?"

"Once more, please."

"Despite their injuries, your parents were striking people. Your mother's face was exquisite, and your father was also handsome. They were very young."

"When she said my name, tell it."

Marina shook her head but went ahead with the story just the same. "They tried to tell us many things, but we didn't understand their language. But we did perceive what she meant at the end. With her strength waning, the very last thing your mama did was to point to you and say Adací. She waited until I repeated the word Adací, then smiled and nodded. It was clear that she was telling me your name."

"Do you like my name?"

"It's not a name or even a word our people would use, but your father and I both loved the sound of it. How could we not use the name that seemed so important to your real mama and papa?"

"Thank you for keeping it. I like it very much."

Adací was grateful that Mother and Father had let her know about her birth parents. They had kept it a secret from everyone else except their two closest friends. They insisted that Adací never tell of her origin. Her adoptive parents had spent the seventeen years of her life raising her as their own—hiding the truth of who she was and where she came from.

No one knew about the crescent moon tattoo on her chest or the silver streak in her hair, which her mother had carefully kept dyed black.

Adací was their child.

CHAPTER THREE

Sister Spider

Pedí held his breath and tried to remain as unmoving as the sandstone, but the fangs of the poisonous spider spread wider. A tiny droplet of venom came out from one of the fangs. Pedí felt its coldness when it fell onto his cheek. On the surface, it wouldn't harm him, but once injected, he was dead.

Pedí silently pleaded to the Adací effigy in his pocket to save him.

She spoke not, but someone else did.

Grandpa?

Pedí heard Grandfather's words a second time or at least imagined hearing them.

"Remember the tale of the Shushuhador."

Pedí recalled the story of the ancient man his grandpa loved to describe. He could see the old Shushuhador sitting cross-legged on the ground, wearing red feathers around his wrists. The man's face was weathered and wrinkled. A striking tattoo of a monkey was etched into his left cheek. The monkey's long tail wrapped artfully around an inked tree limb that circled the man's eye.

There in the dark cave, Pedí fantasized about the grey-haired Shushuhador crawling through to him. The aged man extended his leathery hands and grasped Pedí's arm that stuck out from the crawlspace. Though he knew no one was there, Pedí thought he could feel the feathers circling the old man's wrist brush across his skin.

"Calm, my son. Calm," the imaginary Shushuhador said. *"Be at peace with this beautiful creature on your cheek. Remember, you are family."*

All living things are brothers and sisters, his grandpa had taught him. Even the rocks, the rivers, and the earth itself were part of creation and had their own life.

But would this angry arachnid recognize Pedí as a brother, or would it only protect itself? Still afraid to move and not breathing, Pedí spoke to it with his thoughts.

I'm your friend, your brother.

The spider trembled. One of its front legs came down.

Pedí started to say more but hesitated when he sensed resistance from the dangerous arachnid. Though it seemed to have heard his words, it continued to fear Pedí and was ready to defend itself.

But a squeeze from the hands of the ancient Shushuhador—who still grasped his arm—brought reassurance. *"Be one with the spider,"* the old man seemed to say.

As a young boy, Pedí had played that game with frogs and snakes, pretending to be one of them.

Never with a spider!

But he could imagine himself as a spider as well as a frog. So, Pedí became a Wanderer spider, hiding alongside this one in the cave. As he did, his mind melded with that of the hairy creature on his cheek.

I know you now, sister. I'm your brother and will not hurt you, but I need your help.

A tremor passed through the Wanderer's entire body and then through Pedí. The spider dropped her other three warning legs and closed her fangs.

She didn't move from Pedí's face but remained perched as if waiting for further instruction.

The faint light coming into the cave diminished. One of his pursuers was at the entrance.

Pedí was trapped. He had escaped the spider's bite but had no way out. If Ivo or the old man crawled into the cave, they would surely see him.

Ivo's voice echoed off the sandstone walls. "If you're in there, frog-face, you might as well come out. You're trapped."

Frog-face! That label had plagued Pedí from the day Grandma tattooed his face with the beautiful spotted amphibian. He got the tattoo the day he turned twelve—his transformation ritual. He let Grandma ink his skin without using the cococillo juice that Grandpa had prepared to numb the pain. Pedí had been proud of his bravery for once.

With the frog etched onto his face, he had hoped to finally be accepted—that the people of New Losobon, especially the boys and girls his age, would love the tattoo. To his surprise, it only branded him more as an outsider. The mocking and the insults increased.

The worst ridicule was whenever he worked in the sugar cane fields during harvest. Ivo had also worked there and tormented Pedí with his foul words. When the foreman was away, the bully would strike Pedí in the face.

Other people in the community also seemed to find satisfaction in slinging epithets at the only Idonata boy they knew. He had but one chance to change their scornful opinions of him. If he could finish his experiments with the mushrooms, he might save those suffering from the deadly infections plaguing the people of New Losobon. They may recognize him for doing good and not consider the last Idonata boy worthless.

But that opportunity was soon to be gone. He had no way to escape from Ivo and the old man. They would drag him out, beat him, and he would not be able to stop them. They would force Pedí to show them where the mushrooms grew. The cure would be lost—maybe his life as well.

The spider, still on his cheek, lifted one leg, but not in warning as before. She still waited for instructions.

Could the Wanderer save him?

Pedí imagined himself a spider again, a brother to this beautiful creature on his cheek. It was easier this time. He whispered so Ivo wouldn't hear.

"Dear sister, please attack the man at the cave opening. I know it's morning and time for you to rest, but this man wants to kill us."

The spider crawled off his face and onto the floor of the cave. It advanced toward Ivo, who was unaware he was being stalked. Pedí pushed out of the overhang so he could watch.

The shadow of round-faced Ivo was at the entrance. The distinct swish of a knife pulled from a scabbard resounded through the narrow cavern. Pedí's movements must have alerted him.

A ray of morning sunlight struck the sandstone and flashed off Ivo's knife. Sister Wanderer stopped moving when the sunlight glittered on the cave floor. Too bright! This creature of the night stayed away from the daylight.

Ivo could not see the spider in the shadow and stepped further into the cave.

Pedí put his hand over the pocket that held his Adací figurine. She would help him communicate with the spider. *Forget the light,* he pleaded in his mind with the Wanderer. *Pounce on this wicked man who wants to hurt us.*

The spider raised her front legs high, dropped them, and raced forward into the beam of sunlight. She sprang at Ivo and landed on his lower pant leg. Ivo shook his leg wildly and cried out in terror. Pedí had never heard such a squeal.

Sister Spider lost her grip and slipped off the trembling bully's pant leg, landing on the cave floor.

Ivo raised his knife in the air.

Pedí watched from his place in the darkness. He shuddered, fearing to lose his newfound sister.

Watch out! He screamed to her in his mind.

The Wanderer leaped back just as Ivo threw his knife. The sharp blade missed and buried itself into the cave floor up to its hilt.

The spider reared again with her four front legs, this time in anger, not defense, then jumped again at Ivo.

The coward jerked backward and had to catch himself from falling out of the cave. He scrambled down the rock face, leaving his knife stuck in the dirt.

The Wanderer looked back into the cave at Pedí.

Sister and brother regarded each other.

Then, the spider scampered into a crack near the cave entrance.

CHAPTER FOUR

The Tattoo and the Shining Hair

"Now go to sleep!" Adací's mother left that command as she went out of the room and closed the door.

Despite that order, Adací did not go to sleep but lay in bed, her eyes wide open. She thought of the time she first questioned Mother's restrictions on showing anyone her tattoo and never letting the silver streak of hair go undyed.

"Why do I have to hide my moon?" Adací had asked when she was a small child, her finger tracing the outline of the silver crescent inked into the skin in the center of her upper chest. "And my hair?" She reached and touched her pitch-black braid. "I want to see the silver."

Mother had wrung her hands and sighed twice before she answered. "Oh, Adací! You must never show your tattoo to anyone. You must always keep your hair dyed. Promise me."

"Yes, Mama, I promise. But why?"

"Long ago, when our people first crossed the seas, they encountered a powerful queen with hair like yours and a moon tattoo. She had strange powers and led her people against our soldiers. Under her guidance, some of the natives who could talk with wild things sent forest cats, serpents, and even wasps and ants against our people. Our soldiers were afraid of the queen and called her a witch. But in the end, our people won the war and killed the Idonata witch queen."

"Am I a witch, Mama?"

"You're not a witch, but a special girl—our girl!"

"Will they kill me if they find out I have silver in my hair and a moon tattoo?"

Her adoptive mother had hesitated for a long time before answering. "We won't let anyone harm you! But our people still tell stories about that queen, so if someone showed up looking like her, we don't know what they might do. They would certainly be afraid and mistreat you, as they did to all the Idonata people."

Adací had remained faithful to her promise despite her desire to show off her tattoo and the bright silver part of her braid. Mother had experimented with various dyes from the beginning. The old herb lady at the market had sold her the juice of night berries, and they worked perfectly. Once a month, Adací had to use it on the silver strand.

Mother started braiding Adací's hair once it was long enough. She did this partly because Adací's birth mama had a long braid, but also because it was a good way to hide the dyed part. Adací was now an expert at braiding her hair by herself.

And the tattoo? She wore high-collared dresses, and it was always under cover. It was remarkable, however, that the silver moon, although inked into her as a tiny baby, seemed to grow as she did. And it kept its perfect crescent shape.

Yet, despite her obedience in hiding those signs of her heritage, Adací had still failed her parents. Her peculiar dreams, wild imagination, and impulsive behavior created difficulties. She was a constant embarrassment to Marina and Sergol, frustrating all their attempts to make her a proper young woman.

But not today!

Adací was determined not to disappoint them this time.

Larada Mendin, her best friend, had invited Adací to visit the captain's mansion with her family. The mansion was the most impressive edifice in all of New Losobon. Everyone called it The Big House. It had remained in the Borgesso family since it was built after the conquest. Though elected by the Municipal Council, a Borgesso had been the leader of the New Losobon Captaincy since its beginning. The newest captain was Durgo Borgesso. He had been voted in after his father suddenly passed away last year.

Alstir Mendin, Larada's father, owned a sugar mill and was the wealthiest man in New Losobon, except for the captain. The Mendin family were frequent guests at The Big House, and for the first time, Adací got to come along.

━━━◆━━━

That afternoon, Adací rode to The Big House with Larada and the Mendin family. They got out of the carriage at the massive iron gates that led into the captain's property. Two servants swung them open, and Adací and Larada's family began the long walk through the gardens.

Adací stopped at the passion fruit vines and searched for their strange purple and white blooms. Since the mild winter weather of New Losobon had begun, only a few were left.

She paused next to see a white orchid growing on the side of a tree. The captain's gardeners had attached a woven basket for it to grow in. Like other air plants, this type of orchid did not need soil but attached its roots to the bark of trees. The beautiful orchid and many other fascinating flowers and trees were brought from the southern jungles to create the botanical wonderland around The Big House. The jungles were on the other side of the Blue Mountains and were an immense bowl of forests, rivers, and untamed wilderness.

New Losobon Valley, with its warm climate, had its own orchids and tropical flora, but much was lost when the forest was cleared for the sugar cane and coffee plantations. Only the northern stand of the valley's original woodland remained intact.

Adací continued to slow the procession as she inspected each flower and shrub. Her head swirled as she looked up at the graceful palms lining the walkway. In all this beauty, how did Mother and Father expect her to remember their instructions?

"Make sure to curtsy to the new captain and his wife," they had said. "Be respectful to Chando, and for once, be nice to Bertol."

That last instruction would be the most difficult to obey. Bertol was Larada's twin brother. The twins were six months older than Adací, and when they were toddlers, the three of them were inseparable. Alstir and Pitrassa Mendin were close friends of Sergol and Marina, and the families got together often.

The Mendins were the only ones who knew that Adací was adopted and had been asked not to tell anyone else, even their children. After rescuing baby Adací, Marina had gone into seclusion for a year. All their friends, except for the Mendins, were told it was for Marina to have her baby. Adací's adoptive parents hoped that other than the Mendins, the people of New Losobon would believe Adací was their child.

Adací's close friendship with the twins changed once they were in school together. With Larada, it grew stronger, but it soured with Bertol. Though the twins were a little older than Adací, the three of them were in the same class. They attended the school the sages had built in the cobblestone street part of town, the wealthier section. At school, Bertol and the other boys began to mock Adací.

Her eccentric behaviors brought on the ridicule. Whenever they were outside at break time, and a bird came by, Adací would mimic its song and then wander off, following it. Laughter from the students greeted her when she showed up late to class. It happened over and over again.

Even being in her seat didn't help. Adací lived in her dream world and struggled to pay attention. If the teacher asked her a question, there was no response, even when asked a second or third time—occasionally a fourth. Only when the giggling and insults from her classmates got loud enough would she return from her fantasyland and try to act as if nothing had happened. That only increased the mockery.

The worst taunting began that day in the school courtyard when she was ten years old. Adací had climbed into a tree to check on a bird nest. The boys had come and began climbing the same tree.

Bertol's best friend, Samo, went out onto one of the limbs just below Adací. In her mind, she saw the limb break and the boy fall to the ground. Her accursed imagination was at work again. She wanted to ignore it, but far too often, what she envisioned would soon come to pass.

"Don't go out on that limb!" she had warned him. "It's going to break!"

Samo scowled at her. "How do you know it's going to break?"

Bertol, who was on the branch next to Samo's, shouted at her. "Are you some kind of witch?"

That was not the thing to say to Adací. Mother's story of the Idonata witch queen with her tattoo and silver hair had plagued Adací all her life. She feared that she might become like her.

"Don't call me a witch, or I'll make the branch break."

Those were words she wished she'd never spoken.

The minute she said them, the branch snapped off where it attached to the tree, and Samo fell ten feet to the ground. He cried out in pain, and all the boys gathered around him. They helped him to his feet. Although bruised and scraped, he hadn't broken any bones.

Adací climbed down from the tree and was immediately surrounded by the boys. Bertol, the leader of the mob, told everyone what he had witnessed: "She's a witch!"

"Witch! Witch!" They all chanted. "You made the limb break!"

Adací flew into Bertol with her fists and pounded his chest over and over.

That outburst had only encouraged him and the others. The chants became a daily ritual, with her predictable response feeding their desire to watch Adací explode. She assaulted Bertol every time he called her a witch.

Most often, he easily pushed her away, but on occasion, a good blow would land, and once she bloodied his nose. That got her into trouble. She had to sit with her legs crossed and her nose against the wall while the rest of the class watched on with glee. Bertol never got punished for what he did.

Yet, despite all the past mockery still ringing in her head—for this critical visit to The Big House—Adací would put it behind her. She would not forget to act like a genteel girl!

And Larada would help her. She was so different than her brother. Larada looked at Adací as her rescuer ever since she saved Larada from the poisonous bite of a Lance-head snake. They had been walking on a path together. Larada was in front. The serpent was camouflaged in the grass, but Adací saw it in one of her crazy visions and jerked her friend backward just as the snake struck. Its head brushed Larada's leg, but she escaped its deadly fangs.

Adací and the Mendins finally reached the mansion and stepped onto the central porch. It was made of massive stone blocks, some of which had ancient engravings carved into them. Like so many wealthy houses in New Losobon, the porch and the foundation were constructed from remnants of the temples of the destroyed Idonata nation.

Adací glanced along the length of the three-story building, which stretched out to both sides from the porch. Despite its fame, the structure's outside walls were unpretentious. Plastered and painted white, they had already faded to a dull yellow. The red roof tiles were also unremarkable. Like all the others in the city, they were made of baked clay and had darkened with gray and black lichens.

Though the roof and walls were unembellished, the brown and black hardwoods surrounding each window and doorway were ornate. When the house was built two hundred years ago, captured Idonata artisans had carved the wood with intricate designs, including flying birds with wings outstretched, butterflies poised on flowers, and spotted forest cats stalking their prey.

At the front door, she met the captain. Adací remembered to do all her mother had taught her and survived the formalities of greeting him, his wife, and their oldest son, Chando.

I wish you could see, Mother. I can behave. Today, I'll be a perfect lady.

CHAPTER FIVE

The Girl Who Chases Birds

Captain Durgo Borgesso escorted Adací and the Mendin family to the veranda of The Big House. Like the front porch, the expansive rear patio was paved in Idonata stone. Steps descended in two places to reach a rolling green. Gardeners with scythes were cutting the grass. The sweet scent of the newly shorn lawn wafted on the breeze. Across the green, a stand of age-old hardwood trees broke the horizon. It was a small remnant of the original forest.

Larada's parents joined Durgo and his wife at a canopy-covered table at one end of the patio. Chando led Larada, Adací, and Bertol to chairs arranged in a circle at the opposite end.

The captain's son was tall like his father. His muscles bulged beneath the tight-fitting shirt he wore. Chando was famous for his strength. Stories were told of how the young nobleman had killed a robber with his bare hands.

He was a year older than Larada but had shown interest in Adací's beautiful friend for some time. Although she did not dislike the captain's son, Larada found these visits to The Big House difficult. She was not happy that her father had promised her in marriage to him. Another young man, one she liked much better, had also been pursuing her. But when Larada turned eighteen in five months, her father would announce her engagement to Chando at her Coming of Age celebration.

As the four talked, Adací glanced at the old Idonata watchtower that rose high at the north end of the captain's property. It was the only intact Idonata structure that survived the carnage brought by the invasion of this land. As usual, it took only a few minutes for her out-of-control imagination to take her to another world, another time.

Wearing blue and yellow macaw feathers in her hair and a necklace made of beetle shells, Adací climbed up the stone tower step by step. Her feet found each cut made into the massive boulders the ancient inhabitants brought down from the Blue Mountains. At the top, she joined her fellow Idonata guards. They all cried out the alarm when they saw the soldiers from across the sea enter their valley.

"You're not listening to me."

Bertol's impatient comment brought Adací out of her dreamland and back to reality. Somewhere in the back of her mixed-up head, she knew Larada's brother had been droning on about something or other—probably about how his father had given him some important job at their sugar mill.

She couldn't care less.

Adací still stared at the tower. It annoyed Bertol, but that was okay. She wanted the vision to come back. The Idonata tower had been constructed on the pre-eminent hill of the valley. The first captain—who led the soldiers and settlers from across the sea—built The Big House next to it. He preserved the tower, and it was still used as a lookout.

That first captain's army destroyed all the Idonata villages, homes, and temples—everything except for the watchtower. They killed, drove off, or enslaved any remaining natives, except for a few who stayed hidden in small groups in the valley's forests. Adací's teachers at school said that those remnants were gone now as well.

There were no Idonata left.

Except for me?

"How can someone so pretty be so capricious?" Once again, Bertol interrupted her fantasizing. He was great at using flattery and reproach in the same sentence.

She wanted to say something rude in return but remembered her parent's plea to behave. That was not the only reason Adací decided to hold her tongue. Bertol had been changing toward her—little by little. Larada had even intimated that he was enamored with her.

Adací hoped not, but at least she could try not to say anything too vindictive. "You used to say I was an ugly witch."

"That was years ago." Bertol's voice trembled a bit.

Maybe he actually had some regret.

Adací's thoughts were interrupted by a flash of color. Something red, white, and black flew over their heads. A giant woodpecker landed on a dead branch in the mahogany tree that stood next to the patio. It was the largest woodpecker she'd ever seen. Adací leaped out of her seat and rushed to the tree.

But she moved too fast and scared it. The woodpecker took off, flew across the green, then entered the woods.

Adací ran after it.

She might have heard Larada calling for her to stop, but all other thoughts had left her head. The bird was much too important.

She tore into the forest, following glimpses of the woodpecker through the trees. After bounding over a large boulder, she fell when a fallen branch hidden in the grass tripped her. Adací got up, but she had lost sight of the bird. Then, like a distant drum, a melodious knocking echoed through the forest. The woodpecker was pounding on a tree. She followed the rhythm.

The magnificent bird was halfway up the side of a dead and hollow tree trunk. Adací watched with open mouth. It was so much bigger than any woodpecker she knew. She thought she had already identified all the ones in New Losobon, but this beautiful specimen was more majestic than any she'd seen before.

Adací picked up a rock and pounded it on the side of a tree, imitating the beat—pretending to be an intruder. Besides battering through bark to find grubs, woodpeckers like to drum on dead trees to mark their territory.

The bird cocked its red-crested head to look at her, then twisted its neck back and forth as if in frustration. It took off, winging high and disappearing over the trees.

That was a mistake. I drove it away.

Adací walked back to The Big House. When she came out of the trees and onto the grass, Larada and the others were standing on the patio looking in her direction. Larada came running. Bertol and Chando laughed.

At the other end of the patio, the captain and Alstir Mendin stood up and watched her. The captain's face showed disgust, but the face of Larada's father showed disappointment. She wondered what Alstir and Pitrassa Mendin would tell her parents.

Adací glanced down at the expensive dress her mother had custom-made for this occasion. A large slash rent the floral embroidery work that decorated the bottom. Reddish-brown mud stained the front of the delicate pink fabric.

Her best chance to show her parents she could behave in society had failed.

She must look like the fool she was.

CHAPTER SIX

Nanimoha

Pedí heard a thud as Ivo slid out of the cave, down the sandstone, and landed on the ground.

"What happened?" It was the alarmed voice of the gray-bearded man who had waited below.

"The frog-face is not there. Giant spiders live in that cave. One attacked me."

"Where's your knife?"

"I threw it at the foul thing."

"You leaving it? Not going to get it?"

"Never!" Ivo shouted.

"Then let's get out of here. The fool's long gone by now."

Pedí waited in the dark for half an hour to be sure the men had left the forest. At the mouth of the cave, he looked again at the etching of his heroine, Adací. Next to her, other Idonata writings were engraved along the wall. He hadn't noticed them before. Each symbol was inscribed in a near-perfect square. Remnants of red and white paint covered some of the designs, which included strange faces, stylized hands, and unusual lines and circles.

He wished he could read them. They were similar to the glyphs Grandpa had interpreted on the broken Idonata altar near the captain's mansion. *Nanimoha, the cure that gives life, is hidden by death.* When Grandpa first read those words, something stirred inside Pedí. It was as if the ancient message were written for him and him alone.

Words rang out inside his head. *"Find me, Pedí!"*

That started him on his search for the nanimoha, the powerful medicine of his forbearers.

As Pedí went to leave the cave, the Wanderer spider emerged from the crack in the side of the wall. She pivoted toward Pedí, raised one front leg as if saying goodbye, and headed back into the cavern's darkness.

Pedí nodded toward the hairy creature. "Thank you, dear sister, for saving me."

The words came out without pause or hesitation. His tongue was loose—it flipped and rounded over each vowel and consonant.

Why couldn't he speak that way with people?

Pedí had many animal friends, but he would never have human friends, except for the sages and healers at the Sanctuary. For sure, he'd never have a girlfriend. His words got completely scrambled whenever he tried to talk to a girl. Then they laughed at him.

But even if he didn't stutter, no one would want to associate with a native boy, especially one with a frog inked into the skin of his face.

He shouldn't have chosen his left cheek for his tattoo, where everyone could see it. But that was where Grandpa had wanted him to place his mark. It was the site that was always used by the Shushuhadors. Though Pedí knew he could never be like the ancient men who could talk with the animals, he had wanted to please Grandpa. So, he chose the frog—the reminder of the day he had first communicated with another creature—and had it placed onto his face.

The Idonata people looked upon their tattoos as signs of beauty. Mother's choice was a wild duck. It was colored green, black, and white. It was on the side of her neck, and Pedí never tired of admiring it.

Father's tattoo was huge, Mama had said. A Golden Eagle covered his back. Pedí didn't remember it. He was just two years old when his papa was killed.

The year before his death, Father had brought Pedí and his mother out of the northern forest and built a house at the edge of the city. Father started working as a guard for the captain. He was the first Idonata native ever to do so. It was for Durgo Borgesso's father, the previous captain. That captain was a kind and good man, unlike his son, the present leader of New Losobon.

Father had come to live near the city because he hoped that when Pedí was old enough, he could attend the new school the sages had just built. It was different than their other two schools. It was in the poor part of town, and anyone could attend whether or not they could pay. Pedí had tried to fulfill his father's wish, but he quit going to school when the taunting and scorn became too much.

Pedí pounded his fist against the cave wall. That was a remembrance he wished he could forget!

Pedí climbed down the sandstone and made his way through the forest. It was time to get to the thicket of moura berries, the hiding place of the mushrooms—the nanimoha of his ancestors. He weaved past trees with massive buttress roots, dodged liana vines, and stepped with care through bogs. Though the two men appeared to be gone, he didn't dare follow the open trail again.

When Pedí reached the thicket of moura berries, he listened, watched, and waited to ensure no one was nearby. Yet, he knew his precaution was unnecessary. People feared the deadly moura, and the main forest trail swung wide to avoid the impenetrable growth.

When he first discovered it, he was astounded by its size. The thicket appeared to have been planted by unknown hands as it grew in a massive, almost perfect circle. He suspected that the Idonata people had created it, and he remembered the words on the glyphs describing the nanimoha's hiding place—*hidden by death.*

The purplish-black moura berries were poisonous. Those who ate the dark fruit by mistake would go into a deep coma and never wake up. They'd waste away by starvation.

Pedí looked around once more to make sure he was alone, then climbed into the sinkhole where the Idonata tunnel was hidden. Bats had led him to it. He'd been searching for a way to get inside the moura thicket a few months ago when several of the winged mammals flew out of the depression. Using roots as handholds, he had descended into the tree and vine-covered pit. The bats were coming out of a small opening on the side of a rock wall. The stones in the wall were arranged in rows. It was not a natural formation. It had to be an Idonata structure and was one of the few that had not been found and destroyed by the soldiers and settlers.

The largest stone on the wall was rectangular and had a glyph of Adací carved into it. That stone was like a door and was not cemented to the others. It sat in a narrow channel filled with leaves and dirt when Pedí first found it. He had cleaned out the debris and was able to slide the stone door sideways. It opened to a tunnel that ran straight underneath the moura and emerged in the middle of the vast circular thicket.

Once again, he moved the stone door to the side. After so many visits to gather mushrooms, it was easy now. Pedí knelt to enter the passageway but stopped and looked over his shoulder when branches broke behind him.

Someone had jumped into the pit.

The men must have followed him after all.

CHAPTER SEVEN

Niala

Adací climbed the steps of the veranda but stayed close behind Larada, hoping that the spoiled front of her once beautiful dress would be hidden.

It didn't help.

The captain let out a derisive chortle, then turned away. His wife did the same as if ashamed to be associated with a girl so reckless. But Alstir and Pitrassa Mendin wrung their hands. How mortified they must be that they'd brought Adací with them.

Bertol stopped laughing but then shook his head—his typical response to Adací's strange behaviors ever since he quit calling her a witch. Chando, however, continued to chuckle and grin.

A sarcastic grin.

That hurt.

The people of New Losobon idolized Chando, just like they did his father, the captain. Both would think Adací was not worthy of being among high society. Her parents' plans for her would be shattered once again.

Adací didn't even try to explain her reasons for running after the woodpecker. Larada would understand, but nobody else would. Birds were Adací's friends. She could never pass up an opportunity to meet a new one—especially a creature as wonderful as the giant woodpecker.

Larada went inside and came out with one of the captain's servants. It was a girl who looked to be about Adací's same age. She was adorned with large brass earrings and wore a tattered, yet fascinating multicolored dress—with green, yellow, and blue cloth randomly patched together. It was similar to the type of dress that Heila, Adací's maid, liked to wear. The servant brought a wooden bucket filled with soapy water. Using cotton rags, she scrubbed at the front of Adací's dress.

"What's your name?" Adací asked her.

The girl seemed hesitant to answer and looked first toward the captain, who sat just thirty feet away. She finally said, "Niala."

Adací loved her musical accent. It was the same as Heila's. Niala must also be from the Isle of Mattaçores. "I have a good friend who came from your island."

Niala nodded and started to say something, but she looked again toward Durgo Borgesso and stopped.

"Is something wrong?"

"I'm not supposed to talk with the captain's guests." Niala kept scrubbing and said the words in a mumble without looking up.

"You can talk with me. I'm a nothing, not a fancy lady like most of those who visit here. I'll never be invited back after running after a woodpecker and spoiling my dress. My parents will be disappointed. I promised to behave, but see what I did?"

"But you are a fine lady," Niala spoke louder this time, seeming to forget her fear of the captain. She stood up partway, touched Adací's long braid, and drew back her hand. "Your hair is beautiful. Heila told me all about it. Which part of the braid is—"

The servant stopped herself and looked down as if embarrassed.

"You know Heila? She told you about my hair?"

The girl nodded. "She's my friend, but I don't get to see her anymore."

Heila was one of the few who knew about Adací's silver braid. She often helped dye it. She must have told Niala about it despite promising to keep the secret. But how could Heila not share such a strange thing with an acquaintance from her homeland?

Adací decided it would be best to keep quiet about the hair. She'd talk about something else. "Are you working here to pay for your sea passage?"

Niala nodded.

Heila and her family had also come to New Losobon under contract. Poor people could not afford to cross the great waters. Plantation owners and wealthy merchants would pay their way, but those under obligation had to work for their benefactor to pay off the loan. Far too often, they were forced to work long hours for minimal wages, and it took years to be free of the debt.

Adací's father treated his servants differently. He had bought the contract for Heila's family from another owner and then offered her father, Tavi, a job with good wages. Heila was just a baby then, but when Heila was old enough, she started working as a maid. Sergol allowed them to pay off the debt little by little as they were able. And though Heila worked as their maid, for Adací, she was a friend.

Niala scrubbed at the few remaining spots on Adací's dress. "You're so nice to Heila. I wish you could be my—" She looked toward the captain and didn't finish her sentence.

"You can be my friend. Come and visit me and Heila."

Niala shook her head and started to speak, but she cut herself off when she glanced again at the captain. The servant girl shuddered. Captain Borgesso had stood up and motioned toward someone on the other side of Adací and Niala. He had signaled Chando, who approached.

Larada came with him.

"Shh, miss," Niala whispered.

Chando cleared his throat when he reached them. Niala got up from kneeling, did a little bow, then looked at her feet. Chando eyed her up and down. Niala was a pretty girl with a well-rounded figure. Adací did not like the way the captain's son looked her over.

He smirked. "Done cleaning the dress, Mattaçores girl?"

Adací scrunched her face when she heard the insulting tone of his words. She pictured herself as the giant woodpecker—with red feathers on her head standing on end. She was ready to fly into this proud man.

Niala bobbed again. "Just about, sir."

"Then finish and get inside. You have other work there, no?"

"Yes, sir." Niala bowed a final time, then knelt to scrub at the last spot on Adací's dress.

If Adací could be that woodpecker, she'd pound her beak into Chando like the bird did to the dead tree.

"And a reminder!" The captain's son was not yet finished with the servant. "You can scrub without talking."

Niala nodded without looking up.

"It was my fault!" Adací exclaimed—the imaginary feathered crest on her head growing even taller. "I told her she could talk to me."

Chando smiled as if her words meant nothing. His sarcastic grin grew more prominent when he looked at Adací's clenched fists.

"Be nice," Larada said to Chando. She touched his shoulder as if to rub away his unkindness. Her best friend always came to Adací's aid to keep her out of trouble.

Chando shook his head. "I am nice. This Mattaçores girl is no good, and yet we keep her on. That's being nice, isn't it? It's not cheap to bring Mattaçores rabble from across the sea only to have them fail to keep their part of the bargain."

Niala lowered her head even further as she continued to scrub at the last spot. Adací wanted to take her in her arms and hug her. Why would Chando say such things? Adací hadn't expected him or his father to treat their servants so poorly.

"What do you mean?" Larada questioned Chando. "Aren't she and her family working for you?"

"It's just her, and she's a lousy excuse for a servant. Her father injured his back in the mines and can't work. Her mother stays home to care for him. This girl is the only one in her family who can work to pay off the debt."

Adací could imagine the difficult living situation that Niala and her family must have to endure. They probably lived in the cheap wooden shacks built next to the northern forest.

Niala got the mud out of the last spot and started toward the house. Adací hesitated but then followed her. She glanced back to see Chando, still smugly grinning. She ignored him and hurried that much faster.

Adací went through the back doors, caught up to Niala, and embraced her. "I'm so sorry for how they treat you."

Niala pushed her away. "No, miss, you mustn't hug me. The captain might see."

"He's outside, Chando too."

"Fine ladies don't associate with servants in this house."

"I'm not a lady, just a girl who chases after birds. But I want to be your friend if you'll have me."

Niala backed away. "Having you as a friend would be a dream, but it's impossible."

"It is possible! Heila and I will visit you after you're done working."

Niala shook her head. "I'm here every day from morn till dark. Then I must hurry home to help Mama with Papa and my two young brothers."

"Was your papa hurt bad?"

Niala looked down before nodding.

Adací felt like a songbird whose companion had just been snatched from the air by a hawk. She wanted to rescue Niala but could do nothing. "I'm so sorry about your papa. My father says the men working in the captain's mines are treated like slaves, that some have died in cave-ins."

Niala nodded again but continued to back up. "I'm going to my work, and you must return to the nobles on the patio. I'll be dismissed if the captain sees me talking to you again. We'll have nothing to live on."

Niala turned and ran through another door. Adací took two steps, ready to follow her again, but stopped herself. If she kept trying to help Niala, she'd mess things up as usual and make it worse. Maybe she already had.

Adací walked back through the rear doors and onto the patio.

She looked for Larada but couldn't see her. Bertol was still on the veranda and had joined his parents and the Borgessos at the canopy-covered table. A maid was serving them cake and coffee.

Larada and Chando must have walked off the patio. The primary purpose for the visits to The Big House was to get the two of them together as much as possible—hoping that Larada would become more agreeable to the planned marriage.

But despite her parent's best efforts, Larada preferred to be with Edero Custal. Her pleas to let her choose her future mate had gotten her nowhere. The Custal family owned the other sugar mill in New Losobon. It competed with the Mendin mill for sugar cane from the plantation owners, which created a rift between the heads of the two families. Alstir Mendin did not want his daughter to associate with Edero Custal.

Adací scanned the grounds of The Big House and finally located Larada and Chando. They were talking under the Juvia nut tree, which grew at the end of the house. That towering tree had been brought in from the southern jungles by the very first captain when it was just a sapling. Now fully grown, its fruits were the size of a coconut and filled with tightly packed nuts. The outside husk was as solid as a rock.

Adací's eyes opened wide. She took a deep breath and placed both hands over the front of her dress—right over her crescent moon tattoo.

It was happening again!

Another nightmare!

And in broad daylight!

CHAPTER EIGHT

The Juvia Nut

The huge Juvia nut broke loose from its stem and dropped straight down without touching a branch or even a leaf of the tall tree. It created no sound and headed straight for Larada, who conversed quietly with Chando. The rock-solid nut pod struck the young woman on the top of her head. There was a bone-smashing crunch—like a sledgehammer striking an adobe wall.

Larada went down to her knees and then fell forward onto her face with no attempt to catch herself. Her eyes were wide open, pupils dilated, staring at the ground.

Larada's head was caved in.

Blood was everywhere.

Adací's best friend was dead.

⬥

Adací groaned. She stood motionless on The Big House veranda, hands still clutching her dress over her tattoo.

The vision of the falling Juvia nut had come to her mind in all its gory details.

Adací took off at a full sprint. She had no choice but to believe her premonitions—especially when it was about Larada.

She crossed the patio in seconds, flew down its stairs, and ran through the grass toward Larada and Chando. Adací could imagine the shocked faces of the captain, his wife, and the Mendin family as they observed the deranged girl in action again.

But she had to ignore all that—she only had seconds to reach her friend.

Adací did not slow down. She charged into Larada at full speed, pushed her to the grass, then fell on top of her to protect her. She looked back to see a huge nut pod crash into the ground where Larada had been. It made a six-inch hole in the dirt before bouncing away. It would have crushed her skull.

Larada lay flat on the ground, but like Adací, she sat up partway to look back at the fallen pod. "You saved my life! How did you know it was going to hit me?"

"I . . . I . . ." What excuse could Adací make? "I saw something move high in the tree. The nut was breaking loose. It was right above you."

Larada eyed Adací with lowered brows as if not believing a word of it. Her rescued friend leaned and whispered while slightly nodding in Chando's direction. "You can tell me the truth when we're alone."

Chando had not moved and stood just a step away from where the round nut pod had plowed into the ground. He was not grinning at Adací this time. He looked wide-eyed into the tree as if another pod would fall and land on him.

Running footsteps pounded the grass from the direction of the house. The Borgessos and the Mendins all raced toward them. Adací was sure she'd be sent home and never return to The Big House.

She was a crazy girl who had just assaulted the young woman destined to marry the captain's son.

CHAPTER NINE

Secret Meadow

Pedí's hands gripped the stones of the tunnel entrance. Whoever had jumped into the pit struggled to free himself from the interweaving vines and brush. A dark, moving mass was all Pedí could see. He had to escape before the man untangled himself. But if he went further into the Idonata shaft, Pedí would be trapped, and the mushrooms would be found.

There was only one choice.

He slid the stone cover back over the opening, grasped a vine, and pulled himself up the side of the pit. He expected the second man to be waiting for him at the top, but there was no other option.

Halfway up, he looked back. A red deer limped out of the brush.

It wasn't a man.

A doe had fallen into the pit.

The deer's hind leg was torn open and bleeding. It must have been mauled yet somehow escaped from a forest cat. Running blindly, it had fallen over the edge.

Pedí let himself down and moved toward the injured animal. "Let me help you."

The deer raised its head as if contemplating Pedí's words but then bolted. It slammed back into the tangle of vines and hid behind a small tree that grew in the middle of the pit.

Pedí shook his head. He would never be a true Shushuhador. The poor deer didn't understand him at all. But maybe it was best that his powers were weak. If the captain and his soldiers knew of his ability and thought he was dangerous, they might do the same to him as the first captain, who came across the sea, did to the ancient Shushuhadors.

Despite the efforts of the last Idonata queen and the Shushuhadors to fight back against the invasion of their land, they had no chance. They were outnumbered by the thousands. Captured Shushuhadors were forced off a cliff into the waters of the underground lake just outside the city. Pedí could imagine himself being pushed off that same edge and his bones disintegrating in those deep waters.

Regardless of that risk, he couldn't deny his wish to connect with animals. He had somehow become one with the spider, but he shouldn't be surprised that the red deer ignored him—he was a weak Shushuhador if he was one.

Pedí kicked at a moss-covered rock on the ground. Frogs and snakes were easy for him to bond with, but mammals were always difficult. The hardest mammals of all were humans—especially those with long hair. Pedí picked up the rock and threw it into the greenery.

The poor deer startled and ran headfirst into the tree, then ran circles around it. The frightened animal would never get out of the pit by itself. Pedí corralled it, pushed on its rear end, and guided it up the side. The deer churned its feet, and Pedí propelled it up and over the edge. It disappeared into the trees.

Pedí returned to the tunnel opening, slid the stone door open again, and started through the Idonata passageway. Bats rested upside down above him, a small colony of fifty or so. They were insect-eating bats, not the larger fruit bats. Their roost was to one side where the bricks had dropped off the ceiling, and there were better places to hang on.

There was just enough space to bypass the bat droppings covering half the floor. Pedí talked to the small dark creatures as he went by them. The first time he had crawled through, they squeaked and shifted positions on the tunnel ceiling. Now, they'd grown used to him. At least these little mammals seemed to hear his soothing words.

Every muscle relaxed when Pedí emerged on the other side of the Idonata tunnel. He was inside the moura and looked out at a pool and meadow. He could imagine what a bird must see as it flew over this creation of his ancestors. It was like a giant target. The extensive moura growth was on the outside. Next came a circular pool fed by a spring. The water kept the moura from penetrating any further. Last, in the center of the water, was the magnificent secret meadow.

Chorus frogs jumped out from hiding places near the stones Pedí stepped on to cross the water. They were quiet today as it was not mating season. In the springtime, their high-pitched croaks must fill the air of the meadow. Fat toads moved lazily out of Pedí's way when his feet touched the soft cushion of grass, mosses, and flowers. The warty creatures hardly noticed him, as they had no fear of predators inside the thicket. A small leafhopper landed near a toad and instantly disappeared. The amphibian's sticky tongue gathered up the unwary insect. Bees and butterflies moved here and there, checking out the red and pink flowers. Many were still in bloom despite the approaching colder weather.

When he first discovered the meadow, Pedí was overwhelmed. If this was the hiding place of the Idonata cure mentioned on the altar, which of all the flowers, grasses, and herbs growing here was the nanimoha? And after so many years, did it still exist?

He'd been looking for a treatment for infections—the plagues and pestilences that spread from one person to another. No New Losobon healer had ever found such a potion, but Grandpa said the old Idonata medicine men had such a cure. Was it the nanimoha? Was it still here in this meadow?

Two months ago, he had thought of a way to test each plant that grew here. Pedí moved three half-barrels into a storage room of the laboratory and filled them with pond water, pond plants, and algae. He let the water stagnate until it formed a thick, odorous film. Something living but unseen must be causing the water to sicken and stink, similar to what happens in infected wounds. If he could find a plant that stopped the water from turning bad, it might also work to kill whatever unseen creatures were infecting people.

One by one, he had tried the flowers, the herbs, and the grasses from the meadow. The red flowers inadvertently led to the discovery of the nanimoha. Little yellow toadstools always grew among the crimson blooms. One had mixed in when he collected some red flowers to try in his test vats. He noticed the mushroom when he ground up the flower at the laboratory. He decided to test it and tossed it into one of the test barrels. The next day, when he checked the vats, the red flower had failed to work, like every other experiment, but where the mushroom floated, a circle of perfectly clear water surrounded it.

He had never suspected a fungus would be the cure, but the little toadstool had killed off all the bad stuff floating near it. He repeated the experiment several times, and if he dried and ground up the mushroom, it worked even better. Pedí had found the nanimoha of his ancestors. It had survived for two hundred years in the secret meadow as if it had been protected just for him.

Since his discovery, he had collected, dried, and stored the mushrooms at the infirmary. He needed to collect enough to last through the colder months when the little toadstools would slow their growth. After today, he should have the necessary supply and could complete his experiments.

Pedí knelt, took off his collecting bag, and laid it open near a cluster of the yellow toadstools, his nanimoha. A breeze carried the fresh smell of the meadow, and he breathed it in as he counted the small mushroom caps. They looked like pale marbles fallen across the grass.

He plucked the largest mushrooms from the ground, leaving the smaller ones to grow. He always left several of the big ones as well so they could finish development and spread their spores.

As he prepared to leave the meadow, he watched a group of bright yellow butterflies. There were twenty or more, and they took in moisture from a mudflat along the pool's edge. One left the group and flew erratically across the meadow until it paused momentarily on a red flower near his feet. He tried to talk to it, but it didn't hear him. No insect had ever listened, but at least he had communicated with one of their cousins, the Wanderer spider.

Pedí passed back through the tunnel. He chose the long way to the Sanctuary in case Ivo and the gray-bearded man were still watching for him. He wished he had the strength and courage to fight them. Pedí had been called names, punched, or spat upon for most of his life. Till now, he'd done nothing to defend himself.

He called himself a coward, but Pedí had stood up to defend others before. When he was five years old, he'd saved a little red-haired Itatu girl from bullies. Her name was Ileana, and she became his good friend. He somehow found the courage then. And just last year, he had jumped in front of the ruffians taunting a Mattaçores girl dressed in multicolored but tattered clothing. The girl escaped, but he'd gotten a horrible beating.

He never defended himself, but he defended those two girls. Now, he must fight to protect the nanimoha like he would a friend or a stranger in need. It was being threatened by those who would not use it for good. He had to try and stop them.

CHAPTER TEN

Hiding the Nanimoha

Pedí walked out of the woods when he neared the captain's mansion. The huge house stood by itself at the west end of the city of New Losobon. Its vast, red-tiled roof and the nearby Idonata stone tower stood out from the surrounding trees and gardens. Pedí's little room at the Sanctuary was just south of The Big House. The sages had built their refuge where the Idonata temple used to stand. That ancient temple had been the focal point of the Idonata main settlement before it was destroyed.

Pedí never imagined he would live so near the captain's dwelling. It was where Pedí's father had worked—the father he could not remember but knew only from his mother's stories. His father had remarkable skill with the bow and arrow. He shot faster and more accurately than any of the captain's guards or soldiers could do with their muskets. His courage was legendary, Mama had said.

Pedí lacked his father's bravery and couldn't even shoot a bow and arrow. If his father had lived long enough, he might have helped Pedí learn those skills and gain a little valor.

Then again, Pedí might have just shamed him.

His father died in a battle before Pedí reached his second year. Father had been guarding the captain's coffee harvest when five thieves attacked, intent on stealing this newest money crop. Despite the presence of two other guards, Father singlehandedly routed the robbers. Two of them lay wounded on the ground, his arrows piercing their legs.

The rest fled in fear, but a stray musket ball from a fleeing thief caught his father in the back.

Pedí and his mother had lived in poverty ever since. They might have starved if it hadn't been for Grandpa and Grandma's help.

Now, his grandparents were gone as well. They followed the deer path through the stars to the world without evil. He missed them so much. Pedí and his mama were the last Idonata natives who lived in New Losobon Valley. Even the few scattered bands who had remained in the forest had died off or left for the jungles.

Mama insisted that she and Pedí stay near the city, even though it was in a shack at the edge of the woods. She wanted to fulfill Papa's dream for Pedí to attend one of the sage's schools.

Pedí soon reached the edge of the captain's property. He entered the cobblestone road that went by the front gate. It would lead him past the mansion and directly to the Sanctuary. A green iguana with its dorsal spines and banded tail crossed the road in front of him. He would have followed it and talked to it if he didn't have to put the mushrooms away. He patted the filled bag at his side. He would soon have them safely stored and drying.

When he reached the Sanctuary, Pedí went through a side door and the back corridors to get to the infirmary's laboratory without being seen. He unlocked the door to the storage room and slipped into the space that held the mushroom depository. It was hidden behind his three test vats.

Pedí squeezed past the barrels and opened the old cabinet with his key. Its doors were latticed, allowing it to function as a dryer. He spread the new mushrooms out on a pan on the shelf. The other half of the cupboard was packed with narrow-necked glass bottles full of dried mushrooms that had been chopped and pulverized.

Pedí closed the cabinet doors, made his way around the test barrels, and then looked out the storage room door before leaving. He didn't want anyone, not even the new watchmen, to know where they kept the dried mushrooms. Today's guard, a talkative young man named Calixto, would be outside by the back entrance. Doctor Arias had hired men to watch the lab day and night ever since word had gotten out about Pedí's new cure.

The doctor suspected that the two men who had been following Pedí were under orders from some other person. Perhaps it was a jealous healer, like Breno Torred, or maybe a merchant who wanted to make money from the mushrooms. While hiding in the cave, Pedí heard Ivo mention the captain. If he were the one who was after the mushrooms, then Pedí's worst fears might come to pass. The captain had so much power. He always got what he wanted.

Pedí was willing to share the nanimoha of his ancestors once he knew which infections it would cure and that his dosing of the poisonous toadstool was safe. Many animals had died in the first experiments he conducted, and he was still distressed by the suffering he had caused those innocent creatures. He had prayed over each one as his grandfather taught him when they went hunting and killed a deer or a wild pig for their food. It was a declaration of gratitude for the animal's sacrifice that others might live.

Pedí did not want to be responsible for a human death from the mushrooms. Someone less vigilant, someone just looking to make money off the cure, might not take the same precautions.

Pedí also wanted to use the nanimoha to help those without the means to pay for it—like the people living in the shanty town at the city's north edge. If the wrong person gained control of the mushrooms, they would sell his cure only to the wealthy. The suffering poor would not be able to afford it.

Pedí left the storage room, locked the door, and then turned around. There was movement at the rear of the laboratory. It was Calixto, but he vanished back to his post.

Had he seen Pedí take the mushrooms into the storage room?

Surely, this friendly young man could be trusted.

CHAPTER ELEVEN

Chando's Birthday

"**N**o dreams, no imagining things, and no heedless behavior!"

It was the tenth time Adací had heard the warning. Of course, Mother would give it to her once again before arriving at The Big House. Adací, Mother, and Father sat together in their four-wheeled open carriage. Tavi was driving.

But it was one of my visions that saved Larada and got us invited to Chando's birthday celebration.

Adací wanted to say those words, but she knew better than to get into that argument again. Mother would remind her of the wild trip into the woods after the woodpecker and how it almost ruined her first visit to the captain's house.

After that bird chase and then knocking Larada to the ground, Adací had expected to be forever banned from The Big House and the Mendin house as well. But no, they all praised her for saving Larada.

Larada's parents were extremely grateful. They had questioned how Adací knew the huge nut pod was going to hit their daughter.

Adací just shook her head and said, "I'm not sure. Something moved high in the tree, and I had a bad feeling."

She had glanced to see Larada's raised eyebrows and her lips mouthing the word liar. Except for Larada, Adací didn't tell others about her unusual dreams. Her parents forbade it. And though Alstir and Pitrassa Mendin knew of Adací's adoption, they knew nothing about her strange visions.

Adací's parents demanded, in particular, that she never share the recurring nightmare about her birth parents fleeing from the men in skeletal masks. It was for her protection, they had said. Her adoptive parents wanted people to believe that Adací was their child, not adopted, and not descended from the Idonata people.

It would have been an easier task if not for her reckless nature. Adací's misbehaviors were well-known throughout the town and sparked rumors about how well-bred parents could have such an unmannerly and wild child.

One of the worst incidents happened in the Sanctuary assembly hall when she was twelve. They had gone as a family to attend a community meeting. But Adací left her seat and walked to the center of the building, right under the dome. She raised her arms in the air and yelled out, "Leave us alone! You have no right to take our land! Go back to where you came from!"

She didn't know why she'd said those words or what they meant. But sitting by her parents, waiting for the meeting to start, the urge had come.

She had to do it!

The hall was packed with people, and everyone turned to see the crazy girl. Her father dragged her back to her seat. She had never seen her adoptive parents so alarmed and ashamed at the same time. After the meeting, they had pleaded with her never to do such a thing again. "People are going to wonder who you are," they had said. "And it could lead to something bad."

When Adací questioned what they meant, they made excuses and said she'd understand one day. And though that same impulse to cry out came back every time she was in the middle of the assembly hall, Adací had stifled it ever since.

But notwithstanding her past mistakes, Adací was hopeful that coming to this party would change things and what others thought of her. Her parents would be here to see it, and she could finally make them proud of her.

Larada had promised to be waiting at the door, to stay with Adací and be her guide. Larada was the most respected and desired of all the young women in New Losobon. Her best friend would help Adací succeed.

Tavi let them off at the main gate, and then Adací and her parents passed through the gardens of The Big House. They stopped when they came to the moonflower vines. A few white blossoms had unfurled their petals in the evening shadows. They were Adací's favorite, and they only opened at night. Each new bloom was surrounded by moths fighting to be the first to drink its sweet nectar. Adací wished she could be like the fragrant moonflowers and attract new friends at this party. Too often, she felt like a skunk cabbage whose bizarre and smelly blooms drove everyone away.

When they reached the house, Adací and her parents got behind the line of well-dressed people going up onto the massive stone porch and through the main door. Larada was waiting just outside and took Adací's hand. Her friend was dressed in yellow and wore a headband of jewels. Each gem sparkled, making Larada even more attractive.

Adací's parents went in first, followed by the two girls. In the entryway, a kaleidoscope of colored tiles on the floor and walls reflected the lamplight. Guests were mingling, and everyone took notice of Larada and welcomed her with an embrace. They said nothing to Adací and gave her no formal hugs of welcome.

However, they leaned and whispered to each other after she passed by.

When the girls entered the reception hall, the carved parrots and toucans seemed to fly out of the sculpted hardwoods that decorated the inner windows and doorways. Birds were Adací's friends, but she imagined these wooden ones squawking at her in derision.

Last, they entered the ballroom. Red tiles, waxed to a brilliant shine, covered the floor. Wooden pillars, painted and curved like bending palm trees, were spaced evenly around the room. They held up the domed ceiling. Music from guitar players wafted through the air. They were New Losobon's finest musicians, but for Adací, the plucking of their strings produced sounds more like a funeral march than those for dancing.

All eyes were on her friend, Larada—all pleased to see her. But Adací sensed their disdain that the out-of-control girl was also there.

Marina and Sergol had already found Larada's parents and were visiting. Bertol was with them, and he smiled at Adací. She frowned in return, but that did not stop him from coming over and following Adací and Larada around.

Adací wished he would go away—yet, despite his presence, things got better. Larada's friends welcomed Adací, and several young men who were Adací's age wanted to talk with her. That was a surprise! Whenever they did, Bertol furrowed his brow and turned his head.

Chando, however, was still the main attraction, as it was his nineteenth birthday. He soon found Larada, and the two remained together. There was a buzz of voices from those who looked their way. All anticipated a future marriage between the two most notable young people of New Losobon.

One person who would not want that marriage was absent from this party—Edero Custal. He and his family had not been invited despite being among the wealthier of New Losobon.

Adací liked the Custal boy and wished he were the one to whom Larada was promised. Edero and his mother often went with Adací and her parents to help the indigents at Poor Man's Field. And now that Adací had met Chando—and experienced his sarcastic grin and heard his rude comments to Niala—she wished Larada could choose Edero instead of the captain's son.

Sadly, she knew her friend would never be allowed to make that choice.

Standing next to Larada and Chando, Adací analyzed the captain's son. His words were soft and fawning to Larada, but whenever he spoke to Adací, his tone was full of sarcasm. Adací chose to say nothing in return. Her awkward silence was broken by the approach of a servant girl carrying glasses filled with dark red wine.

It was Niala!

"Good to see you, Niala," Adací said.

The pretty servant girl shook her head and avoided eye contact. Adací decided to say no more. Niala must be afraid of reminding Chando that she'd spoken openly to Adací the other day.

But Chando took notice of her anyway. "Why are you serving and not scrubbing dishes?"

Niala looked at the floor and stammered out her answer. "The steward needed more help out here."

"You're too clumsy to be carrying this expensive wine." Chando took the three goblets from Niala's tray. He passed one to Larada, one to Adací, and kept the last himself.

He eyed Niala up and down like he had done the other day on the rear veranda. "Go back to the kitchen, and no more serving the guests."

Niala shuddered, turned to go, but then dropped the serving tray onto the floor. It clanged against the tile, but instead of staying put, it rolled like a loose wheel across the ballroom. Guests parted right and left to avoid the tumbling tray.

Chando shook his head. "Excuse me." He bowed toward Larada and then handed her his wine glass. "I must escort this servant to the kitchen myself."

He seized Niala's left arm, his fingers digging into her flesh.

She winced.

Chando dragged her through the crowd, following after the rolling tray.

Adací hesitated, glanced at Larada, and then ran after them. The captain's son was humiliating Niala in front of all these people. Adací was determined to stop him. She held her wine glass in the air to avoid knocking it against someone as she weaved through the guests. She glanced to see Larada following behind, trying to keep up despite holding two wine glasses.

The serving tray careened out of the ballroom and into an alcove near the kitchen. It wobbled to a stop. Chando dragged Niala away from his guests and into the recess. He forced her to kneel to pick it up. The Mattaçores girl's knees cracked against the floor tile.

Adací went into the alcove just as Chando pulled Niala back to her feet.

Adací grabbed ahold of his forearm. "Let her go!"

"Keep your voice down, girl!" Chando glanced back into the ballroom.

Adací's voice, though loud, was not noticed by the other guests. The musician's music had masked her shout.

She tried to pull Chando's hand away from Niala's arm, but his muscles were like the branches of an ironwood tree, hard as rock and immovable. Adací held on anyway and forced her fingernails into his flesh. Her other hand still held the glass brimming with wine. "I said, let her go! You're hurting her!"

Chando laughed. "Ha! I'm not hurting my little servant girl, just teaching her a lesson."

"It's not funny." Adací dug harder with her sharp fingernails. One penetrated his shirt and drew blood.

Chando's nostrils flared, and the veins in his neck bulged when he saw the red stain on his shirt's white cloth. His sarcastic grin disappeared. He released Niala, who fell backward onto her rear end. Chando grasped Adací's fingers, stripped them off his arm, and then held tight, pressing them against each other.

Her knuckles burned, but she stared back at him. Adací was ready to lay into this brute, although she knew she could do him no damage even with her strongest punch.

Larada made it through the crowd and entered the alcove while still carrying the two wine glasses. She put them on the floor and grabbed the back of Chando's hand—the one that crushed Adací's. "Don't do this!"

He released Adací's fingers and bowed like a humble servant boy toward Larada. "I'm so sorry."

The now sweet-talking Chando motioned toward Niala, who still sat on the floor. "I was just helping my maid learn her duty when this . . . this . . . thing interfered."

Chando scowled at Adací, his feigned kindness gone as fast as it had come. Adací took a step back. Her right hand, which still held the wine goblet, trembled.

Chando had more to say. "I remember what the boys your age used to call you in school. Witch, wasn't it? They were right on target, as only the Idonata vermin had hair as black as yours. You must be one of them. Did your fake parents find you discarded in a garbage pit somewhere?"

Larada put her hand on Chando's shoulder. "Don't say such things. Adací's my best friend."

Chando turned to Larada and spoke in a softer tone, but his voice wavered as if the effort to be nice was not so easy. "I know how generous you've been to Adací, but I don't trust her. The times she saved you are suspicious. She has some kind of sinister power—just like a sorceress would have. She caused the accidents, then rescued you to gain your confidence—to take advantage of your family's wealth."

Larada's voice choked out her response. "Not true!"

Chando squinted at Adací. "The stories of the Idonata queen said she had a silver moon tattoo on her chest—branding her an enchantress. I don't doubt you carry the same sign hidden under your dress. Should I pull it down, revealing the truth, showing everyone that you are her descendant—the spawn of an evil witch?"

Adací flung the wine from her glass into Chando's face without thinking, without regard for consequences. Dark red liquid splashed onto his cheeks, into his eyes, and over the front of his shirt. Wine dripped off the end of his nose.

Adací prepared for his retaliation, but instead, the captain's son broke out in mocking laughter.

CHAPTER TWELVE

Lily Pads

"What's going on?" The captain's voice roared.

Adací startled and turned to see Durgo Borgesso, who had just entered the alcove. His square chin jutted out. His glaring eyes took in the scene before him. The wine-stained Chando laughed on, continuing to make a mockery of what Adací had done.

The rest of the guests began to crowd in, and a circle formed. Like hens in a henhouse, they clucked back and forth, wanting to know what had happened. One of the captain's butlers brought a white cloth and handed it to Chando so he could wipe the wine off his face. The servant lowered his eyebrows and frowned at Adací.

Niala cowered at the edge of the circle. She shook her head at Adací and whispered, "I'm sorry, miss."

Adací whispered back, "It's not your fault."

"Then whose fault is it?" The captain's loud voice boomed out again, and the murmur of the other voices ceased.

He pointed at Niala. "Are you to blame for the wine dripping off my son?"

The servant girl, who had started to get up, fell backward again. The silver tray she had picked up banged a second time to the floor. Her face was that of a condemned prisoner.

Adací had to protect her. "I threw the wine." She stepped between Durgo Borgesso and the Mattaçores girl. "Niala had nothing to do with it."

Adací still held the empty goblet in the air as if threatening to throw wine at the captain if it were full again. However, she lowered the glass when Father and Mother pushed their way into the circle.

"What did you do?" Mother said.

Why was it always Adací's fault whenever anything happened? Well, usually it was, but not this time. She just needed to explain.

She motioned toward the captain's son. "He-he—"

Chando, the pretend martyr, cut her off. "It's my mistake. I was admiring her beautiful black hair, but I must have said something wrong. I'm awkward with my words."

The liar bowed his head while holding the white cloth the butler had given him. The fabric was covered in wine from his face, and the end draped like a flag of surrender. "I'm so sorry to have offended you."

"But-but . . ." What use was it to try to tell her side of things? Everyone would believe the captain's son, not the crazy girl.

She looked to Larada, hoping she could help. Her best friend's eyes were wide, and her mouth was open. Adací knew she would speak for her. Larada started to say something, but Alstir Mendin grasped his daughter's shoulders from behind.

"You can't keep making excuses for Adací's behavior."

"No, Father, it was not her—"

Alstir put his hand over Larada's mouth, stopping her words. "You're not going to defend her, not today." He looked toward the captain and his son. "Though we love this girl, who has saved my daughter's life more than once, she struggles with self-control."

Larada pulled her father's fingers away from her mouth. "No, Father. You're wrong." Larada broke free and ran out of the hall. The crowd opened, allowing her to pass. She went under the carved wooden archway and into the reception area. She was headed outside.

Adací's only witness was gone.

Adací's father began bowing and using soft words to the captain and the wine-drenched prevaricator. Sergol was good at making excuses for Adací. Lots of practice! But the shaking of his muscles and the bend in his spine seemed worse, as if a heavier weight than usual bore down on him.

Adací looked at the empty wine glass in her hand as if it were the criminal at the scene.

Without a word, Mother grabbed her by the sleeve and dragged her through the herd of highborns, through their scowls, and through their whisperings.

"Wild thing."

"The girl should live in the forest, not the city."

"She's Larada Mendin's friend. Why they allow her . . ."

Mother pulled Adací out of the ballroom and into a side room of the reception hall. Instead of resisting, Adací was a limp baby kitten carried by the nape of its neck in the mouth of an angry mama cat.

Mother shoved Adací into a chair and sat next to her. Her mother spoke in whispered tones, but it was the kind of whisper with a low growl attached to it. The mincing words bit pieces out of Adací.

"You're killing us. We've given half our lives to make something out of you—and this is how you reward us?"

Adací had nothing to say. Marina and Sergol put all their hopes on her, but she only brought them sadness.

"All the young men saw what you did, and their parents, too. How will we ever find someone to take an interest in you."

"I don't care," Adací responded.

"And Bertol was starting to like you," Marina said and sighed. Her following words were spoken even more quietly. "He was our best choice. His parents knew we had adopted you, yet accepted and welcomed your friendship with Larada and hoped it would grow again with Bertol. What will Bertol and the Mendins think of you now?"

"Bertol can go to—"

Father arrived and saved her from saying something stupid. His pale face and deep forehead wrinkles made him appear older than she'd ever seen him.

Adací readied for his onslaught, but he spoke just two words. "Go home." He plopped into the chair next to Mother's. She put her hand over his, and they looked into each other's eyes.

Adací bet they wished they'd never adopted her.

"Have a guard accompany you to the stables." Father's voice sounded so tired. "Tavi can take you home and then return for us. We'll stay and try to lessen the damage."

Adací ran out of the reception hall and through the main door, then shook off the guard who offered to escort her. The light from a half-moon cast long, skinny shadows of the towering palm trees that lined the walkway to the gates. She slowed when she passed the captain's pond. Giant water lilies brought in from the southern jungles reflected the pale luminescence. Some of the pads were six feet across. As a child, she laid on top of one, and it kept her afloat over the still water.

If she crawled on top of one now, maybe it would sink, and then she could disappear into the mud below.

CHAPTER THIRTEEN

Idonata Sorceress

Adací tarried by the captain's pond and gazed across the moonlit lily pads. Something shifted in the trees and bushes on the other side of the water. A pale ghost-like visage came out of the undergrowth and circled the lagoon. Part of Adací said run, but the curious part made her stay. Whoever, or whatever it was, moved silently and remained partially hidden by the bushes and trees that surrounded the pond.

Some people believed in forest spirits, and that when one was alone in the wilds at night, they would find you.

Adací didn't know what she believed, but as the sallow phantom moved through the last of the undergrowth, any fear she had was swallowed up by her despair over what she'd just done. She'd failed her parents, so didn't Adací deserve an encounter with a ghoul? Perhaps this creature of the night was coming to welcome her into a sinister fellowship.

The apparition walked into the moonlight. A band of little reflections flashed off its forehead. This ghost wore a jeweled headband. It was no phantom. It was Larada—her light-colored dress had been the perfect masquerade.

Her best friend ran with arms outstretched, and the two girls embraced, but Adací pulled back.

"You shouldn't be hugging me after what I did."

Larada held on tight. "That scoundrel deserved the wine in his face."

Adací quit trying to pull away from Larada and squeezed her back. "Have I ruined your future? Will you lose favor with Chando because of me?"

"I hope so. I want nothing more to do with him."

"But I thought you liked him some."

"I might have once, but not anymore. Because of you, I know what he's really like."

"Then I'm glad I threw the wine."

Larada let go, turned toward the pond, and then trembled.

Adací touched her arm. "What's wrong?"

"Father will never let me choose. He and the captain have it all planned. I'll have to marry Chando."

"Then there's no chance for Edero?"

"Father despises the entire Custal family. It'll never happen."

"But Edero's kind and so different than Chando."

Larada shook her head. Her face was pale and indeed ghost-like in the moonlight, but the jewels still sparkled across her forehead. "I love Edero, but it'll never be."

Larada flinched as if something poked her. "Unless . . ."

"What?" Adací said.

"One of your dreams!"

"My dreams?"

"You saved me from the Lance-head, then from falling off the cliff, and now the giant nut pod."

"But—"

"You don't talk about it anymore, but I know you had some kind of vision. You saw what was going to happen each time."

Adací hesitated, then nodded.

"You dream things all the time, don't you?"

Adací nodded again.

"I want you to have a vision about Chando and save me from him."

"But I can't control my wild imagination. Mostly, it's just crazy nightmares, like the one about my birth parents."

Larada grasped both of Adací's hands. "But couldn't you imagine something and then bring it to pass?"

Adací shuddered. She didn't want to be the cause of the bad things she envisioned, including the many accidents Adací had seen before they happened. But that was exactly what Chando had just suggested and what the boys at school thought when they called her a witch.

Her trembling worsened the more she thought about it. She shook like a bird taking a bath in a water hole. "If my dreams cause bad things, then Chando was right. I am a witch just like the queen of the Idonata."

"He said that to provoke you. He's jealous of you and knows you mean more to me than he ever will."

"But there was a sorceress, just like Chando said."

"That was two hundred years ago." Larada reached for Adací's long braid and held it in her hands. "You are not like her, and neither are you a witch. And you can't be from the Idonata people. None of them are left."

But I have a silver braid and a crescent moon tattoo on my chest. Adací thought the words but didn't say them. It was best not to tell Larada about it.

Her kind friend ringed Adací's braid around her fingers, almost as if she'd guessed what Adací was thinking. "Besides, you're good, not evil."

"Not if I hurt someone I loved—you, for instance."

"You'd never do that. You always save me, and now you will rescue me from Chando."

Adací hung her head. She felt more likely to hurt Larada than help her. Maybe the giant nut that fell out of the tree was her fault, and she was just lucky to be there to stop it from hitting Larada—the same with the Lance-head snake.

The moonlight dimmed as clouds passed overhead. A breeze blew across the pond and ruffled their dresses. The girls shivered.

Adací peeled off Larada's hands from her braid but held on to them. "Go inside. You'll be missed, and I must get home so Tavi can return for Mother and Father."

She squeezed Larada's hands extra tight before releasing them. "I don't know if my dreams can help you, but somehow, I'll find a way to save you from Chando."

"I know you will." Larada gave Adací a farewell embrace before walking back toward The Big House.

Adací ran to the palace stables.

On the way home, Tavi was quiet. The middle-aged man rarely said more than a word or two. He didn't even ask why Adací was going home early. She was grateful it wasn't Pito driving the four-wheeler. Pito was their chief stable hand and had a word for everything. He was Adací's faithful friend but would be disappointed with what she'd done.

The carriage passed through the cobblestone streets of the wealthy neighborhood of New Losobon. When they reached Adací's house, Tavi turned the horses into the alley at the side of the home and pulled up by the long stable house. It was full of her father's prized animals.

Adací looked around, searching for Pito. A light was on in the bunkhouse where the men slept, but no one had come out. She jumped out, then took off for the back of the house, hoping to get inside before Pito saw her.

Halfway to the door, a gruff voice sounded.

"Stop right now, young lady."

Her feet halted as if caught in a wolf trap. It was Pito. She wanted to keep running but knew she had to face him. She turned as his footsteps approached from behind. Under the moonlight, his gray hair was visible, but she couldn't make out the many wrinkles that creased his weather-beaten face.

"I'm not a lady and never will be."

"Why did you come back alone?"

"I don't have to tell you. Go away."

The older man stood still, not even talking for once. It was too much for Adací, and she gave in. Pito was her confidant, her surrogate grandpa. He led her back to the hitching rack—their favorite visiting spot—and they leaned against it.

Adací told him everything, even that Chando had called her a witch.

"You're no witch, girly, although your beauty could bewitch the most stoic of young men. But damn it, you've got to stop this wild behavior. That worthless burro deserved it, but it must stop. You're destined to be a proper lady."

"Damn it, yourself. I can never be who they want me to be."

"Let your mama hear you swearing again and see where that gets you."

When younger, Adací used to sit near the stables to listen to Pito and the other men. But if she used any of the swear words she had learned, she was sent to her room and had to write "Dignified girls do not swear" fifty times in a notebook.

"Your parents have raised you to become a part of high society. They love you and want something for you that not many have a chance for. It's time to give up your rebellious ways."

Adací nodded but didn't really agree. She could never change. She messed up every time her parents put her in a situation where she had to behave properly.

She went to bed but lay there for hours, even after Mother and Father arrived home and came up to check on her. She was relieved they had nothing more to say.

Adací finally went to sleep, wondering if she was a witch.

CHAPTER FOURTEEN

The Fox

The stables and corral were far away but getting closer as Adací floated down from the sky. She could see right through the roof of the stable house.

Pito was there with Monto, the new stallion Father had just purchased.

A red fox appeared outside the stables. It was headed for the chicken coop, but Lino, the youngest stable hand, chased it away—yelling and throwing dirt clods. The fox tried to escape through the back gate but suddenly changed directions and streaked through the middle of the stable house. Pito was standing behind the horse when the fox ran between its legs.

Monto startled and kicked, his rear hoof catching Pito in the lower leg. The older man fell to the earth, his bones crushed and broken.

<hr>

Adací awoke.

Her right hand was open and draped across her chest, directly over the silver moon tattoo.

She withdrew it.

Something bright shone at her side. A tiny stream of moonlight was coming through her window and had just reached the edge of her bed. Her long hair was unbraided and had swung over into the moonbeam while she slept. The ray of light touched some of the strands of her hair. A few of them glowed silver despite the dye on them.

She pulled them back, and they turned dark.

Adací cupped both hands together and buried her face in them. She spoke out loud to herself. "This can't come true! I would never hurt Pito. If I did, I would not be able to bear it."

Adací sucked in a deep breath, then spoke to herself quietly, in barely a whisper. "But if it does happen, then I'll know I'm a witch, a wicked one."

CHAPTER FIFTEEN

Witch

Adací was late for breakfast. She shuffled to the dining room table and sat across from Mother and Father. They glanced at each other but said nothing to her, not even good morning.

Her breakfast was already laid out on one of Mother's fancy plates, along with a glass of juice and a cup of coffee that was no longer hot. More utensils than she'd ever need were lined up on each side of her dish. Seven empty plates, also arranged with utensils and cups, had been placed in front of the empty chairs.

The dining table would seat ten. Lelia, their cook, and Heila, their maid, set the full table for every meal.

"In case somebody drops in," Mother always said.

Adací believed it was because her adoptive parents still dreamed of having the table filled with their own children. They both had wanted a big family, but Marina could never get pregnant.

Then they got stuck with Adací.

It would have been better if her place were empty, too.

Lelia's voice could be heard in the kitchen, talking to herself. Most mornings, Adací got up early and helped the cook. Mother disapproved, but she had given up trying to stop her. Today, Adací had stayed in bed, brooding over the nightmare.

"Your eyes are red," Mother finally spoke. "Did you not sleep?"

Great! Don't say good morning. Just notice what's wrong with me.

Adací shook her head but kept her mouth shut. She expected an onslaught of criticism and anticipated hearing what else had happened at The Big House, but her parents said nothing. Maybe Adací wasn't worth the effort anymore.

Three times, as she ate, she started to tell her parents about the dream of Pito getting hurt. But her throat went dry with each attempt. What would they think about this new dream and her being a witch? They would want to get rid of her.

Adací shook her head as if having a conversation with someone other than herself. Marina and Sergol loved her despite her disappointing them with everything. Even if children of their own were sitting at all the empty spots, they would have let Adací squeeze in.

That was the problem. She was supposed to make up for the children they didn't have, and she was a lousy substitute. They planned out her entire life, trying to make her into what she could never be. Adací hated the things they made her do—all the training to be a proper girl and all the social activities to make her known among the elite.

Last year, after her sixteenth birthday, her parents wanted to show her off and took her to the town square on weekends, where boys and girls her age would circle the park's fountain and mingle. The boys jostled each other to get closer to her. She didn't know if they were interested in her as a friend or just wanted to say something rude as they walked next to the weird girl. Surprisingly, no mocking words had come. Parents of the young people watched from side benches, and Adací knew they talked about her. She hated it.

Marina and Sergol had also urged Larada to take Adací to some of her rich friend's houses, and she had to admit that a few times, she enjoyed it—at least when she hadn't messed up. But even in the good times, she felt like a marionette, her feelings and actions guided by her parents, who tried to wedge Adací into a wealthy culture she'd never fit into.

And now that she was seventeen, the pressure worsened! It was the year for parents to find a match for their girls in preparation for the big Coming of Age at eighteen. Once seventeen, young men could officially start visiting young women they were interested in. In a way, they were courting both the girl and her parents, seeking their approval.

In all interactions, a parent still had to be nearby. There were many rules, and until they were engaged, young men and women were not allowed to be off alone.

Even before the disaster at Chando's birthday, Adací's parents were worried about finding someone for her. The day before the party, Mother had said, "I see how the young men look at you. They recognize how beautiful you are, but despite that, not one young man has come by to get acquainted, and you've been seventeen for one whole month. They're afraid of you and your crazy impulses. But once you start acting like a lady, everyone will forget your past behaviors."

Those past behaviors had now been re-manifested before the entire wealthy community of New Losobon. Her parents would never find someone who wanted Adací. Girls who weren't matched by their Coming of Age were looked down upon by the well-to-do. They were somehow of less value. Adací hated that tradition and how it hurt those who were not so quick to be matched by their parents. She would be one of them!

But in truth, part of her—actually, most of her—was glad not to get into that game. She would hate to have suitors come by to visit. She would have to sit with a fake smile and entertain them when she'd rather be off doing something else. She doubted that if a young man took an interest in her, he'd want to do what she liked. He'd never take her searching for birds in the forest.

That was her favorite thing.

Pito was assigned to be her escort whenever she went birdwatching. "Proper young girls don't go off alone into the forest," her parents told her the first time she tried. Adací made Pito promise not to tell that she climbed trees to look into bird nests. That would end the expeditions if Mother found out.

Those excursions with Pito would end if her dream came true and he was injured. She needed to warn him, but he wouldn't believe her either. Only Larada thought her nightmares were more than just nonsense. She would have to find a way to persuade Pito—to keep him away from Monto, the new horse.

First, she would apologize to her parents.

"I'm sorry I messed up again at Chando's celebration."

That broke the dam inside of Mother and Father. They got out of their seats, came around the table and hugged her, told her how much they loved her, that they still trusted her, and believed she would do better in the future.

Her own wall of defenses crumbled. Adací hugged them back and told them she loved them too. The hardest part was knowing she would fail them again, despite their words of trust.

"Pito told us what Chando said to you," Father said while the three embraced. "This has been our big fear since you came to us—that the people of New Losobon would guess you're from the Idonata. We can accept them knowing you're not our child, but if they know about your hidden silver hair and your tattoo, then we fear the worst."

"Why, Father? You and Mother always say that but don't explain."

"I don't know if we're ready to tell you," Mother said, "or if we should, but please believe us. It's best if no one knows who you really are."

"But you're not a witch!" Father said with emphasis. "Yet you are a girl who can't control her impulses."

"We need you to stop," Mother added. "It raises too many questions about you."

"Chando is a proud young man," Father said, "and what he did was wrong. But the captain's son is a hero and would be a great choice for Larada."

How could they say anything good about that deceiver? He had everyone fooled except Adací and Larada. But she chose not to say more. Somehow, she would find a way to rescue her friend from the captain's son.

Once again, she almost told her parents the dream about Pito but stopped herself. How could she do it when they had just said how important it was to hide all that she was? It would only make them sad and take away the last faith they held out for her.

She had to prevent the nightmare from coming to pass on her own. "I'm going to the stables. I need to talk with Pito."

Mother frowned. "Don't stay out there and pitch hay or do whatever else you volunteer for. I've told Pito not to let you do it anymore."

You can't stop me from working with the horses and with Pito.

She wanted to say the angry words out loud, but how could she after just apologizing?

"I won't stay long," was all she said.

Adací rushed to the stables, worried that she should have gone sooner to check on Pito. Part of her still wanted to believe it was all a mistake, just a silly dream after all.

She wasn't really a witch.

She pulled open the outside stable doors and looked along the rows of horse stalls. Pito was midway down, tying a rope to Monto. She ran to his side and slid to a stop, kicking up hay that had fallen to the ground.

The horse startled at Adací's approach.

"Whoa." Pito put his hand on Monto's neck to steady him. "What's your hurry?" Pito frowned at Adací, then patted the big horse. "This one's wild and skittish like you. I'm taking him out for his first ride."

Adací breathed hard and fast, taking a minute to respond. She was grateful that she'd made it in time. Pito was with Monto, like in the dream, but there was no fox, no injury. She could save him from getting kicked.

"I may be wild, but I'm not skittish." Adací slugged the old man's shoulder. He winced as if she'd just pounded him with a club.

"Stop it, faker." Adací reached for Monto's rope. She'd get the horse away from Pito, and then nothing could happen to him. She wouldn't even have to tell him about the dream. "Let me take the horse and ride him for you."

"Mmm—no on two counts." Pito pulled the rope out of her hands. "One—I'm not supposed to let you work out here anymore. Two—we don't know how this one's going to behave. I wouldn't dare put you on him yet."

"But you've trained me. I can—"

Adací was cut short by someone yelling from outside the stable house.

"Get out of here!"

It was Lino's voice, and there were dull thuds. He must be throwing clods like she'd seen in the dream.

It was the fox!

She had to help him scare it off and keep it away from Pito and the horse.

"Tie Monto up. Don't get near him until I . . ." She streaked off, not sure what more to say.

"Damned girl!" Pito called after her. "What are you up to now?"

She ran outside the far end of the stables and looked left, then right. Lino was hollering from the direction of the chicken coop. Then she saw it—the fox, a dark red one—bounding toward her, fleeing from Lino. It was running alongside the corral's wood railing.

Adací was in the wrong place. She blocked the open gate the fox was headed for. The fox stopped when it saw her, then turned direction and shot into the stable house.

"No, no, no." Adací ran after it.

It was double vision, as the dream, still fresh in her head, played again, and she watched the same scene before her eyes. Pito had tied up the horse like she'd asked him, only to grab a saddle to place on its back. The gray-haired man was behind the stallion, holding the heavy saddle, when the fox ran under the horse.

The huge animal kicked, and Adací heard the crunch from Pito's leg. He crumpled to the ground, cursing and crying out.

It was as if she felt the pain herself—she also crumpled. Adací fell forward, landing on her palms and forearms, her face just missing the hard earth. She skidded through some fresh horse droppings with her mouth open. She spit out the wet manure and pounded her fists against the hard earth.

I am a witch.

Not only had she conjured up the disaster, but she then brought it to fruition by scaring the fox into the stables. She'd hurt Pito, and without question, it was her fault.

CHAPTER SIXTEEN

Durgo Borgesso and Breno Torred

Pedí had been summoned to Doctor Arias's office. The patient with the injured arm who Pedí was helping would have to wait. When he arrived at his mentor's office, voices of men arguing reverberated through the closed wooden door. Something bad was happening, and it must be Pedí's fault. He took one step back, inhaled, then moved forward and knocked.

When the door opened, the first person Pedí saw was Durgo Borgesso, the captain. He was pointing his finger at Doctor Arias. The leader of New Losobon was a tall man. His square jaw and large forehead were distinct—features of all the Borgesso men. That commanding face matched his demeanor.

Breno Torred was also in the room. The man was even taller than the captain. He had light blonde hair and blue eyes. Torred was originally from Minas, the Captaincy to the north. Though some in New Losobon had light complexions, few were as fair as those from Minas. However, the man's blonde features did not make his face any less menacing.

The captain and Torred were on one side of the wooden desk, Doctor Arias on the other. Behind his thick, round glasses, the doctor's eyes mirrored his frustration. His short mustache was pulled down by a frown, which Pedí rarely saw on his instructor's face. The three men glanced at Pedí and then continued their argument.

Pedí shuffled inside, shut the door, then crowded up against it. Bookshelves lined the walls of the room. They were filled with journals and tomes of past healers, apothecaries, and herbalists. Doctor Arias let Pedí visit and read any time he wished. It was a place of peace for him.

Not today!

"It would be easy to replace you, old man." Durgo's voice penetrated, dug holes, mocked. "If you don't cooperate, the Municipal Council will stop helping the infirmary. Maybe I'll advise them to stop funding the whole damned Sanctuary. The sages will dismiss you in minutes."

"Then you could use the infirmary for your thieving." His mentor stood straight, his customary warm kindness changing and heating into staunch resilience. "I suppose you'd put that sham healer standing next to you in charge."

Torred's hands tightened into fists. His never-smiling face grew even grimmer. Despite knowing he could do little to stop the towering Torred, Pedí moved to the side of the desk to place himself between his mentor and the angry man.

The greed within Torred's eyes showed as he pointed a finger at Pedí. "We heard you saved someone's life with this mushroom you discovered. Why aren't you treating more people and saving others?"

Pedí knew this was not about saving lives for Breno Torred and the captain. It was about money.

He put his hand over his chest and felt for the Adací statue in his pocket. He tried in vain to get his pounding heart to slow down. He was determined to answer these men without stumbling over his words. "I-I'm trying to find out which infections it cures and that it's safe. The mushroom can be deadly if not prepared and dosed correctly. Until I know I've got it right, I can't take the risk on just anyone, but only on those who would otherwise die without it."

Each word came out with a pause in between, but he was proud that he'd answered with only a few stutters.

The captain wasn't impressed. "What . . . a . . . useless . . . scourge."

Durgo spoke each word with an even longer delay, exaggerating what Pedí had done, then used his hand to shield his eyes from him. He scowled at Doctor Arias. "How can you let this frog-faced Idonata scum contaminate the Sanctuary?"

The insulting words hurt despite the many times Pedí had heard them.

Doctor Arias's cheeks were bright red. He was on the verge of exploding. "Your words show how shallow you are."

Doctor Arias's voice trembled, but Pedí knew anger caused the tremor, not fear of these men, despite the power they held over him. No one else dared stand against the captain, but the doctor would defend Pedí once again. Pedí was bringing disaster upon his teacher and friend.

"Pedí's the most intelligent apprentice the infirmary has ever had."

Durgo smirked and rolled his eyes.

Torred remained grim as always. He pounded his fist on the desktop. "If the boy has found something that can cure infections, it should be in my experienced hands and under the captain's and the Council's jurisdiction, not left to the whims of this juvenile with no backbone."

Breno Torred in charge of the new cure?

What a disaster that would be. The slightest error in preparing and dispensing a dose of nanimoha could be fatal. Torred was careless, and even if he did figure out how to make and give it safely, he and the captain would not use it for good.

Pedí opened his mouth, trying to form words to respond.

Doctor Arias gripped Pedí's shoulder and answered for him. "You're not going to get the mushrooms. I only trust Pedí with something so potentially dangerous. He has the skills of his ancestors."

Durgo snorted and guffawed. "His people were all tattooed idiots. Fortunately, they're all dead and in hell, where they belong."

Pedí's chin quivered. Except for Doctor Arias and others at the Sanctuary, everyone felt that way about him and the Idonata.

Doctor Arias's face turned even more crimson. "Mock all you want, but you'll never find the mushrooms despite sending your spies after Pedí."

Torred curled back his lips, baring his teeth. "Why this mystery? Why are you keeping the mushrooms hidden?"

"They're rare. Pedí collects them little by little to preserve them. You'd use them all up in your rush to make money—do the same as you did with the orange frogs."

Torred slammed his fist on the desktop a second time. "It wasn't my fault the stupid frogs disappeared."

Pedí's mentor shook his head. "You're the only healer who sold the frog toxin at a high price for the narcosis it caused instead of using it for pain. Because of you, the jungle people killed every last one of the little creatures in their frenzy to make a few more coins."

Durgo Borgesso smiled. He was enjoying the confrontation.

Torred's blue eyes glared back at Doctor Arias. "You'll never understand my use of the frog toxin. My expertise is beyond your comprehension. But that's not the issue. This foolish Idonata boy must show us where his mushrooms grow."

"You must also give us the supply he's already collected," the captain added. "Torred will soon have the potion doing good, not delaying its use like this forest boy has done."

"I won't need you to show me how you prepare and dose it." Torred patted his chest. "I'll figure that out myself."

Doctor Arias pointed his finger at the proud healer. "Then you and your charlatan friends would have one more way to hurt and kill people."

"Don't call me a charlatan." Torred started around the desk toward Doctor Arias. Pedí held up his hands to stop him. In one movement, Torred shoved Pedí to the side and into the bookshelf. Pedí's forehead and chest slammed against the wooden shelves. Something shattered in his front shirt pocket.

His Adací!

There was no time to check on his precious figurine. He shook off his ringing head and jumped back to protect his mentor before Torred could take another step.

The blond man grabbed Pedí on both sides and lifted him off the ground.

Durgo laughed hysterically. "Stop, stop, my friend. Although you might do the world a favor by tossing this filth out the window, we must be civilized."

Torred dropped Pedí and backed up. "Don't get in my way again, ever."

Pedí put his hand over his pocket and felt his smashed effigy. His insides convulsed, and his head pounded, but he stood firm between Torred and his mentor.

"Get out of my infirmary." Doctor Arias motioned to the door.

"We'll go," Durgo said, still chuckling, "but this is the sages' infirmary, not yours. We'll find a way to get the mushrooms whether you give them to us or not."

The two men slammed the door behind them.

"Are you all right?" Doctor Arias put his hand on Pedí's arm.

"My head's okay, but he broke my little statue of the heroine of our people." Pedí reached into his pocket and felt hundreds of shattered pieces. He pulled out the largest two—part of an arm and a severed head. He held them in his palm. His guiding light was destroyed.

"It was important to you, wasn't it?"

"It's a figure of our first queen and is hundreds of years old. When the ancients made it, they infused it with power from the real queen. I promised Grandpa I'd never lose or let it be damaged."

"I'm so sorry," Doctor Arias said.

Pedí looked at his mentor's kind eyes. "I've brought all this trouble on you. If the sages replace you, it will be my fault."

"No, they'll fight to keep me here. They're tired of dealing with this new captain. What a tragedy that his generous father died so . . ."

Doctor Arias stopped talking and pinched his lower lip.

Pedí waited. There was something his mentor was hesitant to say.

The Doctor began again. "The last captain's death was mysterious— some kind of stroke, they said. Only Torred took care of him. Durgo wouldn't allow any other healer to see his father after he took ill."

The Doctor paused again, shaking his head. "Davi, my friend who works at The Big House, told me the old captain had been well and active one day, but the next, he went to sleep and never woke up. He wasted away until he died."

Pedí took in a deep breath. He could think of one thing that could cause such a death.

Moura poisoning!

It was hard to imagine that anyone would kill his father just for power and wealth. But Durgo Borgesso, maybe? If so, Breno Torred would be the one to help him do it.

Pedí looked at his mentor. "If the captain convinces the Municipal Council to stop funding the infirmary, what will happen?"

"Only part of the Sanctuary's finances comes from those puppets on the Council. If your cure works as well as I predict, we can play the captain and Torred's same game. We'll make those who have money pay for it, but unlike them, we'll treat those who can't afford it for free."

"Doesn't the captain have enough? Does he really need my new potion?"

"It's not just the money he'd make from selling the mushroom cure that interests him. It's how he'll use it for power. He's afraid of the sages. They've been telling the field and mine workers they are treated unfairly. When they're finally free from their debts, the sages help them get into better housing and work with better wages."

"The captain must hate that," Pedí said.

"With their coffee crop and sugar cane becoming more lucrative each year, Durgo and the other wealthy landholders need more and more workers. They're angry when people pay off their obligations, and they have to start paying them fair wages or lose their help."

Doctor Arias pointed one of his bent fingers at the door as if still talking to Durgo and Torred. "If the captain and that charlatan controlled your potion, they would become the saviors of those who are ill. But they'd price the potion so high that no poor person could pay for it except by going into debt again."

The doctor shook his hand in the air. "We have to keep your mushroom potion away from them. And for now, I want you to be the only one giving it to those who might need it."

Pedí agreed and nodded, but he worried. Without his Adací effigy, Pedí had little faith he would succeed with his nanimoha.

CHAPTER SEVENTEEN

Poor Man's Field

"The Black River is flooding again."

Adací's father brought home the news. A large group of people had escaped the rising waters, but they lost everything.

"They've come to Poor Man's Field," Father said.

Mother organized the household to help. Adací and Heila carried freshly baked bread, cheese, and dried meat from the pantry, which Tavi and Lino loaded into boxes in the back of a wagon.

Pito, holding himself up with two crutches, barked out orders. His right leg was cast in plaster.

Lino leaned toward Adací and spoke so Pito wouldn't hear. "He's bossier than ever now that he can't do the work himself."

It had been three days since the stallion broke Pito's leg, but the tenacious old man was already walking on crutches through the stable house and out to the corral, telling the other men what they were doing wrong.

When the wagon was loaded, Adací approached him. "Can I help you back to your bed?"

"Hell, girl. I'm going with you."

"You'll make your leg worse."

"I must be there to keep you from doing something foolish."

"I'd hit you if you didn't have a broken leg."

"Hit away, I'm not a baby. You act as if this stupid accident was your fault."

Since Pito's injury, Adací had constantly checked on him. She stayed the entire time at the infirmary while his leg was set and put in a cast. She made treats for him with Lelia's help and brought them to him daily.

But despite all that, she hadn't told him about the dream or that she had caused the fox to change course and bolt through the stable house. If Pito knew she was a witch and caused his accident, he would no longer be her friend.

Pito shook one of his crutches at her. "The day this happened, you tried to get me away from Monto as if you knew he was going to kick me."

Adací was caught. She was a stranded baby monkey at the top of a tree with a harpy eagle swooping down to grasp her in its talons.

"I don't know what you mean." Adací hunched her shoulders, trying to feign ignorance.

Pito squinted his already narrow eyes, the wrinkles on his forehead and those below the lids showing even more prominently. "I think you know exactly what I mean. You're still worried about what that worthless son of the captain said—that you might be some kind of enchantress. Did you dream about Monto kicking me?"

The eagle's talons ripped into her body, but she resisted, violently shaking her head. "No, No. I didn't dream. I didn't hurt you."

Adací was not just a witch. She was a liar as well.

"Your answer gives you away. You do believe you caused the accident."

Adací looked to the sky, wishing a real harpy eagle would pounce on her and carry her away. She felt a presence behind her and turned, hoping it was a giant bird of prey. But no, it was Mother with her hands on her hips—much worse than a harpy eagle. She had listened to the entire conversation.

Mother's eyebrows were lowered. "If you're believing in your crazy nightmares again, I don't know what I'm going to do with you."

"I'm not."

Liar, liar.

"I didn't dream about Monto."

Lying witch.

"I didn't …" She stopped herself. If she kept talking and prevaricating, she'd only make it worse.

Pito shook his crutch at her again. "Don't blame yourself for what happened to me. If you imagined something, it doesn't mean it was your fault."

But it was. Adací even scared the fox into the stables. She wanted to tell Pito and Mother everything, but her tongue wouldn't move. She'd never get the words out.

"Come on, girl, get in the wagon. I'm going too, to keep an eye on my black-haired beauty."

I'm a black-haired witch, not a beauty.

Tavi, Lino, and Father lifted Pito into the driver's seat at the front of the wagon. Adací tried to help, but Pito batted her hands away. She ran to the house and brought out her pillow to put under his leg, which stuck straight out. He took it but shook his head at her.

Adací, Heila, and Mother climbed in the back among the boxes. Father and Lino stayed home to do chores and care for the horses. Tavi sat next to Pito and then whipped the reins. They were off to Poor Man's Field.

It lay several miles outside the city and was alongside the East Road, which led to Victory Harbor on the sea. The place called Poor Man's Field was owned by one of the wealthy plantation owners. It had once been plowed and planted, but the soil was rocky and never produced a decent crop. Abandoned, it became a place for journeying traders from the jungles or from Itatu to camp while they sold their goods in the city. It had also become a temporary refuge for people from the Black River, where they could stay until the floods subsided and they could return to their homes.

Adací tried to imagine the difficulty of living along the great Black River plains. The river was huge, she'd been told, and often overran its banks. It entered the sea in a massive swampy delta south of Victory Harbor.

Adací flinched when their wagon shifted in a rut and then hit a bump. The East Road was uneven, with deep tracks caused by the heavy wagons carrying bags of sugar and coffee to the ships at the harbor. She glanced toward Pito to see if the bump had caused him pain. If it did, she couldn't tell. He would hide any discomfort from her.

"Why is the Black River flooding?" Adací asked him. "It's the dry season in New Losobon."

"But not in the cursed jungles!" Despite the wagon noise, Pito was easy to hear with his loud voice. "It rains all year in the mountains that ring those lowlands."

"There's been even more rain than normal," Mother added.

"The worst flooding is in the river valley after the falls," Pito said. "Even the houses on stilts are getting water into them."

"The roar at Romingo must be overwhelming." Mother put her hands over her ears as if hearing the water shoot over the cliffs, though they were hundreds of miles away.

Adací had never seen the Seven Cataracts of Romingo. All the jungle rivers came together in one place, then cascaded over an escarpment in seven giant chutes and hundreds of smaller waterfalls. Her parents had been there before they adopted her, but they always made excuses when she asked about going. Marina and Sergol had traveled a lot before Adací came into their family. Everything changed after that. Always overprotective, they'd not let her do anything that might be the least bit dangerous. They wouldn't even take her to see the colorful Itatu villages in the Blue Mountains.

"Do you think any Itatu traders will be at the field?" Adací shaded her eyes from the bright sun with one hand and wiped the wagon dust off her sweaty forehead with the other.

"If any are there, they won't camp near the Black River folk."

"Why are people so mean to the Itatu?" Adací asked.

"Well, they're different, aren't they?" Mother answered. "All freckles and red hair."

Adací had good memories of all the red-haired mountain people she'd met, but throughout her life, she had heard them called derogatory names.

Pito twisted back so his loud voice boomed even more. "The Itatu crossed the seas before our people, but nobody seems to know where they came from."

"They made peace with the Idonata," Mother added, "but moved from the valley into the high foothills. I don't think they wanted to infringe on the land used by their Idonata friends."

Pito spit to the side of the wagon. "If they had stayed in the valley, our soldiers would have chased them off and killed them as they did to the Idonata. Living in the Blue Mountains is hard, so we left them alone. Long ago, the Idonata people taught them how to tame the strange mountain sheep and even the deer. By damn, the Itatu have got herds of deer, if you can believe it!"

The wagons arrived at Poor Man's Field and pulled off the road. An open expanse of tall grass dotted with termite mounds spread before them. A few small groves of trees and thickets were scattered amidst the grass.

The Black River people huddled together in three encampments near some trees. They had built shelters using dilapidated wagons, abandoned wood, and old animal skins. To Adací's disappointment, no traders from Itatu were among them.

While distributing food, Adací noticed a little boy about six or seven years old. The child was off by himself, away from everyone. When the boy saw the food, he started toward the group, but a tall man got up from eating and shouted at him. "You stay over there. I'll bring you some food."

The man walked toward the boy with a slice of bread and a small hunk of cheese, but when he got ten feet away, he flung the bread and cheese at him. The food skidded in the dirt, but the little boy pounced on it and began eating, dirt and all.

Adací walked toward the child with fresh food and a bottle of water, intent on helping him.

"Leave him be!" Adací's mother commanded. "He must be getting punished or something."

Adací stopped, but she couldn't keep her eyes off the boy. He sat in the dirt, eating the soiled food. She saw his tears and inched her way toward him.

"No, Adací," Mother said, guessing her thoughts.

Adací returned to help distribute the rest of the food but kept watching the boy. He looked sad and needed a friend. And maybe more food? Adací stayed back when her mother, Heila, and Tavi gathered armloads of food to take to the last encampment on the other side of the trees. Pito had joined a group of Black River folk around their campfire. No one saw Adací when she got in the wagon and grabbed the last sack of bread and a water bottle. She rushed to the boy's side. He smiled at her and wiped the tears from his eyes. The boy's face was covered in crusty brown and yellow scabs. A semi-clear yellow fluid leaked out of them. Was that why his family didn't want him by them? The sores weren't hurting them, but only the boy. Adací would help him get better. She remembered watching a man scrub sores on a dog once. Maybe that's what these crusty lesions needed. Then he could be with his family again.

She gave the boy a drink of water and a fresh loaf of bread and then ran back to the wagon. There was an old bucket and scrub brush in the corner. Adací grabbed them and returned to the boy. She put some water in the bucket and scrubbed hard at all his dark sores. The boy winced but kept smiling, happy that someone brought him food and was not abandoning him.

When she finished, she heard someone running toward them.

It was Mother.

Pito was ten steps behind, moving as fast as he could on his crutches. A few Black River folk came with them—including the tall man who'd flung the food at the boy. They all stopped fifteen feet away. Their eyes were wide open, their mouths as well.

"What are you doing, miss?" the tall man questioned. "You shouldn't be near my boy."

"What does he have?" Pito asked.

"Jungle rot. It catches easily and causes terrible scarring."

"Why don't you ever obey?" Mother said in her angry voice. "I told you not to go to him." But then Mother softened. Her following words came out with tears in her eyes. "Oh, Adací! If you get those sores on your face, you'll be scarred. It will change your entire future. It will be a very sad one."

Adací looked at the scrub brush in her hand and dropped it into the bucket of water. She looked at the little boy, who still smiled up at her. The scabs were scrubbed off, but now each lesion was bleeding.

She'd only made him worse. Once more, she'd failed to do the right thing.

And Mother was right about her sad future. If she got the sores and scarred her face, she'd look like the old hag she'd read about in a book. Adací had taken the next step toward becoming a full-blown witch.

CHAPTER EIGHTEEN

Scrum

Adací's hands covered her face. She didn't want anyone to see the revolting crusts that spread across her cheeks.

Mother stood at her side and urged her forward, but Adací hesitated at the entrance to the infirmary. The healing wing stood at the south end of the Sanctuary complex. The historic structure had been built by the first sages who crossed the seas. It was composed of many intertwining buildings. They had been added at various times during its two-hundred-year history. The walls were the typical clay bricks covered with stucco, but arches of masonry surrounded each window and door. Sandstone figures of forest animals had been placed in small alcoves above each opening.

Adací glanced up at the lichen-covered roof tiles, which peaked at odd angles. In the center of the two main wings, the silver dome of the assembly hall rose high, contrasting with the darkened tile.

The color of that dome matched the hidden crescent moon on Adací's chest and the part of her braid that was dyed. She could hide the hair and the tattoo, but she couldn't conceal the scourge on her skin—the infection from the immigrant boy.

"Doomed to be scarred," the local healer had said, then fled the house after seeing her. His expensive potion had not helped.

"Imposter," Father said of him when her face worsened. "You have to see Doctor Arias. He knows more than all the other healers."

Adací rocked back and forth in a chair in the infirmary room where she and her mother were taken. The red-tiled floor was waxed to a brilliant shine, and the walls were plastered smooth and painted stark white. Except for a few wooden chairs and an exam table covered with a cloth, the room was nearly empty.

Empty, like her future was going to be.

Afternoon sunlight shone through a large window. Amulets and charms lined the inside of the windowsill. Brought by patients to ward off evil, the healers and sages tolerated it, even though they discouraged the ancient practices.

None of those talismans could stop Adací from becoming a defaced, unsightly hag—the witch she was destined to be.

She looked past the amulets and out at the flowers and trees in the Sanctuary's inner courtyard. Two hummingbirds zipped back and forth among the red flowers. Their feathers shimmered green each time the sunlight struck them. Despite her despair, a little smile emerged—Adací couldn't suppress it. She felt connected to all birds. She fed them, studied them, and sang with them. Her feathered friends would still love an ugly Adací.

But no boys would ever look at her, certainly not any of the wealthy young men her parents hoped to match her with. And for sure, not Bertol! So proud of his handsome face, he would not want to be seen with a blemished Adací.

Well, at least he'd quit bothering her now.

"I hope Doctor Arias can help," Mother interrupted her thoughts. "We should have come here sooner."

What could the doctor possibly do when the lesions were already so horrible? Dark brown painful crusts were scattered over her face, hands, and forearms. A yellow liquid leaked out from them, sometimes running down her face. She carried a small handkerchief to dab them dry.

How would she look when the disease did its damage, and her face was nothing but deep pits with bands of tight scar tissue in between? She had once seen a young girl with such a face. It had frightened her. Soon, Adací would be the freak haunting others.

She reached to grasp her mother's hands but drew back, not wanting to give her any more of the sores. What if the disease spread to her mother's lovely face? Adací would be devastated.

"I'm sorry your hands are getting my sores."

"It's not your fault, it's mine. I should have kept you roped to my side at Poor Man's Field."

"No, Mama, you warned me."

There were voices outside the exam room. A moment later, the door swung open, and Doctor Arias entered. Each step he took was slow as if his joints were in pain, but he smiled, and his mustache moved upward. His eyes danced behind his thick glasses.

"Marina, how good to see you." He leaned in to shake Mother's hand.

She held back and pointed to the sores.

"Oh, I see." He looked at Adací. "This must be your beautiful daughter."

Adací moved her hands to cover her cheeks. "I'll soon be her ugly daughter." Tears rimmed at the corners of her eyes, but she held them back.

"You're afraid of scarring?" Doctor Arias's voice was kind.

Adací nodded. This doctor would help her if he could.

"It's spreading fast," Mother said.

"Let me examine her."

While he looked at Adací's hands and face, she watched his eyes. They weren't dancing now. He didn't touch the sores as if afraid of them. His thick eyebrows lowered, and the skin folded on his forehead. She looked for hope but saw none.

"How did you get the sores?" he asked.

Mother answered for her. "We went to Poor Man's Field to help the immigrants. There was a little boy off by himself. Adací went to him without us knowing. When she saw his sores, she decided she could help heal him by scrubbing them. Of course, it did no good, and a few days later, she broke out herself."

"Was the boy from the Black River?" the doctor asked.

"Yes, his family had escaped the floods."

Doctor Arias took his glasses off and rubbed his bushy eyebrows. Adací held her breath.

"Scrum," he said.

One word, but it sounded like a death sentence to Adací.

"It's called different names in the jungles and along the Black River, but it's an awful disease." His eyes were old and sad without his glasses on, conveying the same bleak message she heard from his lips. "We don't see this type of scrum in our valley."

Adací turned to look out the window. She watched for the hummingbirds, but they were gone. She knew what Doctor Arias was going to say next. She whimpered, then stopped herself.

"I'm sorry," he said. "It does scar. Deep and permanent scars."

"Oh, Adací," Mother said.

The words *deep scars* sunk in like a shovel gouging the soft earth, digging away at her self-worth.

"You have the face of an angel," her mother's sister had always said. That was going to change. Soon, she'd be a witch through and through.

Adací wanted to scream—to say it wasn't fair, but how could she? Didn't she deserve it for what she'd done to Pito? For all her horrible dreams?

Mother put her hand on Adací's arm and looked at Doctor Arias. "Is there anything to treat this?"

His glasses were back on, but his face was expressionless. "There is no potion for scrum."

"Can we . . ." Adací's voice cracked. "Can we stop it from spreading to Mama's face?"

"That, I hope we can do."

Doctor Arias turned toward the window. He sat in his chair with his mouth partly open. The round, thick glasses were off again and in his right hand. With the left, he rubbed his eyes. "I wonder . . ." He spoke just those two words, but he didn't go on. He was not looking at Adací or her mother.

"I'll be right back." He jumped up as fast as his old bones let him, opened the door, and limped into the corridor.

Mother came over and grasped Adací's hands with both of hers.

"But the sores, Mama. I don't want to give you more."

Mother just shook her head and clasped tighter. They waited in silence, holding hands.

Doctor Arias's voice sounded again in the corridor, and the door swung open.

"I've sent for my best apprentice." The doctor's eyes sparkled once again behind the lenses. The pitch of his voice was higher. "He's an Idonata boy, and he made a strange new potion out of a mushroom—a mushroom his ancestors used as a cure before they were all killed off. He's learning what things it might heal."

Doctor Arias waved a hand in the air. "He's cured two people with lung infections and another with bloody dysentery. He gave a dose to a man with a deep wound infection, and the pus is starting to go away."

The doctor dropped the waving hand back to his side and looked at the floor, the twinkle in his eyes diminishing. "But I have to be honest. Some types of infections my apprentice has treated didn't respond."

There was a bump at the wooden door, and Adací watched it swing open. A young man about her age entered, his features catching her attention. He had black hair, cut short. It was as dark as hers, something she didn't see often in New Losobon. His eyes were brown, his face handsome, bright, and discerning. But most striking was the exquisite frog tattoo etched onto his left cheek. It was a perfect rendition and had ten round spots covering its sides.

Adací's hand went to the front of her chest, where her tattoo lay hidden beneath her dress. Stories abounded of the intricate tattoos Idonata people had used to adorn themselves. They could be anywhere on their body, the tales said, but many liked to show them off on their face or neck—like this young healer had chosen to do.

The boy was from the lost Idonata, even though she'd been told none were left. Obviously, that was not right. Perhaps this young man knew the ancient ways. Maybe he would understand how to help her with the terrible visions—even prevent her from becoming an evil sorceress.

That fleeting hope vanished the moment the dark-haired boy looked at her. His face paled, and he took a step backward.

Terror? Or was it disgust? Adací didn't know which was more evident in his expression.

Her life as an ugly, frightening witch had begun.

CHAPTER NINETEEN

Apprentice Healer

Pedí took another step back. His knees buckled, and he put his hand on the wall to steady himself. His lips moved, but nothing came out.

A girl who reminded him of Adací, his ancient heroine, was sitting on the exam table. She had Adací's long braid—as black as the darkest night. But unlike his Adací, there was not a plait of silver.

This girl's face was covered in dark, scabby sores. However, in spite of them, Pedí was spellbound by her countenance. Her eyes, in particular, drew him in but panicked him. He'd never been able to do more than glance at a girl's eyes without turning away. But like the myths of poisonous snakes who could hypnotize their prey with their slitted lenses, Pedí was paralyzed by this black-haired enchantress.

The strange girl covered the sores on her cheeks with her hands as Doctor Arias waved him in. "Come and meet Marina Façillo and her daughter, Adací."

Adací! How could this girl carry that name? People in New Losobon didn't know about his heroine. Only the Idonata used or said that name.

"Good day," the girl's mother said. The mystical, black-braided girl said nothing and looked aside as if she wanted to hide from him. That broke the spell that had bound him to her.

"G-g-g-good d-d-d-day." At least he got that much out. His hand still trembled against the wall.

"Pedí's our finest apprentice." Doctor Arias rubbed his gnarled hands together.

"It bothers him when I brag, but this young man's a genius. He's found many new herbs and roots for cures, but his latest find—a strange mushroom—is the most promising."

His mentor glanced at Adací, then back at Pedí. "I want him to tell you about his new cure, his nanimoha. That's what his ancestors called it. But it may be hard for him. He doesn't stutter anymore with us, but he's very shy and sometimes can't help it when he's around—" Doctor Arias stopped himself from saying more.

Pedí was grateful his mentor had stopped talking about him but noticed the black-haired girl had dropped her hands from her face and looked at him again—the apprehension gone from her eyes. She must have hidden her sores because she thought Pedí was afraid of them, but now she understood that Pedí feared her, not the sores.

Doctor Arias got up and took ahold of his arm. "Do you think your mushroom potion will work for scrum?"

Scrum? Pedí had seen it only once before. Is that what plagued this image of Adací?

He thought about fleeing from the room—from this girl—but his mentor held onto him.

"Adací and Marina need your help."

"But-but, I-I—"

"Please examine their sores and tell them about your nanimoha."

Pedí gave in, not wanting to disappoint his teacher. He started with the mother. That was much safer. His trembling stopped once he began his inspection. His brain pushed out all other thoughts. The scrum he'd seen before was on a traveler who'd returned from the jungles. He knew it was best not to touch the crusts.

After examining Marina's hands, he shuffled over to the girl named Adací but did not look up and only checked her hands and forearms.

"You need to evaluate her face," Doctor Arias said.

Pedí hesitated, afraid to look into her eyes again.

"I'm sorry, I'm so hideous," the girl said.

Afraid he had shamed her, he made himself look at her face. She started covering her cheeks again but stopped when his head tilted up.

"You're not hi-hi-hi . . ." Not another sound would come out.

Stupid Pedí! He couldn't even apologize because of his cursed tongue.

He tried to concentrate on the exam. Four brown scabby lesions covered the girl's right cheek and two on the left. A yellow serous fluid drained from them. Despite his ability to push out other thoughts when doing his healer work, those skills began to fail him. His only thoughts were questions. Where had this girl come from who looked like the ancient Adací and carried her name?

He finished his exam as best he could and then looked at the floor. Doctor Arias put his hand on Pedí's shoulder. "Well, what do you think?"

Concentrate Pedí. Get your focus back. It's not the real Adací sitting there.

"No skin diseases have responded to the nanimoha." He managed a whole sentence with only a few stutters. "Not the man dying from pox, and it hasn't helped those two jungle traders with espundia. Despite giving them several doses of my nanimoha, the infection has spread. It's eating away the nose cartilage on one of them. Soon, instead of a nose, he'll have a deep hole like a skeleton. I'm so sad for him."

"I'm sorry to hear that," Doctor Arias said, glancing toward Adací.

"I hoped it would help those poor men," Pedí added. "It must be a different kind of creature that causes espundia."

"You're still convinced about your invisible life forms."

Pedí nodded. "Infections have to be caused by something living that spreads from one to another person or gets in wounds."

The girl named Adací slumped and would have fallen off the table if her mother had not grabbed her arm. The girl's face was white. Doctor Arias helped her lie down.

She whispered, "Is scrum like espundia? Is my nose going to be eaten off?"

"No, no, my dear." Doctor Arias waved his bumpy hands in the air. "Scrum won't dissolve your nose. Espundia is rare and only caught from a few places in the jungles."

The girl sat back up, a little color returning to her scab-covered cheeks. "I have nightmares of men in skeletal masks chasing my birth parents down a narrow—"

"Please, Adací!" Her mother cut her off. "These men don't need to hear about your foolish dreams."

"But I thought my nose might become a skeleton's nose."

Pedí shook his head. He wanted to comfort the girl, but he'd never get his worthless tongue to speak if he had to address her.

Fortunately, Doctor Arias talked for him. "Your nose is safe."

But the doctor frowned. "However, scrum will scar your lovely face. It hasn't yet, and we might prevent it if Pedí's potion could work for this disease."

Pedí was back to looking at the floor but heard the girl whimper and then whisper. "Please look at me."

He hesitated, then looked up at her.

"Help me," she continued to whisper. "Use your potion, your nanimoha, on me. I don't want to be a ..." She didn't finish her sentence.

"I-I-I'll try. It might work for scrum. For some infections, it's been very effective."

He cleared his throat, preparing to explain the possible risks of his nanimoha. He hoped not to stutter so they'd understand. "I need to tell you something. You have to swallow the nanimoha for it to work. Putting it on your sores won't help. The mushroom I use is poisonous, and until I learned how to prepare and dose it the right way, some of the first dogs and gophers I gave it to died. I didn't give it to any people until I knew I could do it without harming them. But still, I've been cautious with who I give it to."

To his relief, the words came out without a stammer.

Adací's mother stepped between him and the girl. "You are not going to give my daughter something dangerous."

"I-I—"

Doctor Arias came to the rescue once again. "Pedí knows how to use the forest plants like no one else. He experimented with animals first to find the safe dose for the mushroom. He is extremely meticulous in preparing and giving this new treatment."

Pedí's face warmed. The doctor's words of praise embarrassed him. His mentor went on. "He has given it to quite a few people now, and most have had none or only a few side effects. Not one has died, and many have had miraculous cures. His caution is part of what makes him a great healer, but I've told him it's time to begin using his nanimoha on more infections. Scrum would be a perfect disease to try it on. Though scrum doesn't kill people, it's a horrible fate if you get it on your face."

Adací leaned so she could look around her mother to speak directly at Pedí. "I'm not afraid. Please try it on me if there's any chance it might work."

"Only if I take it first," her mother said.

"If you are willing to take it, I'll go m-make a new batch. I wouldn't give it to you if I thought it would harm you, but I wanted you to understand the risk. Even though it's been safe, I still worry with each new person I give it to."

Between a few stutters and stammers, Pedí explained the process he used to make the nanimoha. As he left the room to make a batch in the laboratory, he clutched at the pocket on his shirt that used to hold his clay Adací, then glanced back at this girl named Adací, this living Adací.

How he hoped his potion would work for her.

CHAPTER TWENTY

First Dose

Each lesion on Adací's face pulsed with renewed pain after the young apprentice and Doctor Arias left the room. Pedí had talked about unseen creatures causing her sores. She imagined each little life eating away at her, digging further into her skin, hiding to protect itself before she took the new potion.

She wanted to believe, to hope the healer could kill the creatures and save her from having an old hag's face. But the mushroom cure hadn't worked for any skin diseases. Was her destiny set? Was there was no escape?

When Pedí returned, he carried a glass jar full of a light-yellow liquid. It was steaming. He had told them he had to make a new batch over a stove. "The potion has to be made fresh each time," he had said. "It will stay good for twelve hours but then has to be discarded."

The young healer treated Mother first. He brought out a short glass tube. It was open on both ends and had an engraved line about an inch from one of the ends. The apprentice dipped the tube into the liquid of the jar, and then by opening and closing his finger over the other end, he adjusted the amount that went into the narrow cylinder until it was precisely at the scratch mark. His movements were careful and exacting.

He put the tube into Mother's mouth and let his finger off the opposite end so the potion drained out. Adací watched to see if her mother gagged or spit it out.

"It's not bad," Mother said.

Pedí repeated the process every five minutes and asked if Mother was okay after each ingestion.

After the sixth and final dose, he asked again. "Are you still all right?"

"I don't feel ill."

"May he treat me now, Mama?"

Mother nodded.

With the same caution, the apprentice prepared Adací's first dose using a second glass tube. She tensed when he put it in her mouth and released his finger. The taste was bitter and sweet at the same time. She wondered if he had added something to mask the harsh part of the flavor.

Pedí's tongue stuck out a little each time he drew new liquid into the tube. She couldn't help but smile. His fingers trembled each time he put the tube in her mouth, but she sensed a softness underneath his anxiety. She asked him several questions, but he stammered so much that he never got a complete answer out of his mouth. The young man's face turned a deeper red with each failure to talk with her.

Mother gave Adací's arm a squeeze. She got the message—leave him alone.

Adací sat in silence and glanced back and forth between the apprentice and the old clock hanging on the wall as they waited between doses. The clock's arm swung back and forth. Her future was swinging back and forth on whether this potion would work for scrum.

Just as she was getting the last dose, Doctor Arias returned. When she had swallowed it, he asked, "Any bad effects? Are you feeling okay?"

Adací shook her head.

"We're both fine," Mother said.

"Wonderful!" Doctor Arias's voice rose high. "Now we just have to hope for the best. I will send Pedí to your house tomorrow to check on you and give you the second treatment."

The apprentice's eyes widened. Adací had seen that same look of terror in a fledgling thrush that had fallen out of its nest.

"I c-can't."

"No, Pedí." Doctor Arias's friendly face grew stern. "I won't let you use your fears as an excuse."

The frightened baby thrush look worsened.

"He's never been to the home of a young lady." The doctor's face softened as he squeezed the apprentice's shoulder. "You're going as their healer. It's not a social visit."

Despite the doctor's kind words, Pedí's scared look did not go away. He fumbled for something in his back pocket and pulled out a small jar. "I f-forgot. This is something else to help. This ointment won't cure the scrum, but it will help your skin heal if the nanimoha works to stop the infection. It has plant oils and soothing herbs. Put a little on each sore three times each day. And don't scrub your face hard, just gently wash."

He handed the jar to Adací but then raced past Doctor Arias and out the door without saying more.

Adací started after him. He couldn't just leave. Mother grabbed her arm and stopped her.

"What's wrong?" Adací looked at Doctor Arias. "Did I do or say something that offended him? Is he not going to come and try to cure us?"

"He'll go to your home tomorrow. You can rest assured of that." Doctor Arias rubbed his short mustache and hesitated as if deciding whether to say more. "Pedí's tattoo and peculiarities mark him as different, and he avoids people outside of the Sanctuary as most treat him poorly. Young people his age cause him the greatest fear. He was the only Idonata boy ever to attend one of the sage's schools. But he was mocked and bullied so much that he quit going."

"If the boy quit going to school," Mother asked, "how did he become an apprentice?"

"Jurana and Gabro, two of the sages from the main council, found him in the Sanctuary library, studying on his own. Pedí is smarter than all those who mocked him, but nobody knew. He rarely spoke. The two sages began tutoring him and convinced me to make him an apprentice when he was just fifteen. He's been working with me for two years. It was the best decision I ever made."

Adací listened to every word about Pedí. He was so brilliant, yet so unusual. She wondered why she'd never met him. He must have gone to the new school. The previous captain had been very generous and given the sages money to construct their third school. It was built near the poorer north side of New Losobon.

The Doctor continued. "Pedí has his own scars, but they're hidden inside."

A muted cry escaped Adací, but it wasn't for herself. This young man, who was trying to save her face, had no friends except for Doctor Arias and the sages.

I'll be his friend and help him overcome his shyness. He's an Idonata like me and will save me from becoming a witch.

On the way home in the buggy, Mother held her hands up. "I feel like the potion's already working on my sores."

"I know!" Adací exclaimed. "They're tingling." From her previous despair, Adací now sensed hope. No, it wasn't just hope. This healer was going to cure her.

"If I don't scar, I'll love this boy forever."

"Adací! What are you saying? You're always attracted to the outcasts and those with problems—like the immigrant boy who gave this scrum to you. And your birds—the little ones who fall out of the nest or those with wounded wings—you try to fix them all. This young man has problems you can't fix."

"I didn't mean it that way, Mama. I'll just be grateful. But Mama, since he's an Idonata, would you let him teach me about my heritage?"

"Oh, Adací! How I hoped you would not think and say those words. I'll be forever indebted to this young healer if he can cure us of the scrum, but the more you are with Pedí, the more likely that others will guess your origin. You have to hide your identity for your safety. I know you understand why in part, but there's much more to it."

The buggy turned the corner and skidded on the slick stone road. They passed the park where Adací often went to watch birds. A tall

Signal tree reached skyward above the other trees, preserved in this small remnant of native forest. They were almost home.

Adací glanced to the side. Mother's eyes were peering right through her.

"Don't worry, Mama."

Her parents would never let her be friends with someone not of their choosing. And especially, not a poor Idonata boy.

CHAPTER TWENTY-ONE

Frog in the Infirmary

The wail of a child echoed through the dark Sanctuary corridors. Pedí rounded a corner and ran into Crina, one of the newest apprentice healers.

"There you are." The girl was out of breath. "Doctor Arias is looking for you. A little boy got caught on a thorn bush and ripped a gash in his leg. He won't let anyone touch him."

Pedí and Crina walked side by side the rest of the way. He avoided looking at her, even though he knew she watched his every move.

Crina and her friend Misha, another new apprentice, began bothering Pedí when they started their training a few months ago. They sought him out, then pestered him with questions. Just seeing the two girls walk toward him tangled up his tongue.

Crina began her usual tirade of embarrassing questions, but he somehow got by with yes and no answers, saving himself from stuttering. He took a deep breath and sighed when they finally arrived at the exam room, where the child was crying.

Doctor Arias stood outside the door. "You're late."

"I had to make a fresh batch of mushroom potion for the young woman and her mother." Pedí paused before continuing. "I don't want to go to their house, but I will since you asked."

"I know you will." Doctor Arias smiled. "At noon, right?"

Pedí nodded.

His mentor then pointed at the exam room door. "A little boy has refused to let me and two other healers get near him, so we waited for you. His poor mother is in tears herself."

Pedí could handle children. His tongue worked better, and he knew how to make them smile.

"Doctor says you calm the little ones," Crina said.

Pedí cringed. Was Crina going to be the one helping him? Her long, blinking eyelashes and probing queries were sure to unsettle him.

He walked to a nearby window—away from Crina's side, he might think better. The courtyard pond was visible, shining in the morning sunlight. Spotted frogs were always there in the shallow end.

Pedí turned and asked, "How old is the boy?"

"Five," Doctor Arias answered.

Perfect age for spotted frogs! "Crina, would you get a small jar and put about an inch of water in it?"

She raised her eyebrows. "Okay, but—"

"Wait for me here, and I'll be back."

In the center of the courtyard, water flowed out of an ancient spring and filled a small lagoon. Emerald dragonflies buzzed across the surface, catching unwary gnats and flies. A tiny brook flowed out of the far end of the pond and meandered through the courtyard, then out into the Sanctuary orchard.

Pedí sat by the edge, not moving, waiting. A brownish-green frog with black spots popped up through the algae. Snap! Pedí's swift hands cupped the frog firmly but gently at the same time. He whispered to it, and it quit struggling.

He returned to the infirmary and entered the room with the injured boy. Crina was already there, holding the jar of water.

"Don't touch me," the boy screamed. He lay on the exam table with his trousers off. A jagged laceration split his right lower leg. Blood dripped off the wound onto the table. Pedí evaluated the laceration from a distance for how to numb it, clean it, and the best suture to use. The mother was trying to console her child without success.

Pedí hoped his plan to calm this little guy would work. "Look what I have in my hands."

The boy stopped crying when he saw the frog peeking out from Pedí's fingers.

"I need you to watch my friend for me until I fix your cut."

The boy held out his hands, his fears forgotten.

"What are you doing?" The child's mother raised her hands as if to push Pedí away. "I see your tattoo. You must be a survivor of those Idonata people. I don't want you near my boy."

Pedí touched the frog on his cheek, embarrassed that something so important to him would cause distress to this mother when she realized he was Idonata.

Crina walked over to her side. "This is Pedí, the best apprentice in the whole infirmary. He's also the best at fixing cuts and knows how to quiet the little ones."

Crina's compliments plagued Pedí. He didn't know if she meant them, but it helped soften the mother this time.

"May I?" he asked, showing the mother the frog in his hands and motioning toward her son.

She nodded.

Pedí let the boy touch the spotted amphibian. "Let's put him in Crina's jar of water. Then his skin won't get too dry."

Pedí had the boy help him transfer the frog to the jar. "You'll have to keep your hand over the top."

The boy giggled as the frog bounced against his palm.

"Don't let him escape."

With the boy happily distracted, Pedí washed his hands in a basin and went to the side table where the instruments and supplies were stored.

He soaked a cloth in andiroba oil and stood near the boy's leg. The wound appeared to only go into the superficial fat layer, not the muscle, so he wouldn't need any deep sutures. It would require some cleaning, but first, he'd let the oil numb the injury.

"I am going to put this over your cut. Then it won't hurt when I fix it. Keep watching our frog, even if this oil causes a little stinging."

The boy enjoyed the hopping frog in the jar while the oil did its work. Pedí swallowed and tried to loosen his tongue. He wanted to tell stories to distract the child, but it wouldn't be easy with Crina and the boy's mother listening.

He started slowly, trying to keep each word steady. "When I was your age, my grandpa taught me how to catch f-frogs. They became my best friends."

Pedí checked, and the cut was numb. He poured water over it and washed it clean.

"One day, I shocked Grandpa when I caught something else. Something scary!"

The boy's eyes got big. He didn't notice as Pedí chose a suture from a container of various sizes and threaded the curved needle. Pedí pinched the skin edges together and slipped the needle through both sides.

"It was a racer snake, blue on top with a yellow belly, and I didn't let it go, even when it bit me."

Pedí glanced at the boy, whose eyes widened further and mouth plopped open.

"Racers have tiny teeth, so it didn't hurt much, and they aren't poisonous. It also became my friend."

As he placed and tied each suture, Pedí told stories about monitor lizards and fat salamanders.

When he finished, he bent to be near the boy. "Your cut's all fixed. Thank you for watching our frog friend. Do you have a name for him?"

The boy closed his eyes for a moment, then nodded. "His name is Obi."

"That's a good name. I can take him to the pond now. When you come back to get your stitches out, we'll go there and find Obi again. Okay?"

Pedí took the jar and whispered a few words to the frog. It quit trying to jump out and looked relaxed, floating in the water.

"Isn't he the best?" Crina blinked her eyes at Pedí.

His hands, which had been so sure with each needle stick and tie a moment ago, grew cold and shaky. It was time to leave.

At the pond, the frog leaped out of the jar and dove into the dark mud at the bottom. Long-legged water striders danced on top of the water. A scarlet dragonfly with banded wings patrolled the air near Pedí and briefly hovered at his side.

Pedí scanned the air for the Blue Dragonfly, the mythical giant one. He had searched for one for his entire life at every pond and swamp he visited. Grandpa had insisted the legends were true and thought he might have seen one as a child. It was supposed to be three times as big as any other dragonfly. Its color was an iridescent blue that would glow even more in the sunlight.

Pedí worried that none were left alive.

His Idonata ancestors had worshiped the Blue Dragonfly and drew pictures of it inside their temples. It was the last of an age-old type of dragonfly, rarely seen, but it appeared when the Shushuhadors called for its help. According to legend, there was a connection between the queen, the Shushuhadors, and the Blue Dragonfly. Some said the ancient men could communicate with the insect world when the dragonfly assisted them. It had started with Adací, the first queen of the Idonata, and continued down to the last queen, who had died two hundred years ago. But with no queen and no Shushuhadors left, there were unlikely Blue Dragonflies either.

The Sanctuary bell tower began tolling. Nine chimes. In three hours, he would have to go to Adací's home. The vision of the Blue Dragonfly was driven from his mind and replaced with a braid of black hair. Like a vine from a strangler fig, the thought of that braid circled and constricted his neck. Pedí could barely suck in air as competing thoughts fought each other inside his head. He wanted to help Adací but was afraid of her. Who was this girl? Where had she come from, and why was she named after the heroine of the Idonata?

He was drawn to this girl, yet wanted to run from her at the same time.

A water snake prowled the edge of the pond. Its appearance interrupted Pedí's thoughts and broke the imaginary braid that choked him. He took a deep breath.

The spotted frog he had released popped back up to the water's surface, not far from the roving snake.

"Hide, little friend."

The frog dove back into the mud, and Pedí returned to his work at the infirmary.

When noon arrived, he stopped by the laboratory and picked up the jar of nanimoha potion. He left the Sanctuary grounds and made his way toward Adací's house. He scuffed his shoes on the worn cobblestones. In this affluent area, the streets were not dirt like the rest of the city, nor like the muddy trail that ran by his mama's shack.

He had learned that Adací's father raised horses. He must do well to live in the nice part of town. Pedí could only imagine how glorious their house must be. It would be made of stones, hardened brick, or finely trimmed wood—not plastered over clay like most of New Losobon, nor like the wooden shanty where he had lived with his mother.

As he neared Adací's home, he glanced again at the paper with the address scribbled on it. His hand holding the paper trembled. With his other hand, he clutched his shirt pocket and pleaded to an Adací effigy, which was no longer there. "Please help me cure this girl, but save me from her."

She had been kind yesterday, but a wealthy, refined person like Adací would think of him the same as all the other people of New Losobon did.

The last day he had attended school was when Rita—a girl he hoped would like him—shamed him in front of the class.

"Why must we allow a tattooed Idonata boy into our school?" Rita had asked the sage who was teaching them. "He's not like us."

The sage started to answer. "We want to be kind to—"

Rita interrupted. "He saved a snake from the boys beating it with sticks. Then I saw him talk to it. And he carries a doll in his pocket. He talks to it, too."

Pedí had taken his Adací statue out to show her to the sage. He tried to explain who she was and how she had saved the world from the six evil spirits at the beginning of time. But he only got out a few stammers when his words were drowned out.

Rita had begun a chant. "Pedí talks to snakes. Pedí talks to dolls."

Everyone but the sage joined in.

He ran out of the room to jeers and jokes. Rita's voice was the loudest. "I hope you never come back."

He didn't.

He quit school and started working in the cane fields. If Jurana and Gabro hadn't found him in the Sanctuary's library, trying to study on his own at night, he never would have been anything—never could have made a little money as an apprentice to send to his mother. She was grateful when the sages and Doctor Arias asked him to move to the Sanctuary, where he could better complete his training. Doctor Arias had proposed that his mother come and live at the Sanctuary with him, but his mama declined. "I'll be happier in the little house my husband built for us."

Pedí had worried about not being home to help.

"I'll be fine," Mama had said. "Make something of yourself. Help others. Papa would be proud. Just come home as often as you are able."

And Pedí did go home often. He fixed things in their little shack or worked in the garden. Each time he went home, Mama praised him and said he spoke better than ever. That was only because she didn't hear him try to talk to other people.

It was partly true, though. With Jurana, Gabro, and Doctor Arias, the stuttering disappeared. They treated him like an equal. No one else ever had. In addition to the medical training he got from Doctor Arias at the infirmary, Jurana and Gabro also made time for him. They visited with him daily on the sandstone bench at the end of the inner courtyard. They taught him what he missed from not being at school and shared their favorite books. Every day, he learned something new.

Jurana and Gabro asked him to tell them about his Idonata beliefs. They told him never to forget what he'd learned from his mama, his Grandpa, and his Grandma.

CHAPTER TWENTY-TWO

Second Dose

A loud squawk brought Adací out of a deep sleep—the first good rest she'd had all night. The annoying sound had come from outside. She stretched and looked toward the window. The gray of early morning came through it and lightened the room.

Another squawk, even louder, penetrated her room. She recognized it this time—a pesky green parrot. She knew their calls, this one a screech of frustration. The bird feeder must be empty.

Too bad it wasn't an orange thrush. Its beautiful song woke her up during the summer months. She had learned to imitate the thrush's voice and could sing with it.

Adací lay back on her pillow. The recurrent dream about her birth parents had disrupted her slumber on and off throughout the night.

The parrot called out again, and she was startled. Thinking about the vision of the warriors in death head masks had set her nerves on edge. Fortunately, her face was not going to become skeletal. She didn't have espundia and wouldn't lose her nose. The horrible scrum was bad enough.

The scrum?

She put her hands on both cheeks and shivered. Adací hopped out of bed and went to sit at her dressing table. She took a deep breath before looking in the mirror, afraid of what she might see.

She sat up straighter. The sores were better, much better. The surrounding redness had lessened. No more oozing! No new crusts! She reached her arms out wide as if searching for someone to hug. Adací pictured the young healer's concentration, his tongue sticking out a little as he gave her each carefully measured dose. He was going to save her from becoming deformed—maybe even from becoming a witch.

She tossed her nightgown in the clothes basket and put on her work dress—her baking dress—as she liked to call it. She hoped Lelia would let her help in the kitchen today. The cook had forbidden it once the scrum showed up. Even when healthy, Lelia would scold and tell her she shouldn't be there. But Adací knew the cook loved to have her help and to have an ear to listen to her non-stop talking.

Adací tried to learn something new from Lelia each morning, but baking was her favorite. She loved to make extra bread and take it to the widow who lived down the street. The neighborhood children came daily to see if Adací had made a sweet for them.

The days when Adací's mother planned a trip to help the poor were the hardest in the kitchen but the most fulfilling. The wood-fired ovens would be loaded and hot as she and Lelia made extra bread loaves. Adací's clothes would be drenched with sweat before they were done.

Father and Mother no longer complained that she helped the cook. At first, they tried to tell her it was not what a cultured young woman should be doing, but they gave up.

Adací went down to the kitchen, but as soon as Lelia saw her, the cook held up her hands. "Wait till your sores are a little better."

But she did let Adací stay and watch.

Adací hummed and sang bits and pieces of a song she was composing, a song to thank Pedí. It was the first music that had come to her since the scrum started. The disease had squelched all melody out of her.

"It's good to hear you singing again," Lelia said.

Later, when the noon hour approached, Adací was still humming her new song. The big clock in the sitting room chimed twelve times. Adací went to the front window to look out again. It was the third time she'd checked. Still, no one was on the porch or in the street. She turned and stiffened when she saw her mother watching from the dining room door.

"Are you afraid he won't come?" Mother asked.

Mother must have watched Adací repeatedly go to the window. The mama cat was scrutinizing the disobedient kitten again. If she knew that Adací wanted Pedí not just to be her healer but also a friend, she'd stop her. Adací pointed to the sores on her cheeks and held out her hands. They had marveled earlier at each other's improvement.

"I just want to get the next treatment."

"Me too. He'll be here soon."

That worked. Mother left the dining room, crossed the entryway, and climbed the curved stairway to the upper level, probably to check on Heila.

Adací returned to the window and stayed this time, holding the curtain back. A movement caught her attention. It was Pedí on the cobbled street. He glanced, first at something in his hand, then toward the house.

He must be checking the number. He did it a second time. Thorough, that one.

She could wait no longer and flung open the door. "Good afternoon, Pedí."

He looked once more at the paper as if her presence hadn't been enough confirmation that he was in the right place.

"We've been waiting." Adací's mind whirled with ideas to help Pedí not be afraid of her so she could talk to him about being Idonata. But how could she ask her questions in front of Mother? It wasn't going to happen.

Pedí started up the walk, his head hanging. It was like his feet were covered in sticky syrup, and he dragged them along the pathway to her door. He reached the polished stone steps of the porch but then stopped, his head still down. He appeared stuck. Or maybe he was ready to turn around and flee?

But no, he breathed in, then stepped onto the porch. Adací got ready to sing the song she had made up but hesitated. He would not be expecting a song, and it might scare him off.

Instead, she turned a cheek toward him. Surely, even this shy boy would notice and say something. But no word came.

He was looking at his shoes.

Her lips drew tight, and she tapped her foot. "Look at my face."

He glanced toward her, and she caught the glimmer of a smile.

"The p-potion didn't make you sick?"

"No, only better. Mama, too."

She motioned him inside and took him to the sitting room. It was crammed tight with upholstered chairs, dark hardwood tables, and curios on various shelves. Two magnificent paintings adorned the walls. They were the only things Adací liked about the room. One was of the Blue Mountains, its highest peaks covered with snow. The other showed the seven chutes of the Romingo waterfalls. Both were places she longed to visit. Pedí glanced at each illustration.

She motioned for him to sit down.

He moved slowly, touched the chair's upholstery, and glanced again at the paintings before taking his seat.

"I'll just get Mama."

She found her mother upstairs in her bedroom. "Hurry up. He's here."

Mother followed her to the sitting room, where Pedí sat stiffly but stood up when they entered.

Mother presented her hands to him. "I don't know how to thank you enough. The sores are so much better in just one day." She turned over her hands so he could examine each lesion.

"Now look at mine." Adací unbuttoned her cuffs and pulled up her sleeves. He checked the sores on her hands and forearms but did not look up.

"Are you not going to inspect the sores on my face, too?"

She leaned toward him, forcing him to look at her. His eyes opened wide, and he seemed paralyzed, no longer examining her. His lips moved, but he said nothing.

Mother's presence was like a dark cloud, watching, worrying.

He's just checking my sores. Let him be.

Pedí closed his eyes and took two steps back.

"Am I getting better?" she asked, hoping to put him at ease. She may make him nervous, but he knew what he was doing when it came to healing. "Will I scar?"

He shook his head. "With more treatments, no sc-scarring."

"Thank you!" She took a step towards him, her arms held out. She'd just give him a little hug—a formal show of thanks.

His hands came up as if to ward her off, and he stumbled backward, nearly falling to the ground.

Adací gasped. Now I've done it. I've scared him.

Mother glared at Adací before moving to help Pedí. "Are you okay?" she asked him.

Pedí regained his balance, nodded, and then pulled out a handkerchief to wipe his eyes. "I'm fine. Just-just happy you're better."

He walked backward out of the room. "I-I should go."

"Wait." Adací moved to stop him. "What about the next dose?"

Pedí's face reddened. He pulled out a jar of the mushroom potion from his pocket. "It's here. I made a new batch this morning."

He also brought out a pouch that held two glass tubes. Mother and Adací received the potion in measured doses every five minutes, just like yesterday.

Adací smiled again when his tongue stuck out with each tiny draught. It wasn't a smile of mockery but of admiration that this young man, so shy and afraid of her, would still come and give her his special potion. He probably worried that Adací would mock him as others did and laugh at his speech, his awkward ways, and his tattoo.

She would never laugh at the healer saving her face, and Adací loved his spotted frog. She wished she could show him her moon tattoo.

When he finished, Pedí put the jar and tubes back in his pocket and started to leave.

"How many days will we need treatment?" Mother asked.

He hesitated as if searching for words, perhaps words that would help him stutter less. "Most illnesses the nanimoha potion has worked for have needed four or five doses to resolve."

"Should we come to the infirmary tomorrow?" Mother asked.

Pedí took a deep breath, looked at the wall, the floor, and then back to Mother. "Doctor Arias insists that I c-come here. He wants me to l-learn not to be so . . ."

Adací and her mother waited, but the final word never came out.

Mother set a time for Pedí to come tomorrow.

On the front porch, he reminded them to apply the ointment. "As the crusts go away, the ointment will help the skin heal. Remember not to scrub too hard when you wash."

Adací saw herself scouring away at the little boy at Poor Man's Field—hard enough to make him wince and cry, even bleed.

Selfish Adací had forgotten the boy and never told Pedí that he would need to treat him also.

"The boy, the boy at the field. I—"

"I went there yesterday and treated him. I'll go again after work today."

Pedí had remembered the child. Why hadn't she?

"Will he scar? I scrubbed him too hard."

There was a new look in Pedí's eyes. Was it worry or disappointment? Maybe both. Worry for the boy, disappointment in her.

"The boy may scar some because he's had it longer than you. It wasn't your scrubbing."

Pedí was trying to be kind. She knew what he must think.

"I'm sorry for what I did," Adací said, then ran back into the house. The apprentice healer would never want to be the friend of someone so careless, who always makes mistakes, who always harms others.

CHAPTER TWENTY-THREE

Hognose Snake

Crina dragged Pedí by the arm toward the circle of sages and healers who had gathered in the courtyard of the Sanctuary. When they got within a few feet of the group, Crina let go. She pushed him forward and then stepped back. Pedí slipped between two of the sages to see what was happening.

Minutes earlier, Crina had met him at the stables. She was shaking her head and mumbling. Pedí had just returned from Poor Man's Field, where he'd gone after work and treated the little boy with a second dose of his potion. As Crina pulled Pedí from the stables to the courtyard, the only word she had said was "snake" over and over.

Once in the middle of the circle, Pedí saw the cause of the alarm. A fat brown serpent with black blotches on its back was hissing angrily. Its head was raised and neck spread. Jonol, the Sanctuary gardener, approached it from the edge of the crowd. He held a shovel in the air. It shook in his hands.

The chief sage was barking out orders. "Careful, Jonol!"

The chief motioned with his hands to the healers and sages surrounding the snake. "Keep your distance, but don't let it escape. Can't have a poisonous serpent free in the courtyard."

When Jonol got closer, the snake became even more violent. It hissed louder, spread its neck wider, and made striking motions toward the man.

"Stop!" Pedí exclaimed.

He had been watching the snake, taking in each marking and mannerism. He ran and got between Jonol and the angry serpent. "Don't hurt the hognose."

"What are you doing, Pedí?" the chief sage shouted. "You're too close. It'll bite you."

Other warning voices cried out when Pedí knelt to face the snake. It lunged at him, narrowly missing.

When the snake hissed and reared again, preparing to strike, Pedí weighed his options. He knew he could talk to the hognose and get it to calm down, but this snake was unique and had an unusual behavior. Pedí decided to let everyone see what this snake would do, hoping they'd lose their fear. People in New Losobon hated all snakes. They remembered the stories of the poisonous serpents the Idonata Queen and her Shushuhadors had sent against the soldiers many years ago.

The angry snake once more thrust its head at Pedí. This time, he slapped it on the side—but not too hard. Instead of raging, the snake drew back and dropped to the ground. It rolled on its back and writhed in convulsions, ending with a spasmodic wriggling of its tail. Then, it lay still.

The people in the circle murmured and seemed confused. "It's dead," one person exclaimed. "He killed it," another said. "But how?"

"Not dead." Pedí turned to face them. "It's faking. It's a toad-eater, a hognose snake."

He pointed to the snake's turned-up nose.

"Isn't it poisonous?" the chief sage asked. "It was so violent."

"It's not poisonous. It was all bluff. You had it surrounded, and it couldn't get away. When cornered, this snake fakes being angry like a poisonous snake but never bites. It's a survival strategy."

Jonol was still nearby and pointed his shovel at the snake. "Why's it not moving if it's not dead?"

"It's a strange snake. If the angry bluff doesn't work, it plays dead. It won't move till we're gone. But it has one problem."

Pedí turned the snake onto its stomach. It immediately flipped onto its back again, then lay still like before.

"The snake thinks it has to be on its back to play dead."

Pedí turned it over again, and once more, it rolled onto its back. Pedí and Jonol chuckled, and the crowd's tension broke into laughter.

"Will you take it away?" the chief sage asked. "We can't have a snake like that in our courtyard."

Pedí picked up the limp snake, pleased that it was safe. "It must have come here looking for toads. I know a farmer's field with lots of toads. I'll take it there."

He carried the snake to his apartment in a pillowcase from the infirmary, tied shut with a string around the top. He hung it on a hook. "Rest, my feigning friend. I'll take you to a toad heaven in the morning."

Pedí poured himself a cup of water from a covered jug he'd filled before going to work, then saw the carved wooden turtle on his table. He smiled as he pulled off his shirt, covered in the dirt and sweat of his day's work. Jurana and Gabro left the turtle as an invitation for him to eat with them. He was always welcome, but he'd never miss a wooden turtle night.

His sage friends were the wisest people in New Losobon. He never understood why they acted like he was something special, not a poor Idonata boy.

On the way to their cottage, he stopped by the laboratory to check with the night guard and make sure everything was in order. Calixto was on duty again and stood in place by the outside door. Pedí warned him to be extra vigilant.

"What's in that storage room?" the guard asked. "The one built on the side. I passed through the lab and checked the door, but it was locked."

Pedí's gut writhed like the feigning hognose snake. Why was Calixto interested in that part of the lab, the hiding place? He must have seen Pedí go in with the mushrooms. Was he—

Pedí mentally shook his head, answering his own doubts. The man was doing his job, just being thorough. Calixto had been curious the other day and wanted to know all about the potion he was protecting. He had even asked where the mushrooms grew in the forest and when

Pedí would collect more. Of course, Pedí didn't tell him where they grew but had mentioned that he was going before sun-up the next day.

Pedí considered a way to answer the guard's question about the storage room. "That old place is where I did my experiments."

"So, nothing in there for me to protect?"

The snake inside him twisted again, but Pedí told himself to relax. *You're just nervous because of the men who keep following you. Don't doubt your guards.* "Nothing to protect. It still stinks from my test vats, so we keep it locked."

Pedí went on to dinner with Jurana and Gabro. He was soon eating his favorite foods—slow-cooked beans, chicken breast pounded flat and spiced with garlic, and a traditional chopped salad of tomatoes, onions, and bell peppers seasoned with salt, vinegar, and oil.

When they finished, Pedí looked at the sage's black stove. Nothing was cooking. Only a steam kettle sat on top. He eyed the sideboard. No pie or cake was set out. Jurana watched him, and his face warmed.

On wooden turtle nights, she had usually made some special dessert, but maybe not tonight. He glanced her way again and thought how beautiful his hostess was despite being in her late sixties. Her elegant hair was a mix of black and gray.

"Looking for something?" Jurana asked.

Gabro's hand touched Pedí's forearm. He looked into his surrogate grandpa's dark eyes. He liked his white hair and neatly trimmed beard.

"Our guava tree just peaked for the winter crop," Gabro said.

Pedí jumped out of his chair. "That means—"

"Jellied guava!" Jurana got up to open the cupboard. "We hid it so you wouldn't guess."

She pulled out a pan of sweetened and pureed guava fruit, which had thickened into a round, red circle. She cut slices and added a soft cheese in the middle before putting the guava sandwich on Pedí's plate. His favorite dessert.

When his mouth was full of a second helping, he noticed Gabro stroking his beard. Pedí knew what that meant. Something concerned him.

"What?" he said, after swallowing the cheese and guava.

"Doctor Arias told us about the two men who followed you, and that the captain came to the infirmary demanding your mushrooms."

Pedí swallowed several times even though his mouth was empty. "I'll be all right. Please don't worry."

"You know we will," Jurana said.

Gabro got out of his seat, walked to the stove, then turned around to return to his chair. His hand still stroked his beard. "This new captain is not anything like his father. He only cares about increasing his wealth and power, no matter who it hurts."

Pedí's back straightened. His battle with Durgo Borgesso and Breno Torred was just beginning, but he was determined to protect his nanimoha. He was through running from bullies.

Jurana began clearing the table, and Pedí got up to help. When he put his dishes in the wash pan, she grasped his wrist. "Tell me about this girl you visited today."

One thought of Adací and his supposed newly found bravery melted like a batch of jellied guava left on a hot stove. "I-I . . . Not a visit . . . Just went as a healer."

"Tell us about her." Jurana dragged him by the wrist back to the table.

He was speechless.

"We know her parents." Gabro poured hot water from the stove over the dirty dishes and then joined them at the table. "This is a chance to get to know someone your age."

"I'm just her healer."

Jurana still held his arm. "But if she invites you to stay and talk, don't run away."

"We want a report tomorrow night," Gabro said. "There's guava left if you'll come and tell us."

Pedí's shoulders drooped. He'd try but knew he'd fail if he had to stay and visit with Adací.

The three friends stayed up late talking. The sages laughed hard when Pedí told them about the hognose snake in the courtyard.

CHAPTER TWENTY-FOUR

The Lost Bottle

There was a rustling sound inside of Pedí's apartment. Someone was there!

After returning from his supper with Jurana and Gabro, he had just opened the door. His knuckles turned white from where he gripped the doorknob.

The noise repeated, and the pillowcase hanging on the wall hook moved.

His hand relaxed.

"So, you're back from the dead." He went over and patted the writhing snake through the cloth of the bag. "Best to rest for now. I'll let you go in the morning."

Pedí lit his lamp and opened the bound journal he had brought home the other day from the library. It was written by an explorer who had gone deep into the jungles at the headwaters of the Ipixuna River. The narrative was one of the few books about the jungles he hadn't read.

Half an hour later, his head drooped, and his fingers slipped down the pages. The book fell and thumped on the floor. Pedí woke and stumbled to his bed. But the minute his head rested on his pillow, the hognose began writhing again.

"Go to sleep."

The command didn't help—the snake was not going to listen to him. Each time he drowsed off, the serpent woke him. Pedí shuffled over to the pillowcase. "Looks like neither of us can rest."

He parted the curtains and looked at the shadows created by a three-quarters moon. "There's enough light to find our way to your new home. Might as well do it now."

Pedí dressed, grabbed the snake bag, and then took the west trail that led away from the Sanctuary and the city. The air was damp, and the moon highlighted the eerie night mists that clung to the farmer's fields and the edges of the groves of trees. It would be easy to imagine a phantom hiding along his path.

Pedí felt his empty shirt pocket. His Adací was not there. He no longer had her protection. But it wasn't the spirits of the forests and fields that worried him. He knew how to take care of himself in the wilds. It was caves that he would hesitate to enter without his precious Adací. Without her help, he wouldn't have escaped the day he hid from the captain's men in the sandstone cleft.

It was strange that Ivo and the gray-bearded man knew he was going so early that day. Doctor Arias was the only one who should have known of Pedí's plan.

Except . . .

He had told Calixto as well!

The young guard was alone on watch. There was no second guard with him tonight. If he were an informant for the captain, he could let someone in to steal the nanimoha. And if he had watched Pedí come and go from the storage room with the collected mushrooms, he'd know where to send them.

Pedí changed directions and ran back the way he had come. He held the snake bag close to his body so the serpent would not be injured by a bush or branch along the way. He was breathing hard by the time he reached the Sanctuary. Pedí passed through the orchard and moved from tree to tree, staying hidden. The entrance to the laboratory came into view.

Calixto was there.

Standing guard.

All was quiet.

Pedí's fears were unnecessary.

But something flashed from a laboratory window. Then, a second flash. Two lanterns were lit and moving inside. They shone through the windows near the room where the mushrooms were hidden. Pedí looked back at Calixto. He was standing guard, not to protect the mushrooms, but to protect the men who would steal them—maybe the same ruffians who had followed Pedí into the forest.

He should go for help, but by the time he woke anyone, the thieves would have already stolen everything. The outside service door could get him into the storage room. If he could get inside ahead of the thieves, he'd be there to stop them.

He moved in the shadows of the last few trees. When Calixto was looking away, Pedí dashed for the back side of the building. The bagged snake bounced against his body. He should have left it hanging in the orchard.

He made it without Calixto seeing him. The moonlight was blocked on this side, so he felt along the dark wall until he found the old door. His fingers found the knob, then the keyhole. He searched his pockets and located the right key.

Scraping and grinding came from inside. The thieves were breaking the lock on the inner door. They would soon be inside. All was lost if they saw the cabinet behind the barrels. His months of collecting, drying, and pulverizing the mushrooms would be for naught.

Pedí unlocked and twisted the handle of the rarely used door, but he didn't pull it open. The rusted hinges would grind and creak. He waited until he heard the crash of the inner door being forced open, then jerked hard. The old door screeched, but bolts breaking on the inside masked the sound. He ducked in, swinging the door closed behind him.

Pedí lay down on the side of the cabinets, his nanimoha's hiding place. The only things between him and the thieves were the three test barrels and some empty boxes.

Light from their lanterns pierced the darkness of the room when the two men came through the inner door. It also pierced through Pedí's crazy plan. His racing heart ignited as panic replaced the little courage he had. What was he thinking? He couldn't stop these men. They would get his mushrooms and kill him at the same time.

He should slip back out the service door. It was the wise thing to do. Staying was suicide. But he didn't move. He would stay and fight for his mushrooms even though it was hopeless.

The light increased as the thieves came further into the storage room. They rummaged through the boxes.

"Nothing here." It was the older, gray-bearded man.

"What's that stink?" It was Ivo.

"It's the barrels. Something's rotten."

A light glared down onto the top of the cabinet. They must have raised their lamps above their heads to see over the casks. Pedí pulled his legs in closer and tucked against the mushroom repository. He bumped against the snake bag lying next to him on the floor.

"There's a storage chest in the back," the gray-bearded man said. "That's the likely hiding spot."

It was too late, too late for anything. Pedí wouldn't scare them off just by being there.

"Let's move this barrel out of the way." The older man coughed as he said it.

"If we can stand the stench," Ivo said.

They put their lanterns on the floor. The light glared between the casks, where they narrowed at the bottom and shone onto Pedí. The men were standing, and at that angle, they couldn't see him. But Pedí could see their legs and feet on each side of the middle barrel as they shifted it away from the cabinet.

"One more time," the bearded man said.

The snake moved in the bag. It was awake and nosing around. Could it save him like the spider had done? He doubted it would pretend to be dangerous again. When he was younger, he'd kept a hognose snake as a pet for a few days, and it quit bluffing. Maybe this snake would only pretend to be dead instead of dangerous.

But it was his only chance.

He untied the sack. The snake crawled out and headed for the light shining between the barrels. The men shifted the cask again just as the snake brushed by Ivo's feet.

He jumped. "A snake. A snake's in here."

The hognose was now between the thieves and their lanterns. Ivo was still hopping up and down. Pedí watched the snake's shadow. It stopped by the lights, then turned and raised its head.

Please pretend to be dangerous. Pedí tried to communicate with it through his thoughts. *Don't play dead.*

A loud hiss followed. The shadow from the snake's head bobbed, striking at the men. It was a great performance.

"A blow viper," the old man cried out.

"Poisonous snakes are guarding his mushrooms."

"They'll kill us."

"Let's get out."

Shadows from the snake's head followed the men as they inched their way around the sides of the room. When they reached the door, the older man turned and flung his knife—just like when Ivo threw his knife at the Wanderer spider. But Pedí had no time to warn the hognose. Fortunately, the knife missed the snake and bounced off the tiled floor.

The hognose lunged forward, striking and hissing louder. The men bolted through the dark laboratory. Without their lanterns, they knocked things over as they searched for the back door.

Pedí crawled out between the casks and picked up the hissing snake. He chuckled. He had been saved by a spider and now by a serpent. Animals were indeed his friends.

He put the hognose back into the bag and tied it shut. "Sorry. I'll get you to your toad heaven tomorrow. Thank you for saving me and my nanimoha."

Pedí crept through the lab until he could see the door to the outside. No one was there. They had all fled, including Calixto.

Pedí ran to Doctor Arias's cottage and pounded on the door. He cringed with each knock echoing off the door and into the darkness.

Talia, the doctor's wife, answered. She was in her nightgown.

"I-I . . ." He couldn't get the words out.

"Come in. My husband will be right out." Talia was always kind to him, and here he was, waking her in the middle of the night.

The doctor soon joined them. He suggested they move all the dried mushroom powder to Jurana and Gabro's cottage. "No one will think of finding your potion there."

The sages agreed to the plan, and all the mushrooms were moved to their cottage before anyone else at the Sanctuary was awake. Pedí kept one bottle in his pocket. He would need it in the morning to make a new batch of nanimoha for Adací, her mother, and the little boy at Poor Man's Field.

As the sun arose, Pedí took the snake to the farmer's field. When it crawled out of the bag, he bowed to it. "Thank you, Sir Hognose. Have a good day."

He returned to the laboratory and pulled out the bottle from his pocket. It was then that he remembered. There should already be a bottle of dried mushroom powder on the lab counter. Yesterday morning, in his hurry to get to the infirmary, he had left the bottle out after making the potion. He was going to put it away at noon, but he forgot.

He searched the tops of all the work counters, pushed aside the bags of sweet herb, and looked behind the grinder. A tight knot formed in his throat. He searched again, opening every drawer and cabinet, scanning the counter a second and third time. The partially used bottle of dried mushrooms was nowhere.

The label on the bottle said: *For Pedí's use only.* The captain's men must have seen it and recognized it for what it was. That means Durgo Borgesso and Breno Torred would soon have it.

Pedí hesitated to consider the possibilities. That sham healer might mix it too strong and kill someone. He had to hope that wouldn't happen.

Pedí made another potion batch using the mushroom powder bottle he'd kept back from Jurana and Gabro's cottage. He then returned the bottle with its remaining contents to the sage's cottage and rushed to the infirmary in time to begin seeing morning patients.

But Doctor Arias sent him away. "Go home and sleep. We'll get by without you. I'll send someone to wake you in time to go to Marina and Adací's house."

Pedí started down the corridor but turned to look at his mentor. He should have told him about the lost bottle, but he continued walking, unsure what to do. When he got to his apartment, he collapsed on the bed. Exhaustion pushed every worry from his mind, and he fell into a deep sleep.

CHAPTER TWENTY-FIVE

Cake and Chocolate Beans

Adací assumed it was her fault that Pedí had remained silent when he gave her and Mother the third dose of his cure a few minutes ago. She hadn't given him a chance to say anything but had talked nonstop. She kept praising him while waiting for the five minutes between each dose. Although Adací's and her mother's sores were still red, the oozing and crusting had cleared completely.

"Your potion's like magic," she had said.

Her words, however, only embarrassed him. His face had turned a deeper crimson with each compliment.

Now that the doses were all in, Mother herded Pedí toward the front door and seemed anxious for him to be gone. Had she guessed Adací's plan?

Pedí was at the door and reached to turn the handle. Adací had to act fast. She stepped toward him. "Please don't go yet!" Adací grabbed his arm. "I made a cake to thank you for curing us."

Without giving Pedí or Mother a chance to say no, Adací dragged Pedí toward the dining room. Mother followed but stayed silent, not intervening—thus fulfilling Adací's scheme, knowing that Marina would be embarrassed to stop her.

Adací glanced at Pedí, then Mother. Pedí looked scared. Mother looked angry. But Mother's look turned to shock when they entered the dining room. As planned—without Mother's knowledge—Lelia had set up a small table for two, and a coconut cake rested on a plate in the middle.

Adací pulled Pedí to one of the seats, and he sat down. Adací took the seat opposite. There was no seat for Mother, who half-smiled at Pedí before frowning at Adací. "I'll be nearby," she said, "in case you need me."

Mother had emphasized the "nearby."

When Mother started out of the room, Pedí raised a finger as if to protest being left alone with the wild black-haired girl, but no words came out of his mouth. Adací was glad he was speechless. He couldn't ask Mother to stay.

"Lelia, our cook, has water boiling for some chocolate." Adací had plenty to say for both of them. "I just have to pour it over the ground beans. Then we'll visit while it's steeping."

She stepped into the kitchen, took the teakettle off the stove, and poured the hot water over the roasted chocolate beans.

Did Pedí like his chocolate strong? With sugar added? Would he like the cake I made with Lelia?

Adací spilled some water when her hand started shaking.

What's wrong with me?

She had never been so nervous.

Adací left the chocolate to steep and returned to the dining room. Pedí didn't even glance at her when she sat down but kept looking at the huge painting that hung on the wall. It was a jungle scene with a river, palms, and flowering trees.

Maybe he'd talk about the painting. It could be a way to begin learning about him and the Idonata. "Have you been to the jungles?"

Pedí shook his head. She waited. His lips moved like he wanted to say something, but nothing came out.

"You want to go there?" she said, guessing.

He nodded.

"Me, too."

He took a bite of cake and looked around the room but never at her.

Maybe this aversion to her was more than just his shyness. Perhaps he didn't want to be around the girl who scrubbed the little boy too hard and then forgot him.

"Are you unhappy with me because of what I did to the little boy at Poor Man's Field?"

Every muscle in Pedí's body tensed.

So that was it. She waited to be chastised, but when he said nothing, Adací started to hum. It always calmed Father when he came into the house exhausted at the end of the day. If Pedí was angry with her, she needed to hear it.

The humming worked. He finally talked.

"Don't blame yourself for the b-boy. You tried to help him. He's doing better."

But his muscles didn't relax, so she kept humming.

"Someone stole a bottle of my dried mushrooms that I forgot to put back in hiding. They're dangerous if dosed wrong. It'll be my fault if someone's hurt."

Adací's own tense muscles relaxed. He was upset with himself, not her. "Does Doctor Arias know?"

"I haven't told him yet."

"If you need my help, I'll do anything. Your potion is so wonderful. It must be protected."

He looked right at her face. "Thank you."

It didn't last long. He turned away again, but not before giving her a little smile.

It was a perfect time to ask her questions. "Doctor Arias said you know all about the forest and the animals. I know about birds, but not other creatures. Will you tell me about them? And will you also teach me about the Idonata people?"

Adací's mouth plopped open when Pedí started talking with hardly a stutter or a stammer. "Frogs are my favorite animal. I can talk to them and a few other creatures."

Adací put her hand over her mouth and pressed her lips together to keep from smiling. "I sing with birds. Maybe I'm a little bit like you."

"A few of ancient Idonata could communicate with animals. They were called Shushuhadors. I'm trying to be like them. A poisonous spider saved me from the men who were after my mushrooms, and then a hognose snake did the same thing."

Adací's pressed lips couldn't keep the smile away when he told her what happened with the hognose snake. She laughed out loud but then remembered the steeping chocolate beans.

"Excuse me. The chocolate should be ready."

Adací glanced over her shoulder as she walked to the kitchen. He was watching her. When she was next to him, his eyes were anywhere but in her direction. Then, when she turned her back, he couldn't keep his eyes off her. She shook her head and ducked into the kitchen.

Lelia was right behind the door. Adací nearly knocked her over.

"You've been listening." She used her growly voice, hoping to sound angry. But Adací could never be upset at Lelia.

"Just a wee bit. I couldn't help but overhear a little."

"When you stand by the door with your ear cocked, it's hard not to overhear a little." Adací frowned, but Lelia saw right through her pretend anger and gave Adací a guilty smile.

"Did Mama ask you to listen?"

The cook looked away and didn't answer, meaning Adací had guessed right.

"Is Mama mad at you for helping me bake the cake and setting up the table and chairs?"

"I can work that out. But tell me, do you like this young man?"

Adací leaned to whisper, to make sure Pedí or Mother, if she were also listening somewhere, couldn't hear. "He's a funny boy. Awfully shy. But I will get him to teach me about his animal friends and the Idonata people."

Adací brought the brewed chocolate back to Pedí in two steaming cups. She blew across the top of hers and took a big sip. The bitter flavor was soothing. Pedí did the same and drank his without sugar, just like she did.

He told her next about the legend of the giant Blue Dragonfly of the Idonata. "Would you help me find one? You must watch every time you're near a pond or stream."

"I will."

He told her of many other animals, and she loved each of his stories, but the darn boy still wouldn't look at her. He was back to observing the jungle artwork on the wall.

"Do you like the painting?"

"I've read lots of books about the jungles. I want to see the colorful poison dart frogs and the big snakes."

Adací examined the painting herself while Pedí talked, but out of the corner of her eye, she could tell he was no longer looking at the jungle scene but at her. When she turned, his eyes jumped back to the painting.

"Does my face frighten you? Are the sores still so bad?"

He looked down and shook his head.

"If it's not my face, is it me? Are you scared of me?"

It was an unfair question. She already knew the answer. Pedí's eyes closed, and his forehead wrinkled. She imagined he'd rather face a forest cat than her.

"I'm k-kind of scared. I thought you might laugh at me like they did at school."

"Have I laughed at you?"

He shook his head.

She decided to risk another difficult question. "Do you have a special girl as a friend?"

Ah, this looked even harder to answer. His hands gripped the edge of their little table, and his eyes looked left and right. Adací thought she already knew the answer to this one, too, but she was wrong.

"I had a very close friend who was a girl. Her name was Ileana. She was from Itatu and moved back to her homeland when I was six years old. I think of her often. She didn't have any friends either and was the only one who would play with me."

Still loyal after ten years to the only girl who was nice to him. Adací wondered if he'd ever think of her in the same way.

"After you give us the potion tomorrow, will you visit with me in our backyard? I want to learn more from you and wonder if it might be easier for you outside. I love to listen to you, so you can talk and talk and never be afraid of me."

"Thank you for being kind to me," Pedí said. But her last questions must have worn him out. He stood up. "I think I should be g-going."

They walked together to the front of the house, and Pedí thanked her for the chocolate and cake. Mother joined them at the door and took Adací's arm. There was a definite stiffness to her. The criticism would come after Pedí left.

The young healer checked his pockets to make sure he had all his supplies. "I need to come two more times to treat you."

"Tomorrow at the same hour should be fine," Mother said.

He went out the door and down the walkway.

"Goodbye," Adací called out. "I'll be waiting for you tomorrow. We'll talk by our avocado tree."

Mother stayed at her side, watching Pedí walk away. When he was out of hearing range, she leaned toward Adací. "What are you doing? I couldn't stop your cake and chocolate trick today without hurting him. The boy certainly deserves our gratitude, but you'll create problems if you're too friendly. You can't be seen with him except as your healer, and you know why. It will make it easier for people to guess you're Idonata like him. Then they'll treat you the same, or much worse."

"I know, Mama, but he needs a friend, and I just want to learn from him. He's the only Idonata in New Losobon besides me. It's important, Mama."

"As long as it only happens at our house during his last two visits, we won't stop you. But you can't be seen in public with him. Do you agree?"

"Yes, Mama."

"And be careful. This boy has no experience with girls. He'll misinterpret your kindness and think he could become your suitor and that we would somehow approve of him. That will never be."

Adací waved her hands back and forth, palms facing Mother— overly demonstrative but hoping to be believed. "I know your plans for me. I just want to learn from him. That's all. He knows our interaction is temporary."

"Just don't go too far in befriending this boy. You don't know when to stop—when enough is enough."

Mother's words were a punch in the belly.

Her mother went back inside, but Adací stayed and gazed down the street long after Pedí had disappeared.

CHAPTER TWENTY-SIX

The Avocado Tree

Adací sat on one of the hewn hardwood logs that circled the avocado tree. It was her place to daydream, to make up songs and sing them to the birds.

But today, she was not singing.

"They can't tell me who to be friends with." She spoke to the tree, which waved in the breeze.

Pedí had come the final times and treated Adací and her mother. All that was left of the scrum was a pink color on the skin, which he said would fade in time. However, even though her mother had reluctantly agreed to it, her parents were not happy that she and Pedí had visited under the avocado tree yesterday and then again today.

They were afraid of him—and, of course, they didn't trust Adací.

Did they think she would run off with the boy? With this scared apprentice who would talk about his animal friends for hours but couldn't look her in the face? With this kind and gentle young man who struggled to say a word if she asked any question that was not about his potions or his wild things?

"I'm not in love with him!" she said to the tree, which continued to ignore her.

"He's just a friend," she whispered, not wanting the tree to hear anymore.

An hour ago, in a formal sit down, her parents had repeated all their plans for her future, which didn't include Pedí. "You can be seen with

Bertol and a few other boys we choose, but that's all," Father had said. "You know what's expected of a well-bred young lady. You can't be with just anyone if you want to be a part of the nobility."

"We love you," Mother had added. "We only want what's best for you."

That was the hard part. They made her angry and were controlling, but she knew they loved her. With no other children, Adací was all they had, and all their hopes were on her. Keeping her origin hidden and keeping her from Pedí was for her protection, they told her once again. She understood why in part but not entirely. Either way, Adací would devastate them if she did anything to jeopardize their plans for her to one day be married to someone accepted in New Losobon's upper classes.

Adací got off the log and walked into the garden, which stretched from the avocado tree to the rear wall. A scattering of red and green tomatoes remained on the vines. She picked one of the ripest and held it in limbo, her fingers surrounding it tightly—ready to crush it and let the juice and seeds drip down onto her dress.

Ready to crush her parents' hopes and wishes for her!

She couldn't do it.

Instead, she bunched her skirt and formed a pocket. She put the tomato in, then picked several more ripe ones and added them to her collection. She selected only those that were the roundest and the juiciest. When her Coming of Age came next year, she would have to pick and choose from among those her parents favored.

But would any of those rich boys want a witch for a wife? What would happen when they learned of the silver tattoo on her chest or saw her hair without the dye? Her parents seemed to ignore those problems, but she assumed they already had a plan to explain it away. Perhaps that was why they favored Bertol. He had witnessed enough of Adací's strange behaviors that he would be more likely to accept the rest of her peculiarities.

Still holding the bunched skirt, Adací carried the tomatoes to an old basket on top of the woodpile and placed them in it. She stood on her tiptoes and looked over the fence into the back of the stables. A horse was running in the corral, and Lino was chasing it.

Pito's gruff voice sounded as he came out of the stable house. He was on his crutches, his casted leg held out in front. He cursed and yelled at Lino. Adací could still remember each of the cuss words he used when he taught her to ride a horse. Instead of scaring her, each expletive made her love him that much more.

Adací watched Pito's awkward steps with his crutches. She hadn't meant to harm him—to make the horse kick him. Who was the next person her dreams would injure?

She walked back to the avocado tree and put the basket down. Without thinking, her hands found her cheeks, and she felt the sticky ointment Pedí wanted her and her mother to continue using on the healed scrum sores.

"For several more days," he had said. "To keep the new skin from drying out."

She shifted to the log seat nearest the rock wall separating their yard from the neighbors. A wild beehive was nestled into a crevice of the wall. Pedí had sat by it and had taught her about the wild bees. There were many species in New Losobon, he had said. Some made long flute-like openings to their hives, and others had fan-like entrances like the one in her wall.

She put her hand near the hive and watched the little black bees circle in and out around it. Pedí had shown her how to do it. Unlike beekeeper's bees, this type of wild one never stings.

For a moment, Adací was happy. She imagined herself a tiny black bee and flew into the crevice, into the honeycomb, to hide. Hide from her parent's lectures. Hide from Bertol and the other rich boys. Hide from becoming a witch.

I have to hide from Pedí as well.

She would miss learning from him. She had loved hearing about the animals he knew and the herbs he collected for his potions. They also talked a lot about the southern jungles. She wanted to know what he had learned from his reading and what his grandpa taught him.

Pedí said there were legends of strange tribes and even cities hidden in the tropical forests, but it was hard to know what was truth and what was fable. He hoped his Idonata ancestors might have survived deep in those wilds. Most explorers, he had said, believed the escaped Idonata had all died off or blended in with the jungle natives.

She had wanted to ask him if he knew anything about witches and how to stop becoming one. But each time she started, she choked and stammered as if she'd become Pedí. She never got the words out. She was afraid of what he might think of her.

Adací did teach him about birds. Pedí loved birds like he loved all animals, but she knew a little more than he did. It made her proud, and he seemed pleased as well.

Yesterday, she had shown him her bird feeder. Her hair was unbraided—a rare occurrence. Some strands got caught in the tree branches above the feeder. When she untangled it, some of her hair pulled out and fell to the ground. It was from the center of her scalp, most of it from the silver part that had been dyed. Pedí picked up the strands and put them in his pocket when he thought she wasn't watching. It was strange, as if he knew about her hair.

When he left earlier today, Adací had given him her final *thank you*. She hoped it was her most sincere. His simple *it was nothing* brought a smile to her lips. What he'd done for Adací was so much more than nothing.

As he went out the front door, she could tell Pedí wanted to ask if he could come again, but he was too shy. Mother was by her side, and Adací couldn't say anything. Mother's tight smile had barely concealed her displeasure at seeing Pedí stay and visit the last two days. But it was over, and Mother and Father should stop worrying.

Now, she wished Pedí's hand and hers had not accidentally touched while they were visiting. It had stopped them both—from thinking, from talking. Pedí even looked into her eyes for a short time without turning away. What if he thought that she could become his special girl? He would be hurt when he learned that Adací could not look at anyone other than a rich boy. He might think she was mocking him like all the other girls had.

Adací looked toward the distant Blue Mountains, the snow on their tops shining reddish-pink with the blush of the setting sun. She wished she could escape there or to the jungles—to hide from what she was and what her future would be.

CHAPTER TWENTY-SEVEN

A Substitute for his Broken Adací

Pedí's mother put the last stitch in the cotton pouch she'd sewn for him. She tested the drawstring and then handed it over.

Pedí checked it himself, opening and closing the small bag several times.

"Will it fit?" Mama asked.

He tucked it in the deep pocket on the front of his shirt, then nodded.

Mama gently touched his arm. "You have something for the pouch to replace your heroine Adací, haven't you?"

Pedí delayed his answer. The living Adací's hair was going into the pouch, but Mama didn't know about her. Yesterday, when he came home to stay for a few days, he told her that the figurine of Adací had been smashed.

They had mourned together.

Other than Papa's bow and arrow and feathered armbands, which hung on the wall of their tiny shack, the little statue of Adací had been the last reminder of who they were, of Grandpa and Grandma, and of all their beliefs.

Mama's hand was still on his arm. "Please tell me what the pouch is for."

Pedí went to his wooden cot in the corner and searched under the pillow for the folded paper in which he had hidden the strands of Adací's hair. He brought the coil of hair to his mother, unwound it, and then handed it over. Pedí had rubbed off some of the black dye. Underneath, the hair almost glowed; the silver color was so bright.

He told Mama how he had met Adací and then cured her and her mother.

"The first time I saw her, I thought I was looking at the ancient Adací. Except for not having a silver strand, her braid was just like the one on my little statue."

Mama listened in silence. The light from the open window highlighted her soft skin and dark hair, which was long, straight, and reached nearly to her waist. Mama was beautiful.

She touched the hair that Pedí held in his hands. "This is intriguing. There are a few strands that aren't dyed. They are as dark as yours and mine, but these others—the ones from which you removed some coloring—are exquisite. Only Adací and her descendants, our queens, had such locks. Look how it shimmers when I angle it toward the light coming through the window."

"I know, Mama. It frightens me! She frightens me! And her parents named her Adací. How would they know that name? They're from the people of New Losobon, not from the Idonata."

"Does she look like her parents?"

Pedí shook his head. "She looks more like you. She's so pretty."

"Maybe she isn't their child."

"Oh!" Pedí pulled the pouch out of his pocket, curled the strands of hair, then put them inside. "I remember now that she mentioned a nightmare about her birth parents the day I first met her."

"She must be adopted."

"But even if she was, how could she have descended from Adací?"

Mama took the pouch from Pedí's hands and pulled the hair back out. "There must be a secret to this new Adací's story."

Mama repeated the legend of ancient Adací for him. He knew it by heart, but he loved to hear it as told by his mother. In the beginning of time, the Moon Goddess came to Adací. First, she inscribed the tattoo of the crescent moon onto her chest. Then, the Goddess taught Adací to weave her hair in a long, tight plait. She touched one of the interwoven braids. It changed to a bright, shining silver. The Goddess also gave her the jade moon stones to adorn her interlaced hair.

Adací began to have visions, which she used to protect her people. But in the end, she sacrificed herself to save them from the six evil spirits who had escaped from the underworld. Before she died, Adací had a baby girl. That girl was born with a patch of silver amidst the black, just like her mother's. When the girl turned twelve, she chose for her tattoo that of the crescent silver moon and had it put on her upper chest. For centuries, descendants of Adací, each with a plait of silver hair among the black, had led the Idonata nation. They all chose the same tattoo. But the last queen was killed by the soldiers from across the sea.

Mama concluded her story.

That last woman with a silver braid had died two hundred years ago. It confirmed Pedí's doubts that it made no sense to associate this living Adací with the original one or with the queens of his people.

He shook his head. "Grandpa said the legacy of Adací died with the last queen and that the jade stones went missing."

"But missing where?" Mama uncurled Adací's hair again and let the strands drape down from her fingers. "Maybe the final queen also had a baby girl, and the child survived with those who escaped from the soldiers."

"But wouldn't Grandpa know?"

"When your grandpa was young, he traveled to the jungles with a search party. It was organized from the remnants of the small bands of Idonata who had remained in the forests of our conquered land. They failed to find any trace of our lost people, yet still believed they existed."

Mama re-curled the hair and gave the strands back to Pedí. "Grandpa's search party was not the first, but it was the last. There were not enough Idonata hiding in the forests to go again. And now that your father and my parents are gone, you and I are all that's left."

Pedí slipped the hair back inside the pouch. He had wanted something to believe in, something to replace the lost statue of Adací, but he was being foolish.

"Saving this hair makes no sense. I should throw these strands away."

Mother took him by the chin to make him look at her. "Just because no one has found our lost people doesn't mean they didn't survive."

"No, Mama. I was wrong to think that just because this girl is named Adací and has a braid with a few silver hairs, she could be like our heroine."

Mother let go of his chin but grabbed his shoulders and shook him. "I know your instincts. Why would you replace your Adací statue with this girl's hair if you didn't feel something special about her? Your Grandpa and I both believe you were born with the skills of the ancients. You are a Shushuhador."

"I'm not, Mama."

"But you are, and I want you to bring this girl here so I can meet her."

"I'll never see her again. She's a rich girl. I only got to know her because I was her healer."

"Was she kind to you?"

"She acted like she wanted to be my friend, but I don't know why. I'm an Idonata boy with a frog tattoo on my face. Except for Ileana, no girl has wanted to be my friend."

"Adací must sense in you what I do. Go to her again. Find out about her."

"I don't have the courage."

CHAPTER TWENTY-EIGHT

A Family from Itatu

It had been one week since Adací last visited with Pedí by their avocado tree. She tried to think of an excuse—some feigned illness—so she could go to the infirmary. Once there, she hoped to see and talk with Pedí again. But despite her best scheming, she knew her parents would see right through her plan.

Today, she had to put those thoughts aside. Larada had come to Adací's house. It was their first time together since Adací contracted the scrum. All visitors had been forbidden to prevent it from spreading.

It was a happy reunion for the two girls, even though Bertol had tagged along as if he was welcome. Adací suspected her parents invited him without telling her. Marina and Sergol seemed more intent than ever on pairing Adací with someone of their choosing since Adací troubled them over her friendship with Pedí.

Despite Bertol's presence, it was a wonderful time catching up with Larada until her best friend shared some bad news. Larada had been forbidden from receiving any more visits from Edero. The boy she loved had been coming to see Larada from time to time despite her being promised to Chando. But now, Larada's parents ended those encounters. "It's too close to your Coming of Age for you to be seeing someone other than Chando," the Mendins had declared.

"All we can do is write notes to each other," Larada said. "Bertol has been kind enough to deliver my letters and bring back Edero's response. Our parents don't know that he's doing it."

What she said next troubled Adací.

"Edero believes in your powers to save us even more than I do. You are our only hope."

Adací hated to hear of their confidence in her to rescue Larada from Chando. So far, she had had no visions showing a way to change the promised marriage. And how was she to do it? Her dreams came randomly, without her direction. She had no idea how to get one of her strange visions to do what she wanted it to do and worried that any of her dreams would only bring disaster.

"I'm trying, but nothing yet," was Adací's answer.

Just then, there was a knock on the door. Heila answered it, and the maid came to the sitting room a few minutes later. "There's someone here to see Adací."

"Who is it?" Adací asked.

"It's a slender young man wearing an overcoat."

"Edero!" Larada and Adací said his name at the same time. They ran to the front door.

Edero Custal stood in the doorway, dressed in a finely tailored overcoat. His body was so slender that it nearly engulfed him. The two girls continued running toward him, but he held up his hands when Larada got within a few feet. She stopped.

"Alo, Larada. Alo, Adací."

Adací loved his accent. Edero's grandparents had crossed the sea from northern Losobon, where they spoke a different dialect. Edero had the kind of face you like to look at, even though he wasn't that handsome. There was a kindness in his eyes that was sincere and real.

The opposite of Chando Borgesso.

"I didn't know you were visiting Adací today," Edero said. "I shouldn't be here. I don't want to cause problems."

"But why did you come to see her?" Larada asked.

"To ask her if she'd had any dream to help us. I keep thinking about it and how her dreams have saved you in the past. I know she can do it again. I wanted to give her encouragement."

At that moment, Adací's mother came into the entryway. "Edero!" she said. "You're here, too?"

He explained that he had come to ask Adací a question and didn't know Larada was visiting. He asked Marina if she knew the decision to restrict him from seeing Larada.

"I do," Adací's mother said. "And I'm sorry for you." Marina rubbed her hands together. "But I'm glad you're here. We need your family's help at Poor Man's Field."

Mother explained that Father had just learned that another group of Black River people had arrived at the Poor Man's Field. Like the others, they had been flooded out but were even more destitute. "We need to go there today, but we don't have enough supplies for their needs. Could your family add to our provisions?"

"I'll go home right now," Edero said, "and get whatever extra food we have. Mother will want to come, and I'll bring some of our servants."

"We're coming too," Larada and Bertol said simultaneously. Unlike Edero and his family, they had never been to Poor Man's Field.

"We'll get supplies from our house as well," Larada said. "But Mother may not let me go with you if Edero's coming."

"I'll write you a note explaining what happened and that we need your help," Marina said. "It's not a social visit, so I think your mother and father will allow you to come."

***

It took several hours, but everyone gathered back at Adací's house. Then, they were off to Poor Man's Field in three supply wagons. After arriving, Adací broke off from the others. She walked to the small group of trees where the previous group of people who had escaped the floods remained. She wanted to find the little boy that had scrum.

He saw her first, then ran and hugged her. "I'm better. A healer came."

The scrum sores were gone, but three deep scars were left on his face. The boy would be pockmarked for the rest of his life. He seemed happy, the defects not bothering him, but they bothered Adací. She blamed herself for scrubbing too hard and causing them.

The boy left to get his mother just as Bertol's voice sounded behind Adací. She turned and swiped her hand across her eyes.

Bertol saw. "Are you okay?"

She shook her head. "The little boy who gave me the scrum got scars even though Pedí cured him."

She told Bertol about the mistake she'd made.

Bertol insisted it wasn't her fault. That was a change, Bertol defending her. He even sounded like he meant it.

But it didn't help.

Even if the scars came because the boy had scrum too long, as Pedí had said—and it wasn't her scrubbing—she'd forgotten to tell Pedí about him and only thought of herself. In one way or another, Adací was at fault. Her face had been spared, but she would carry the boy's pockmarks inside her for the rest of her life.

The boy's mother came out of their shelter with her arm around her son. She nodded toward the box of food in Bertol's hands. "You need to save some of that. There are Itatu on the other side of the ridge. An Itatu mama came begging, but we had little to give. Her youngest is dying from some kind of fever the Itatu are plagued with."

When they finished helping the rest of those in need, Adací and the others got back in their wagons and drove over the elevation that split Poor Man's Field. Adací knew the far side of the field well. It was where her birth parents lay buried.

The Itatu family that the Black River woman had told them about was living under an awning of colored cloth that was stretched from poles attached to the top of their wagon. The father sat beneath the canopy, wrapped in blankets and shaking with chills. He was on a makeshift chair and leaned against the wagon box. Two older children helped their mother care for the father and for a young girl who looked to be about five years old. The girl lay on a bed of folded blankets placed on the ground near the wagon's rear wheel.

Adací jumped down and ran to help. She approached the Itatu mother, whose freckled face was streaked with sweat and dirt. The young daughter wasn't moving except to shiver intermittently. Her nose was bleeding, slow but constant. The mother dabbed the girl's nose with an old rag and used the same cloth to wipe sweat off the girl's forehead. Adací didn't know what to do or what to say.

Marina came to Adací's side. "What does she have?" Marina asked the woman.

"We call it winter fever," the Itatu woman said. "It always comes this time of the year. Our little one has gotten much worse today."

Marina knelt by the girl and placed the back of her hand against the girl's forehead. Marina's eyes widened. "She's like a stovetop," she whispered to Adací.

"I can sponge her with wet cloths, Mama," Adací said. "Is that okay?" She was trying to be careful after the scrum episode.

Marina nodded and motioned for Adací to go ahead. "Our people don't get this fever, so I think it's safe for us to help."

"Here's some clean water." Edero gave Adací a bottle of water as she knelt by the sick girl. Bertol brought some cotton rags. Adací began wetting the rags and sponging the girl's forehead. Adací had helped sick people before—she'd even seen a few people die—but this girl's pale face and hot body looked worse than anyone she remembered. "Is she going to die?" Adací asked.

Mother held her finger to her lips to hush Adací's words.

"Just keep sponging her with wet cloths," Mother said.

Edero and Bertol carried a wooden box out of the wagon to use as a seat for the exhausted mother. Elana, Edero's mother, helped the woman sit down.

When Adací opened the girl's blouse to dab her chest and abdomen, everyone gasped. A red rash covered her skin, and frightening dark blood spots were scattered beneath it. The rash and blood spots were not crusts and sores like the scrum but were even more alarming. Something terrible was happening to this girl.

"We must send someone to get a healer," Elana said.

"Get Pedí from the Sanctuary infirmary," Adací pleaded. "Have him bring his new potion."

Mother agreed.

The fastest horse was taken off one of the wagons, and Bertol raced off.

While Adací sponged the child with wet cloths, she fingered her braid and whispered to herself. "Pedí has to come with his nanimoha. He can save her."

The girl's mother slid her box seat closer to her child. She sat opposite to Adací. The Itatu mother's eyes were hollow and dry as if no tears were left. Adací gave her a clean cloth, and each time a drop of blood gathered on the girl's upper lip, the mother would dab at it.

"My Luciana is going to die, isn't she, miss? Uai, she's our sweetheart. Her papa adores her. She waits for him to come home each day, then rushes into his arms."

"There might be a chance. There's a young healer with a new potion."

But would Pedí's new cure work for this child's illness? He said it hadn't worked for all infections, and this little one was so far gone.

"Uai, if there's a potion to help my girl, it would be a miracle. Just look at her." The mother covered her eyes with her hands.

Adací sensed the profound love this mother had for her dying child. She thought of her birth parents and how they had given their lives to save her. She loved Mother and Father, but there would always be a part of her that longed to know her birth parents. She wished she could hug them to thank them for preserving her life. Whenever she was at Poor Man's Field, and Mother let her, Adací would go to the graves. Their bodies lay under a tree not far from where this family was camped. She would sit between the small mounds of earth and talk to them.

As Adací cared for the child, she glanced at the rest of the Itatu family. Larada and Edero had prepared a meal for them from the last of the food supplies. The father and other children pressed the food into their hungry mouths, not tasting, hardly chewing, just filling the emptiness of their bellies.

Adací looked back at the dying girl and watched her chest and abdomen rise and fall with each breath. She worried that if she looked away, the shallow movement would cease. Adací refused to eat when Mother brought her a plate. What if she stopped sponging, and the girl died? Each dab with the wet cloth seemed to slow the growth of the imaginary scrum scars that had been enlarging inside Adací ever since she saw the pockmarks on the immigrant boy's face.

Kneeling in the dirt, hoping to save the life of the small, freckled-face child, seemed the most important thing she'd ever done. What if Pedí could teach her to be a healer like he was? She could work by his side, helping others. She might not become a witch.

Mother brought Adací a clean cloth. Mother's brow was wrinkled, and she shook her head. The girl was going to die. It was taking too long for help from the infirmary to come. Each minute was like an hour.

The clop, clop of approaching horses interrupted the vigil. Adací looked out from under the canopy. It was Bertol.

Pedí was with him.

Adací glanced back at the girl's ashen face—her only movement, an occasional shiver.

The apprentice healer had come too late.

CHAPTER TWENTY-NINE

Too Sick, Too Little

Pedí tied his horse to a tree behind the parked wagons and then walked toward the Itatu camp. He was unsure what he would find. When Bertol Mendin came to the infirmary, he talked first to Doctor Arias. The doctor summoned Pedí and asked him to go to Poor Man's Field.

From the description of the ill girl, his mentor predicted she might have the Itatu winter fever. Five years ago, Doctor Arias had gone to Itatu during an outbreak. "While there," he said, "I saw many people die and could only reduce the suffering with potions for fever and elixirs for pain. Take your new cure. Perhaps it will work for this horrible disease."

Pedí ducked under the colored cloth awning draped from the top of the Itatu family's wagon. A little red-headed girl lay on folded blankets. An Itatu woman sat to one side of her. On the other side, a girl with a long black braid sponged the child with wet cloths.

Adací!

Pedí placed his hand over the pocket holding the cloth pouch with her hair. He had not thrown it away. Every day, he had tried to find the courage to go see Adací but hadn't succeeded. He could only picture himself stammering at her front door—then being sent away.

If he didn't go there as a healer, he would not be welcome.

Pedí tried to put Adací out of his thoughts. He had work to do, and she would only distract him. He approached the child and her mother. "How long has your daughter been ill?"

"Uai, three days. Each day, she's got worse." The woman covered her eyes.

"May I examine her?"

The mother nodded, and Pedí knelt by the child. He was right next to Adací. She crowded up against the wagon wheel to give him room.

"Am I in your way?" she asked.

"Please stay. You're helping bring her fever down."

The freckled-face girl had a red rash with blood spots just under the skin, which matched Doctor Arias's description of winter fever. He examined the child's abdomen and found her spleen and liver were slightly enlarged—more confirming signs. She whimpered occasionally and shook from chills.

A louse was crawling on her blouse. Pedí picked it off.

"Uai, I'm sorry," the mother apologized. "My husband brought the lice with him from winter camp. Luciana slept on his lap, and the lice found her."

Pedí was about to crush the louse but stopped. The lice could be the cause—or, more likely, it was some invisible creature inside them. Smashing it in his fingers might spread the infection into any of his little cuts or scrapes. He put the louse on the ground and smashed it with a rock.

He could tell that Adací watched his every move but was afraid to look her way.

Instead, he addressed the mother. "Your child does have the Itatu winter fever."

Pedí hesitated before saying the next part. "She's very ill and may not last many more hours."

"Uai, I knew it." The mother leaned and hugged her dying child.

"Isn't there something you can do?" The words came from the father, who was behind him. Each word was spoken with difficulty. "Uai, this young lady told us you have a new potion."

Adací grabbed Pedí's forearm, her nails digging in. "Tell them about it."

He shook his head. He had never used his potion on a child. And this one was nearly dead. If he didn't get the dose right, the poisonous mushroom would finish her off.

"I-I-I—"

Adací interrupted his stammering. Her voice cracked as she spoke in short bursts. "He has a potion. It cured my face. A miracle."

"No, Adací. She's too sick, too little."

She dug her fingernails in tighter.

Maybe if he told Adací what happened with the lost bottle of mushroom powder, she'd understand his hesitancy. "Not only am I worried that this ch-child is too small for the nanimoha, but there's something else. Remember that lost bottle of mushroom powder? Breno Torred did end up with it, and he treated a prominent man in the city using the mushrooms from the stolen bottle. Just as I feared, he didn't dose it right, and the man died."

Pedi stiffened, remembering the anguish he felt when he heard about it. "Torred and Durgo Borgesso are blaming m-me for his death. This child is too ill to respond to my potion, but if I use it and she dies, the captain might find out. He'll have the excuse he needs. He'll use his power with the Municipal Council to send soldiers or the police. Not only will I harm this child, but they'll take my nanimoha away, and I won't be able to treat others who need it."

Adací shook her head as if she hadn't even listened. She brought her other hand to his arm and dug in with another set of fingernails. "But you're not like Breno Torred. You know how to dose it right. Save her!"

"I don't even know if my nanimoha will work against winter fever."

The child's mother groaned.

The father dragged his feet on the ground as he came up behind Pedi. "Uai, is there a chance your potion will work?"

Pedi shook his head. "I doubt it. She's too ill."

"Is Luciana going to die whether or not you use your potion?"

Pedi nodded.

"Then use it."

Pedi stood up to face the father. Adací let go of his arm, which now had ten red crescent moon marks where her fingernails had dug in.

"I don't want to hasten her death."

"Please!" the mother cried. "She's already dead without it."

"You can cure her!" Adací exclaimed.

Those words from the black-braided girl shook him. It was as if the ancient Adací had spoken to him herself. He had to obey her.

"I will try," he said.

A supply wagon was moved close, and the tailgate was let down and secured horizontally to use as a table. Pedí pulled his equipment and a bottle of dried mushrooms from his saddlebag. He measured the dose and weighed it on a scale. He added it to an exact half-liter of water that he brought to a boil in a small pot over a fire. He let it simmer for five minutes, then removed it from the heat.

As the solution cooled, he added the sweet herb, stirred it, then strained it through a sieve.

His hands trembled as he carried a cup of the potion back to where the girl lay. Adací helped her sit up and gently shook the child. She opened her eyes.

Pedí bowed his head, put his hand over the pouch with Adací's hair, then whispered. *"Nanimoha, pianu-ha somyu-i"*

"What did you say?" Adací asked.

"I spoke to the potion in Idonata, asking it to cure the girl. Grandpa taught me some of their language."

"It will work." She took his arm again but didn't dig in with her fingernails this time.

He imagined the real Adací at his side, guiding him, but then shook his head at his foolishness. Pedí gave the Itatu child the nanimoha potion over the next half-hour but measured each dose a centimeter under the line on the tube marked for an adult. Adací gently prodded the dying girl and managed to keep her awake long enough to swallow each small amount. Then, they laid her back down.

"Please keep sponging her," Pedí said to Adací. "Now we wait to see what will happen. I fear she'll not tolerate the potion in her weakened condition."

Pedí stood up while Adací sang lullabies and dabbed the little redhead with damp rags. The girl's father scooted his chair over and sat beside his wife.

"When did you first get sick?" Pedí asked him.

"Uai, after returning from the winter camp."

"Did you get better after the initial fever but then sick again?"

"Uai, how did you know? I got well enough to make the trip here to sell some of our cloth and blankets, but the fever returned."

The mother leaned over to adjust her little girl's position. "That's when our Luciana got the fever."

Pedí nodded. "Winter fever can have two or more bouts of sickness with normal days in between. The first one is the worse, the one that may ..." He didn't say the last words.

He knelt again and searched through the child's clothing. Several more lice were crawling on her. He picked them off and crushed them into the dirt with rocks.

The father got down to help. "Uai, I brought the lice to her. At winter camp, we sleep in crowded cabins. If one man has lice, soon we all do."

"The lice might be the cause—or something inside them," Pedí told him.

The freckled face girl had been twisting side to side in weakened movements whenever Adací dabbed her skin with the moist cloth, but then the child stopped moving.

His potion was killing her.

Adací sang her lullabies a little louder. Pedí knew she was trying to calm him, the parents, and everyone else who stood in a circle around the sick child.

Suddenly, the tiny redhead jerked and shook with renewed force. Pedí checked her pulse. Her heart was beating faster, and her skin was hotter than before.

The mother reached for her child. "Luciana's dying."

Unable to face the parents, Pedí talked to the ground. "I'm so sorry. The potion's not working, or it's too strong for her."

The father held his wife in his arms as she wept.

Adací placed one of her hands on the girl's forehead and the other on Pedí's arm. A surge of warmth passed between the dying child, Adací, and Pedí. For a moment, he felt hope, but it was a fool's hope.

The chills only worsened. The girl opened and closed her eyes with each shaking motion, but they weren't signs of consciousness. Her breaths were shallow and further apart. She took one deep gulp of air. Pedí waited to see if it would be her last. All movement stopped. Her eyes closed and stayed shut.

Adací gasped, as did the others in the circle of onlookers.

"She's gone!" the mother cried out.

Pedí was still checking her pulse, but it did not cease. Instead, it beat slower, stronger, and at a steady pace. Her chest and abdomen rose and fell with each breath, but now in proper timing. Beads of sweat formed on the girl's head, and she flushed red.

"Her heartbeat is back to normal," Pedí said. "Her fever's breaking."

The father let go of his wife and reached out to touch his daughter. "Uai, you mean she's not dead? But she's so quiet. And before—"

"She was in crisis and should have died. But now . . ." Pedí looked at Adací, then at the parents. "The nanimoha may have worked. It seems to have resolved her symptoms after first making things worse."

The girl's clothes and blankets were soon soaked from her sweat. Her eyes flickered. She was waking.

Adací and Pedí stepped back as he motioned for the parents. "Come near. I want her to see you first."

The girl's eyes opened. "I'm thirsty, Mama."

The air was filled with whoops and cries—the loudest came from her family. The small redhead looked wide-eyed at the people gathered around her.

Adací ran to get fresh water, and the child drank several cups. Adací's black braid swung back and forth as she wiped the sweat from the child's face and sang to her. Pedí clutched his pouch with the coiled hair. He no longer had his clay Adací, but it was as if his ancient heroine had come in person to make the nanimoha work.

Pedí wanted to prevent anyone else from getting the Itatu fever. He suggested boiling water and helping the family wash their bedding and clothes. He may be wrong about the lice, but until he knew for certain, it was best to get rid of them. The tricky pests hide in the folds of clothing, but boiling kills them and their eggs.

"When you get home, check for lice and boil your clothes," Pedí told everyone from New Losobon. "If you find any lice, don't crush them with your fingers. It may release whatever causes the disease inside the louse onto your skin."

He treated the father with his mushroom cure and told him he would return tomorrow to see if he and his little girl needed another dose.

After putting his supplies back into the saddle bags, Pedí went to his horse to re-attach them. The others were preparing to leave as well. He looked for Adací but couldn't see her. She must still be at the girl's side, singing her lullabies.

He wanted to say goodbye but was uncertain if he should. Adací's mother seemed changed toward him. She had not been as friendly the last two times he'd treated them at their house, and today, she frowned whenever he was near her daughter. He didn't want to cause problems for Adací.

A poor Idonata boy should never associate with a wealthy girl.

CHAPTER THIRTY

Invitation to the Festival

Adací sat by the recovering child, stroking her hair and singing songs. The little redhead smiled at each new one. The wagons and horses were nearly ready, and they'd soon be leaving, but Adací didn't want this feeling to end. She had helped Pedí heal this child, this wonderful freckled-face girl. If she could spend more time with the young healer, Adací would escape from becoming a witch—or at least become a good witch instead of a bad one.

She glanced around, looking for Pedí. He was on the other side of the wagons getting his horse ready. She had to ask him her question before he got away.

Adací half-walked, half-ran to reach Pedí. But she slowed her pace when Mother looked her way. She stopped completely when a hand slipped into hers.

"Oh, Bertol, it's you."

"Are you on your way to talk to that healer?"

"Uh . . ." She nodded. This conversation needed to end, or Pedí would be gone.

"Are you in love with him?"

Adací shook her head. "Of course not. He's just a friend." She glanced in Pedí's direction. He was making a final adjustment to his saddlebags. This encounter with Bertol was taking too long. Why did he have to bother her now?

He still held her hand. "I saw how you looked at him. You do like him, don't you?"

"I'm just grateful; it's nothing else."

Bertol squeezed her hand even tighter. "I've enjoyed being here with you, though you were busy helping the little girl." He looked at the ground. "And the healer."

Why was Bertol acting so nice and so humble? What was wrong with him? Adací glanced again to check on Pedí. She couldn't see him anymore, but his horse was still there.

"Thank you for coming," she said to Bertol, then tried to pull her hand away.

"I . . ." Bertol started to respond but stopped. He was looking behind her.

She turned. It was Pedí.

He was already backing away. "S-sorry to interrupt," he stammered. "I came to say goodbye, but-but I see you're b-busy." Pedí spun around and walked away, not even waiting for her response.

"Wait!" Adací jerked her hand out of Bertol's grasp and rushed to Pedí. She grabbed him by his shirt sleeve and then twisted back to look at Bertol. "I need to talk to Pedí alone."

She walked the healer around the wagon, keeping a firm hold on his sleeve. He pulled from her a bit.

When they reached his horse, Adací let go. "Thank you for saving the little girl. Your potion is magic."

Pedí made circles with his shoes in the dirt. Adací gave him time, even though she knew Bertol waited on the other side of the wagon.

"You and your mama saved her."

What did he mean? Without Pedí, Mother and Adací would have just been there to see the girl die.

"You found the girl. You came here to help. Not many do that."

Adací bounced on her toes, grateful that Mother and Father had taught her to care for others. Now she could ask him. In two days, it was the Winter Solstice Festival. He might be free that day.

"You talked about taking me frog hunting. Can you do it on Festival Day?"

His face turned bright red, but he smiled and nodded.

"Come to our house after breakfast that morning. We'll take horses and go to the forest. I want you to teach me more about your animal friends, and I'll even try to catch a frog."

Adací grinned but shook her head. "Not snakes yet, especially not hognose snakes."

She saw Pedí's own little grin. "Make sure to come early," she added. "We have to be back by noon. I'm going to the festival with my parents."

The next words came out like a loose bullet from a soldier's musket. "You can come with us to the festival. Mama and Papa won't mind."

She should not have pulled that trigger. Of course, her parents were going to mind. But this was more important. Pedí was going to change her whole life and save her from her evil destiny.

Adací waved as Pedí got on his horse and rode away.

When she turned around, Mother and Bertol were twenty feet away. They had come partway around the wagons. Mother's hands were clenched. Bertol's were loose and at his sides, but they were shaking. His eyes drooped. His proud look was gone.

They must have seen and heard everything.

On the bouncy wagon ride home, Mother kept quiet but trembled like a volcano ready to explode. When they got back, everyone left for their own homes. Adací walked with her mother toward the back of the house. Mother leaned toward her, and the lava began to flow out of the volcano. "Bertol was heartbroken that you ignored him and went to talk with Pedí. Are you so blind not to see that Bertol likes you?"

"No, he doesn't." Adací shook her head.

"He's not the little boy who used to make fun of you."

"But—"

Mother cut her off. "I know what Pedí did was a miracle. He deserves our thanks. But not the type of thanks you're giving. Have you forgotten so soon what your father and I told you? He's a good boy, but he can't be your friend. You would be treated poorly, just like he is. And something terrible might happen if the wrong people find out about you. We couldn't bear it."

Mother grabbed Adací's upper arms so she couldn't turn away. "You're deceiving Pedí, and you're going to hurt him. You certainly confused and hurt Bertol."

Adací bit her lower lip. Her interest in Pedí was different. She just needed to find a way to explain it to Mother.

But Mother wasn't done yet. "How many times can we make excuses for you? If Bertol sees you at the festival with Pedí, he'll quit wanting to be your friend."

"Bertol's not my friend or my boyfriend, so I don't care."

Mother squeezed Adací's shoulders even tighter. "Bertol likes you. Everyone knows it. Everyone but you!"

No, no! Adací didn't want Bertol to be her boyfriend. What if Pedí also thought that was so? With his shyness, Pedí would be even more afraid to be with her.

Mother continued. "Bertol would be the perfect young man for you to marry one day. Don't ruin everything we've planned over your desire to be kind to that healer."

"I just want Pedí to teach me. That's all! It's nothing else."

"Now you're deceiving yourself. You know it's more than that."

Adací shook her head, broke free from Mother's grasp, and ran up to her room.

CHAPTER THIRTY-ONE

Outbreak in Itatu

Pedí's sleep was infused with visions of a girl with a beautiful face and a long black braid. When he woke, Pedí felt like he was still in that dream world. Tomorrow, he would go frog hunting with Adací and later to the Winter Festival. He had a friend, a friend who liked him. It was hard to believe, but it was true. And this wonderful friend reminded him of his heroine, the original Adací.

Though it was still early, Pedí got up, went to the Sanctuary stables, and saddled a horse. He rode with a smile to Poor Man's Field to check on the Itatu family. The little girl was up and about helping her mama. Neither she nor her father had any more symptoms. One dose appeared to be all that was needed to cure winter fever.

When Pedí returned to the Sanctuary, Doctor Arias waited at the stables. Despite his swollen joints, his mentor had come all the way out to meet him. His knobby hand gripped the fence rail. "Are the girl and her father well?"

"The nanimoha cured them with a single dose. Winter fever responded like the man with bloody dysentery— resolving with just one treatment. I'll recheck the little girl and her father tomorrow to make sure."

"Perfect! Just what we need to save the Itatu."

"Itatu?"

"You have to take all of your mushrooms there."

"What happened?"

"A rider from Itatu arrived this morning. He rode through the night. Luco, their leader, sent him. The chief of the Itatu is begging me to come. There's been a horrible outbreak of the Itatu winter fever."

Doctor Arias released his grip on the fence and opened and closed his gnarled hands as if checking to see if they still worked. "It's the worst epidemic they've ever had, much worse than the time I went five years ago. Many are dying."

"The girl and her father at the field!" Pedí gasped. "The nanimoha worked so fast. It might save others."

"That's why you have to go."

The doctor's forehead wrinkled. Something else concerned him. A few stable workers were nearby. He motioned for Pedí to move away from them, and they walked into the orchard.

"Davi Gonço is my old friend. He came to talk to me last night. As chief butler at The Big House, he's around the captain often enough to learn what things he's planning."

Doctor Arias cleared his throat and looked around before continuing. "The rumor we heard is more than just gossip. The captain is blaming you for the death of the man that Torred killed with your mushrooms."

Pedí gulped. He'd told his mentor about the stolen potion bottle the day after it had happened. Guilt swept over him again for his negligence and what it had caused.

"They're spreading tales that you gave him the mushrooms with the wrong instructions on purpose, intent on having him fail."

"But-but—" Pedí tried to interrupt.

"The truth won't matter. The captain will find witnesses willing to say anything."

Doctor Arias put his hands on Pedí's upper arms to steady him for what came next. "He and Breno Torred will convince the Municipal Council to send soldiers to confiscate the mushrooms you've already collected and then force you to show them where they grow in the forest."

Pedí's head swirled. He leaned against a papaya tree.

"If the captain and Torred can't make you tell them how to use the mushrooms safely," Doctor Arias continued, "they'll declare you a fake and destroy your nanimoha. They don't want anyone to benefit if they can't use it for their nefarious purposes."

Pedí slid down the scarred bark of the papaya tree and sat on the ground. His nanimoha was soon to be no more, just when he knew he could safely give it to people—even children.

A band of leafcutter ants trailed through the grass near him. He picked up a stick and held the end of it in their path so they had to go up and over, and he could see them better. Each ant carried a segment of a chopped-up leaf, like a little parasol. When discouraged, Pedí looked to his insect and animal friends to help, but this troop of striking red ants would not deflect the despair soon to overwhelm him.

Pedí looked up at his mentor. "Durgo and Torred will blame you as well. It will give them an excuse to have you replaced."

"I didn't want to say it, but you may be right."

Pedí dropped the stick when a leafcutter soldier ant climbed onto it and almost reached his hand. He'd learned from painful experience that he could never talk ants out of biting or stinging. Their relatives, the wasps and hornets, were the same. Even the old Shushuhadors couldn't communicate with them without the help of the Blue Dragonfly.

"Is there anything we can do?" Pedí asked.

"I have a plan. That's why I came out to meet you." Doctor Arias's frown changed to a subtle smile. "Let's get the rest of the dried mushrooms ready. I'll get some of the new apprentices to help. You can leave for Itatu tomorrow on Festival Day. You'll be gone before the soldiers come to take them from you."

Festival Day! He'd miss his date with Adací! By the time he traveled to Itatu and visited all the mountain villages, he could be gone for two or three months. Adací would forget him.

Pedí looked at the ground, not even at the ants.

"Is something wrong?" Doctor Arias asked.

Pedí shook his head. He couldn't tell the doctor about wanting to go frog hunting with Adací. It was no excuse. He had to save the Itatu and protect his potion from Torred and Durgo.

"Nothing's wrong. Just thinking of all we have to do to get ready."

They walked back to the laboratory, and Pedí began the work to prepare the remainder of the mushrooms. Everything was brought back from Jurana and Gabro's cottage. The dried toadstools, which were not yet ground, were pulverized into small pieces.

As he put the cap on each new bottle of mushroom powder, Pedí thought of Adací. He might not even have time to say goodbye and apologize for not taking her frog hunting. The joy that had expanded inside him since Adací's invitation began to disappear. He could feel it escaping, bursting out. But he kept grinding mushrooms and packing bottles—there was nothing else he could do.

When Doctor Arias stopped by to check on his progress, Pedí told him about the lice he found on the Itatu girl. "I've often wondered if ticks, mosquitoes, and lice spread infections by biting a person who is ill and then biting another person and giving them the same disease. It would be something from the first person's blood—the miniature creatures I've talked about."

"I don't know," his mentor said after Pedí explained his theory. "But you've been right before. Perhaps you'll learn more about the lice when you get to Itatu."

"Will the soldiers follow us?"

"I don't think so. It won't do them any good if you get there first and have success. Once people know the potion works, it'll destroy Durgo and Torred's lies."

Pedí heard murmuring voices from the other side of the lab. It was Crina and Misha. Why did the doctor ask those two to be the ones to help get the supplies ready for Pedí's trip? They listened to everything he and the doctor said, then whispered back and forth.

Doctor Arias had picked up a bottle of the dried mushrooms. He shook it, then watched the small pieces settle down to the bottom. "I want you to take every bottle. The soldiers may not follow you but will come to the infirmary seeking the mushrooms. I don't want to have to lie to them."

"You're not coming with me?"

Doctor Arias put the bottle back on the table and looked at his hands. "My joints aren't well. I'd only slow you down. You've seen winter fever now and can recognize it. And for the first time, we have a potion to treat it."

Pedí had expected his mentor to come with him. Now, he'd be without his Adací figurine *and* his teacher.

Doctor Arias held up his gnarled hands. "I wish I could go. If there was still some orange frog toxin left, it might have been possible. It gave me relief to use it from time to time."

Pedí thought of a way to give something back to his mentor. "I'll go into the jungles after I fight the fever in Itatu. I'll find some orange frogs."

"I'm afraid there're none left."

"What about the Ipixuna River? I just read about it. It's the least explored region of the jungle. The river has a series of waterfalls that have kept the traders out of its upper branches."

"It would take you too long to get there."

"Not if I can find the old trail. The book said an ancient pass runs through the Blue Mountains from Itatu. I wouldn't have to go down to the Romingo Falls and up the Ipixuna."

Doctor Arias shook his head. "I don't want to put that burden on you."

The sound of breaking glass interrupted their conversation. Crina had dropped a bottle she'd been holding onto the countertop.

"Sorry," Crina said. "I didn't mean to."

"It wasn't mushroom powder," Misha added. "Just sweet herb."

"Don't worry," Pedí said. "We have plenty of sweetener."

Crina grabbed Misha's arm, and the two walked over to Pedí and Doctor Arias. "We heard you say jungles. Is Pedí going there too?"

"Is he going to find orange frogs?" Misha asked. "Aren't they bad?"

Doctor Arias shook his head at the two girls. "Only if misused. In the right dose, their toxin can help the worst pain cases."

Pedí's thoughts spun of frogs and jungles, but all too soon, they settled back on Adací's black braid and kind smile.

Doctor Arias must have seen the look on his face. "Something's still bothering you."

"It's nothing."

"I know what his problem is." Crina butted into the conversation. "He's going to miss his new girlfriend."

Pedí wished she'd stay quiet. Crina and Misha had pestered him worse than ever once they found out he'd been to Adací's house a few times.

"Forget her, Pedí." Crina winked at him.

Misha brushed her hand across his arm. "We'll still be here when you get back."

Crina and Misha pretended to like him. But whenever he talked with them, whispering and giggling followed. They laughed at his stuttering while Adací waited patiently for him to form his words. They made jokes about him while Adací talked about birds and the Blue Mountains.

"Leave Pedí alone." Doctor Arias shooed them away. "Go clean up your mess."

The girls left, but they had brought out Pedí's nervous sweat. He swiped his forehead.

The doctor put his hand on Pedí's arm. "It is about Adací, isn't it?"

Pedí shook his head but then nodded.

Instead of saying more, his mentor turned toward the laboratory wall. He took his glasses off and rubbed his eyes.

Pedí must have disappointed his mentor by thinking more about Adací than the importance of this trip. "I'm sorry. It's just that . . . Well, she . . . I promised her I would go frog hunting and to the festival."

Pedí took a deep breath and cleared his throat. "I need to let her know I'll be gone. Will there be time to go to her house?"

Doctor Arias put his glasses back on and turned around to face Pedí. "Come outside, away from listening ears. I've delayed telling you something."

Pedí followed him out the back door and into the orchard. He had his hand over the pocket where he kept the pouch with Adací's strands of fallen hair. What was Doctor Arias going to say? Was there more danger from Durgo and Torred than he'd let on?

Or was this little talk to set Pedí straight, to let him know that he was a fool to think Adací might like him?

Doctor Arias cleared some leaves off a bench under a banana tree and motioned for Pedí to sit down. "Adací's father came to see me this morning."

Pedí slumped. It was to tell him he was a fool.

"Sergol Façillo is very grateful for what you did to cure Adací and his wife," Doctor Arias began. "He wanted you to know that Adací enjoyed visiting with you the last few days, but it must end now. When Adací is old enough, they already have plans for her to be engaged to Bertol Mendin, who is from one of the wealthiest families in New Losobon."

Pedí closed his eyes. He could see Adací and Bertol holding hands when he had come to say goodbye at Poor Man's Field. Why was he so stupid not to realize Bertol was her close boyfriend and planned fiancé?

The doctor put his hand on Pedí's shoulder. "Adací is kind and wanted to thank you for what you did for her. But it's over. She doesn't want to see you anymore."

A void began growing inside Pedí as if termites were gnawing at his heart. How foolish he had been to imagine that a girl like Adací could like him. Though she was Idonata and maybe even descended from the ancient Adací, she was now part of New Losobon's nobility. That would be much more important to her than befriending a fellow Idonata, especially someone as defective as him.

"Why would I ever imagine a beautiful and cultured girl like Adací would take an interest in lowly forest scum?"

"You are anything but that. You have a goodness that few have. I'm sorry I ever had you go to her house. I didn't know it would lead to this."

"I'd better finish up in the lab." Pedí got up off the bench. "I'm leaving first thing tomorrow for Itatu and going to the jungles after I'm done there. I'll find some orange frogs." His voice was abrupt and determined, but inside, he was hollow. The termites had done their work.

CHAPTER THIRTY-TWO

Rotten Avocado

Adací sat under their avocado tree. She watched the sun go down, its last rays giving the western clouds a pink and orange hue.

It had not been a good day.

She hadn't even seen Father. He left before breakfast to meet with someone and then went off selling horses. Mother might as well have been gone, too. She had treated Adací like a shunned baby duckling that wandered into the wrong nest.

Now, both parents were away from home. Tavi had driven Marina in the carriage to join Sergol at the house of one of the families that bought Father's horses. They had been invited for dinner.

But not Adací.

Her reputation for causing disturbances must be spreading.

Mother had given her a new book to read, but instead, Adací put on some old clothes and went to help in the stables. It boosted her spirits to be around Pito, though seeing him on his crutches was hard. Her old friend protested when she asked to help but then gave in. Lino found her a pitchfork.

When the stable work was done, she came to the avocado tree to reflect on what had gone wrong. The problems started when she went with her mother to Poor Man's Field to take additional food to the family from Itatu. The child who'd been dying ran to meet her. She and her father were well, with no signs of illness. Adací smiled while she sang songs again to the little girl. Adací was waiting for Pedí to arrive, knowing he was coming to see if the little girl and her father needed another treatment. But then she learned that the apprentice healer had already come and gone.

Adací's smile disappeared.

Mother noticed.

Her parents wanted her to end the relationship with Pedí, but she was nearly in tears because she had missed him.

Mother had stopped talking to her after that.

A loose stick lay on the ground underneath the avocado tree. Adací picked it up and scratched Pedí's name in the dirt. She needed to persuade her parents to let her be his friend and let him teach her about the Idonata people, about being a healer, and about the animals and plants of the forest. More importantly, he was the only person who might save her from becoming a witch—but she couldn't tell them about that.

A cool breeze ruffled the leaves above her. It brought a change, an apprehension with the murmuring sound of the wind. She looked at the empty log seat where Pedí had sat a few days ago, then at the beehive, whose tiny black occupants were still busy going in and out. A whispering sadness crept inside her.

You will never see Pedí again.

It was just the wind circling her ears—her silly fantasies, nothing more. But she pricked up her ears and listened harder to the breeze. It spoke not a second time.

A door opened and closed at the rear of the house. Her parents must have come home. She went in and approached the kitchen, but she paused when she heard her mother's voice.

"Do you think he'll still come tomorrow?"

"No, I'm confident he knows by now," Father answered.

Adací waited a bit longer, wondering who they were talking about. When they said no more, she opened the door to the kitchen. Her parents startled. They had that look of being caught in a deception before finally smiling at her.

Lelia was behind them, boiling something on the stove. She was the first to speak. "I'm just finishing some rosemary tea. May I get a cup for each of you?"

"Yes," Mother said, then gave Adací a quick hug. "How was your time alone? Did you do some reading?"

Adací started to nod, then glanced at her hands and hid them behind her.

"Let's see them," Mother said.

Adací held out her palms. She hadn't got the grime from the stables off. She felt like a small child caught stealing from the sweet jar.

"You haven't been reading, have you?"

Adací shook her head.

"I must talk with Pito again."

"It's not his fault, Mama. I insist on helping, and then he finds me something to do."

Both parents shook their heads.

"Wash your hands, then come into the sitting room," Mother said. "Let's talk while we drink some tea."

Adací followed them after scrubbing in the basin and sat in one of the upholstered chairs. Her parents sat across from her with a small oval table in between. Adací held her braid in one hand and fidgeted with it. Lelia brought in the steaming tea, already poured into three cups. Adací picked one up and stirred it with a spoon before taking a sip.

Her parents asked about Larada and when she would be coming to the house again. They glanced at each other as they talked. They were leading up to something else.

Father cleared his throat. Adací braced herself.

"You seem to have forgotten our little chat the other day. We still think it wonderful—how kind you've been to that strange healer—but we need to talk about him once again."

The tone of the sentence pierced straight through—sham praise for her, but disparagement for Pedí. She was ready to say something angry but stopped. Ever since she'd thrown the wine into Chando's face, Father had seemed more vulnerable, as if another one of her big mistakes would break him.

She gave a softer response. "He has a name."

"I'm sorry to sound rude, but any continued friendship with Pedí will interfere with your future, and worse, it might put you in danger."

Adací's knuckles whitened where she gripped her teacup.

Father continued. "We talked to some people who know more about him."

Adací put her cup down and started to put her hands over her ears to block out his words, but she decided against it. It would only make things worse.

"Except for Doctor Arias and a few of the sages at the Sanctuary, he has no friends. He may have a gifted intellect, but sadly, he doesn't have the social skills to be with people, and you won't cure him with your kindness."

Adací shook her head. "You're wrong, Papa. He talked to me for hours about his animal friends, his healing herbs, and the Idonata people."

"That's just it, Adací," Mother said. "You know how to help him discuss the few things he's interested in. No one else ever will. The only friend he'll ever have is you. Because of your soft heart, you'll throw away everything we've done to have you accepted in New Losobon. And you'll drive away those who want to be your true friends, like Bertol. He was devastated that you ignored him and talked with Pedí instead."

That raised the hair on Adací's neck. She thought of a swear word but held it in.

"I understand you plan to go off alone in the forest with the healer tomorrow." Father wagged his finger. "You're too young to be doing that. You are not eighteen, and you have not been promised yet. And when you are, it will not be to that boy. You know our customs. If people heard, they might say the worst possible things."

"I don't care what they say."

"But you must care," Mother said. "And you invited him to the festival without asking us."

Father leaned toward Adací and put his hand over hers. He spoke in his soft voice and choked on the first few words. "We've hidden your past, your origins, on purpose. You know why, don't you?"

Adací nodded. "People still hate the Idonata, and I would be mocked just like Pedí if they knew where I came from."

"And it may be more than just mocking if people associate you with the Idonata queen," Mother said. "There are intolerant people in New Losobon who carry deep fears of the Idonata. They will find out about you if you keep associating with Pedí."

Father squeezed Adací's hand. "You must think we're unkind not to want Pedí around, but it's because of our love for you. We have to keep you safe. We don't feel any prejudice against him, but others do."

"Already your wild behaviors have cast a bad light on you," Mother said, her voice also choking on her words. "This relationship with Pedí will end all our hopes. We don't want you to suffer. You're all we have."

Part of Adací wanted to scream at her parents, but the other part—something deep inside her—broke when she saw how much they were hurting. It was all because they loved her and were trying to protect her. She held in the angry thoughts.

"I know you love me, Mama. I know you love me, Papa. But you've taught me to be kind to all people—even those shunned by others."

"We want you to be good to everyone, it's true," Father answered. "But to be seen at the festival by the side of a known Idonata boy—others won't see it as we do. It will not end well."

Adací wanted to fly out of her seat and dive like a raptor with talons outstretched. But it wasn't her parents she wanted to strike. It was at the beliefs and class system of New Losobon—labeling who was good and who was bad. It wasn't fair.

But she couldn't dispute that Father and Mother's words were true. Adací would embarrass them if she brought Pedí to the festival. To be with a poor north sider and an Idonata would cause all sorts of gossip, especially among the elite.

She picked up her cup again and gripped it even harder. Her knuckles blanched. Mother reached over and took the cup out of her hand.

The possibility of learning from Pedí and becoming his friend melted like a burning candle, drop by drop onto the floor. She sat in wretched silence while the wax oozed out of her. She had bungled everything. Instead of helping Pedí, she was leading him down a path that would go nowhere, for him or for her.

"What can I do? I promised Pedí to go frog hunting and then to the festival."

"Why don't you go outside to your thinking spot by the avocado tree and consider some solutions," Mother said. "You need some time. Take your sweater. The weather's changing."

Adací wore her sweater, went outside, and sat under the avocado tree again. It was already dark, so she took a lantern with her. The wind was blowing and almost put out the light until she sheltered it to the side of one of the logs.

She shivered when she looked at the place where Pedí had sat, then at the beehive. It was quiet, its inhabitants at rest, but Adací's thoughts were like the wild bees, coming and going randomly, swirling inside her head.

She'd been crazy to imagine that Pedí could be her friend—that he could save her from becoming a witch.

Lightning flashed behind her, and a deep-pitched thunder soon followed. She chilled as the breeze passed through the fabric of her sweater. She looked at Pedí's name that she had drawn earlier on the ground. It was harder to see in the flickering lamplight.

A gust of wind rushed through the garden. She startled when a flock of small birds burst out of a nearby bush. Rain was coming. She drew her sweater around her and got up to return to the house. The wind caused her to stumble forward. She looked down and saw that her foot had smudged out Pedí's name.

A forgotten avocado—trapped for months between the branches overhead—blew out of the tree and landed on the log where Pedí had sat. The dried, hardened shell exploded, and remnants of the rotted insides sprayed all over Adací. She bowed her head as rain began pelting her, and she rushed into the house.

CHAPTER THIRTY-THREE

Pedí is Gone

The bird's song woke Adací. She recognized the notes—a tanager, the first one this year. She looked out her upstairs window. The morning sun was already up. Last night's storm had passed.

The tanager was on one of her bird feeders, which swung back and forth on the tree limb to which it was tied. The bird was a brilliant yellow-orange with contrasting black wings. It was sampling the fruit Adací had left. It took small bites, then raised its head and sang.

"You've come from the north, small friend. Do you like our warmer climate and the food I left for you?"

Adací breathed deeply. The long night and the worries about what to do seemed distant. The tanager's melodious song erased the ache inside.

"I can do this," she told herself.

At breakfast, she readied to tell her parents about her plan to resolve the problem with Pedí. She swallowed the bread she was chewing and looked back and forth at her mother and father. They were watching, waiting, anticipating her to speak.

"I've decided what I should do. I'll go frog hunting with Pedí as I promised, but I'll ask Pito to go with us—to be our chaperone. And then, I'll tell Pedí it would be best if he went to the festival alone."

Her parent's faces were blank when she finished. She looked down at her food, waiting for their response. When they remained silent, she sipped her orange juice but still stared at her plate. Why didn't her parents respond? Shouldn't they be pleased?

She glanced up. They weren't looking at her but at each other. There was something they weren't sharing. It was the same look as last night. She knew now what it was.

"He's not coming, is he?"

Both parents shook their heads.

"It's better this way," her father said. "We took care of the problem for you."

"What did you do?"

Her father took a bite of food, delaying his answer. "I talked to Doctor Arias yesterday morning and told him to tell Pedí that *you* . . ." Father stopped and cleared his throat. "That *we* didn't want him to see you again."

Adací stood up from the table and walked back and forth, her long braid swinging wildly each time she turned.

"We're sorry we didn't tell you sooner," Mother said. "We wanted to give you time to decide on your own. Fortunately, you did."

"Not that way, Mama. I was going to tell him, but not that way."

"What did you want to happen, Adací? You said you were ready to tell him you couldn't go to the festival with him."

"But now he'll think I didn't want to go frog hunting."

She continued to walk back and forth. Three steps, then turn. Three steps, turn. Her breaths came faster and faster.

Father got up and grabbed each of her shoulders. "Stop, Adací. You're making me nervous."

She shook her head while he held her. "He'll think it was me. He'll think it was me. I didn't want it to happen this way. I have to go see him."

"You'll undo what your father did for you," Mother said.

"No. I'll tell him I can't see him very often, but I want him to know that he's still a friend."

I need him to help me.

"You're going to confuse the boy even more," her mother said.

"You shouldn't go." Father still held her shoulders.

Adací jerked away. "You'll have to lock me in my room to stop me."

"Adací!" Mother's voice was raised. "You know we wouldn't do that. But think what you're doing."

"I'm going to the infirmary now!"

She rushed upstairs to her room, opened the doors to her oak wardrobe, and ran her fingers through the dresses, pulling out the blue one.

Larada says it shows off my hair the best.

What was she thinking? Why did the dress matter? She was saying goodbye to Pedí forever. He could never be her friend.

She put the blue dress on anyway and went to the stables. With help from Lino, she hooked a horse to their buggy and soon rolled up to the infirmary.

The doors were locked.

It was closed for the festival.

Adací wandered along the front of the Sanctuary until she reached the door to the assembly hall. She glanced up at the massive silver dome. The main auditorium was always unlocked, so she went in and made her way down the center aisle. The spacious room was abandoned, and the only sound came from her shoes clicking against the paving stones that covered the floor. She stopped midway and looked up at the domed ceiling adorned in scenery painted gold, blue, and green. A row of windows at the base of the dome brightened the colors. Other windows of stained glass filtered sunlight into the rest of the hall.

It was here, in the center of the vast room, that she'd embarrassed her parents as a twelve-year-old. The urge came again today, to raise her arms above her head and shout. And she knew what she wanted to say—an angry outburst against the world.

She raised her arms and opened her mouth, but only a single word came out.

"Pedí."

The name echoed through the empty hall.

Adací hung her head.

A door opened, then closed behind her. Two young women came in from a side door. They were laughing and talking as they walked down the aisle. They nearly ran into Adací.

"Oh, hello," a girl with long eyelashes said. "We didn't see you."

"May we be of help?" a puffy-cheeked girl asked.

"I came looking for someone, but the infirmary's closed. Do either of you know Pedí? He's a young—"

Her words were interrupted when both girls began giggling. They looked at each other and kept putting their hands over their mouths as if it were some secret joke.

"Of course, we know Pedí," the long-eye-lashed girl said. More giggling followed. "We were talking about him."

The girl held her hand out to shake Adací's. "I'm Crina. I work with Pedí at the infirmary. I'm a new apprentice healer."

"I'm Misha," the puffy-cheeked girl said. "I'm going to be a sage and teach at the schools."

Misha poked Crina with her finger. "And he likes me best. He's just too scared to say it."

"Stop it," Crina said. "He's scared of all—"

She interrupted herself. She looked more closely at Adací and leaned to examine her long braid. Crina's smile disappeared. "Are you—"

"I'm Adací. Pedí cured my scrum."

Misha gasped. Crina took a step backward.

"I need to talk with him. Is he here?"

Crina's eyes widened. "You don't know?"

A shaft of fear pierced Adací. "Has something happened to him?"

"He's gone."

"Gone?"

"To Itatu."

"He can't be gone."

She had to see him and let him know she still wanted to go frog hunting. Why didn't he come and tell her he was leaving? Then she remembered what Father had done.

"He left early this morning," Crina said. "Doctor Arias sent him with his new potion. People are dying there."

"Oh." It was all Adací managed to say.

"I thought he would tell you," Crina said. "He's going to be gone for months because he's going to the jungles after he fights the fever in Itatu."

Gone for months!

Those three words began reverberating inside Adací's head. She shook her head, trying to cast out those words, but they only bounced harder against the inner table of her skull.

"I need to see Doctor Arias. Is he around?"

"Follow us. We're going that way."

The girls walked Adací out a door at the back of the assembly hall, then through the courtyard and orchard to Doctor Arias's cottage. He was working in the garden at the side of his house.

The doctor wore a wide-brimmed hat and held a hoe. A hedge of thorn bushes surrounded the garden.

He looked up as they approached. "Hello, girls. And Adací, how nice to—"

"She didn't know Pedí went to Itatu," Crina interrupted. "She was waiting for him to come to her house."

"Oh my," Doctor Arias said. "Let me unlatch the gate. Be careful as you come through. The thorns are sharp, but keep a few of the rabbits and other critters out."

The three girls entered the garden. Adací glanced down each row of groomed vegetables and flowers as if searching for something. Something lost.

"Did your father not tell you that he talked to me?"

"Not till this morning."

Adací leaned to look down a row she hadn't checked. "I . . . I needed to talk to Pedí."

She turned to look behind her. "And tell him I didn't send Father."

She twisted to try and see around Crina and Misha. "But that we couldn't go to the festival."

She turned back again and once more scanned the rows by Doctor Arias. "But I did want to go frog hunting with him."

Her search ended, and she looked at Doctor Arias. "Now he's gone."

"Just a minute." Doctor Arias glanced toward Crina and Misha. "I need to talk to Adací alone."

"She needs us," Misha said.

"We know Pedí better than anyone." Crina waved her hands. "We can help."

"You know how to bother him better than anyone," Doctor Arias said. Both girls frowned.

"Go get ready for the festival. I'm sure you have things you need to do."

"But we've got—"

"I need you gone." Doctor Arias ushered them out the gate. They mumbled as they left.

He waited until they were out of hearing range. "Those two admire and adore Pedí, but he can't see it. He thinks most people are just mocking and making fun of him."

It was as if Doctor Arias's sharp-edged hoe cut straight through Adací. "Did he think I was making fun of him?"

Doctor Arias shook his head.

"Did he want to come to see me?"

Doctor Arias looked away. He hoed a few more weeds before nodding. "You were an exception—one of the few people besides me and the sages he trusted would be a true friend and never treat him poorly."

Adací hung her head. What would Pedí think of her now?

"Those two girls," the doctor waved his hand toward Crina and Misha, "were jealous of you—that Pedí wanted to be with you and wasn't so afraid anymore."

"I just wanted to learn from him. I didn't want him to think it was more than that."

Adací knew she was lying. Everything she'd been telling herself and her parents about her reasons for wanting to be with Pedí were nothing but lies.

Doctor Arias put down his hoe and took hold of Adací's hand. "Your kindness was good for him, so don't feel bad. This trip to Itatu and the jungles will help him get over you. He's used to being rejected."

Adací had been holding back the tears, but those words, *he's used to being rejected,* unstopped the plug. Hot tears ran down her cheeks.

Doctor Arias helped her to a small bench just outside his back door.

His wife, Talia, came out of the house. "What have you done to this girl?" She sat by Adací and put her arm around her.

Adací tried to stop. She accepted a small towel from Talia. "I don't know why I'm so emotional." She wiped dry each eye. "Pedí needed a friend, but I've hurt him just like everyone else. He'll think it was me who didn't want him to come."

Talia patted Adací's back.

The doctor knelt to be closer. "Maybe it's best if he thinks it was you. He can move on, and so can you. He'll be okay. I promise he'll forget you. You need to get on with your life and associate with the fine young men your parents choose for you, like this Bertol, your father mentioned."

The tears wanted to come back. Adací covered her eyes with the towel to keep them at bay. She had been unfair to Pedí. She tried to get him to like her and encouraged the friendship even though she knew her parents would never allow it to continue.

But he would get over it, Doctor Arias had said, and even promised that Pedí would forget her. That was the real difficulty, wasn't it? She didn't want him to forget her.

CHAPTER THIRTY-FOUR

Frog Hunt

After giving Adací a few more hugs and a glass of water, Doctor Arias and Talia walked her back to her buggy. She started for home. On the way, Adací remembered a pond at the south end of her father's fields.

She changed direction. Perhaps there were frogs there. She would go frog hunting on her own.

Was it penance for what she'd done to Pedí? Would he somehow know what she was doing? Adací shook her head. It was a useless act, but just the same, she had to do something to try and pull the sadness out of her heart.

At the cattail-filled pond, she walked along the edge. Two dull-colored brownish-green dragonflies chased each other and swooped down near the water's surface. They were good sized, but nothing like the Blue Dragonfly Pedí had told her about.

She scanned the pond, looking for others, looking for a giant blue one. A flash of blue caught her eye, but it was just a small damselfly. It flew lazily and landed on a bare weed stalk just in front of her. When she bent to look at it, a big green frog with a brown stripe down each side jumped out of the grass near her feet. She tried to grab it, but in two short hops, it plopped into the clear water.

While sitting by the avocado tree during his last visit, Pedí had taught her that if you weren't fast enough to catch frogs before they jumped into the water, you needed to watch where they dove into the mud. The frog had disappeared into the pond bottom under a floating clump of duckweed. The tiny green plants formed a perfect hiding place.

"If you have enough patience," Pedí had said, "they always come up for a breath, usually right where you last saw them."

She would wait, but the frog's hiding place was about three feet out from the pond's edge. How would she get close? She looked down at her blue dress. The bottom edge was already soiled from walking by the pond.

It didn't matter. She would catch the frog for Pedí. Adací rolled her long sleeves up. She glanced around to make sure no one was watching, then gathered the dress so that it was above her knees. She knelt down and slowly inched her hands into the water.

The black mud squished between her fingers, and several small insect creatures emerged from the bottom muck and swam around her hands. She sucked in a deep breath to keep from panicking. Eventually, her hands got within a foot or so of the duckweed.

Then she waited.

And waited.

Her left sleeve unrolled partway and touched the water, but she couldn't move to push it back up. She focused on the task before her. If she thought about Pedí being gone, she would fail.

A few bubbles came up from where the frog dove in. Something moved. The frog appeared out of the mud and rose slowly to the surface. Its eyes and nose poked through the floating duckweed.

She held her breath. Her muscles tensed. She readied for the lunge.

As quickly as she could, she pulled her right hand out of the mud and grasped at the frog. But it was too fast for her. Adací ended up with a handful of duckweed. Her whole body teetered on the left hand for a moment, and then she went down, face first.

She came up sputtering. Water, mud, and duckweed covered everything, ruining her beautiful dress. She backed out of the water and sat on the pond's edge. Cold, wet, and covered in black, oozing gunk, she might have laughed at herself another time.

Adací held open her empty right hand. A few duckweeds clung to it. She wanted to cry but didn't even have the capacity for that. She had failed, failed at everything.

She sat. Not thinking. Not doing anything. Just cold, filthy, and miserable.

An hour or more passed before she got up, walked to her buggy, and started for home.

As Adací neared her house, she heard shouting and slowed the horse. Pito hobbled out on his crutches from the front yard. Lino came and grabbed the horse's collar, then helped her down. Tavi rode up from behind, his horse covered in a sweaty froth.

Mother and Father, followed by Lelia and Heila, came off the porch. Adací was surrounded by everyone in her household. They stared at her wet and soiled clothing.

Mother spoke first. "What happened to you? Your dress? Are you all right? Where have you been?"

Too many questions for Adací's muddled head. "I . . . I . . ." She glanced down at the ruined dress.

"When you didn't come back," Father said, "we sent Tavi to the Sanctuary. They said you'd left two hours ago, and we've been searching ever since. When we heard Pedí went to Itatu, we worried you tried to follow him."

"No, Papa. I know he's gone. Forever."

"Where did you go?" Mother asked.

"I . . . I went frog hunting. I . . . I promised Pedí."

"Alone?" Mother asked.

Adací nodded. She opened her right hand and gazed at it. Some duckweed was still stuck to her palm. "Pedí got away. I mean, . . . I mean, the frog got away."

"You're not making sense," her father said. "None of this makes sense."

"Come in the house." Mother grabbed her arm. "Let's clean you up."

"I'll try to salvage the dress," Heila said.

Adací bathed and was helped into another dress. She was moved around like a puppet on a string. Her parents hurried her so they could still make it to the festival.

Adací shook her head. "Go without me. I'm starting to feel sick to my stomach, like I may throw up." And she wasn't lying. Whether from the sadness or something else, her insides were churning, and she was ill.

Her parents left without her, and she went up to her room.

CHAPTER THIRTY-FIVE

At the Grill Pit

Durgo Borgesso, the captain, was at his grill pit. He supervised the three servants cooking large chunks of beef over wood coals. The outdoor grill was built of stacked rocks with iron grates on top. It was located in an alcove at the side of The Big House. A tall, curved hedge surrounded the pit. Clouds of smoke rose above the foliage and into the air each time a worker turned over a piece of meat.

A feast was being prepared for the men of the New Losobon Municipal Council. They would soon arrive at the captain's mansion. It was a planned event to celebrate Festival Day.

Breno Torred stood at the captain's side. Durgo spoke with him. "Everyone on the Council has to believe our story about that Idonata boy's mushroom."

Durgo poked at a piece of meat with the metal skewer he held, checking to see if it was done. "It has to be the boy's fault that you killed Jama Olivodo."

Torred also held a skewer and used it to check a piece of browning meat. "I still think that forest scum is lying, and we're wasting our time. I doubt he cured anyone. I did my best, but Jama died in minutes after swallowing that mushroom stuff."

"You're overcooking that piece!" A loud voice interrupted the two men. It came from Chando Borgesso, who was also supervising the servants. The captain's son leaned back in a recliner on the barbecue's opposite side. He also held a long skewer but used it to poke—not at the meat—but at a female servant whenever she got near him. The poor girl was also the recipient of his frequent verbal insults.

It was Niala.

Her hair was tied back in a multi-colored cloth. Sweat dripped off her face and even her brass earrings as she worked near the hot coals.

Chando twisted from the edge of his recliner to reach the servant girl with another of his skewer stabs.

"Leave her alone," Durgo yelled at his son. He had no concern for the girl, but he feared that in her efforts to avoid his son's taunting jabs, she might knock another piece of meat off the grill and into the dirt. She had already done it once and received Durgo's well-deserved rebuke for that mistake.

This Mattaçores girl was nothing but a plague. The captain blamed her for the incident that disrupted his son's birthday celebration. Though that unstable friend of Larada Mendin had thrown the wine into his son's face, Niala had once again been talking with that crazy girl. The servant girl's guilty face proved that she must have been the underlying cause of what had happened.

"Captain! Captain! I must speak with you!"

What! Another interruption! This was not what he needed when it was almost time for the men of the Council to arrive. Someone was waving their arms from just outside the entrance to the grill pit. Through the smoke, Durgo recognized who it was.

His spy from the infirmary! This would be important, or the man would not be here.

"Come with me." He motioned to Torred.

The two men left the pit and pulled the man into a small grove of trees to talk privately. Chando came running to join them.

"Sorry to disturb you," his spy said out of breath. "I came as soon as I could get away."

"What happened?"

"Arias sent that Idonata boy to Itatu. There's a fever outbreak there, and the people are all dying. The young apprentice left early this morning and took all the mushrooms with him."

"Stupid Arias!" Durgo ground his teeth. "Let the damn Itatu die!"

"They will die." Torred laughed. "That mushroom will only add to the death rate. It's a poison, not a cure."

The messenger from the infirmary started to say something but stopped himself and looked at the ground.

"What?" the captain asked.

His informant still hesitated but finally spoke. "The boy healer used his mushroom potion on a man and his daughter at Poor Man's Field. They both had this Itatu fever. The girl was almost dead, they said, but he cured them both."

Torred, who still had his skewer, stabbed it into a tree with such force that it stuck and hung straight out. "That chump has got some secret. The mushroom's so stinking deadly."

"We're going to be the chumps, not the boy," Durgo said. "The rumors we spread of his incompetence will come back at us. We should have found a way to force that Idonata trash to do our bidding long ago. But Arias is always there protecting him."

"Father!" Chando interjected. His face was red, his eyes narrowed. "Don't let that old man at the infirmary and a frog-faced native boy make fools out of you. You should have gotten rid of Arias long ago."

"We would have, but some on the Council think that ancient healer is worth something." Torred twisted the end of his skewer, trying to drive it further into the tree.

"And now it will be worse," Durgo added. "If that mushroom potion stops the Itatu outbreak, Arias will be praised for sending the boy there. Even that tattooed idiot will gain notoriety."

"Send our soldiers to stop him," Chando said. "You can get the Council to approve it."

Durgo shook his head. "By the time they catch up with the boy, he might have already used the potion. If it heals the Itatu fever, the soldiers will look like fools, and we will look like fools."

"Is there not another way to disrupt the boy and interfere with his work in Itatu?" Chando jerked Torred's skewer out of the tree and poked repeatedly at the bark with it. "Send someone in secret to prod the boy, make him tell how to work the potion, even reveal the mushroom's hiding spot. Then . . ." Chando raised the skewer high above him and drove it deep into the tree, "kill him."

Durgo stabbed his own skewer into the same tree. "That may work, and I know just the man to do it."

Tadol Machad, with his hollow eyes and dark whiskered face, filled Durgo's memory. The man had lived by himself in the mountain wilderness for years. He could become one with the forest, hide in it, and live off it. And with enough money, he would do anything the captain asked. Twice, he had killed for Durgo, and no one had a clue who'd done it.

"I'll send Tadol Machad after him." Durgo smiled at Torred and Chando. "He'll do the job without fail, and no one will know he's even been there."

"Whoever you send has to have brains," Torred said. "Those Itatu aren't as stupid as people say."

"They won't find or catch this man."

Durgo, Torred, and Chando returned to the grill pit and helped the servants transfer all the cooked meat to two large serving trays. Chando gave Niala a parting jab with his skewer.

Durgo put his hand on Chando's shoulder when she had walked away. "You must take more caution with that girl. I know you enjoy harassing her, but the other servants are watching. What if one of them talked to Larada Mendin?"

Chando frowned. "They wouldn't dare."

"I hope you're right," Durgo said. "But your future fiancé seems to like that Mattaçores rubbish for some reason. I already worry what Larada might have thought when you dragged Niala across the ballroom at your party."

"If Larada questions anything, it's that black-haired witch who's at fault. Soon, I'll expose her for what she is."

"Be cautious, boy!" The captain shook his head. "That strange girl is Larada's close friend. I'll not forgive you if you ruin this chance to unite our family with the Mendins. You know how much it means to get in on both sides of the sugar profits."

Durgo changed his frown to a smile and slapped his son on the back. "But enough of this. I know you'll do me right."

The three men left the grill pit and talked about their plans to send Tadol Machad after the Idonata boy and how to lie to the men of the Council about the cause of Jama Olivodo's death. Somehow, they would convince them that it was the fault of the Sanctuary, of Arias, and of that Idonata apprentice. The damned sages needed to lose their influence over the people. Once the captain had control of this new mushroom and Torred learned how to use it without killing someone, they'd have a cure everyone wanted. It would be in their power, and they would use it for personal gain.

Durgo, Chando, and Torred entered the banquet hall and joined the arriving guests for a feast of roasted beef, greens, tomatoes, and pickled palm hearts.

CHAPTER THIRTY-SIX

The Idonata Queen

Adací stayed in her room after her parents left for the festival. She sat on the bed, her back against the headboard. Thoughts would come and go but never coalesced, never penetrated her despondency.

Inside her darkened mind an unwanted candle glowed, trying to tell her the truth. She didn't want its light to shine because it would become a blinding, destructive light. It would say to her that if, by some miracle, her parents let her see Pedí when he came back, he'd never want to be her friend and never trust her again.

Twice, Heila came to her room, wanting to know if Adací was coming down to eat or if she could bring lunch and, then later, supper to her room.

"No, thank you," was Adací's answer both times. The nausea that had begun earlier had worsened. Her stomach spun and twisted, and twice she had retched. Food was not going to stay down.

When evening came, there was a knock at her door, and it swung open. Mother entered. She and Father were home from the festival. Mother carried a tray with a glass of water, a loaf of bread, and a wedge of cheese. She put it on a side table and lit a lamp.

"Will you eat a little? Heila said you've had nothing all day. We bought your favorite cheese at the festival. Some bread, too."

"Later, Mama. I'm sick."

"Be careful, then. You throw up so easily."

Adací nodded.

Mother had a leather bag at her side. It had a long strap that went over her neck and shoulder. She took the bag off and placed it on the bed before Adací. Strange designs and markings were cut into the old and weathered leather.

"Do you remember this?"

Adací started to shake her head but paused. She picked up the bag and brought it to her nose. The smell of the worn leather reached into her brain and pulled out vague memories. There was something familiar about it.

"It was your birth mama's. You used to drag it around and play with it. I put it away in the cedar chest when you turned four, and there it has stayed. You would have worn it out otherwise. Look inside."

Adací undid the lacing. Her fingers trembled, and her mind stretched backward through the years to recall any memory of her real mama and papa. But other than her nightmares about them, there was nothing.

From the bag, she pulled out three multicolored baby dresses. They had been sewn from dyed cotton. A design was stitched onto the front of each one. It was the face of a woman with a dark black braid. One plait of the woven hair was silver.

Just like mine.

Green strands of thread were woven around the hair, interspersed with tiny green knots forming bead-like balls. Something billowed out of the top of the woman's head. Adací wasn't sure if it represented clouds or feathers. Four moons in different phases circled the figure— the crescent moon was at the top.

"Why have you never shown me these dresses?"

Mother looked away before answering. "We worried the figures on the dresses might stoke your wild imagination as a child. It was already out of control. But we saved them as keepsakes to give you when you were older. They are a link between you and your birth parents."

Mother held one of the tiny dresses. It was more worn than the others. "You were wearing this very one when she laid you in my arms. See the round cutout in front? The edges aren't finished. I think your mama had just made the opening to show off your crescent moon tattoo. I didn't let you wear the dress because we didn't want anyone to see the mark on your skin. Your mama had a similar cutout on her clothes, but it was carefully stitched. It showed off her silver crescent moon."

Adací reached and took the worn dress. "Why would my birth mama give me a tattoo when I was so little? It must be painful to get one."

"I know," Mother agreed. "In your parent's belief, it must have been critical for you to have that tattoo."

Adací tried to picture herself as a baby getting the tattoo, and she wanted to see her birth mama and papa watching. What were they thinking and feeling when the moon was inked onto her skin?

Mother pushed the old leather bag toward Adací. "There's something you missed deeper inside."

Adací reached in and pulled out a handful of dark green jade jewels. They were perfectly round and strung together on green-colored twine.

"One of the last things your mama did was unhook these jade stones from her braid. She handed them to me, then pointed to your short black and silver hair. After giving me the jade, she told me your name."

Mother wiped a tear that had rolled down her cheek. "Your mama and papa smiled, then closed their eyes when I repeated your name back to them. Their injuries were so severe, I don't know how they were still alive, but somehow they clung to life until they knew you were safe and that we knew your name. I was holding you in my arms when they passed away."

Adací clasped the jade against her chest and reached for the little dress. That's when she saw the reddish-brown stain on the back side of the fabric. "Is this blood?"

"It's your birth parents' blood that got onto your dress," Mother said.

"What happened to them, Mama?"

"That's what I came to tell you—the part of the story we've been afraid to relate. Sergol and I decided you needed to hear it now to help you understand why you can't be seen with Pedí."

Adací readied herself to be crushed, to learn something that would forever plague her heart. It was evident in Mother's eyes.

"We told the truth about going to Poor Man's Field the day they gave you to us, but it all happened before we got there. It was just outside the city entrance, not at the field. We came upon a convoy of sugar wagons on their way to Victory Harbor. They had stopped, and the men on the wagons had gotten out and surrounded two people at the side of the road. They were beating them with sticks. We ran to see what was happening. Pito was with us and grabbed an old pitchfork from the side of the wagon. Pito and Sergol drove off the men. It was your parents the men were beating. Your mama and papa were huddled together as if protecting something. But they weren't moving. Blood was everywhere."

Adací started sobbing. It interrupted her mother, but Adací sucked it in. "Go on. Tell me. I have to hear this, though I don't want to."

Mother told her that Sergol had yelled at the men to know why they were beating the two people, and Pito jabbed the pitchfork toward the wagoners, keeping them back. The chief wagoner yelled back, saying they had to kill the witch queen and the animal talker. He claimed the man had attacked them with a poisonous serpent, just like the old tales described. Their leader contended that the witch and her Shushuhador had come to kill the people of New Losobon with their magic powers. He and his men were only doing their duty, protecting themselves and the city.

Another wagoner who had been off to the side the whole time stepped forward. He had not participated in the attack. "That can't be true," he argued against his boss. "The woman and the man were hobbling and barely alive. They showed no aggression until you threatened them with your sticks and clubs. Only then did the snake come out of the bushes, and the man talked to it and sent it toward you."

Marina said his words caused an uproar from the other wagoners, who jeered at him because he was from Mattaçores and didn't know their history. They pointed out the silver in the woman's braid, with the jade stones and the moon tattoo. "She is a witch queen!" their leader declared. "Just like the one our soldiers fought against." He told them his ancestor had fought the old witch queen two hundred years ago and had been killed by a lance-head snake controlled by one of her Shushuhadors.

Pito and Sergol told the men to go on their way—that they had already killed the two travelers. Indeed, the two people hadn't moved and remained in a tight ball, and the lance-head snake lay dead on the ground. The wagoners left but complained, saying it would be Sergol and Pito's fault if the witch lived. The man from Mattaçores did not go on with the wagons but stayed to see if he could help. It was Taví.

"Your parents were still alive when we checked them," Adací's mother said. "Underneath their bruised and bloodied bodies, you were wrapped inside a cloth sling, sucking on a honey-soaked cloth to keep you from crying. They had kept you hidden from the wagoners, but some of their blood had soaked through, staining your dress. They took the blows themselves to prevent any from reaching you."

Adací started crying again.

Mother continued despite Adací's sobs. "Their old injuries were evident—the arrow in your mama and the deep gashes in your papa— the ones you described in your nightmare. Those injuries must have already brought them near to death, so it didn't take many blows from the angry wagoners to finish the process. But your mama and papa clung to life until they gave you to me and said your name. Then they quietly closed their eyes and didn't open them again."

Mother folded her arms as if holding a tiny baby. "As I held you, it only took a glance from Sergol to know he agreed with my desire to adopt you and make you our child. We begged Pito and Tavi never to tell anyone about your origin, and Pito suggested that Tavi begin working for us. We needed another stablehand at the time. So, Tavi never went back to work for the wagon master. Sergol bought his contract."

Adací found a handkerchief and tried to dry some of her tears but was unsuccessful.

Mother said more. "After we buried your birth parents at Poor Man's Field, we tried to find out where they might have come from. The wagoners' violent response to seeing your mother and father was disturbing. The hate and fear that our people have of the Idonata witch queen has not gone away despite the many years. We had to prevent that same hate from destroying our new daughter, so we hid your silver hair and your moon tattoo."

Marina reached and touched Adací's braid. "We also sought out information on the Idonata Queen and her people, your people. There are so many farfetched tales about the queen that we didn't know what to believe. An old librarian at the Sanctuary found a written history about her."

Adací sat up straighter but then nearly swooned. She bowed her head, and the swirling cleared. The overwhelming sadness of learning what her birth parents had done to protect her added to the weakness she was already feeling from not eating or drinking all day. But she held off asking for the glass of water, doubting her stomach would keep it down.

Mother didn't notice her near faint and went on. "The librarian pulled a bound volume off a shelf in the back of the library. It almost fell apart. A sage who came here in one of the first crossings had recorded the story of the queen and her powers and those of her Shushuhadors. He told about the forest cats and snakes sent to attack the soldiers. He also described how the captain's army eventually overcame the Shushuhadors and killed most of the Idonata people, though they enslaved a few. The sage's history said the queen and the last survivors hid in their largest temple."

When Adací heard the word temple, she brought her head up again. "Where was the temple, Mama?"

"It was right where the silver dome of the assembly hall sits today. The temple was torn down, but the sages used the stones for the foundation of the Sanctuary."

"What happened to the queen?"

"The account said she came out of the temple and stood on a platform at its top. The queen was alone, her long black and silver braid hanging nearly to the ground. The moon had just come above the horizon, and the silver part of her hair glowed almost like a burning fire. She raised her arms above her head and spoke strange words to the soldiers, which they didn't understand. They trembled as they watched her. They did nothing because they feared the queen and believed she was a witch."

Adací fingered her braid. "Then what happened?"

"The legend said that while the queen distracted the soldiers, the rest of her people escaped from a secret exit."

"And the queen?"

Mother's eyes widened. "She…she…" Mother cleared her throat before going on. "When they found out she'd tricked them into letting the others get away, three soldiers put away their fear and ran up the steep temple steps to get closer. They shot the queen in the heart with their muskets, and she died."

The moment Mother said those words, Adací felt a sharp pain in her own heart. She clasped her hands over her chest.

"What are you doing?" Mother shouted, then trembled. "Are you all right?"

Adací opened her hands, expecting to see blood, but there was nothing, and the pain subsided. "I'm okay."

Mother's eyes widened even further. "You felt pain in your heart, didn't you?"

Adací nodded, still holding her hands open and examining them for blood.

"You create such images in that brain of yours." Mother shook her head. "You can see why we've been afraid to tell you everything."

Her mother sighed and then finished the story. "The soldiers hung the dead queen by her long hair from a tree to show they were no longer afraid of the Idonata witch. They tried to follow her people who had escaped from the temple but never found them."

"Do you think my birth mama and papa descended from those who got away?"

Mother nodded. "Though we didn't understand their language, we sensed your parents were trying to tell us that there was something extraordinary about you. We believe you are a direct descendent of that queen who died."

So, Chando was right about me!

Mother grasped Adací's hands. "For me and your father, you are indeed a queen."

I'm a moon-haired, moon-tattooed witch, not a queen.

Mother let go of Adací's hands. She picked up one of the little dresses and smoothed its folds. "To honor your birth parents, we raised you as our child—afforded you every opportunity in New Losobon's society."

Mother's following words came out between short sobs. "I hope this helps you understand why your father told Pedí not to come again and why we must keep your past hidden. We've protected you for seventeen years and won't fail now. We are sorry that Pedí is treated poorly, but we won't allow you to join him in that suffering—because, in your case, if the people of New Losobon find out about your hair and tattoo, someone will try to kill you. If that happened, it would destroy us too. Your father and I love you more than you can imagine."

Adací's heart, which had just felt the pain from the musket balls of two hundred years ago, ached in a different way. She'd never be the same now that she had learned of the suffering her birth parents went through to save her life. Adací felt unworthy of both sets of parents who had done so much for her. And though she was unhappy with what her parents had done to keep Pedí away from her, what could she say? They had done it to protect her, and being angry about it would only cause more hurt to the two people who had treated her like something special, who had given up so much to raise her as their own and to protect her from harm.

"I know you and Papa love me, Mama."

Mother hugged Adací then left the room.

Adací put the baby clothes back into the leather bag except for the more yellowed dress. She placed it on the bed in front of her and looked closer at the string of jade.

How clever! The top and bottom of the twine had a small bone hook, and near the last jewel on each end, there was a place to attach it. The twine passed twice through a hole carved into the back of each jade ball. Behind each one was a row of even smaller bone hooks attached to the twine.

Adací stumbled to her dressing table while holding the faded baby dress and the string of jade. She had to stop once to keep from fainting. Her stomach churned, and she retched again before making it to the chair in front of her mirror.

Adací looped the top part of the jade's string through her hair, hooked it, and then wound it down the rest of the braid. The twine between each piece of jade was just the right length so that the next stone came to the outside. She pushed the small bone hooks into her hair to secure each one. The pieces of jade got progressively smaller. She looped the twine from the last stone and attached it about three inches from the end of her braid. Perfect.

She touched the balls of jade and wondered how they must have looked on her real mama.

Adací picked up the baby dress and hugged it tight. She tried to picture her birth parents. "Oh, Mama! Oh, Papa!" she spoke to the dress. "Thank you for saving my life. Can you tell me where you came from and how to find my people, if any are left?"

Instead of an answer, her faintness worsened, and her head swirled. She stumbled back to her bed. She looked over at the bread and cheese but still had no appetite. She didn't have the strength to get up again anyway. The jade was still in her hair, and she was holding onto the baby dress when she went to sleep.

CHAPTER THIRTY-SEVEN

Nightmare

The young couple stumbled and fell but got up again to keep going. They looked back, their eyes blinking, their ears straining. Adací could see what frightened them—the men in skeletal masks were getting closer every minute. The mother carried baby Adací in the red cloth sling. But there was something different in this dream. Another woman was with her birth parents. She was also ill and injured and carried a young child in her arms.

They fled together down the narrow canyon with the howling winds. When they arrived at the large cave, the dream didn't end as it always had before. This time, they entered the cavern. In its depths, they encountered a huge monster with long, dangerous claws. It was a creature Adací had never imagined. It attacked but stopped when her birth father spoke soothing words to it. The giant beast let them pass and hide in the back of the underground chamber.

When the warriors in the deathhead masks entered the cave and tried to get by the creature, it tore them to pieces.

Then, the nightmare shifted.

Adací seemed to float to another place, another time. She saw the face of a man. He had no mask, but his thin, whiskered face, sunken eyes, and sinister grin created a skeletal look, even that of a deathhead. A knife was in his hands—he fingered it. His evil, hollow eyes were fixated, stalking someone. Adací saw who the man was watching.

Pedí!

The apprentice healer was standing on a path in the mountains. By his side was a little red-haired girl. The man was going to kill them.

***

Adací woke and cried out, "What have I done? Is my dream going to bring harm to Pedí?"

Something pushed on the back of her head. She reached with her left hand and felt the jade beads attached to her braid. Her right hand still clutched the baby dress. Thoughts of her real mama flashed in Adací's head, and she imagined her birth mama standing before her with a long braid adorned with jade, just like Adací's.

"Please, Mama. Don't let Pedí be hurt."

Her mama opened her mouth as if to speak, but the apparition faded to gray and disappeared.

"No, Mama, don't go."

What was Adací to do? She had failed to protect Pito from her evil vision that broke his leg, but this time, she had to find a way to save Pedí from the skeletal-faced man.

She'd go after Pedí, warn him, then stay and protect him.

But her parents wouldn't believe her. No one would. They'd stop her.

She'd leave tonight while they were asleep.

CHAPTER THIRTY-EIGHT

Ride to Itatu

Pedí rode side-by-side with Barco, his freckled, red-bearded companion. They were nearing the Boundary Cliffs that separated New Losobon from the high country of Itatu. Two horses pulled the old cart from the infirmary, packed with Pedí's nanimoha and other supplies. Barco's horse, which he had ridden to bring the message about the fever outbreak, followed behind, attached by a rope.

It was early evening on the second day of their journey. Last night, they had stayed at an inn. The road they followed emerged from a dense forest and climbed through an open savannah. The air was calm but cool, the temperature gradually dropping as they began the ascent into the mountains. Once through the pass in the cliffs, the road would go even higher.

Pedí glanced to the west, where the sun was going down. He squinted to see better when he perceived the distant outline of a horse and rider on top of a ridge. The figure was silhouetted by the red and orange sunset.

"Is there a road up there?" Pedí touched Barco's shoulder and pointed toward the horse and rider.

Barco pulled on the reins, stopped the cart, and then rubbed his short red whiskers. "Uai, the old trail passes through those bluffs. That route is shorter but not good for wagons. It will join us at the pass."

Barco put his hand over his eyes to shade the setting sun. "Must be a stalwart horseman with plenty of supplies. The inns on that path shut down when this new road was made."

The silhouetted person was watching them. Pedí sensed it and shivered. It could be one of the captain's spies. Doctor Arias had warned him that when Durgo Borgesso found out that Pedí had taken all the mushrooms to Itatu, he may send someone to try and stop his work.

Pedí would need his heroine's protection. But instead of invoking her name, he reached into his front pocket and touched the pouch that held the strands of the living Adací's hair—the hair that tormented his thoughts.

The night before last, despite preparing throughout that day for this journey, he had not been able to sleep. All he could think about was the girl with the black braid. He thought she was his friend, but she rejected him like all the others. He had gotten out of bed and gone outside his apartment, intent on throwing the coiled hair away. He wanted to rid himself of all reminders of Adací.

When he took the strands out of the pouch, the light of the moon shone on them. The parts of the silver hair where the black dye had rubbed off glowed an even brighter color. Pedí collapsed to the ground.

His mama was right. This new Adací may have descended from the original Adací. But even if she were, Adací wanted nothing to do with him and cared nothing for the Idonata as a real descendent of his heroine would. He tried to toss the shining hair to the ground, but he couldn't do it.

Pedí continued to finger the pouch in his pocket and looked toward the silhouetted figure. As he did, the dread that a spy watched them was crowded out with a ludicrous impression.

It was Adací up on the hill!

She was in trouble and needed him!

Where did that come from? Adací would be home holding hands with Bertol Mendin.

Barco whipped the reins, and the horses started forward. Pedí looked away from the rider on the hill and tried to forget the bizarre forebodings.

His riding companion pointed ahead to the notch cut into the rising land and described the Boundary Cliffs they were approaching.

Long ago, a massive upheaval created the escarpment, which ran from high in the Blue Mountains to the Black River plains.

The cliff face was on the Itatu side and not visible except at a V-shaped gap half a mile away. Large boulders and chunks of solid rocks were thrown up from underground when the cliffs were formed and poked through the grasslands they were crossing.

When they reached the pass, their cart was inspected by the border sentries. Since Barco was from Itatu, he had to declare his purpose for travel and if he had bought or sold anything in New Losobon. The guards asked if they wanted to camp at the side of the road near the stone house where the sentries slept.

"Uai, no way I'll sleep near these men," Barco whispered to Pedí. "I know they're under orders, but they don't trust anyone with red hair and freckles."

"The inspections are our captain's doing," Pedí whispered back.

Barco knew a place further on. So, they passed through the cliffs and set up camp when they reached the top of the first hill that climbed into the Blue Mountains. After eating a supper of rice, beans, and dried meat, the two men sat around the campfire.

A voice from far away floated with the breeze. "Pedí, wait for me, I'm coming."

"Did you hear that? Someone called my name."

Barco shook his head. "Uai, I heard nothing."

The two men looked down the hill and saw the road winding back and forth to reach the top. No one was in sight. At the bottom, the road stretched back toward the Boundary Cliffs, which they could barely make out in the gathering darkness.

"Uai, wait," Barco said. "There's a horse on the road but no rider."

A lone horse emerged from a clump of trees that shaded the bottom of the hill. The animal wandered from one side of the road to the other as if lost.

"Strange," Pedí said.

He blinked several times to clear his eyes, to make them work better. A whispering inside told him there was more to see, that someone needed his help. Once again, he put his hand over the pouch with Adací's hair.

"Could I have heard a cry from the bottom of the hill?"

"Uai, no way," Barco said. "Too far. Look, someone is coming."

Five horses with riders were on the road that led from the cliffs. They moved fast in the direction of the lone horse.

"Uai, the horse must have got loose and wandered off from the pass."

Four of the riders stopped within the cover of the trees. One came out and went alongside the wandering horse. He tied a rope to it and led it back under the trees.

"You're right," Pedí said. "It was just a loose horse."

"Let's get some sleep," Barco said. "Long road ahead of us tomorrow."

Pedí went to bed, but his apprehension did not go away. Several times during the night, he got out of his tent and looked back down the hill. There was nothing new to see. The riders and their horses had gone back to the pass.

Yet even so, he could not shake the suspicion that someone was following them, and he kept having fears for Adací's safety.

CHAPTER THIRTY-NINE

Through the Pass

Adací was on top of a ridge, sitting on a horse. She looked toward the east. The sun descended behind her, creating long shadows that crossed the narrow road she was following. Far below her, she could see the new road, the route she should have taken. It appeared from out of the trees and crossed a broad savannah.

Her illness and the nausea that had started yesterday had worsened. Twice, she'd nearly fallen off the horse from being lightheaded. She rode on Suza, her father's strongest mare. Yet despite its strength, the horse was also ready to drop after carrying Adací through the night and all day with only a few short rests.

Neither could go any further.

After her dream, Adací made her way to the stables in silence. It was dark in the house, and no one stirred. Afraid of waking her parents, she didn't go to the pantry—she just wrapped up the cheese and bread Mother had left in her room and took some money to buy food on the way.

She left a letter on her bed, telling her parents she had a dream and needed to warn Pedí. Of course, they would send someone after her. Her parents had no trust in her and thought Adací lived in a make-believe world of her own creation. But with the head start, she hoped to reach Pedí before anyone could catch her.

In her hurry, Adací hadn't brought enough water. Her mouth was parched, her lips cracked and bleeding. She had taken the shorter route, the old road, to try and catch up with Pedí. That was a mistake. The two inns she passed were boarded up. Nowhere could she get food or water. No villages or houses lined the old road.

Not a single rider had crossed paths with her. Alone all day, the dream of the thin-faced, hollow-eyed man stalking Pedí repeated in her mind. Despair crowded out the little hope she had left. She was a fool and worried that soon she would be a dead fool.

Dust appeared on the savannah, and a wagon, or cart, came into view. It was on the new road and headed toward the pass. Two horses pulled it, and two men sat in front. A single horse followed, attached by a rope.

The cart came to a stop.

She sensed that whoever was on the cart was watching her like she was watching them.

It was Pedí! It had to be!

The cart started up again on its way to the pass.

"Can we go a little further, my friend?" Adací whispered to Suza. She hoped to catch the cart at the break in the cliffs where the two roads came together.

Instead of holding the reins, Adací lay against the horse's neck and held on, her face against its mane. The horse took a few steps and then faltered. Her faithful mare could go no further.

Adací tried to get off but fell, landing on her back. Her breath was knocked out of her. It took five minutes before she could sit up. She pulled herself to her feet using Suza's leg and opened the saddlebag. She scooped out some of the oats she'd brought from the stables. Suza ate them from her hands.

With Suza fed, Adací rummaged in a side pouch of the bag and pulled out her knapsack. The little food she'd brought was gone except for a few breadcrumbs. She poured them into her hand and licked them off. The slightest effort made her head swim. She breathed in short, staccato breaths.

Though dizzy, Adací gave Suza a few more oats and wondered if she could eat them herself. She pulled out another handful. With her head leaning against Suza, Adací rubbed the oats in her hands to remove the chaff. She put the dried oats in her mouth and tried to chew. With no saliva, the effort was too much, and she spit them out. Pieces of partially chewed oats stuck to her dry lips. She didn't have the energy even to wipe them off.

A small amount of the water was left in the water bag. Adací unhooked the bag but stopped before drinking. Though Adací needed the water desperately, her horse would need it more than her. It had been some time since Suza had drunk from a small stream. So, Adací drank only a mouthful, saving the rest for the horse. But when the water hit her stomach, Adací retched.

This was not good. Ill, dehydrated, and unable to drink, she was in trouble.

With what little strength she had left, Adací cut open the water bag with a small knife and held it out for Suza to drink. When finished, the old mare nudged Adací's shoulder as if telling her she could go a little further.

However, Adací didn't think she could go on, whether or not Suza could. Adací's braid had swung across her shoulder, and she saw the jade stones wrapped around it. She hadn't taken them off. She fingered the last stone and remembered the dream, the need to warn Pedí. Resolve surged through her, power seeming to come out of the jade. She'd fight on.

Adací struggled back into the saddle, and the horse trudged onward until they reached the end of the road at the clifftop. The pass was below and to their left. They'd have to go down a narrow ravine they had just gone by to reach it.

But Suza seemed unable to take another step. Adací slid off and then led the horse to a patch of grass and a depression in the rock where water had collected from a rainstorm. Suza drank and then began grazing.

Adací tried to walk to the cliff edge but stumbled. Her vision blurred until she sat on the ground. She crawled toward the edge of the escarpment and peered over. All was quiet on the main road that went between the clifftop she was on and a matching clifftop forty feet away. A small stone cabin stood to the side against the opposite cliff face. One of the sentries who guarded the pass was lighting a lamp on a post. He was thirty feet below her.

There was no other movement. The cart with the two men was nowhere.

She needed to call for help. The men would give her food and water. If she could keep it down, she could go on. They would know if Pedí had gone through.

She opened her mouth to call out but stopped when the rumble of hoofbeats sounded on the road. Adací's weakened body felt the vibrations thunder up the side of the cliff. The sentry came to attention. Another guard came out of the cabin. "What is it?" he yelled.

"Riders coming hard," the first man said.

Both raised their muskets as five horses with riders pounded to a stop. The face of the lead rider was just visible in the fading light.

It was Father.

Tavi, Lino, and two other men had come with him.

Adací's head drooped against the cold rock. She was finished. If she called out for help now, Father would find her and take her home. She would have cried if there had been any water left in her body to make tears.

The sentry shouted at the riders, his voice echoing up the side of the rock. "What in the devil are you doing racing your horses at the pass?"

Father held up his hand to calm the guards. "Has a lone girl gone through? A girl with a long black braid?"

The guards shook their heads. "The only people through the pass today were a young healer on a cart with an Itatu man—about an hour ago."

Adací trembled. It was Pedí.

"The girl's following the healer," Father said. "She's confused and ill."

Adací wanted to deny what her father said. She almost shouted down the cliff: *I'm not confused! I'm not ill!* But she looked at her quivering hands and knew he'd spoken the truth.

"The healer's just ahead," the guard said. "Went to camp at the first rise into the mountains."

"The healer doesn't need to know about the girl. We just need to find her. We should have caught up but must have passed her in our rush. We changed horses twice so we could keep going at full speed."

"Set up camp on the side of the road," the guard said. "No one gets through without us knowing."

Although her brain was still hazy, a few thoughts meandered inside, forming a plan. Adací would wait until Father and the others took the saddles off their horses. It would give her a chance. Pedí was close by—just the first hill after the pass. She'd get by the guards and reach him before Father and the others could catch her. She could warn Pedí about the skeletal-faced man before Father took her home with him.

This little hope gave her limp body enough energy to move. She crawled back to Suza. Using a large rock to help her, Adací scrambled into the saddle.

Riding back a little, she found the fork in the road that descended from the escarpment through the ravine. Adací clung to the horse's neck until the path leveled at the bottom and joined the new road. The opening in the cliffs came into view.

Her timing was right. Father and his men were setting up camp near the small house. Their horses were tied to a hitching rack.

But the sentry was still on the road, just sixty feet away. He saw her. "Who's there?"

Adací whipped the reins and took off straight at him. He waved his arms. The other sentry joined him, and they stretched across the road.

"Stop," they called out.

She kept the horse going at full gallop, and the men jumped out of the way at the last second. Her heart leaped with renewed hope as she went through the pass. Pedí's camp would not be far.

The road was straight, and there was just enough light for her to keep the horse racing at top speed. Suza's strength surprised her despite how tired the mare must be. But the gallop was too much for Adací. She was hanging on but feared that she might fall at any moment.

After a quarter-hour of full-speed riding, a hill appeared directly ahead. She could make out the road, which wound back and forth to reach the top.

"The first rise into the mountains," the guard had said.

Not far to go, but the nausea and cramps worsened in the pit of her stomach, and her hands loosened from the reins. Little lights flashed in her eyes.

"No, no," she cried out. "Not now! You can't pass out now."

The bottom of the rise was ahead, just past a small grove of trees along the road. A campfire was burning on the hilltop, and she could make out two people. Pedí would be one of them.

But her vision shimmered. The hilltop, the fire, and the people became a blur.

As her horse entered the grove of trees, she called out with her last bit of strength.

"Wait for me, Pedí. I'm coming."

The cry was more from her heart than from her dried-up throat.

She felt herself floating through the air. It was a strange sensation as everything was dark—her vision gone.

Then, a sharp pain on the side of her head.

Then nothing.

CHAPTER FORTY

Itatu

Two days had passed since Pedí and Barco went through the Boundary Cliffs. They had continued their climb with the loaded cart into the foothills of the Blue Mountains.

Pedí kept looking back, expecting to see someone following them, but it was always just his whim. No one was ever there. Thoughts of Adací came far too often. He wanted her out of his head, but she wouldn't go away. Most disquieting was the odd feeling that he had abandoned her, not the other way around.

When they reached the high valleys of the Blue Mountains, they passed through the first Itatu villages. Their houses were painted bright colors—blues, greens, and yellows. Smoke billowed out of each chimney, which was placed in the center of the sloped roofs.

In one village, the first person to see them raised a cry, and people poured out of their homes to meet the healer who'd come. Pedí had never imagined so many shades of red hair. Some had dark burgundy, others a fiery orange, and a few had a blend of brown and crimson. All had freckled faces.

Children wanted to come to the cart to touch Pedí, but their parents held them back.

Barco chuckled. "Uai, New Losobon merchants pass through from time to time, but it's always a novelty for the children to see someone without red hair and freckles. They are even more fascinated with that frog inked onto your face. They've never seen anyone with a tattoo."

Pedí and Barco did not stop in the smaller villages but pushed on to reach Belmonte, the largest settlement.

There, he met Luco Simol, the leader of the Itatu.

The initial encounter was awkward.

Pedí couldn't blame their chief for distrusting a healer so young—and especially one with a frog tattoo and dark black hair. Fortunately, Doctor Arias had sent a letter vouching for him and describing his new potion. Once Luco read it, Pedí was welcomed to their home. He sat at their table eating venison stew with Luco, his wife, Alina, and their three children.

The table was located in a central room next to an iron stove. It was used for cooking but also supplied heat to the dwelling. Small bedrooms were located at the periphery of the central area.

There was a shuffling from behind. Pedí turned to see another child. She looked to be around seven or eight. Her hair was a deep burgundy, her cheeks covered with the usual freckles, but it was her eyes that caught his attention. Their bright green color reflected the lamp light.

"Uai, Mirela," Luco said, "it's good to see you out of the bedroom. Join us for supper and meet Pedí. He's a healer who has come to save our people from the fever."

"Another daughter?" Pedí looked back and forth between Luco, Alina, and the child.

"Not ours," Alina said. "We've taken her in. Her family was killed when their wagon tipped over. Only Mirela survived."

"Uai, it happened just three days ago," Luco added. "She hasn't spoken since and has refused to come out of the bedroom."

The girl walked over to Pedí. "Uai, did you know my mama and papa?"

He shook his head, not knowing what to say.

"They put them in the ground with my brothers."

Pedí brushed back some of her hair that covered her eyes.

Mirela reached up with both hands, grasped his cheeks, and pulled his head close to hers. She held on while inspecting the tattoo on his face.

"I'm sorry," Luco said, getting up from his seat. "She's never seen anyone with an animal painted on them. At least she's talking again."

Luco put his hand on Mirela's shoulder. "Let go of him."

She did, then climbed into Pedí's lap and snuggled against him. Pedí glanced at Luco to make sure it was all right.

Luco nodded.

Alina brought a bowl of stew for Mirela and set a place for her at the table. "Get down so Pedí can eat."

Mirela shook her head.

"It's okay. I can eat with her on my lap."

When Pedí picked up his spoon, Mirela took it out of his hand and started eating from his bowl.

Alina brought another spoon for Pedí and shifted the bowl she'd prepared for Mirela over to him. "This is good," Alina said. "She's hardly eaten a bite since the accident."

The two bowls were side by side, and Pedí and Mirela finished theirs simultaneously.

The girl stayed near Pedí until it was time for sleep, then hugged him and followed Alina into the bedroom with the other children. After helping them settle into bed, Alina came out of the bedroom. She whispered to Pedí so Mirela wouldn't hear. "I don't understand this sudden attachment to you, but I couldn't be happier. When her family was killed, I feared the little girl was going to die herself—as if she had lost her reason to exist. Whether it's your tattoo or something else, she's latched onto you."

Early the next morning, Pedí sat in the driver's seat of his cart, waiting for Luco to get his horse. The door of the house swung open. Mirela rushed out and clambered up beside him.

Luco rode up. "What are you doing, Mirela?"

"Uai, I'm going to help Pedí."

Alina had followed Mirela out of the house. "Uai, remember you said, 'We are helping Pedí with the sick today.' Mirela figured that the 'we' included her."

"It would be best for you to stay home, Mirela." Luco fingered his long red mustache with one hand and held the reins with the other. "I'm glad you want to help, but what we're doing is not work for little girls."

Mirela didn't budge and shook her head.

"I'm sorry, Pedí," Luco said. "She's determined, and I'm not sure I can get her off the cart or if I should. It's good to see her functioning again."

Pedí put his hand on Mirela's shoulder. "We're going to be taking care of sick people. I can find something for you to do, and you can help me. But you have to follow my instructions. I don't want you to become ill."

Mirela's green eyes sparkled, and her burgundy hair bounced. "Uai, I'll obey you."

Alina had them wait until she brought out additional food and a warmer coat for Mirela.

The healing journey began through the hills and valleys of Itatu. In some houses, no one was ill. But in most, Pedí would find several family members lying hot with fever and a red rash.

At the home of a couple with five children, two of their little ones had been ill for three days. Mirela—her face knit with concentration—got out the little pot, carefully measured and added the correct amount of water, then put it on the stove. She already knew the routine.

While Pedí examined the sick children, he glanced to check on Mirela. She was still watching the pot but had pulled a large knife out of a sewn pocket on the side of her leather boot. She touched the sharp edge with her finger and then made stabbing motions in the air. He had never seen such a knife or someone so young using one. The girl was only seven.

The boy whom Pedí was examining picked a louse off his skin, crushed it with his fingers, and then scratched where the louse had bitten him. The child's fingernails were bloody from scraping his skin and crushing lice. Pedí searched through the child's shirt and trousers and picked off more lice. He smashed them with his shoe. So far, every patient with the fever also had lice on them and had been scratching at their skin. But some people had lice but were not ill. Winter fever spread randomly, and not everyone in a family got the disease.

Pedí wondered about his theory. If a tiny creature inside the lice caused the disease, the entity was inefficient in getting from the louse and into the next person. Perhaps the louse got the disease-bearing creatures from biting a sick person, but they could only spread the disease entity if they were crushed, and then the louse remains scratched into sores or cuts on the skin. Those who just picked the lice from their clothes without crushing them and digging at their skin might not become ill.

When the boiling water was ready, he added the precisely weighed dose of the ground mushroom pieces. When it was done and cooling, Mirela asked again if she could add the sweet herb to the mushrooms. She liked to lick off spilled leaf flakes that stuck to her fingers and hands.

After helping strain the batch through the sieve, Mirela carried the finished potion to the bedside of the sick children. She assisted Pedí in giving the dose using his glass tubes.

That evening, after all the homes in the small hamlet had been checked, Pedí waited while Luco gathered the townspeople to the village square. Luco pulled a box off the cart and had Pedí stand on it and face the crowd. Mirela climbed up at his side.

"I-I..." Pedí's tongue grew thick. He swallowed to free his vocal cords, but his mouth was as dry as the scales of a horned lizard. He had been proud that until this moment, he had not stuttered among the Itatu. But speaking in front of a crowd—impossible.

Mirela's green eyes met his. She squeezed his arm as if trying to force the words out. Maybe she would speak for him. He leaned and whispered into her ear.

Mirela raised both arms high above her. "Uai, Pedí says lice carry the fever."

He whispered to her again.

"Uai, when you crush lice and scratch your skin, you put the fever inside you."

Mirela cocked her head as he told her the final words.

"Uai, crush the lice with rocks, or sticks, or shoes, not fingers. Boil clothes. Boil bedding. Kill all lice, and the fever will not spread."

Pedí patted Mirela's head and then looked up to see a wide-eyed crowd running for their homes. Despite the cold evening air, some were stripping off clothes as they went.

The chimneys in the village smoked hotter as the families boiled water on their stoves and washed everything.

At each Itatu village, the pattern repeated itself.

Late one night, Barco and his scouts came to give another report. Luco had asked him to find a few other men and be on the lookout for any strangers that might have followed Pedí to Itatu.

"We saw a lone rider on the road from New Losobon," Barco said. "When we approached, he took off with his horse into the forest. We followed and eventually found his horse, but the man was gone. He disappeared. We searched everywhere but there was no sign, not even a footprint. We'll search again tomorrow."

Pedí was glad that Barco was the one in charge of the scouts. He trusted his red-bearded friend.

But who was this man they'd lost in the forest?

Like a louse, this worry crawled through Pedí's thoughts and prickled at him. He couldn't scratch it away.

CHAPTER FORTY-ONE

Adací Wakes Up

More than a month had passed since Adací fell off her horse and hit the side of her head on a rock. Her father had found her unconscious and brought her home. She had fractured her skull.

"I'm so sorry," Doctor Arias had said after examining her. "She might never wake up. The blow was so bad that she must have bled inside her head."

For two weeks, Adací lay not moving, not responding, kept alive by tiny drops of bone broth given to her either by her mother, by Heila, or by Larada. One of them was constantly at her side.

Then, at the beginning of the third week, Adací opened her eyes.

She was back.

But not really back.

Things were different.

She couldn't remember following Pedí. The long horse ride was lost from her memory.

Mother confined Adací to her room after she woke up. Food and drink were brought up the stairs. It took Adací several days to get enough strength to walk. At first, it was just steps around her room. The headache from the fracture worsened when she got up, and some days, it caused her to vomit.

Her only entertainment was to watch birds from her bedroom window, but Adací didn't sing with them. She didn't sing at all.

Mother, Larada, and Heila took turns sleeping on an extra bed brought into the bedroom. Mother was afraid that Adací might get up on her own and fall.

Other than her household, Larada was the only person Adací would see. She did not want to visit with anyone else. Bertol knocked on the door of her house every day. Sometimes, he came with Larada, other times alone, but Adací refused to see him.

⬥

Finally, on the third week after wakening, Adací was deemed well enough to be alone. No one needed to stay and sleep at her side. That night, she sat on her bed, surveying her surroundings. The lamp was still burning.

She spotted the old leather bag with strange markings cut into its side. It lay partially hidden in a corner. She crossed the room to retrieve it, walking slowly to avoid flaring the headache.

Back on her bed, she pulled out the worn baby dress she held the night she'd gone after Pedí. Although Adací could not remember her horse ride, she had not forgotten what Mother had told her about the queen of the Idonata. Neither had she forgotten the story of her birth mother and father and the suffering they went through to save her. She remembered clutching this same little dress as she fell asleep that night.

The jade beads?

Where were they?

Adací had put them on her braid but did not recall taking them off. She searched the bag and found them wrapped in brown paper under the other two dresses. Father must have taken them off when they found her unconscious.

Adací tried once again to remember that night. They said she had traveled past the Itatu border on a horse. To her, it was all a blur. Not even bits and pieces would come.

She gave up. She put out the lamp and lay back on her bed. She put the baby dress back into the bag but held onto the jade stones when she fell asleep.

⬥

Steam flew out of Suza's nostrils with each breath. Her faithful mare was galloping with all her might. Adací could feel the sweat on the horse's skin as she clung to its neck.

The hill was just ahead, the road winding to the top. The young healer was there.

"Faster, Suza, faster," she urged the mare.

"Pedí, wait for me, I'm coming," she cried out.

A voice answered.

Was it Pedí? Did he hear her?

The voice came again, louder this time, shouting at her. It was … It was … Pito's voice!

━━━◆━━━

Something bumped against Adací's foot. She opened her closed eyes and looked down. Her toe had stubbed the edge of a loose cobblestone. She gazed at her bare feet, standing on the dark cobbles.

There was no Suza, no hill, and no Pedí.

No, no, no! It was just a dream, and she must have walked off in her sleep.

A sharp pain began pounding inside her head, and she teetered and stumbled forward. Adací was going to land face-first on the road, but someone caught her and stopped her fall. She felt the rough skin on the person's hands and glanced at the wrinkled face. It was Pito.

"Oh Adací!" His voice trembled. "I feared I'd find you bleeding on the side of the road like they did last time."

Despite still needing crutches, faithful Pito was the first to find Adací's track and reach her side. He held her tight until the others arrived and carried her home.

Her head throbbed all the way but subsided once she rested against her pillow.

When Mother had gone to check on Adací in the middle of the night and found her gone, the whole household was alerted and fanned out to search for her. She had wandered off in her sleep, dreaming, the jade stones clutched in her hands.

CHAPTER FORTY-TWO

Sharpening the Knife

After a month of travel through the Itatu highlands, Pedí, Luco, and Mirela reached the last village. The nanimoha potion continued to heal those who suffered from the Itatu winter fever. Those treated responded similarly to the little girl at Poor Man's Field. Symptoms worsened before the fever broke and returned to normal. Many nearing death recovered, but for a few, even Pedí and his nanimoha were too late.

That evening, after they'd visited the last of the homes, Luco pulled Pedí aside. He nodded toward Mirela, who was washing her face in a basin of water. "Uai, she's your puppy dog. She rarely leaves your side."

It was true. Besides shadowing Pedí in all the work, Mirela sat by him when they ate, curled up on his lap in the evening when everyone huddled around a stove to keep warm, and when it was time to sleep, she pulled her bedding next to his.

"She was as wild as can be before the accident." Luco waved his arms. "You've seen the knife she carries in her boot pocket. She made it out of half of a broken sheep shear. She's threatened people with it."

Mirela was indeed an enigma. She ate with her fingers at meals, interrupted older people with her questions, and appeared to have never been taught a single manner.

Luco fingered his red mustache. "Uai, she won't do a thing I ask, but she listens to you. Her mama was a real beauty but so different. Stayed to herself. Rarely talked. Not sure she was well. Her papa could never make a living on his own. Uai, they were starving until I hired him to help with my herds. No one else in Itatu wanted much to do with the family. They were different and true loners. But Mirela was fiercely loyal. She watched out for her younger brothers like she was the mama."

Pedí wondered if Mirela's mother had suffered from severe melancholy or another emotional illness. Perhaps she was not able to teach Mirela or help with the younger brothers. Despite being only seven, Mirela had to assume the role of mother in the home and figure out her way of doing things.

Luco put his hand on Pedí's shoulder. "Sorry, but you are her new family. I don't know what will happen when you return to New Losobon. I watch her pride in mixing the potion. She copies everything you do, including your kindness to those who are sick."

Luco sighed. "Yesterday, she overheard Barco talking about the men who tried to steal the mushrooms at your laboratory. Out came her knife and her little sharpening stone. She's watching out for you like she did for her family."

CHAPTER FORTY-THREE

Crazy

Once again, Mother, Heila, and Larada began taking turns sleeping in Adací's room. Before, it was to keep her from falling. Now, it was to prevent her from wandering off.

Mother took the jade stones and hid them. She feared the green gems and believed they had caused Adací's wild ride after Pedí, and now the sleepwalk.

Ashamed to be a burden, Adací tried to convince Mother and Father that she could be alone, she wouldn't go off again, the dreams would not come back.

The sleepwalking dream was the only one she'd had since waking from the head injury. The other nightmares and visions were gone. The blow to the head knocked them out of her. Since a young child, Adací could not remember a night without some kind of dream. Now, she woke each day with an empty head.

At least, maybe now she wouldn't become a witch.

But had she truly been an evil witch? Her dreams, the same ones that had vanished after her head injury, had helped her save Larada three times! She bit her fingernails, something she never did—the uncertainty gnawed at her.

Adací thought her nightmare was the cause of the skeletal-faced man stalking Pedí, but maybe it wasn't so. That vision gave her the chance to try and warn him, even though she had failed when she fell off the horse.

But now, if there was any good in her dreams, they were gone.

When Adací got stronger, Mother let her help Lelia in the kitchen. Adací liked being there, but she didn't smile, sing, or even hum while she helped bake bread or cut up vegetables. At least once each morning, Lelia would complain of something in her eyes and go to a corner. The cook would find an old rag to wipe her eyes and blow her nose, then come back trying to smile.

Adací knew that Lelia, Larada, and everyone else wanted the old Adací back.

But she was gone.

Adací didn't know where.

As days passed and things didn't change, her parents stopped talking whenever Adací approached. They gave her worried looks when they thought she wasn't watching. They asked daily if other friends could visit, and mainly if she would be willing to see Bertol Mendin. Adací just shook her head.

When they asked why, she couldn't answer.

Perhaps it was her fear of having to explain why she'd followed Pedí. No one, except Larada, would believe or understand. Despite not remembering the horse ride, Adací recalled all the details of the nightmare. She remembered the part with her birth mama and papa escaping into the cave with the other young woman, and then the skeletal-faced man stalking Pedí. That last remembrance haunted all her waking moments.

One day, Adací got enough courage to tell Marina and Sergol what she saw in the nightmare. When she finished, they looked away, shaking their heads, not thinking she'd notice. Adací knew what they thought of her—an unstable girl whose mind was gone, whose head injury had knocked the last bit of sense out of her.

Late one afternoon, Mother came through the back door after going to town. She slammed it behind her. She didn't see Adací, who was watching from the kitchen.

"Those gossipers, how cruel!" Mother spoke out loud.

Adací went to where Mother hung her jacket.

"What gossipers, Mama?"

Mother's hand went to her mouth. Her eyes widened. "You might as well know."

She walked Adací to the dining room, and they each took a chair. Mother's eyes narrowed, and her forehead scrunched. Adací knew that look. Bad news was coming.

"A few months ago, you were becoming the talk of the town because of your beauty. We had such high hopes for you—for finding you the best out of all the young men in New Losobon."

Mother took Adací's hand, but her touch felt cold.

"Now you're the talk of the town because of your reckless actions. In the past, we were able to make excuses for your wild behavior—the times you fought boys at school, or ran off from your friends to chase birds, or yelled out in the assembly hall."

That was the shortlist. Mother could have gone on for an hour.

"These last incidents were too much—throwing the wine in Chando's face and then running off after that healer and nearly killing yourself."

Mother covered her face with both of her hands. The worst was coming.

"Some say you're a danger to others and that the Mendin family should forbid Larada from being your friend."

"No, Mama, no!" Adací jumped up from her chair. "She's the only friend I have left."

If I lose Larada, then I wish they'd left me to die at the side of the road.

Mother stood up and wrapped her arms around Adací. This time, her hands felt not as cold. "I had a chance to talk with Larada's mother. She's your defender and said she'd never let anyone separate you and her daughter."

Mother scrunched her eyebrows again. There was more coming. "You're not getting better. More melancholy every day! Your father talked with Doctor Arias, and he's picked out two of the best from the Council of Sages to try and help you. I'm taking you to the Sanctuary tomorrow."

Oh, no! I don't want to see someone on the Council of Sages.

Adací was familiar with the sages who taught in the schools but had never imagined talking with a sage from the Council. Adací had heard them speak at meetings in the assembly hall. They seemed to know so much. The sages in the schools got their training and knowledge from those on the Council. And worse, those on the Council of Sages helped people with personal problems. Even crazy people! That's why Mother and Father were taking her there.

⸻◆⸻

The next day, Adací sat by her mother in their carriage. With each uneven cobblestone the wheels rolled over, Adací's stomach rolled, too. She was going to lose her breakfast before they ever arrived at the Sanctuary.

The carriage entered the narrow lane that ran straight at the assembly hall with its shining silver dome. Tavi, who was driving, turned left instead of right at the fork, which was a surprise. The sage's counseling rooms were on the right side of the assembly hall, and the infirmary was to the left.

Tavi pulled up in front of the drop-off for the infirmary. Instead of helping them out, he ran inside. Mother seemed in no hurry, so Adací waited. She gripped her knees to keep them from quivering.

In a few minutes, Tavi came out with Doctor Arias at his side. The doctor came to the carriage and reached in to shake Mother's hand.

"Nice to see you, Marina," he said. "I'll take good care of Adací. I believe they're already waiting for her."

When Tavi helped Adací step down from the carriage, she whimpered. Mother was not getting out. She wasn't staying. Adací was a prisoner being dropped off at the dungeon. She had heard of people with severe mental illness being locked up.

She shook as Doctor Arias took her by the arm. She turned to look at her mother, but Mother's eyes looked straight ahead. The carriage was pulling away.

"No, Mama, don't leave me," she wanted to scream, but the words stayed frozen inside her.

CHAPTER FORTY-FOUR

At the Winter Camp

Pedí and Mirela followed the faint trail that climbed to the top of a ridge. Mirela hiked in front, her leather boots making tracks in the snow that had fallen during the night. It was Pedí's first time to experience a snowfall. Although New Losobon was further north than Itatu, it only rained in the mild climate of New Losobon Valley. The elevation of the Blue Mountains made the difference, even though its peaks were closer to the equator.

Pedí glanced back at the Itatu winter camp below them. Bonfires were burning, water was boiling, and the men were bathing despite the cold weather. A group of sheep the Itatu called longnecks grazed nearby. It was the smaller variety of mountain sheep, with a thinner, longer neck but whose fleece was even finer.

Pedí marveled at the organization of the Itatu people at the high camps, where they spent month-long rotations and moved the longnecks around to help them survive the cold season. The longnecks did not do well in the lower valleys where the Itatu took their deer herds and larger mountain sheep in the winter. The longnecks survived by eating bunch grasses and fescue, which grew only on alpine slopes. They also licked rocks and ate lichens for nutrients.

Once all the fever-stricken people had been treated in the villages, Pedí convinced Luco that they needed to go to the winter camps. The small cabins, where the men slept in close quarters and often didn't take a change of clothing, must be the recurrent source of the lice that plagued the Itatu.

Luco organized volunteers, who hauled large tubs for bathing, new bedding, and changes of clothes to each mountain camp. Pedí and Mirela treated any of the men who were already ill with the nanimoha potion.

Then, while the men bathed, the two of them went hiking.

Pedí followed the footprints of his freckled-faced friend. She had raced ahead and was thirty feet further up the ridge. He could see the sheep shear knife sticking out of the pouch on the side of her boot. If needed, she would use it to protect Pedí, and that worried him.

Fortunately, no spy of the captain had followed, and no threats had come to him or those helping. The man Barco and his men had seen on the road from New Losobon was never found. Whoever he was, his purpose must have had nothing to do with Pedí.

Mirela paused at the top of the ridge and waited for him to catch up. The two of them watched out for each other. Pedí had become a substitute for her lost family. Sometimes, Mirela treated him like a brother, but most times, she acted as if he were her father. Either way, he knew Mirela loved him, and it was the pure love of a child.

He took the last few steps to the ridge top. Mirela was looking at the mountain gorge on the other side. It dropped sharply off the trail. Jagged granite rocks, like sword-tips, poked out of the fallen snow. Dark evergreens and leafless trees also contrasted against the white.

Mirela took Pedí's hand as they gazed together. Then she let go and continued on the trail, skirting the edge of the chasm. Pedí followed. At a section of the trail that ran extra close to the drop-off, Pedí made sure that Mirela got safely across, then remained at the spot.

He had been waiting for this moment. The small pouch came out of his pocket. His fingers stretched the opening, a motion he could now do without looking. The coiled hair lay inside.

This was the perfect place to be rid of the fake Adací, to throw away the constant reminder he carried with him. He could do it this time.

Pedí glanced first to check on Mirela. She was a little further ahead and safe.

His fingers found the hair. More of the black dye had rubbed off the silver strands, and each day, their color seemed brighter, especially when contrasted against the few filaments of pure black hair. That fact made getting rid of the hair even harder, yet he was determined to succeed. Pedí held onto the end of the strands. The wind blew from behind, and the hair stretched out over the gorge below. He desperately wanted to let go, but like each other time he had tried, an image of the ancient Adací came to him, and the hair stuck like glue to his fingers.

"Uai, what are you doing?"

He startled. Mirela had doubled back.

"Uai, it's shiny silver hair. Can I see?" She grabbed the strands from his fingers. He hoped she would let them go—that she would do what he couldn't.

"Uai, some hair is dark black like yours, but most have sparkly silver. Uai, whose hair is this?"

"Her name is Adací. No one has hair quite like hers. She tried to hide the silver part with dye, but it has mostly rubbed off."

"Oh! I will tell her not to dye it. This is special hair." Mirela gave the strands back to Pedí. "Don't hold them over the cliff. You might lose them. Put them back in the pouch."

Now that Mirela knew about the hair, how would Pedí ever get rid of it—get rid of the girl who'd taken the name and place of his heroine?

"Is Adací your friend?"

"I thought she was, but she never wants to see me again."

"Uai, that's too sad." Mirela stretched her arms, pushed up on her tiptoes, and hugged Pedí as high as she could reach.

They started back down the trail to return to camp. Mirela lagged behind, exploring each rock and tree. Pedí turned when he heard a muffled cry. What he saw froze him in fear.

A thin and bony man had captured Mirela. The man held his right hand across her mouth and cheeks, preventing her from calling out. His left arm crossed her chest and pulled her little body against him. His left hand held a short knife.

The man's deep, hollow eyes glared mockingly at Pedí. White teeth, surrounded by a short, grizzly beard, showed through his sarcastic smile. If not for the whiskers, it might have been a skeleton's deathhead peering at Pedí.

CHAPTER FORTY-FIVE

In the Sanctuary Courtyard

Adací's stomach churned as she watched Tavi and Mother drive away.

Doctor Arias held her arm in his gentle but gnarled hand. "You'll like Jurana and Gabro. I wanted to introduce you to them personally."

Oh!

Maybe she wasn't going to be locked up.

At least not today.

Adací did like Doctor Arias. Her parents said he had checked on her every day while she was unconscious.

But he must also think she was crazy like everyone else did.

The doctor was quiet as he led her inside the infirmary and through the corridors toward the assembly hall. Instead of passing through it and to the other side where the sages worked, the doctor led her down the middle aisle toward the podium. Adací paused at the center point—where the top of the Idonata temple had stretched above them so long ago.

She could see their queen standing tall, arms raised, crying out against the soldiers. Then smoke billowed out of three muskets. Bullets pierced the queen's heart. Adací grabbed her chest when she felt a jolt of pain, just like when Mother first told her the story.

"Are you okay?" the doctor asked.

Embarrassed, Adací jerked her hands back to her side. She nodded that she was fine, and the vision of the Idonata queen went away. Since her head injury, it was only the second time her imagination had created some kind of vision. The other time was when she sleepwalked holding the jade stones.

The doctor led her through the rest of the assembly hall and into the courtyard. Adací covered her eyes to adjust from the dark interior to the bright sunlight. They passed through the trees and by the side of a pond.

A small hawk cried out, its shrill voice chilling Adací. The bird of prey dove at a tree, and songbirds exploded out from it. The hawk knocked one to the ground. Its talons grasped the tiny flapping creature and carried it off.

The songbird's helplessness weighed on Adací as she continued to the far end of the courtyard. Two people were standing near a stone bench waiting for her. It was Jurana and Gabro. Adací knew who this couple was. Whenever she'd heard them speak at the assembly hall, they had captivated her; they were so brilliant.

But what would they do to her? She wanted to flee, to fly away like the songbirds from the hawk before it was too late, before the sages grasped her thoughts and dreams and tore them out from her.

But as she looked at their kind faces, another consideration emerged. What if they helped squeeze the truth out of Adací and helped her understand the past visions about her birth parents and about Pedí? Maybe they could help her with the sadness. That was something she wanted and desperately needed.

Doctor Arias introduced them to each other, then left. Adací's lips quivered as she watched him walk away.

"Please sit down," Jurana said. How elegant and stately this older woman was, yet there was a softness to her.

Adací sat in the middle of the red sandstone bench, its surface worn smooth through years of use. The sages sat on each side of her.

"Pedí liked to sit right where you are," Jurana said.

Adací almost jumped off the bench but instead placed her hands on the slick stone and rubbed back and forth. "You knew Pedí?" There was a shakiness in her voice as she looked at Jurana and then turned to look at Gabro.

"We love Pedí. He's like a son to us."

Adací's hands continued to rub the stone as the couple coaxed her to tell them about herself and all that had happened. Her fear subsided the longer she was with them. She told them everything but stopped before relating her dream after putting on the jade. Adací's eyes oscillated back and forth, and then she looked down at her feet.

"Is there something else?" Jurana asked.

Adací's hands gripped the edge of the stone seat. "I don't know if I'm ready to tell you about the last dream. Will you first share more about how you know Pedí?"

Gabro told her about meeting him in the library and how Pedí became an apprentice healer and moved to the Sanctuary. Jurana told her about the many times they met with him, taught him, and all the times he'd been to their cottage.

"You're the sages he told me about," Adací said." He never said your names, but I could tell he loved you." She looked down at her feet. "No wonder he loves you."

"We truly do think of him as our third son, and he's the one we see every day. Our two boys live with their families in the far western part of the valley."

Adací's hands had not moved from her sides and held on to the stone seat. "Did Pedí tell you about me?"

Adací watched the two sages look back and forth at each other. They seemed hesitant to answer, but she saw a slight nod from each of them.

"I hurt him, didn't I?"

Jurana turned away, and Gabro cleared his throat. Neither of them responded, and neither of them nodded. But Adací already knew the answer. Doctor Arias had told her that day in his garden. She had asked, hoping that somehow the answer would change.

"I didn't mean for it to happen," Adací said, her voice cracking. "He was just my healer, but we visited each time he came to our house. I was astonished at how shy and awkward he was. Then he talked to me about the things he loves—his animal friends, his herbs, his nanimoha, and all of nature. When he did, his stuttering stopped. It didn't take long for something to change in me. I liked everything about this boy and wanted him to be my friend. And I think he accepted me as his—as he let me into his world. But my parents were not happy. They respect Pedí but worry that my association with him would bring only disgrace and sadness—that I would be treated like he is."

Adací twisted the end of her braid. "There's something more that frightens my parents worse than just being shamed, but I don't know if they want me to tell you about it."

Gabro turned toward her. "Marina and Sergol talked to us in preparation for our counseling with you. They told us about your birth parents and what happened to them but asked us to keep it a secret."

"Then you know I'm an Idonata girl!"

The sages both nodded.

"Oh!" It took Adací several minutes before she could speak again. "A part of me knew that a lasting friendship with Pedí could never be, as it would shatter my parents' carefully laid plans. They have tried to mold me all my life to marry into the nobility of New Losobon. They believe it's the best way to protect me. It's not what I want, but how can I betray them? They've been so good to me."

She pulled hard on the end of her braid, on the part dyed silver. "But I hurt this tender-hearted boy. I misled him and chose to do it when I knew our relationship was impossible."

She waited for the sages to chastise her and tell her how wrong she'd been. But they said nothing. Adací put her hands over her ears. The silence was deafening! Jurana reached and took one of Adací's hands away from her ear and squeezed it tenderly. But they still said nothing.

Since the sages were too kind to criticize her, she might as well tell them all that happened. "Do you know what Father told Doctor Arias and what the doctor told Pedí?"

"We do."

Adací's cheeks felt hot. The sages must know everything about her.

"Pedí must think I was just pretending and never wanted to be his friend. He might even think it was my way of mocking him like so many people do."

Jurana squeezed Adací's hand a little tighter. Gabro patted her other hand that Adací had taken off her ear and placed back on the bench. It was their kind way of answering, but she knew the truth. Pedí would never trust her again.

"Tell us about your last dream," Jurana said. "Did it involve Pedí?"

Adací told them first about her mother's Idonata queen story and her birth mother's jade stones that Adací had put in her hair. Her entire body shook when she related the nightmare of the skeletal-faced man following Pedí. "The vision was so vivid, so real, I couldn't doubt it," she added at the end of the narration.

"So, that's why you went after Pedí on the horse," Jurana said.

Adací pulled her hand away from Jurana's grasp and hugged herself, trying to stop the shaking. "But I didn't get to warn him. Do you think the dream will come true? Will the skeletal-faced man find and kill him? I worry about it every day. I failed Pedí."

"You didn't fail him," Jurana said.

"You tried to save him," Gabro added.

"But the nightmare! It will be my fault if—"

Jurana interrupted Adací when she put an arm around her trembling body and pulled her close. "Don't blame yourself for what you see in your dreams and visions."

"But I'm too much like the evil Idonata witch queen!"

"No, Adací!" Jurana squeezed her tighter. "Don't think that way!"

"You are not evil!" Gabro said. "But you are like the last Idonata queen, perhaps in ways you've chosen not to share with us."

"But I don't want to be like her."

"What she did was not evil," Jurana still hugged Adací's shaking body. "She was only protecting her people from destruction by our soldiers."

Jurana released Adací from her embrace and then reached for Adací's long woven hair, which had swung around to the front. "Your braid is beautiful. May I hold it?"

Adací nodded.

Jurana followed the strands with one of her fingers, seeming to search for the dyed silver part, even though Adací had not told them about it. "Didn't Pedí ever tell you about his ancient heroine?"

Adací shook her head.

"I'm surprised he didn't. She was called Adací, just like you."

Adací took a deep breath.

"Because you had the name of his heroine—it must have frightened Pedí," Jurana said. "Maybe that's why he didn't tell you about his ancient Adací."

"Everything about me scared him, I think," Adací said.

Gabro chuckled. "I'm sure that's true."

Jurana told her more about the ancient heroine. "The Adací that Pedí worshipped had a crescent moon tattoo on her chest, and part of her long black braid was bright silver."

Adací's skin tingled. Had the sages guessed that she had the same marks?

Jurana let go of Adací's braid. "Pedí told us that this ancient Adací rescued her people from six evil spirits. He once carried a little figurine of her, but it was broken."

Gabro added to the story. "The Idonata Queen that ruled her people when our soldiers and settlers first crossed the seas must have been a direct descendent from the ancient Adací. Pedí said that each of their queens would have a baby girl with silver hair who would become the next queen."

Gabro stood up as if to emphasize the next part of his story. "I want you to know that the last Idonata queen was not evil. She did have unusual powers and directed those strange Shushuhadors, who could communicate with wild things. But she was only defending her people against the invasion and destruction of all they had. Jurana and I are descended from those who established this Captaincy, but we're not proud of what our ancestors did to the Idonata people. Many in New Losobon honor that first captain and his soldiers, but they were ruthless and cared nothing for the Idonata nation. Sadly, our new captain is too much like his ancestor of two hundred years ago."

Jurana took a deep breath. "So, like the Idonata queen, who our people killed, and the first Adací, whose powers were good, we believe you are the same. We know you want to prevent what you see in your visions but can't always do so. But that doesn't mean you caused what happens in your dreams."

Adací was not sure what to believe. She couldn't deny the times she'd saved Larada, but she failed Pito and now Pedi. "Why did I have to fall off the horse? I never got to warn Pedí."

"How hard that must be for you," Jurana said. "Gabro and I will add our hopes and silent pleadings to yours, that Pedí will return safely."

"Your visions are a special gift," Gabro said, "I want to learn more about these jade stones your birth mother had. Do you still have them?"

Adací shook her head. "Mother hid them."

"Hmm," was the response she got from both sages.

"Pedí believed that the ancient Adací had jade stones given to her by the moon goddess," Gabro said. "Could your stones be the same, and did the Idonata queen also have them?"

Jurana grasped Adací's hand again. "We'll try to find the old manuscript your mother said was in the Sanctuary library. Perhaps it will help us understand more about your heritage and powers. Will you meet with us once a week? Your parents want you to keep coming here."

"I will."

"In the meantime, please don't castigate yourself over what happened with Pedi."

"But even if the nightmare wasn't my fault, Pedí left thinking I never wanted to see him again. Doctor Arias said maybe that's best. But I can't bear it. What if he never comes back?"

Jurana took ahold of both of Adací's hands and held them tight. "I feel your kindness of heart. How you ever came to see past our Pedí's shyness in so short a time speaks much of your character."

"He's a good boy," Gabro said, "and has depths of character that few recognize. You are the same. No wonder he liked you so much."

"Don't tell me that!" Adací jumped off the bench and looked out across the orchard. It only made it worse each time she heard that Pedí liked her.

"We can't even be friends. What I did was wrong."

She turned to look at the sages. Jurana's eyes were soft and caring as they looked back. Gabro rubbed his short, dark beard. They still weren't going to say it, to let her know how unkind she'd been.

"What if I can never tell him I'm sorry?"

Jurana stood up and put her arm around Adací. "Believe in his and your goodness. It will help soothe the worry and sadness."

Gabro got up and added his arm to the hug Adací was getting from Jurana. "We miss him just like you do. When you come each week, we'll tell you more about Pedí and teach you some of the same things we taught him."

The sages informed her that her mother was returning to pick her up, and they walked her back through the courtyard. Adací remembered the main reason her parents had brought her to see the sages. "My father and mother think you are helping drive Pedí out of my head. Will you be in trouble if we still talk about him?"

Gabro put a finger to his lips. "Shh. We're just helping you sort things out. Let's keep it a secret between us."

CHAPTER FORTY-SIX

The Sheep Shear Knife is Lost

Pedí remained powerless, still frozen in fear for Mirela as he gazed at the skeletal man who had seized her. But somehow, Pedí managed to pull his feet out of the stifling terror. He ran toward the man. Despite having no weapon, Pedí would do whatever he could to save Mirela.

"Stop," the man shouted, "or she's dead."

Pedí halted. He watched Mirela's eyes bulge when the man pressed harder with his hand across her face. Mirela squirmed and kicked her feet against him.

The man pulled her into him even tighter. "Tell this red wildcat to quit kicking, or I'll snap her neck."

"Mirela, stop!"

She held still.

"Please let up on her. She'll suffocate."

The man smiled tauntingly but relaxed the hand on her face a little.

"If you want her to live, tell me where to find your precious little mushroom and how you make your potion work safely. Then the girl goes free."

He twitched the hand holding his knife, flashing it at Pedí. "If you lie, I'll come back to Itatu and kill this little she-cat you seem to care about."

Pedí shuddered. He was choking, not getting enough air. The dread of losing Mirela was too much. He had no choice. There was no way out except to comply with this fiend who held Mirela's life in his hands.

But once the man had the potion's secrets, what would stop him from killing Mirela and himself?

Nothing.

He had to buy some time. Luco and Barco may come.

"I have some paper in my pack. I'll write down directions. It's complicated and hard to find the mushrooms."

Pedí pulled the pack off his back and rummaged through it. "Here it is."

He pulled out a small notebook and then glanced at Mirela. He could only see her eyes, her green eyes. The rest of her small, freckled face was covered under this man's filthy hand. Pedí expected to see fear in those eyes, but that's not what was there. It was rage and revenge. Mirela was not afraid, even though, in a split second, her life could be taken.

This was not comforting. What foolish thing would this girl do? He scanned the area, hoping for someone to appear, but there was no one. Did he dare shout? What would this hellish man do to Mirela if he did?

Pedí fumbled with his pack again, trying to buy some more time. "The ink is right here. I just have to find it."

Pedí glanced down the trail.

The man must have seen him do it. "No more stalling. I don't need you to write it down. Just tell me out loud about the potion. But tell me, good. I've warned you. If I don't find the mushrooms, and the potion doesn't work, this red dog is dead meat."

Pedí began to describe the mushroom meadow but paused mid-sentence when he saw what Mirela was doing. The man still held her tight against him, but her right hand was free. She was reaching with it, trying to get to her boot. She was bending her leg to get the boot up to her hand. Pedí knew what she was after.

No, Mirela, he wanted to scream. If the man saw what she was doing, he would kill her.

But too late. The knife was in her hand. Before the skeletal-faced man could react, Mirela plunged it deep into his thigh and slashed upwards.

Blood spurted out. The man screamed and relaxed his grip.

Just enough.

Mirela broke free.

She dashed headfirst into Pedí, and the two sprinted down the trail, ignoring the chasm at their side.

The man hobbled after them with Mirela's sheep shear knife sticking out of his leg. He cursed and threatened. "Next time I catch that little red animal, I will kill her."

Pedí and Mirela yelled out for help as they descended from the ridge. Luco, Barco, and other men heard them and ran up the trail. But when Pedí looked behind, the injured man was gone. The men from the camp found and followed his trail of blood. It, too, disappeared. They searched for hours, but he was nowhere. He was like a phantom.

That night and every night while visiting the rest of the winter camps, Pedí was extra vigilant. He and Mirela never ventured out alone—the skeleton-like man could be watching, waiting to take revenge. Mirela wanted her knife back and said she was going out by herself looking for it. Pedí convinced her that it wasn't a good idea.

CHAPTER FORTY-SEVEN

Ileana

Pedí was relieved when the mountain camps had all been cleansed and the work finished. They returned to Luco's home in Belmonte, and the villagers held a celebration—thanking their leader and Pedí for ending the epidemic. People from the surrounding settlements came. The gathering lasted two days.

The night it was over, Pedí entered Luco's home with Mirela at his side. Two people, an older man and an older woman, were waiting for him. They stood by the table near the stove.

Luco introduced them. "This is Anton and Elisada. You saved their granddaughter from the fever."

The man had a long wooden staff and pounded it against the floor. "Uai, we heard you want to go to the jungles. You'll need a guide, and I'm the best in Itatu."

"He goes there once a year to trade," Luco said, "and knows the old trail through the mountains better than anyone."

"Uai, I'm coming too," Elisada said. "To cook for you on the way and try to repay you in some small way for saving our little Sulia."

"Thank you." It was all that Pedí could think to say.

Anton held out the strange staff for him to observe. Intricate figures of jungle cats were carved along its length. "It's a welcome stick—a gift from a village chief. Uai, tribes along the Ipixuna River will accept you if you have one."

There was a knock at the door. Alina opened it, and an Itatu girl about Pedí's age entered. A young man was with her. Pedí had noticed them during the celebration. Whenever he had looked her way, the girl was looking back. He felt he knew from somewhere but did not remember treating her or going to her house.

"I have to ask the healer something," the girl said.

She walked forward and stood a few feet away. "Uai, did you have a little red-headed friend named Ileana when you were five years old?"

Blood rushed to Pedí's head as if a giant constrictor snake had wrapped itself around his body. The girl who stood before him had the same hair color as the five-year-old Ileana, but she combed it differently. The freckles lined up on the nose and the cheeks just the same. The lips, although quivering, were Ileana's lips.

He nodded, and she rushed to hug him.

"It's you. It's really you," she said.

Pedí was speechless.

Mirela tugged on his pant leg as if to remind him she was there.

Ileana saw her. "Who is this beautiful girl holding on to you? Have you found a new friend? Another Itatu friend?"

Pedí knelt and pulled Mirela close. "She's my friend like you were. You're both my special Itatu friends."

To himself, he whispered, "*The only friends who haven't tricked and rejected me.*"

Luco and Alina invited everyone to stay and eat supper. They crowded around the table. Mirela sat on one side of Pedí, Ileana and her friend on the other.

Ileana talked about the year her family had lived in New Losobon. She described the difficulties they'd had being accepted and how she'd been bullied just because of her red hair and freckles. "Pedí always came to my aid and got the beatings intended for me."

The young man at Ileana's side reached for her hand, and she turned and smiled at him, her face turning red.

She looked back at Pedí. "I forgot to tell you about Elisio. He's my intended and soon will officially become my fiancé. My family was not ill, and you never came to our house, but you saved his mama. He wanted to be at the celebration to thank you, and I came along. Uai, I'm so happy I did and got to see you again."

With her free hand, she reached for Pedí's. "Do you have a special girl, your own intended?"

The giant constrictor was back, coiling itself around him. But this time, it was crushing him. He shook his head.

"Uai, he carries moon hair from a girl." Mirela pointed to the pocket that held the little pouch. "Part of it is bright silver."

Pedí shook his head at Mirela, hoping she'd not say more.

"She made him sad," Mirela added.

Ileana still had her hand over Pedí's. "Tell me about this girl. Was she not kind to you?"

"She was very kind, too kind. That's the problem because I thought we were friends—good friends. But one day, I was told she never wanted to see me again."

"Uai, it's hard to fake kindness. Maybe it was her parents' wish, not the girl's."

Pedí shook his head. "It's impossible. She's a rich girl, and no one in New Losobon, especially a rich girl, wants to be seen with an Idonata boy."

Ileana squeezed his arm. "I'm so sorry."

CHAPTER FORTY-EIGHT

The Soapstone Monkey

There was a knock at Adací's bedroom door.

"There's someone here to see you." It was Mother. Usually, she just came in after knocking. What was up?

Adací put down the book she'd been reading and started toward the door. She glanced around the room, which had been rearranged—the extra bed taken out. She was back to sleeping on her own.

Bertol must have come by again. If it were Larada, Mother would have sent Heila to tell her. Why did he keep showing up? Well, she could guess. Mother and Father put him up to it.

"No, Mother." Adací jerked open the door. "I won't see—"

She stopped when she saw her mother's lips twisted in a quizzical smile.

"It's Larada," Mother said.

Oh!

Adací was just being stupid again. "But why didn't you send—"

Adací paused again. Mother's unusual grin was still there.

"What?"

"Someone is with her."

Adací shook her head. "You've tried that trick before. I still won't—"

"Stop, Adací! It is Bertol, but Larada brought him and begs you to see them both. They need your help with something."

Until now, Larada had dutifully respected Adací's wish not to have other visitors—including her brother. Her best friend would not have brought Bertol unless it was necessary.

"Okay, Mama. Tell them I'll be right down."

Adací redid her braid and changed out of her baking dress. She hurried down the stairs and joined the visitors in the dining room. Lelia must have heard there were guests. A bowl of cut-up fruit and three slices of cake were already set out on the table.

Adací glanced back and forth between the twins. Both appeared nervous, unsure of the reaction they might receive from Adací. Neither showed any interest in the food Lelia had brought them, and no one spoke, not even Adací. She was also unsure what to say.

Larada broke the silence. "I'm sorry to bring Bertol against your wishes, but he's been helping me by visiting Edero, since I'm forbidden to do it. He has something to share that I felt would be best coming directly from him."

"Hi, Bertol," Adací said. "Forgive me for being unfriendly, but it's not about you. I haven't wanted any visitors except Larada. The recovery from my accident has been difficult."

"I understand," Bertol said. "I hope you're doing better."

"Thank you. I am."

Larada took a deep breath. "Let me explain why we're here. I've tried every possible argument, but Father won't change his mind. He promised the captain, and there's no breaking it. He will announce my engagement to Chando at my Coming of Age."

"No, no!" Adací had not forgotten her promise to save Larada from that terrible fate but had done nothing. And now, since the accident, she felt utterly powerless. "I've failed you, Larada. My accident took away any power to see things that I had. I have no idea how to help you."

"Don't say that, Adací!" Larada exclaimed. "Please listen to what my brother has to say."

Adací glanced at Bertol. His lips were quivering, and he hesitated before speaking. "When I take letters from Larada to Edero, I often stay and talk. We always discuss the power of your dreams, knowing how often you've rescued my sister. When I told Edero what I witnessed you do to that tree limb in the schoolyard, his belief that you can save Larada from Chando got even stronger."

"But I didn't mean to make that branch break. I just knew it was going to happen and tried to warn Samo."

"I know that now," Bertol said, choking some on the words. "It was my fault for calling you a witch. I'm sorry I ever did."

"Thank you for saying that, but why does that story give Edero more hope? I don't dream anymore, and even if I did, I worry I would only hurt Larada instead of help."

"Not true." Larada scrunched her eyes. "You always save me and have done it time after time through one of your strange visions."

"I don't understand this unusual ability you have," Bertol said, "but I know you have a power in you that no one else has."

"Even if what you say is true, it doesn't matter. I haven't had a single dream since my accident."

"Yes, you have!" Larada grabbed ahold of Adací's braid and yanked on it. "You dreamed the night you held the jade stones and wandered into the street."

She was right. The stones had caused Adací to dream, and it was a clear, vivid dream. The jade even helped her see part of her forgotten horse ride.

But would they work again with her empty head?

Larada let go of Adací's braid and pulled something out of a small cloth bag she'd brought. She held up a small figure carved out of soapstone. It was a perfectly formed howler monkey. "Remember when you borrowed my ceramic doll and went to sleep with it? You dreamed all night about me."

Larada handed the figure to Adací. "This monkey is the one thing I have of Chando's. His grandpa gave it to him when he was a little boy, and Chando gave it to me."

Adací tried to give the soapstone monkey back to Larada, but Bertol reached and pushed it back. "The other thing Edero asked of me was to convince you to use the jade stones and hold this monkey when you sleep. He believes you'll dream about Chando—something to keep him away from Larada."

"You're all as crazy as I am." Adací's hand, which held the monkey, trembled.

Larada cupped her fingers around Adací's, making her hold the memento even tighter. "Please, you have to save me!"

"But Mother hid the jade stones."

"You can find them!" Bertol said.

Adací hesitated, then nodded. "I'll try to find the stones. I'll try to dream again."

CHAPTER FORTY-NINE

An Embroidered Handkerchief

After Larada and Bertol left, Adací searched the house for Heila. While talking with her friends, Adací heard the kitchen door crack open. The moment she glanced at it, the door closed, but she saw the many colors of the person's dress.

It was Heila.

She had been listening.

Adací didn't mind that the maid overheard them. Heila would not tell Mother that Adací was going to search for the jade stones. In fact, she hoped the girl from Mattaçores would help her.

But nowhere in the house could Adací locate the maid, so she returned to her room. When she opened the door, the girl she sought was sitting on the bed, waiting. Heila did not look up when Adací approached.

"What's wrong?" Adací asked.

Heila raised her head. "Forgive me, but I listened to you talking with Larada and Bertol." Heila took a deep breath. "There is someone else you also have to save with one of your visions."

"What do you mean?"

"Niala is in trouble."

Heila told her story. She had gone to the open market to buy fruit and vegetables for the kitchen and ran into Niala. Her fellow Mattaçorian was there selling embroidered handkerchiefs her mother had made. She was trying to make a little extra for her family.

"Why aren't you at work at the captain's house?" Heila had asked.

"I couldn't face going there today."

"What happened?"

"I'm afraid of Chando. He's getting more and more aggressive. I'm not sure what he intends to do to me."

"Won't his father stop him?"

Niala shook her head, then bowed it. "He lets Chando do whatever he wants and doesn't care at all for me."

"But what will become of your family? What about the debt you owe the captain?"

"We'll lose our home and be sent out on the streets. Father won't bear it in his condition."

"But—"

"Don't worry," Niala interrupted. "I'll go back to The Big House. I don't have a choice."

"Maybe Adací's family can do something to help," Heila said.

"No one can influence the captain or Chando. I'm like a slave to them."

"Will you get into trouble for missing today?"

"The steward knows what's going on with Chando but said he can't stop him. The steward gave me some time to take a break, to recover from the abuse, at least a little. He'll make excuses for my absence but can only do so for a few days. I promised to return by noon in two more days."

"I'm going to tell Adací," Heila declared.

"No! Please don't! And don't tell my family either. It would destroy Papa and Mama to know of my suffering at The Big House."

Niala had then handed one of the embroidered handkerchiefs to Heila. "Give this to Adací as my thank you for wanting to be my friend, but tell her to stay away. It will only make things worse."

Finished with her story, Heila grasped Adací's hand like she was clinging to a lifeline. "You have to save Niala, please!"

"This is all my fault!" Adací pounded her chest right over her tattoo. "Because I talked with her, I got her into trouble. I always make things worse for people."

"It's not your fault, and you make things better, not worse." Heila stood up and wrapped her arms around Adací. She held on so tight that Adací could hardly breathe.

Heila whispered into Adací's ear. "I believe in your dreams like Larada, Edero, and Bertol."

"No one should believe in me. I wish I could do something, but—"

"Find the jade stones!" Heila interrupted her. "Use the soapstone monkey to save Larada, and you can use this handkerchief to dream about Niala and save her too." She gave Adací the embroidered handkerchief.

Heila's confidence in her did not change Adací's belief that if she did have visions again, she'd just put everyone in danger. Yet even so, she had no choice but to try. "Will you help me find the jade?"

Heila released her from the hug, and the search began.

They rummaged through the house secretly that day and halfway through the next.

All of Mother's potential hiding spots were empty. In the hutch behind her special porcelain—nothing. In with Lelia's pots and pans— nothing. In the back of the linen closets—nothing.

Perhaps Mother had given them to Pito. That would make sense. He was off his crutches now and working again. When he and the others had taken the horses to the south fields, Adací and Heila searched outside. In the stable house—nothing. The bunkhouse—nothing. They even checked the chicken coop—nothing.

The jade stones were nowhere, and tomorrow was Niala's last day. She was returning to The Big House at midday, and she'd have to face Chando's abuse all over again.

CHAPTER FIFTY

Into the Jungles

Pedí sat by Luco at the table near the stove.

He had spent the last two days preparing for the journey into the jungles. Anton and Elisada had helped get all the needed supplies. The three of them were leaving in the morning.

Mirela came out of the bedroom, dragging a bag behind her. "My clothes are ready."

"You're not going with them," Luco said. "Uai, how many times do I have to tell you?"

"You're not my papa. Uai, I don't have to obey you."

"Uai, you don't obey anyone except maybe Pedí."

Pedí brushed Mirela's hair back from her eyes. "Wait in the bedroom for a bit. We'll talk about it, okay?"

Mirela nodded, then scowled at Luco. She walked backward until she reached the bedroom, then closed the door.

"I don't know what to do with the girl," Luco said. "I don't want her to be a burden, but she's going to run away after you, no matter what I say."

Elisada approached from across the room. "Mirela would be a help to me."

Anton joined his wife. "If you let Mirela go with us, we'll protect her and bring her back unharmed."

Luco drummed his fingers on the table, then pulled the end of his mustache. "Uai, it's true that she's a good worker, but Mirela is too much of a free spirit. She's belligerent and disobedient with me, but for Pedí, she'll do anything."

Luco looked toward the bedroom where Mirela had gone and shook his head. "I've never seen anyone like her. What she did with her knife to that evil man astounds me. An eighteen-year-old girl wouldn't have the courage to do that, and this one's not even eight."

"She wasn't frightened of the man," Pedí said. "Just angry."

"She's still upset that she left her knife sticking in his leg," Luco said. "I found her another knife, but nothing's like the one she fashioned from the broken sheep shear."

"If you're okay, we'll take Mirela with us. She'll be a help."

Luco nodded. "She can go. I don't think I have another choice."

Luco called Mirela back into the room. When she heard the news, she jumped up and down and went back and forth several times between hugging Luco and then running and hugging Pedí.

* * *

Before they went to bed that evening, Barco knocked on the door. His horse was covered in sweat. "My men and I completed another circuit around the villages but found no sign of the man who attacked Mirela. Uai, I thought I was good in the wilds, but this man's better."

"Maybe he went back to New Losobon," Luco said. "Or better yet, died."

"That's possible." Barco stroked his beard. "Even if he tries to follow, Mirela's knife wound should stop him. The trail through the mountains is not an easy one."

Pedí hoped they were right, but the man's hollow eyes haunted him, and he remembered the angry threat against Mirela. Only the captain could have sent a man who seemed willing to do anything to get Pedí's nanimoha. But Luco and Barco seemed convinced he was gone, so Pedí tried to forget him.

* * *

They left the next morning on three horses. Anton led the way on the first horse, with two loaded mountain sheep attached and trailing. Elisada was on the second horse. Mirela rode with Pedí on the third.

They followed the ancient trail through the Blue Mountains. After five days, they began their descent and could look out at the immense bowl of tropical forest stretching south toward the equator.

Waterfalls and small streams gurgled and sang as they descended with the travelers. The Blue Mountains became a series of broken cliffs, and they had to walk the horses down steep switchbacks and around rockfalls.

The rain and snow that fell in the mountains fed hundreds of jungle streams and tributaries. Soon, they could see the Ipixuna River below them, cutting a dark curving ribbon through a sea of green. Far to the east, the Ipixuna would join the other large rivers to form the massive Black River, which at Romingo dropped over a two-hundred-foot escarpment in seven chutes and hundreds of small cascades.

As they descended, Pedí often looked behind. Twice, he thought he saw something move far back and above them where the trail crossed open space. When he stopped to have the others look, nothing more appeared.

Nine days after leaving Itatu, they reached the base of the cliffs and entered the heat and humidity of the jungles. Before continuing, they tied up their horses, and then Anton led them through the trees and along the edge of the bluff to a large open cave.

There was something inside that their guide wanted them to see.

A musty, dead smell met their noses at the cavern mouth. It was not the overwhelming stench of the recently dead but the mildewy, penetrating odor of something that died long ago.

Elisada stopped. "I don't like the smell," she said, shaking her head. "I'm staying outside."

Mirela pinched her nose. "It stinks. I'm not going in either."

Prickling sensations went up and down Pedí's spine. Instinctively, he looked for an engraving, a glyph of his heroine Adací, but there would be none here. His ancestors would never have been to this cave.

But maybe he shouldn't worry. This was more of a grotto—an open space that went into the side of the cliff—not a deep cave. Light penetrated to the back wall. There were a few dark holes in the sides and one in the back, but they could avoid those. And besides, Anton had been here before and said it was safe.

They stepped inside and moved among the remains of thick animal hides covered in long hair. Large bones lay scattered among the hides. The animal remnants were what Anton had brought them to see. The crawling, tingling sensation that had started in his spine spread to all of Pedí's body. He shook it off. His curiosity was piqued.

He fingered the yellow-brown hair still attached to the hardened skin of the hides. An enormous skull was lying by itself on the ground. He picked it up and traced its outline with his finger. He had never seen an animal like this. From the size of the skull and a nearby backbone, he estimated the creature could have been fifteen to twenty feet long and weigh as much as three or four giant bears.

Mirela screamed! But not from the opening where Pedí thought she was. It was from the back of the grotto. She had entered the cavern without telling them. Her curiosity overcame her dislike of the smell.

Pedí and Anton sprinted toward her.

Mirela bounced from foot to foot. "Look what I found! Look what I found!" She held a nine-inch-long curved claw, perfectly formed.

Pedí stopped by her side and breathed again. "That claw is huge! What were these animals?" he asked Anton.

"Uai, the jungle people called them Mapondos. They were the last of the giant sloths. The villagers protected them at one time, even revered them, but their meat became a delicacy in Romingo and the lower jungle towns. Hunters searched for and killed them all."

Mirela bent down to look for more claws.

Anton knelt with her. "These creatures were slow-moving but not as slow as the tree sloths. They were powerful and dangerous if you got too close to them or threatened their young. Their claws were used for pulling down vegetation, digging roots, or making caves, but not for aggression unless provoked."

Pedí glanced at the black cavity in the back wall of the grotto. Mirela was just six feet away from it, searching for more claws. The dark opening was about four feet across, and no light penetrated it. The crawling, tickling sensation returned, but he knew now it was just his imagination. They were safe.

Elisada called out from the entrance. She must have heard Mirela's cry. Pedí moved toward her and waved. "Mirela's okay. We're—"

He spun back around. Something wasn't okay. He felt it from behind—from the black hole.

Mirela had moved even closer to the dark recess. Two yellow eyes were watching her. Something as black as the hole was inside.

"Mirela," Pedí whispered, "move towards me, away from the opening behind you. Do it slowly."

He put his hand over the pouch with the living Adací's hair and pleaded for help—help from his ancient heroine.

Mirela glanced at the cavity, shuddered, and stepped backward toward Pedí. The yellow eyes moved forward, and an outline of a creature began taking shape.

A head appeared, the square-shaped monstrous head of a forest cat. It was pitch-black—not the more common spotted kind. The rest of its ebony form still blended with the darkened cave.

Anton had seen the cat and was moving backward at the same time as Mirela, but he was further away. With each cautious step the girl took, the forest cat moved in cadence with her.

Pedí did not back up but moved toward Mirela and the giant feline. Grandpa had said the forest cat's bite was the most powerful of all creatures. They could crush right through the shells of river turtles. One chomp of Mirela and she'd be gone.

Pedí reached Mirela's side and swept her behind him. He faced the cat, which had come halfway out of the cave. Its massive shoulders and short but powerful front legs showed. Long claws gripped the floor of the cavern.

Its black jaws opened, and a line of yellow teeth appeared in a sardonic smile. When the creature stepped closer, the long tail of the forest cat appeared. It swished back and forth, not in friendship, but in anticipation of a meal. Pedí was just a few feet away.

Each breath of the cat was harsh—the air almost heaved out. The nostrils moved up and down, sniffing its victim. The cat bent down, preparing to leap.

Pedí bowed simultaneously and reached again for the pouch with Adací's hair. He spoke to the cat in Idonata. It was foolish even to try. Mammals didn't listen to him, but what else could he do? At least now the black cat would attack him first, and Mirela and Anton could escape.

Surprisingly, the creature hesitated, acted confused, but then crouched again, ready to spring.

Pedí hadn't moved except to motion for Mirela to keep backing up, but she had stayed close behind him. He worried she'd put herself in jeopardy when the cat jumped on him.

Pedí remembered that Grandpa had taught him how to growl like a forest cat. It was a deep chesty sound, almost a cough—an angry *huh-huh*. Pedí made the sound as best he could.

The black beast raised its head and responded with a similar but even deeper *huh-huh*.

Pedí began backing away, taking Mirela with him. He continued to talk in Idonata and then growl out repeated *huh-huhs*.

The cat echoed Pedí with its own growl each time, and it didn't move, except for its tail, which swished back and forth, striking against its flanks.

When they reached the cavern mouth, Anton whispered for them to run.

"Not yet," Pedí said. "Go toward the trail, but slowly."

Pedí continued to face the animal, talking and growling. The giant cat gave a final deep *huh-huh*, then turned and disappeared into the dark hole.

"Now we can run," Pedí said, and they took off toward the trail where they'd left their horses. No one said a word until they'd mounted the saddles and started off. When Pedí lifted Mirela onto their saddle, he noticed she'd kept the Mapondo claw. She put it into the pouch on her boot, where she used to keep the sheep shear knife.

"What were you saying to the cat?" Anton asked.

"I told it we were friends in Idonata."

"And the growls. Do you know how to talk its language?"

"Just how to mimic the sound. I have no idea what they meant."

Pedí thanked his ancient heroine in a whisper to himself, then felt the cloth pouch in his pocket. He had sensed a power coming out of the pouch and couldn't help but believe that this new Adací's hair had saved them. He wanted to get rid of the hair and forget this girl, but he could never throw the silver and black strands away now.

CHAPTER FIFTY-ONE

Jade Stones

"Mother will never tell me where she's hidden the jade," Adací said to Jurana and Gabro during her weekly visit with them at the Sanctuary. "Heila and I have searched everywhere for two days without success. And tomorrow, Niala has to go back to The Big House."

Adací sat on the sandstone bench in the courtyard with a sage on each side of her. "Even if I find them, I'm worried I'll hurt Larada and Niala instead of helping them."

Jurana scooted closer. "We don't believe that, and we'll tell you why. We found the old manuscript in the library about the Idonata queen the soldiers killed."

Jurana looked at Gabro as if asking for him to continue her story.

He cleared his throat. "The queen had jade beads in her hair. The soldiers who shot her stripped the jade off before they hung her from a tree."

Adací imagined the queen hanging by her long braid with blood dripping down her chest. Just like when Mother first told her the story, Adací felt a burning in her chest, though not as severe.

Gabro went on. "The story in the manuscript gets even stranger. The three soldiers argued over who would get the queen's jade. That night, they went to sleep in the same tent, unwilling to trust each other with the gems. In the morning, they were all found dead. Poison darts were stuck in their necks. The jade stones were gone."

Adací's chest and heart, which had been burning, now felt cold.

Jurana let go of Adací's hand and reached to touch her braid. "After two hundred years, you show up with jade stones."

"But where did my birth mama get them? Could they be the same ones the queen had?"

"There is no way to know for certain, but we wonder if the jade has been passed down through the ages. They could be the same stones worn by Pedí's heroine, the first Adací."

Adací tried to imagine her namesake, the original Adací, attaching the jade to her long braid. As Adací created that vision, it was suddenly replaced by another. She saw where the green gemstones were hidden. It was a clear picture in her head. The stones were coiled together and tucked deep in a hole in the broken stonework underneath the bellows.

They were in the blacksmith shop, the one place she hadn't checked.

The one place Pito would know she'd be afraid to go. Of course, that's where he'd hide them.

Adací rushed home, then watched and waited until Pito and the other men were out in the corral. They didn't see her go into the blacksmith shop.

She hated the place—the fire, the smoke, the banging on metal when the men worked in it. Her irrational childhood fear of the shop had never left her.

Pito tried to help her overcome it when she was five years old. Using a piece of hardwood, he carved a little jungle boy with feathers on his head, then said the figure was hers if she could find it.

The wooden boy had not been in any of his regular hiding spots, and the blacksmith shop was the last possibility. She had entered trembling and then saw the deep hole. She knew the carved boy was there that day, just like she knew the jade was there now.

And like that day when she was five, Adací's hand started shaking. The tremor began the moment she saw the hole. As a five-year-old, her arm had gone in up to her shoulder. She had expected to be bitten by a snake or a rat at any moment, but she had captured the little wooden boy. She still guarded him in her room—one of her prized treasures.

Taking a deep breath, Adací reached in—this time just up to her elbow—and pulled out the stones. She heard footsteps and quickly dropped them into a pocket in her dress.

Pito had walked into the shop. From the look on his face, he must have seen her pull out the stones.

Adací grimaced and shook her head. "They're mine. Mother took them from me."

"Your mama's afraid of them damn stones. We all are. Afraid if you put them on again, you'll dream something crazy and go off on a horse to hell or beyond. I don't want to bring you back dead this time."

Pito looked away. When he spoke again, the gruffness was gone, and his voice cracked. "I . . . I couldn't bear it."

Adací could handle the angry Pito, but she didn't like it when he softened—he'd win her over every time.

Not this time!

She put her hand over the pocket with the stones; she wasn't giving him the jade. "I won't go off—at least not without telling you first. But promise me you won't tell Mama that I found them."

"I won't lie if she asks."

"I don't want you to lie. Just don't tell her until she asks."

Pito nodded his agreement. "Be careful, damn it! If something happens to you—"

"I'll be careful, but I need these."

Adací ran to the house, afraid of giving in and turning over the jade to Pito if she talked to him any longer.

⬥

That night, she put them on, attaching each round jade ball as before. The little bone hooks still functioned and were not damaged from her fall off the horse.

Would they work again? Could she dream something to help Larada and Niala? She had to try, even though she feared the jade might bring back another nightmare of her birth parents or that she might put Pedí in more danger. But the ancient Adací and the Idonata queen had helped their people. This Adací would do the same.

She lay in her bed for a long time, holding the soapstone monkey and the embroidered handkerchief, one in each hand. Sleep finally overcame her.

When Adací awoke the next morning, she remembered she had dreamed. The same vision repeated itself several times.

She had seen herself standing at the gates to The Big House. She was trying to get inside to be there when Niala arrived at noon. But the guards wouldn't let Adací in. So, she had wandered along the high wall surrounding The Big House and its gardens, trying to find a way inside.

But it was impossible. The wall was twelve feet high, made of thick adobe bricks, and covered with a slick stucco surface. The first captain had used captured Idonata people who hadn't been killed or escaped to do most of the work. They built the wall around his entire property, including the forest remnant in the back. At the top of the wall, they had stuck sharp glass into the mortar. It was unclimbable.

In the dream, Adací continued her journey around the wall until she reached the north side and spotted the Idonata watchtower, perched on a hill within the barricade. A sudden flash of vibrant blue caught her attention. It was the giant Blue Dragonfly that Pedí had told her about. It hovered before her and was huge, as big as three regular dragonflies combined. It glowed with the most pleasing azure color and was the most beautiful thing she'd ever seen.

The astounding creature flew back and forth, leading her to a spot on the wall where the stucco had fallen off, exposing the adobe bricks. The watchtower was just on the other side. The wonderful dragonfly flew away at that point, and Adací woke up.

What did it mean?

In the dream, she sensed the need to be at The Big House when Niala returned. Despite that feeling, she had no idea how to get inside the wall and reach The Big House or how being there would make any difference. Nevertheless, she believed that the dream promised help from the Blue Dragonfly. With its assistance, she would surely find a way inside, and then she'd have a chance of saving Niala.

To her disappointment, however, no vision had come to her about how to rescue Larada from Chando. The soapstone monkey must not be the right connection to the captain's son.

CHAPTER FIFTY-TWO

Cashihua

Pedí couldn't see much in the darkness of the thatched hut except for the outline of the young woman lying motionless in a hammock. Her name was Cashihua, and her thick hair hung off the edge. Her husband, Payaku, huddled in the corner, waiting for his beautiful new bride to die.

Pedí had been brought to see her by Jabuti, the village healer. Jabuti had tried to save Cashihua's life with his herbs and root potions, but she was only getting worse. When he learned Pedí was also a healer, he asked for help.

Pedí and his companions from Itatu were deep in the jungles and had come five days upriver from the town of Ipixuna, the largest settlement on the river with the same name. In Ipixuna, they had stabled their horses and pack sheep.

While they were in the town of Ipixuna, Pedí asked about the orange frogs. He was told that none were left in the jungles. There were other kinds of unusual frogs, but the orange ones had all been killed in the rush to obtain their toxin and sell it to the drug traders. That same bleak message was repeated at every village they stopped at along the river—no orange frogs.

Anton had hired rowers, who brought them upriver on balsa rafts. They could take them no further when they reached the village of Kuloduru. Steep waterfalls broke up the Ipixuna River, and all water traffic ceased.

Kuloduru was where they met Jabuti. Three perfectly straight yellow spines, like the whiskers of a cat, pierced his face. Made from palm splinters, two were at the corners of his mouth, and one just below the center of his lip. His stocky chest was painted with black, white, and red circles, the colors of which were extracted from tropical plants.

Jabuti could speak the language of New Losobon. The jungle natives had learned it in order to barter with the traders who came up the river from Romingo, the largest jungle settlement. They sold them bananas, mangos, tropical hardwood, and the brightly colored cloth they wove from cotton grown in small plots.

Cashihua shifted in the hammock and shook with pain. Jabuti showed Pedí her swollen right thigh. It was twice its normal size and hot to the touch. Pedí recognized the cause. The young woman had an abscess in the deep muscles of her leg. Doctor Arias had taught him about these dangerous jungle infections. Unlike most pockets of pus, they sometimes occurred without any proceeding injury. But like all trapped muscle abscesses, unless drained, the disease would spread, and Cashihua would die.

Jabuti was frantic. Although the young woman was not his child, she had lived with Jabuti and his family after Cashihua's mother had died. She had become like one of his children.

"Her leg needs to be opened with a knife to let the pus out," Pedí explained. "And I have a new cure for infections—my nanimoha."

Cashihua raised her head and turned in the hammock to face Pedí despite writhing in pain. "Nanimoha! You have nanimoha?"

Pedí nodded.

"Give it to me."

He spoke more in the Idonata language to Cashihua, and she answered him. But the effort was soon too much, so she closed her eyes and sank back into the hammock.

The name nanimoha had meant nothing to Jabuti. Pedí had tried to speak the Idonata language at Ipixuna and the other villages along the river, hoping to find some of his lost people. But no one had understood. The jungle tribes spoke in tongues different than Idonata.

"Where did you learn the ancient language of my people?" Pedí asked Cashihua, but she didn't respond.

Jabuti answered for her. "She and her mama came out of Rowai-ra with the moon witch. Cashihua learned the Idonata tongue from her mama before her mama died."

"Did the moon witch have a braid of silver hair and a moon tattoo?" Pedí asked.

Jabuti nodded but looked down at the ground and spoke quietly. "We were all afraid of the moon witch. Rowai-ra is the Valley of the Wind Spirits, where she and her people lived, but they were all killed off. It's forbidden to go there because it's still dangerous." Jabuti's eyes widened, and he shook his head. "I don't want to talk anymore about the witch or Rowai-ra. It will bring bad luck."

Pedí honored Jabuti's request not to ask more questions but realized the moon witch must have descended from the lost Idonata. The Valley of Wind Spirits could be where his ancestors escaped when they fled New Losobon two hundred years ago. But the tale of their demise troubled him. He would try to find out more later. For now, he had to help with Cashihua.

Jabuti went to the corner of the hut and lifted a large woven basket off the ground. It was filled with flowers that he and Payaku had gathered from the forest. "I will perform the blossom ceremony for Cashihua, and then you can use the knife and the nanimoha."

Jabuti and Payaku covered Cashihua's body with the flowers cut from the forest. They also attached delicate purple orchids to her long hair.

"Now she's ready," Jabuti said when they finished.

Mirela had helped Pedí prepare the nanimoha, and he cleaned a long knife.

Cashihua's dark eyes opened wide when Pedí plunged the blade deep into her swollen thigh, but she only flinched, as Jabuti had promised. He held tight to her lower leg. Thick pus flowed out.

Pedí compressed the leg. Pus shot a foot into the air.

Cashihua sat up and cried out.

Mirela rushed to her side and held her hand.

When the pus stopped draining, Pedí placed a small hollow bamboo piece inside the incision. It would allow any new pus to flow out and not build up. Then Pedí and Mirela, using his glass tubes, gave her the first dose of the nanimoha.

When Cashihua drank it, she made a face and gagged but still swallowed it down. "I know the nanimoha will help me."

As she said those words, Pedí's hand went to the pocket that held the pouch with Adací's hair. *Please save this young woman,* he pleaded silently to the coiled locks.

After giving her the other five draughts, Pedí bound Cashihua's leg with strips of cotton cloth that Jabuti provided. From his experience treating a person who had an abscess in New Losobon, Pedí knew Cashihua would need daily doses of the potion. Infections with pus were not the same as the winter fever of the Itatu, which had responded with a single treatment.

He smiled when he thought of his nanimoha. It truly was the cure his ancestors had used. Next summer in New Losobon, he'd harvest more mushrooms and heal people there with severe infections. The people would no longer scorn him and would recognize the good of the Idonata.

That Adací wasn't his friend didn't matter anymore. He would save her strange hair, but otherwise, the jungles had helped him forget her.

At least, that's what he told himself.

CHAPTER FIFTY-THREE

The Wall and the Watchtower

Adací saddled Suza and rode through the cobbled streets near her home. It felt good to be on her favorite horse again. Except for Tavi taking her to meet with Jurana and Gabro each week at the Sanctuary, Adací had remained housebound since her head injury. Now, she felt like a fledgling bird, ready to fly out of the nest for the first time.

She got away without her family realizing she was going to The Big House. Father, Pito, and the other stable hands had gone to the south fields to repair fences. Mother had left to go shopping.

Adací's spirits were lifted even further by the flowering trees that lined the sides of the road. Spring had come to New Losobon. Morning sunlight filtered through blossoms of red, yellow, and purple. Adací's favorite was the Tabebua tree. Clusters of giant yellow flowers adorned its branches. It was one of the few trees in New Losobon that lost its leaves during winter. The bright blooms appeared first before the new leaves grew.

She breathed in deep. Like the fingers of a hand, the scented air reached down her throat and pulled out the melancholy. For the first time since her injury, Adací had a purpose.

Adací's anticipation of seeing the Blue Dragonfly also pushed back her sadness. The incredible creature would come and guide her and help her know how to rescue Niala. Adací was disappointed that Pedí would not be here to see the mystical insect he had looked for all his life.

In her mind, Adací could see the exact spot along the wall where it had led her. The old watchtower was just on the other side. Only Heila knew of the vision. This morning, the maid had rushed to Adací's room to ask if the tokens had brought any dreams. But when Heila learned that Adací was going alone to The Big House, she was concerned. "Take Larada with you," the maid had said. "Then they'll let you in at the main gate."

"But that's not what the dream showed me," Adací countered. "I was alone, and the same vision came to me three times during the night."

⬥⬥⬥

When Adací and Suza reached The Big House gates, they did not stop. The guards would never let her in. She continued on the horse and followed the wall surrounding the captain's property. At the Northeast corner, the wall turned west, and Adací pulled the reins and stopped. She surveyed her surroundings.

The cobblestone street continued northward but would soon branch into three dirt roads. The one that went east bordered the north end of New Lososbon and passed between the adobe houses and the wooden shacks of the poorest part of town. The branch that continued north would reach the old forest. The road west would lead to the western valley covered with expansive plantations and farmer's fields. The west road paralleled the captain's wall and was about a hundred feet from it. Short trees and sprawling bushes grew on the wall side of the road. On the opposite side, the captain's coffee grove spread out northward until it reached the forest.

A narrow trail ran closer to the wall than the road and wandered through the trees and bushes. That is the track Adací should take. When the Blue Dragonfly appeared in the dream, it was along a trail, not a road. Adací led Suza off the cobbles and onto the faint trail.

She began to watch for the dragonfly. It would come soon. When she reached the spot where she could see the top of the old Idonata watchtower rising above the wall, she stopped Suza. This was the place in the vision where the dragonfly appeared. She waited for ten minutes, but nothing blue showed itself.

She urged Suza to go forward, and Adací continued to watch for the dragonfly. The further she went, the doubts grew. Was the dragonfly only a creature of her dreams?

She arrived at the place on the wall where the adobe bricks were exposed. Adací looked left and right for the Blue Dragonfly, but it was nowhere. Yet, this was the exact spot. She could remember it distinctly. Why hadn't the Blue Dragonfly come?

The former excitement she had experienced—the heightened senses, the belief that she had a purpose—left her. Adací felt all alone. She needed that mystical blue creature as a companion.

Then nausea hit! She retched, then covered her mouth to keep from vomiting. Without guidance from the Blue Dragonfly, Adací had no idea how she would get inside the captain's wall and even less of an idea of how to rescue Niala from Chando, even if she did get inside. But she couldn't go home without trying. There must be something about this spot that would make it easier to climb the wall. First, she led Suza into a nearby circle of trees. She tied the mare to one of the trees with grass growing around it. The horse could remain hidden and have plenty to eat.

Adací crept back through the trees, staying as low as possible. She could hear workers nearby, trimming the coffee plants. They would alert the captain's guards if they saw her trying to get over the wall.

As she neared the last of the tree cover, Adací came up against a large stone pillar. It was partially hidden in bushes. It stood about five feet in height but must have been much taller in the past, as half had been broken off and lay sideways on the ground. The part still standing was covered with intricate chisel marks, a form of ancient writing. She remembered Pedí telling her about the broken stone altar near The Big House. Its glyphs described his nanimoha. Could this be it?

Adací choked, then wiped her eyes to clear the pooling tears. Thinking of Pedí doubled, no tripled, her feeling of being all alone. There was no Pedí and no Blue Dragonfly to help her.

She sucked in a deep breath, then keeping low, Adací scampered across the last open space between the trees and the wall. She reached the damaged section, but there was no opening, just loose stucco that had fallen off. The adobe bricks were intact, and the broken area was not large enough to aid in climbing the wall. She'd never get over it.

Why had the dragonfly brought her here in the dream?

Then, her foot slipped, and she stumbled into a hole. It was right beneath the damaged section of the wall and seemed to extend underneath it. Adací cleared out some loose rocks and debris and found that the hole went under the wall, creating a narrow passageway.

During storms, water must have rushed off the tower and the hill on the other side, then gone under the adobe structure, creating the tunnel. The opening was almost big enough for a small person to climb through.

Adací's heart pounded as she glanced back toward the coffee plantation. She could hear the workers but couldn't see them, so they were unlikely to see her. She got on her belly and slid under the wall. It was a tight fit, but she could squeeze through. On the other side, the stone watchtower rose high from the top of a hill, beckoning her onward.

Adací approached the bottom of the tower. Though she'd seen herself in dreams—adorned with feathers and climbing up the steep steps many times—Adací had never been to the tower. She rubbed her hand along the gray-black stones, which fit tightly together without any mortar. The craftsmanship was remarkable.

As she circled to the front of the structure, a row of glyphs appeared near the first steps leading to the top. A speck of blue showed on one of the glyphs, which were etched in the stone and surrounded by squares. As she got nearer, she could see a dragonfly carved into that glyph. Two flecks of azure paint remained on its body.

Adací put her hand over the glyph and felt strength and hope coming out from it. Though the dragonfly never appeared except in her dream, it had guided her inside the wall. Would the beautiful creature help her find a way to save Niala?

She startled when she spotted another glyph adjacent to the dragonfly etching. A woman's figure was intricately carved into the rock. She had a long braid and a small crescent moon on her chest. Could this be the first Adací, her namesake?

She put her other hand over it. An energy emanated out from both glyphs and into her. She knew now that she was not alone and could rescue Niala. The Blue Dragonfly and the first Adací would help her.

Adací glanced up at the sun. It was nearly noon, and Niala would be coming. She took off running toward The Big House, trying to stay hidden by the bushes, trees, and flowers of the captain's gardens.

CHAPTER FIFTY-FOUR

Race to The Big House

Adací saw two guards patrolling the grounds as she dashed through the bamboo hedge. They spotted her and shouted for her to stop, but she only ran faster. They followed.

Adací knew that Niala would come through the stables and then go to the servant's entrance at the back, near the kitchens. Adací had to escape the guards and reach that doorway before Niala arrived.

As she circled the house, she saw the back entrance. Adací was out of breath, exhausted, and ready to faint, but she had outrun the guards chasing her. When she arrived at the door, two of the captain's guards came out of the house. It was easy for them to grab her arms and restrain her, as she had no energy to fight them. At least she could yell. "Let me go!" she shouted.

"Who are you?" one of them shouted back. "Why are you here?" the other said.

Adací twisted and turned, but it was without much force, and they only tightened their grips on her.

The door to the servant's entrance opened again. Chando walked out, his eyes opening wide. "By the gods above, it's the witch! I thought I heard shouting."

He nodded toward the guards. "Good job, catching this wild woman. Keep a tight grip. She's good at digging with her fingernails and throwing wine." He laughed.

The other two guards who had been chasing Adací arrived. They surrounded her as well.

"Does it take four of you to control a little girl?" Adací stuck out her chin at them.

Chando chortled even louder. "Answer me this, witchy girl. How did you get past the watchmen at the gate? They have strict instructions to keep you out since that wine-throwing escapade."

"I'll not tell you."

"Of course you won't, you little hag."

At that moment, Niala approached from the stables. Adací saw her and tried harder to break free and to go to her. "Let me loose!" she cried out again.

Niala came closer, shaking her head. "Oh Adací! Why are you here? Are they hurting you?"

"I came to—" Adací stopped herself, unsure what to say."

Chando looked back and forth between the two girls, a sarcastic smile crossing his face. "So that's it! You came to try and rescue our little Mattaçores wench." He took a step toward Niala. "Where have you been, anyway? The steward said you were coming back today at noon. That's why I'm here at the servant's entrance—to welcome you!"

Niala shuddered.

"Leave her alone, you monster!" Adací shouted.

"Why, I'm surprised at you, witch girl. You should be happy to see me show kindness to this island-born maid." Chando went to Niala and grabbed her arm.

Niala winced.

"Welcome back to work!" Chando laughed as he said it. "I missed you."

The guards holding Adací paid more attention to Chando's actions than securing her. The one holding her right arm let up on his grip. Adací twisted that arm loose, bent down, picked up a rock from the ground, and threw it at Chando. The rock hit the big man squarely in the back.

"Umph!" Chando startled. "I told you not to let up on her. That witch is crazy!"

The guards immediately restrained Adací, holding her even tighter than before.

The servant's door opened again. This time, Captain Durgo Borgesso stormed out.

His brows were furrowed. He looked around at all those present before speaking. "Someone said there was a disturbance at the back." He walked over to Adací and put his face close to hers. "Why am I not surprised to see that you're the cause of it?"

The captain put his hands on Adací's shoulders as if the guards securing each arm had not already restrained her enough. "But how did you get inside my property? Can't my guards get it right?"

One of the men who had chased after Adací explained, "I think she found some way over the wall. We saw her running through the grounds near the old tower."

The captain's eyes widened, and he jerked his hands away from Adací as if suddenly afraid of her. "Is that true?" he asked, the words said with a slight stutter. "How did you—"

"You can go jump off that tower!" Adací interrupted, gritting her teeth at him.

The captain laughed, but it was a nervous laugh. Chando and the guards joined in the merriment, gloating and cackling.

Durgo Borgesso took a deep breath before addressing Adací again. "You're quite the girl. You have no respect for anyone. You've shamed your father and mother many times. I guess you plan on doing it again—sneaking into my property and causing this disturbance."

The captain rubbed his hands together. His smile and laughter were gone. "But how did you get over the wall, and why are you here?"

Adací didn't know what to say or do to save Niala or herself. Her angry reactions to the captain and Chando had only worsened the situation. Adací needed to change her behavior.

Chando dragged Niala over to his father. He still had a tight hold on her arm. "I believe the black-haired girl came to intercept this little strumpet, who has been skipping work. But I'm not sure what the witch intended to do."

Then it came to her! Adací knew what she was supposed to say. The Blue Dragonfly and the first Adací were helping. "We need another servant. Father sent me to buy Niala's contract."

"She's not for sale!" Chando shouted.

"Ignore her, son," the captain said. "Of course, the witch girl is lying. If it were true, her father would have come. He would have entered through the gate. There's something else going on here."

Adací struggled even harder to break free. "You're wrong. We want to buy Niala's obligation and let her work at a home that would respect her. Your worthless son is abusing her, and you let him do it, just like he's hurting her now."

Chando took two steps toward Adací and balled his fist, but before he could do anything, his father grabbed his arm while nodding toward two approaching people. "Hold on," he whispered. "Look who's here."

It was Larada Mendin and Edero Custal. They were about twenty feet away. They must have entered by the main gate and then come around the side of the house.

Chando still had ahold of Niala, but he released her and gently patted the arm he'd been squeezing. "I'm so sorry if I held you too tightly." He bowed his head toward the maid as if actually apologizing.

What a liar, Adací thought, but didn't say it. It was time to hold her tongue. But why had Larada and Edero come? Heila must have gone to Larada and told her what Adací was doing. Her friends had arrived at a critical moment. How much had they heard and seen?

Edero spoke as he and Larada drew closer. His words confirmed that he and Larada had listened to at least some of what Adací had said because Edero followed Adací's ruse. "I am sorry to interrupt. But just like Adací, I came to purchase Niala's obligation to you. My family also wants Niala to be our maid. I brought Larada because I wasn't sure I would be allowed inside without her help. But sorry, Adací, I'm going to outbid you."

Edero came within a few feet of the captain and Chando and addressed them. "My family will pay double the price you paid the shipping merchants for Niala and her family."

"Look here, Custal!" Chando spit out the words. He reached and grabbed ahold of Niala's arm again. "This Mattaçores maid is not for sale."

Niala flinched when Chando's fingers circled her arm. She shuddered.

"*Get your filthy hands off of her!*" Adací wanted to shout at Chando but stifled the urge. She twisted again to try and free herself from the guards but couldn't.

Larada had gone to Niala's side. She put her hand on Chando's arm and gently pulled it away from Niala. The maid leaned into Larada, who circled her with her arms. "Niala is afraid of you. I'm certain you don't mean it, but perhaps you are a little too rough with her."

He does mean it, and you know it as well, Larada. That evil behemoth has hurt her repeatedly. But Adací realized that Larada and Edero were being judicious in defusing the situation, something Adací did not have the capacity to do.

Chando's father went to his son and whispered into his ear. Chando nodded and then managed a fake smile. He bowed toward Larada and Niala. "I don't mean to scare our little island girl. She's been absent from work, and I came to the servant's entrance to welcome her back and make sure she was okay."

"You lying piece of—" Adací stopped herself from saying more and wished she'd constrained her words.

Durgo Borgesso took a step forward, ready to take control of the situation. But his jutted-out chin had withdrawn a little, and there was a tremor on his lips and sweat on his brow. He was not happy that Larada was witnessing his son's ill-treatment of Niala and Adací. But would it be enough for him to capitulate?

He addressed Larada. "I apologize if our words and actions have been unfriendly. But how could we not be upset when this black-haired girl mysteriously shows up and creates a disturbance."

The sweat on the captain's brow was now dripping down his cheeks. "Many people in this city fear her. The girl's unusual behaviors have caused many to believe she's a witch. No one has climbed over our wall before, but this girl magically manages to do so. Then, after trespassing, she comes and makes repeated false claims against my son. He only wants what is best for our servants, including Niala. The maid was absent, and Chando came precisely to ensure she was okay when she returned to work. Perhaps his words seem harsh, but it's just his nature. He only wants what is right and fair for all the servants."

Adací could barely contain herself from not yelling liar again and adding a few swear words to it.

The captain wiped the sweat off his brow and face with his handkerchief. "This dark-haired, out-of-control girl claims she is here to purchase Niala's contract. I don't believe it. She is here for some other purpose—to create havoc, it would seem."

"My friend means well," Larada said. "Please tell your guards to let her go."

Edero bowed toward Chando and Durgo. "If Adací was misinformed about your son, forgive her, and forgive us as well for intruding."

Unlike Adací, Edero was diplomatic.

He continued. "Please let Adací go and please let my family purchase Niala's contract. That truly is why I have come."

"You'll not get her," Chando said, his counterfeit smile turning back to a frown.

The captain shook his head at his son. "Give us a moment to discuss your offer. But until we return, I would be more comfortable restraining this unusual girl. I'm sorry if it seems unkind, but I have no idea what she'll do next."

He took ahold of Chando's arm and led him into the house. "We'll be right back."

A few minutes later, the captain and Chando exited the house.

"Again, I apologize for seeming unfriendly," the captain said in a somewhat humble voice, "but it was all because this frenzied girl stole onto our property and then verbally abused my son."

He motioned toward Niala. "Although we are sad to let this fine girl go, we'll consider your offer on one condition—this crazy girl has to stay away from The Big House."

Was Niala going to be released from her servitude to the captain and Chando? This was the miracle that Adací had hoped for. The Blue Dragonfly and the first Adací made it happen—giving her the strength and the words she needed and bringing Larada and Edero to The Big House. Adací was relieved she had not totally botched it.

Chando's scowl showed that he disagreed with his father but had been forced to accept the charade.

Edero bowed again. "We understand." He motioned toward Adací. "Our friend will agree to stay away."

Adací nodded, trying to be a peacemaker like Edero.

"I'll send you a bill for the servant and her family," Durgo said to Edero, then motioned with his hand to his guards. "Let that girl go."

Edero bowed once again. "Thank you for your generosity." He led the girls, including the now-freed Niala and Adací, toward the front gate.

Adací glanced back at Chando. His face was red and ready to burst. He hurled out some parting invectives. "Custal! You are shaming my future bride by coming alone with her. I understand why Larada might be here, but not you. She thinks that black-haired witch saved her once. But Larada is promised to me! Stay away from her!"

Adací watched Edero grind his teeth but then take a deep breath and smile before turning back to respond. "I just asked Larada to get me through the gate. It's nothing more."

Adací could see he wanted to fight Chando, but the skinny boy would be beaten to a pulp if he did. But as always, Edero was tactful.

As the four young people went along the palm-lined walkway toward the iron gates, Adací hugged Niala, who had begun to cry. Niala looked her in the face. "If you had not come and created a disturbance, they never would have let me go. The captain is afraid of you. I can tell it. You saved me. All of you saved me. I can never repay you enough."

CHAPTER FIFTY-FIVE

Guasúpe Beetle

Pedí and Mirela gave Cashihua six small doses of the nanimoha each morning. The potion did not cause the increased fever and elevated heart rate as it had with the winter fever. Pedí wondered if it was the Itatu fever itself and not the mushroom cure that caused the unusual reaction.

When Cashihua could finally walk on the recovering leg, she led Pedí and Mirela to the riverbank. The three sat together on a downed tree and watched the village boys teach Anton to fish with a bow and arrow.

Mirela pulled out her Mapondo claw and showed it to Cashihua. "Uai, are there any left alive?"

Cashihua glanced to both sides, checking that no one else listened. "Only in Rowai-ra. But you must not tell. The hunters might kill them. My mama and I came from Rowai-ra."

She motioned toward the Blue Mountains.

"Mama lived in the hidden city and served the moon queen. Jabuti calls her the moon witch, but our queen was not a witch. She used her powers for good. When masked warriors attacked our village, the queen sent her people to hide in the deepest canyons of the Blue Mountains. The queen faced the warriors alone, with no one except her mate at her side. But my mama and papa did not escape with the others. They stayed to help the queen."

Cashihua adjusted her position on the log. "The queen decoyed the evil warriors away from her people, and they followed her, her mate, my mama, and my papa down into Rowai-ra. But at an ambush, my papa was killed, and the queen's mate was beaten with clubs and nearly died. My mama and the queen both had arrows shot into them. But they escaped again, though they were barely alive. All their efforts after that were to save their babies. Mama carried me. I was two years old. The moon queen carried a tiny moon baby. The baby had a tuft of silver hair among her dark black locks."

Pedí put his hand over the pocket that held the pouch with Adací's hair.

Cashihua continued. "Jabuti was hunting. He saw us all come out of the forbidden valley. Jabuti was frightened. He had heard stories about the powerful witch who lived in Rowai-ra. He pointed his bow and arrow at the queen but was too afraid to shoot."

Cashihua held her arms as if pointing a bow and arrow and then throwing them to the ground.

"My mama couldn't walk any further. The moon queen motioned for Jabuti to help Mama and me. He took us home and tried to heal Mama. He feared the moon queen but still treated her and her mate with their injuries. They only stayed for a few days, then said they had to go."

Cashihua stopped talking. She surprised Pedí when she reached and touched the tattoo on his cheek. "I like your design. My mama had yellow butterflies inked onto each of her cheeks, and she had little blue ones on her lower legs. She did the blue butterflies herself. Mama was an artist and tattooed many in our village before they were attacked."

Cashihua touched her cheek and then lowered her eyes. "Mama was going to paint a design on my face when I turned twelve, but she died when I was just eight."

"Uai, what animal were you going to have?" Mirela pinched her cheeks. "I want a Mapondo claw on both sides of mine."

Cashihua shook her head. "I wish you could, but there's no one left who knows how to do it. Mama was the last one. I wanted a red-billed toucan, and I asked her to ink my cheeks at every birthday, but she wouldn't."

"Why not?" Mirela questioned.

"Mama said tattoos were only painted on children at a special ritual when they turned twelve. Only once did Mama not follow that tradition. It was the last tattoo she ever painted and was on a tiny child. She put a tattoo on the moon baby."

Pedí felt as if something inside his chest leaped out. There was a pulsing right under the pouch with the black hair. "She tattooed a little baby—the queen's baby?"

"Though Mama was very ill, the moon queen begged her to do it. She said her baby had to have the royal mark. Mama guessed that her queen knew that she and the baby would not survive, but she wanted her offspring to be given all that belonged to her heritage."

"It sounds cruel to tattoo a tiny baby," Cashihua said, "but Mama smiled when she told me the story. She said the queen's mate made a poultice of Dojo leaves and put it on the baby's chest just before Mama drew the tattoo. The moon queen cried and couldn't watch while Mama inked the tattoo, but the baby didn't cry. She smiled, babbled, and even laughed as if it tickled her skin."

"Was the moon baby a witch, or was she a good baby?" Mirela asked.

"She was the best baby, Mama said. After the baby got her tattoo, the queen and her mate took her away. The queen had a vision and said she was supposed to take her baby to their original homeland. Mama cried when they left. She knew they would never make it to their destination. They were too injured and ill. Mama said the moon queen and the moon baby are no more in this world."

"Uai, that's too sad," Mirela said.

Pedí hung his head and marveled at the story, but he wondered about that baby.

Just then, there was a loud splash in the river. Anton had mistaken a ten-foot-long Arapo catfish for a rock. It was resting in the shallows, and Anton stepped on it by mistake. The giant fish flipped him into the air, and he landed hard on the riverbank.

Pedí ran to help. Anton's ankle was injured. Pedí felt each bone and determined the ankle was not broken but badly sprained. With bark stripped off a tree and cotton strips for ties, he fashioned a splint. One of the village boys handed Anton a long pole to use as a crutch.

"I'm afraid your fishing days are over," Pedí said.

That night, they gathered around the small fire in front of Payaku's thatched dwelling to eat supper. The main course was the Arapo catfish that had injured Anton. The village boys had shot it with their arrows. It was wrapped with banana leaves and baked in the coals. While they ate, Mirela kept getting up and whispering to Cashihua.

Earlier, the two of them had gone off alone into the forest. When they came back, Pedí noticed that Mirela could barely contain herself. Her normal high energy was three times elevated.

When he had asked her what had happened, she shook her head. "Uai, wait till later."

When the meal was finished, Mirela jumped up. "Now?"

Cashihua nodded her approval.

Mirela ran inside the thatched hut and came out carrying a small cage she and Cashihua had woven from vines and fibers. Something moved inside it, and Mirela bounced up and down as she brought the cage to Pedí.

"Uai, look what we found."

A giant black beetle was inside the cage. It had huge mandibles and long antennae that extended the length of its body. Pedí had never seen an insect so large.

"Guasúpe," Cashihua said, giving the name of the beetle. "It means giant. It's the biggest kind and can be used as a weapon."

Cashihua told them that when she was younger, she had been walking alone in the forest. A warrior from an enemy tribe found her. He knocked her to the ground and threatened to kill her with his club unless she came with him peaceably. He was going to make her his second wife.

While on the ground, Cashihua spied a Guasúpe beetle and picked it up. She shoved the insect into one of the warrior's eyes.

Cashihua interrupted her story to demonstrate. She opened the cage and grabbed the beetle by its thorax, just behind its head. It thrashed its legs, and the large mandibles opened and closed, but Cashihua maintained control of the creature.

Pedí and the others followed her to a small tree by the side of the hut. When she shifted her hand and squeezed the beetle's abdomen, it became furious. She pushed its head toward the bark of the tree. The jaws clamped on the soft bark, and the beetle suspended itself with the mandibles locked tight.

"This happened to the warrior. The Guasúpe grabbed his eye and didn't let go. The warrior ran away, screaming. I went home."

Cashihua then grabbed the suspended beetle by its thorax, tapped on its head with one finger, and the jaws released. She put it back into the cage.

Mirela was bouncing up and down again. "Uai, can I tell about the frogs now?"

"Back at the fire."

They returned and sat around the coals of the fire. Payaku added a log, and it was soon burning bright.

Mirela could contain herself no longer. "Uai, Cashihua knows where some orange frogs live."

Pedí sat up straight. *Was it possible to find some after all?*

"I waited to tell," Cashihua said, "until I was better. I'll take you there."

"Where are you taking them?" Jabuti held a stick out over the fire. His eyes were wide and reflected the flames.

"Rowai-ra."

Jabuti shook his head. "Rowai-ra, no. Too dangerous. You must not go."

"I will take them," Cashihua said. "We will find the orange frogs."

"You will die. They will die. The spirits will kill you."

"Mama took me to Rowai-ra once before she died. Though we didn't go that far into the canyon, we were safe. And since then, I've explored it on my own. That's how I found the orange frogs. I'm not afraid of Rowai-ra."

"But you and your mama came from Rowai-ra with the moon witch. It might be safe for you, but not for others. I will not go with you. Payaku will not go with you."

"I'll take them alone," Cashihua said.

CHAPTER FIFTY-SIX

Fork-tailed Flycatcher

Though Adací had worn the jade stones several more times, no dream had come about Chando. Yet now more than ever, she wanted to rescue Larada from that worthless son of the captain.

Sadly, Larada's father had not changed his determination to have his daughter wed the muscle-bound rogue. When Larada tried to tell him that she had learned that Chando had been unkind to one of the captain's servants, her father dismissed it as a vile rumor. Larada could not tell her father what had happened the day they rescued Niala. It would expose that she went there with Edero and was alone with him.

Edero Custal and his parents insisted on paying the captain for Niala and her family. They welcomed her into their home as one of their servants and found a better house for her family. Adací had been to Niala's new home twice, and the Mattaçores girl had become another friend.

Adací met Niala's father, Afondo, and learned more about his back injury. Afondo was still in pain but had recovered enough to do a few chores around the house. "You should go to the infirmary and see Doctor Arias," Adací told him. "He can help you."

Adací told them about Pedí. "There's an Idonata healer that used to work at the infirmary, but he's gone to Itatu. If he ever gets back, he will have lots of ideas on how treat your back pain. He's the greatest healer of them all."

"I know who he is," Niala said. "He rescued me once from a bunch of bullies and took a horrible beating in my place."

Adací felt even more pride in Pedí. However, any word or recollection of him threatened to bring back Adací's melancholy. She worried every day that because of her vision about the evil man with the knife, the apprentice healer might not return. Every time she wore the jade stones, she feared she'd have another dream that would harm Pedí. But no new vision had come about him—either good or bad.

Instead, every night was a nightmare of her birth mama and papa, the men in skeletal masks, and the cave with the monster. The other young woman was there too, fleeing with them and carrying a young child.

But no dream about Pedí. And the Blue Dragonfly never appeared again in any of her visions, though she wanted it to come back.

Worst of all, she had no dream about Chando, even when she held the new token that Larada had given her—something else from that horrible man to whom her friend was promised.

Against her will, Larada had been to The Big House several more times with her parents. She had no choice but to spend time alone with Chando.

He had also come to visit Larada at her home. To her dismay, the captain's son acted more solicitous and kinder than she thought possible. His pretend gentleness only added to her apprehension as he gained more and more of her father's affection and trust. Underneath the façade, Larada and Adací knew what type of person he was.

At the last visit, he had worn a new pin on the lapel of his coat. It was a medal of honor given to him by his father for having fought alongside the captain's guards. They had gone after some men who had stolen gold from one of their mines.

Larada asked if she could keep the pin. She had to squelch her self-respect, knowing the narcissistic man would think she liked him. When he handed it to her, he bragged again about his bravery in the brief fight with the thieves. He took pleasure in describing the gory details of how he had killed one of them. It nearly made Larada gag.

But she swallowed her pride and accepted the medal.

In one of his letters, Edero had begged her to do it. "If your doll caused Adací to dream about you, and if Niala's handkerchief did the same for her, then we just have to find the right connection for Chando. The soapstone monkey isn't working."

Edero seemed to believe even more than Larada in the power of Adací's dreams. However, that trust had not helped her have a vision to stop the planned marriage. Instead, she worried Chando's pride had only been stoked when Larada asked for the medal. He would believe that Larada loved him over anyone else.

That evening, when it was just getting dark, Adací went to the avocado tree. She sat and meditated, wanting to find a way to rescue Larada. Was it her lingering lack of faith in herself that prevented her from having a rescue vision for Larada?

A fork-tailed flycatcher flew out from a dead limb and hovered above the garden. The bird's white body, black wings, and split tail contrasted with the colorful spring flowers growing amidst their vegetables. With incredible skill, it picked a moth out of the air and then flew back to its perch.

Adací could be like that bird and act confidently and skillfully. The Blue Dragonfly dream helped her rescue Niala. She needed to stop believing that her nightmares came from an evil power. Jurana and Gabro told her over and over again that her dreams were a gift.

She went to bed that night with renewed confidence. After attaching the jade stones to her hair, she held the Chando medal and the soapstone monkey. This time, she made fists with both hands around the tokens and went to sleep thinking about how she'd like to fight the brutish man and punch him in the nose.

Adací fled through the woods. Something or someone was after her. She looked around for her birth parents, but they were not to be found. She was all alone.

She paused to look back, expecting to see the men in skeletal masks, but that was not who appeared around the bend in the trail.

It was Chando.

She ran and ran and ran.

The horrible man chased after, threatening to kill her once he caught her.

<hr>

Adací opened her eyes. The nightmare was over, but her entire body ached as if Chando had, indeed, caught and beaten her with his powerful fists. She checked her arms and legs and even her face for bruises, but there were none.

Her dream had nothing to do with rescuing Larada from Chando. Instead, Adací was going to suffer. She trembled. Was she destined to be like the ancient Adací and the Idonata Queen, who gave their lives to save others?

But this dream wasn't going to save anyone. The vision didn't prevent Larada's marriage to Chando.

Was Adací going to fail her best friend and end up dead?

CHAPTER FIFTY-SEVEN

Valley of the Wind Spirits

A moan woke Pedí. He opened his eyes to the palm frond ceiling of the shelter they had built last night. The moan repeated. It came from Elisada.

Pedí sat up. His head slammed against one of the wooden poles of their lean-to. Rubbing the bump, he peered to his side. Just enough morning light was coming through the narrow entrance to see his three companions sleeping. Elisada was closest.

She lay on her back in the cushion of leaves they had gathered for bedding. Her head was tilted, looking at something curled up on her blouse. She glanced at Pedí. "Save me. It's a snake."

He crawled over to inspect. It looked more like a shoelace than a snake, but she was right. A long, thin serpent with diamond markings of brown accentuated by tan borders rested on top of her. At its thickest part, it was not as round as the tip of his little finger. It wasn't moving. Its square-shaped head with large bulging eyes rested on one of its coils.

"Don't worry, it's a vine snake. It's enjoying the warmth of your body."

Pedí picked it up. The creature woke and began gliding across his fingers.

"Let me hold it." Mirela awakened and reached for the serpent.

Cashihua also sat up and spoke its name. "String snake."

"See the eyes." Pedí pointed them out to Mirela. "They're slits, not round, which means it's a poisonous snake."

"Poisonous!" Elisada tried to roll away. Mirela was holding the snake right above her.

"It's safe." Pedí tried to reassure Elisada. "It only has rear fangs and won't bite us, just the small creatures it finds for food."

Elisada did not seem comforted and crawled out of the shelter.

Mirela kept the vine snake all morning, and although she usually helped with cooking and camping, she did nothing but play with her new pet.

Pedí, Mirela, Elisada, and Cashihua were on the second day of their journey from Kuloduru. Yesterday morning, they crossed the Ipixuna River in a dugout canoe and followed game trails through the forest on their way to Rowai-ra—the Valley of the Wind Spirits. Cashihua limped on her recovering leg but led them on paths that ascended around the falls of the Ipixuna and then toward the Blue Mountains.

Pedí had tried to talk Mirela out of coming when he saw the alarm in Jabuti and Payaku's eyes. But she wouldn't listen. Anton couldn't come because of his injured ankle. Elisada insisted on being part of the journey. Pedí saw the fear in her eyes and told her it was all right for her to stay back.

"I want to help you find the orange frogs," Elisada had responded.

He admired her courage.

No one else from the village of Kuloduru dared get near Rowai-ra. Jabuti predicted they would all die. Cashihua had scoffed at him, but Payaku also believed he would never see his new wife again.

After a breakfast of mangos and shelled Juvia nuts, the second day of the trip to Rowai-ra began. Pedí hoisted his small backpack and swung a cloth bag over his shoulder. It was full of extra food for the journey.

Mirela let the vine snake go, but she gathered up her other pet— the Guasúpe beetle. Cashihua had made her a sling to carry its cage. The sling was similar to the ones the villagers used to heft their babies. It was made of spun cotton and dyed red from the seeds of a plant. It draped across Mirela's neck and shoulders with the beetle's cage tucked inside. The scratching sounds of the giant insect accompanied them with every step they took.

As they walked, Elisada talked to Mirela. "Uai, I see your mama's face when I look at you—same green eyes and burgundy hair. Your mama was the prettiest woman in all of Itatu."

Mirela said nothing. Whenever someone mentioned her family, her face took on the same look—inscrutable and melancholy, her eyes at half-mast, but tears never came.

Pedí picked her up, and the little redhead buried her face in his shoulder. He carried her for the next half mile. Despite the uphill slope of the trail, hefting Mirela was never a burden.

When he put her down, she told Cashihua about her family. "Uai, they put my mama and papa in the ground. My baby brothers, too. The wagon fell on them."

"My mama died when I was your age," Cashihua said. "She was hurt and sick when we came out of Rowai-ra. Jabuti took two arrows out of her body and helped her stay alive until I was eight years old, but Mama was never well. The one time she brought me to Rowai-ra, she felt a little better. She wanted to return to search for any who might have escaped the attack on our village. But the long walk was hard for her, and we only went part way into the canyon. She became suddenly afraid that the masked warriors would find us and decided that our people were all dead anyway."

Cashihua smoothed Mirela's dark red locks. "Your mama, papa, and brothers were good people, so they will go to the happy place. One day, you'll see them again. Jabuti and all of the village believe the spirits of bad people go to Rowai-ra."

They began walking again, but Pedí stopped when he realized Elisada was not with them. She was fifty feet behind, looking from side to side. They retraced their steps.

Cashihua took the older woman's hand. "Come. Don't be afraid."

Elisada went with them again but never stopped glancing wide-eyed into the surrounding trees. She stayed tight to Cashihua.

That afternoon, Pedí asked Cashihua why they saw more wild pigs and red deer than elsewhere in the jungle.

"We're close to Rowai-ra now. No hunters will come this far."

"Are you not afraid?" Elisada asked.

"I was born in Rowai-ra. The spirits leave me alone."

"But what about us?" Elisada's eyes blinked rapidly.

"Stay with me, and you'll be safe."

There was a scuffling sound in the trees behind them, and Elisada jumped. They all turned their heads to look back the way they'd come. Nothing appeared, and the noise did not repeat. Pedí thought he had heard the same noise twice yesterday.

"Just an injured animal," Cashihua said.

Around the next bend, they heard something else. It drove out all thoughts of the other sound.

Wailing.

An inhuman wailing.

It grew louder with each step forward. The swelling sound stopped them when they came out of the deep woods and into a clearing. The hair rose on Pedí's neck. Mirela grasped his arm. Elisada cried out.

They had come to the bottom of the Blue Mountain cliffs. The escarpment towered before them—two hundred feet into the air. The stone walls were bluish-black, and in places, huge pieces had broken off and fallen to the ground. Tropical shrubs and small trees vied for toeholds and fought each other for space in the cracks on the cliff face. Mists swirled at the top of the massive stone wall. The sound, the chilling noise, struck them in full force. It emanated from a fierce wind that created a crying sound as it passed between a giant fissure splitting the rock walls.

"Spirits are angry today," Cashihua said. She did not pause but leaned into the blast and led the group on a faint pathway through the cleft.

Pedí shook his head but pressed forward. The eerie sound must be the cold air coming off the top of the Blue Mountains and then passing through the narrow canyon. Yet even so, with each change of pitch in the wailing, crying wind, he could picture a wraith warning them to stop.

Mirela clung to his side. Elisada held onto Cashihua's hand and moaned with each rise and fall of the wind's cry. The chasm where they walked was twenty feet across. Rock falls, trees, and bushes caused them to take a zigzag course through the canyon. They often had to step across a small stream that trickled alongside them.

When the passage narrowed, Cashihua had them halt behind a piece of stone thirty feet tall that had broken off the cliff. It provided a windbreak. Ahead of them, the cleft was only ten to fifteen feet across and darkened. Trees growing at the top blocked light from above. Their long branches extended across the chasm.

"This is the special place." Cashihua breathed deeply and pointed to the opposite canyon wall. "There, you can climb to the top."

The spot where Cashihua pointed had cracks and fissures that split the rock wall in many places. Pedí could make out a zigzag trail that ascended the cliff face.

"From the top, the view is beautiful. I saw the orange frogs in the trees that grow along the edge."

Mirela pulled the Mapondo claw out of her boot pocket. She held it toward Cashihua, then pointed it at the cliff top. "Are the Mapondos up there?"

"No," Cashihua patted Mirela's head. "They live further up the canyon."

"Can we find them, too?"

"They have new baby Mapondos, so it's not safe. Today, you must find the orange frogs."

A plan was made. Because it would be too hard for Cashihua to scale the cliffs with her healing leg, Pedí would go alone. But Mirela demanded to go with him. So, Elisada stayed with Cashihua, and Pedí and Mirela started the climb. Pedí brought his backpack with a cotton bag Cashihua had made to put frogs in if they found any, but Mirela left the beetle behind. The climb up the cliff would be too hard with the beetle cage sticking out from her side.

They soon accomplished the steep ascent. On top, the breeze was lighter, but they could still hear the moaning wind from the canyon below. It was an astounding sight as they looked down into the narrow chasm. They walked by the side of ancient hardwoods which grew along the edge. The massive trees extended branches over the open space to catch the sunlight. Most of the limbs were covered with moss and flowering plants.

"Rain collects in the leaves of the attached plants," Pedí told Mirela. "Small tree frogs use the water caches to lay their eggs. It's a perfect place for us to find some orange ones."

They looked for a tree that would be easier to climb. The first promising one was near a huge old tree that had fallen across the chasm and formed a natural bridge. Sunlight filtered through the leafy canopy onto the gnarled bark of the tree bridge, also covered with bright green moss and flowering plants.

Like long brown ropes, several liana vines hung down over the dead tree, adding to its beauty. When the tree toppled, the vines must have torn off from the bark and out of the ground. The liana's vast network in the treetops would keep it suspended indefinitely.

Pedí went to the tree they had planned to climb. He started up, grasping the grooves in the bark for support, but he lost his grip and slid down the trunk. Mirela laughed.

He started up again but felt a tugging on his pant leg. "Uai, you're too slow," Mirela said. "I'm good in trees."

"Okay," Pedí said. "But if you find any frogs, don't pick them up. You have to be cautious with their toxin. I'll come up to catch them. And don't go out on any limbs that hang over the gorge."

Pedi boosted Mirela partway up, and she scampered up the trunk like a monkey. In their hunt for the frogs, it would be much faster to let her be the climber.

As Mirela ascended, Pedí glanced at the tree bridge that crossed the chasm. He saw a flash of color. Two orange tree frogs jumped out of one of the flowering plants growing on the fallen trunk. They were halfway across.

CHAPTER FIFTY-EIGHT

The Wild Bees are Dead

Adací tried to forget the nightmare about Chando chasing her. She didn't tell Larada or anyone about it. Adací worried that telling it might make it come true. She preferred to pretend that it never happened.

That afternoon, Father brought home news that helped her put the horrible vision aside, at least temporarily. A messenger from Itatu had arrived at the Sanctuary. He carried a message of gratitude from their leader. Pedí's potion had stopped the epidemic of winter fever and saved many lives.

Adací almost shouted out for joy.

"Rumors say the captain is not happy," Father said. "Ever since Doctor Arias sent the young healer to Itatu, Durgo has complained to the Council and even sent letters to prominent people denouncing what Arias had done. His letters claimed the apprentice's potion was dangerous."

Father gave Mother a quick hug but went on talking. "This new captain is not like his father. He doesn't like the sages, nor Doctor Arias. Only Durgo Borgesso would not be pleased that the potion saved the Itatu. Everyone else hopes it can now be used for our people."

Father rubbed his hands together. "The sages will announce the miracle of saving the Itatu in all the schools. Doctor Arias will be honored for sending the new potion there. He'll be even more famous. The captain has threatened to replace him with another doctor. Now, he'll be afraid to do it."

Why hadn't Father said more about Pedí? Had the skeletal-faced man in her nightmare harmed Pedí after he saved the Itatu?

"What about Pedí? Is he not famous, too?"

Her father hesitated as if he didn't want to answer, but with a frown, he mumbled, "he'll be famous, too."

That means Pedí was alive and was a hero. People would esteem him like they did Doctor Arias. They'd forget he was an Idonata boy.

Maybe her parents would let her be his friend.

Adací mentally shook her head, knowing that could never be. Just watching how long it took Father to answer her question about Pedí confirmed that impossibility.

But why had he not come back with the messenger? "And is he . . . is Pedí coming home?"

"The apprentice healer went to the jungles to search for orange frogs. No one knows when he'll return."

She'd forgotten about the jungles, that he was going there too.

Her joy over Pedí's success in Itatu flew away as fast as a swallow swooping to catch an insect. Adací rushed outside to the avocado tree. She sat on a log seat and watched the little black bees going in and out of the hive. If Pedí had come home, she would know he was safe and that the skeletal-faced man had not found him.

In the jungles, there were even more places for the man to hide and ambush him.

She needed to protect Pedí. But how? Another dream? But if one nightmare had sent the evil man after him, would a second one not make it worse?

Jurana and Gabro kept saying that her dreams had a purpose—that she wasn't the cause of the bad things she saw.

She wanted to believe them and hope her dreams could do good things.

She did have a vision that helped save Niala.

But nothing to save Larada from the captain's son. Just a nightmare where her own life seemed in jeopardy. But that dream couldn't be true, could it?

Adací watched her bee friends and tried to believe in herself. The darkened surface of the log seat where Pedí had sat caught her attention. The smashed avocado had blackened in three splotches. It reminded her of the eyes and the hollow nose of a skeleton. Men in death head masks and the bony-faced man stalking Pedí were all she could see.

Any trace of confidence disappeared. Instead of saving Pedí, Adací would kill him.

Mother was right. The jade stones were dangerous. They might have helped save Niala, but what disasters would they bring to Adací, Pedí, and others? Tomorrow, she would return the jade beads to Pito and let him hide them away—this time where she'd never find them.

In her room that night, Adací paused before crawling under the covers. A faint whisper said her name, "*Adací*." It was coming from the old leather bag in the corner.

The jade stones were calling to her.

Why couldn't she silence her relentless imagination?

She stormed over to the bag, pulled the beads out, shook them hard, and then walked to the window. She opened it. She was ready to toss the jade out, but as she leaned forward, the moonlight caught the hair in her braid, which had swung around to the front. The dyed silver strands glowed brightly in spots where the coloring was less.

Adací hesitated, her mind a whirlwind of conflicting thoughts. She had noticed the shine of the silver hair underneath the dye before— always when in the moonlight. Maybe the shining moon was the key to using the jade after attaching it to her hair. Mama had worn the jade. Her last act had been to take the green gems off her braid and give them to Marina to save for Adací. They must not be evil. Whenever Adací imagined seeing her birth mama, she thought her mama wanted to tell her something, but then the vision faded. Maybe Mama was telling her to put on the jade in the glow of the moon. Perhaps then,

Adací could control her visions, direct them to help Pedí and change the nightmares.

Adací cupped the jade in both hands and held them tight against her chest. She would put them on and sleep in the moonlight. After attaching the jade, Adací looked up at the nearly full moon. She held out her braid, stroking each stone. They glowed an intense green as if fed from the moon's power and from the silver hair, which glowed here and there where the dye was less.

As Adací stared at the moon, she imagined she could see herself as if looking in a mirror. But then she realized it wasn't herself she saw. It was a young woman, the very likeness of Adací, but just a little older. A man appeared behind the woman, holding onto her shoulders. They looked out of the moon at Adací.

Her papa and mama.

She blinked, and the vision shifted. Her parents faded and were replaced by the Idonata Queen, whom the soldiers had shot with their muskets. She was at the top of the temple, calling out against the invaders. She wore a dress with an open circle in front, showing off her crescent moon tattoo. Her black braid was long and hung nearly to her feet. One strand glowed silver. Jade stones encircled the top half.

But that image also blurred and then disappeared. Another woman appeared in the moon with a braid the exact length of Adací's. But her clothes were like those worn anciently. She was from long ago. The woman's plaited hair was wrapped in the jade stones, and she pointed to them as if telling Adací how to use them.

It was the first Adací—the first queen of the Idonata.

Adací blinked again, and the lunar portrait disappeared. Only a round moon was left. Adací glanced at her hands, which held her braid. Her fingers pointed at the stones as she'd imagined the ancient Adací to be doing.

She shook her head, almost ashamed. Had the accident damaged her brain so much that she made all of this up?

No, she wouldn't believe it. Her visions were real. With the jade and the moonlight, she was going to rescue Pedí.

Adací ran to her bed, grabbed her blanket and pillow, then returned to the window. If she lay down in the right place, the yellow glow of the moon coming through the window would catch her braid and the stones.

Adací yawned, closed her eyes, and went into a deep sleep.

Alone under the avocado tree, Adací looked around at each log seat. All were empty. The one where Pedí had sat was changed. The skull-face pattern from the smashed avocado had become more distinct, looking even more like a death head.

She turned from the image, trembling, and sought comfort in the wild bees. But the beehive was quiet. No little black friends. Nothing moving in or out. She went to the hive. Piles of dead bees lay on the ground next to the wall—hundreds of tiny creatures, all lifeless.

As she gazed at the bees, she thought of Pedí. He couldn't be dead like the bees, could he?

The vision shifted as if she took herself to where he was!

Adací was no longer under the avocado tree but on the edge of a precipice. She peered down into a deep chasm in the midst of jungle trees.

Pedí was hanging by a vine over the chasm. She could see sharp rocks far below him. She tried to call to him, but her voice was mute. She could see his eyes. They were sad, so sad. Then he lost his grip, and his body tumbled downward, spiraling through the air.

He struck the rocks.

Leaves, branches, and vines floated down to cover his lifeless body.

Adací woke.

The moon still shone onto her braid adorned with the jade. She sat up, tore off the stones, then threw them on the floor. She stumbled to her bed, sobbing.

CHAPTER FIFTY-NINE

Orange Frogs

"**D**o you see them?" Pedí called to Mirela.

The little Itatu girl was high in the tree branches, trying to look down at the log bridge.

"There's two. Stay where you are until I can help you down. I'm going to creep out and grab them before they get away."

Baby style, one hand at a time, one knee forward, then the other, Pedí crawled onto the fallen tree. The massive trunk was at least three feet across, which made his crawl easier. He tried to sense the sturdiness of the old wood with each movement and made his way to where he had last seen the frogs. He had to dodge around three liana vines draped loosely over the dead trunk. When he got past the last liana, he stopped crawling. He was at the spot where he'd seen the frogs. He straddled the giant log for stability.

Mirela called out, "Uai, be careful!" She had moved onto the limb directly above him, disregarding his command not to go out on the branches over the chasm.

"I will be careful, but you must get off that limb. It's right over the gorge." Pedí glanced up to see if Mirela had moved. As expected, she stubbornly remained where she was.

An air plant with pink flowers grew right in front of Pedí. Its roots were wrapped into the weathered and fraying bark. The orange frogs had jumped out of it but now had disappeared. They must be hiding under its leaves. He whispered to the frogs in Idonata. A bright orange one hopped out. Pedí bent forward with an outstretched hand and captured it. The second frog appeared from under the leaves and made a getaway toward the other side of the chasm. But with another bend and reach, he had a frog in each hand.

As he sat back up with his legs still straddling the giant trunk, there was a cracking sound beneath him. The trunk of the fallen tree bent downward several inches right where he sat.

"Pedí!" Mirela cried out. "It's going to break!"

He held both frogs against his chest, against the pocket with Adací's hair, pleading silently for his ancient heroine to save him. The sag in the log bridge stabilized, but he could see that most of the wood was rotted underneath the old tree's fraying bark.

Pedí took in a deep breath and looked up at Mirela. "I'm okay. The trunk is ancient, but it's too thick to break."

He said the words to comfort Mirela but knew it was time to get off the fallen log. In slow motion, Pedí placed each frog in the cloth bag Cashihua had prepared. He added some moss to keep them moist. Working at the same pace as a tree sloth, he reached and pulled the pack off his back and put the cloth bag inside.

After carefully maneuvering the pack onto his shoulders, he wiped his hands off on the moss clinging to the bark. He did not want to get any frog toxin from his hands into his mouth. This was not a time for drowsiness.

His heart raced when he peeked over the side to the jagged rocks at the bottom of the gorge. Pedí brought his knees back up and onto the trunk from the straddling position. With one hand and one knee, he made his first backward crawling motion.

Boom!

The rotting wood blew up like a bomb directly beneath him. Pedí dropped straight into the abyss. He fell amid exploding wood particles and moss. As he fell, he remembered the liana vines. He twisted, turned, and grabbed the closest one. It swung wildly, back and forth, but he held on, using his knees and thighs also to hug the vine.

Now in two pieces, the log bridge broke loose from the cliff on each side with a loud pop, then tumbled into the chasm. Far below him, there was a thunderous crash as they collided with the canyon floor. Pedí expected to join them soon. He hung from the swaying vine in the middle of the chasm, twelve feet below the cliff edge. He couldn't reach either side. When his strength gave out, he would fall to his death.

Yet, despite his precarious situation, he could not stop worrying about Mirela. Holding as tight as he could, he looked up and saw her legs and arms curled around the limb she was on to keep from falling. Leaves and branches cascaded down around her—having been broken loose from the forest canopy by his moving liana.

Mirela peaked over the side of the limb, and her voice filtered down from above. "I'm coming to help you."

"No, Mirela!" he called back up to her. "Climb down from the tree and go back to Cashihua. There's nothing you can do to help me."

Pedí's damp hands loosened and slipped down the liana a foot or two. He wrapped his legs even tighter around the vine beneath him. Pieces of rock and dirt cascaded down the face of the cliff to his side. His weight must be pulling the liana vine off its attachments in the branches above him, causing broken pieces of vines and limbs to fall onto the precipice. But even if the liana wasn't breaking off, he would surely fall. Pedí spun with vertigo, and his grip weakened. He couldn't hold on much longer.

CHAPTER SIXTY

Back to the Sanctuary

Adací was an hour late for breakfast. She stirred the food on her plate with a fork.

Mother was still at the table, sipping a cup of coffee. Father had finished eating and had gone out to work with the horses.

"What's wrong?" Mother asked.

"I . . . I put the jade beads on again."

"You what? You found them?"

Adací nodded, still moving her food with the fork but not eating it. She hadn't told Mother about finding the jade under the bellows. Mother didn't know she'd used them and had a dream that helped her rescue Niala.

"Why would you do that?" Mother said.

"I was going to throw them out the window, but there was a moon, so I put them on instead. With my braid adorned with jade and in the moonlight, I hoped things would be different. I wanted to have a vision to save Pedí from the evil man in the first vision. But instead, I brought new harm to him. I saw Pedí die, and it will be my fault. My nightmare will kill him!"

Mother rolled her eyes. "Stop this nonsense. The jade stones do something to you, not others. They cause you to do foolish things. You nearly died because you believed in your outlandish dreams."

"But this time, I made Pedí fall into a deep canyon in the jungles."

"You don't cause things by dreaming." Mother's face was red. "The jade stones have to go. I insist you give them to me."

Adací's head was bent over the table, but she looked up when Lelia and Heila entered the dining room. They were holding on to each other and must have been listening from the kitchen.

"The stones are on the floor by my bedroom window," Adací whispered.

Mother motioned for Heila to get them.

When she returned, Mother held out a sack. "I don't want to touch them."

Heila put them in the bag.

Mother tied it shut and then held the bag away from her body as if it contained a poisonous serpent. "I'll hide these where you'll never find them again. Maybe I'll destroy them."

"Please don't, Mother! I'm afraid of them, too, but they were my birth mama's. I just don't know how to use them."

"No one does, and there's no one left to teach you. They're just evil."

"Jurana and Gabro have been trying to learn more about them and want to see them. Let me show them the stones first. Then, if they say so, you can smash them."

"I'll wait to get rid of them, but only if you take them to Jurana and Gabro today. Aren't they supposed to be helping you with your dreams and your obsession with Pedí? What have they been doing?"

"They're trying, Mama."

"You must leave the jade stones inside this bag until you show them to the sages. I'll ask Tavi to take you to the Sanctuary. You're in no condition to go there by yourself."

A few hours later, Adací waited outside Jurana and Gabro's offices, where they were counseling others. She hadn't gone to the sandstone bench when Tavi dropped her off as it was not her regular time to meet with them.

When Jurana came out of a room, she leaned to look into Adací's face. "You need to talk?"

Adací nodded.

"We're just about done for noon break. I'll find my husband, and you can tell us what's troubling you."

When they were free, they led Adací to the end of the courtyard. On the way, she held up the bag with the stones. She told them how she had found and used the jade to dream and save Niala. Then, she described sleeping with the jade in the moonlight to try and save Pedí. "The jade glowed, and even part of my hair glistened where the black dye had rubbed off."

Jurana gasped. "You must have hair like the ancient Idonata queens. Your story gets more and more mysterious."

Gabro stroked his beard. "My goodness!" was all he said.

Adací swallowed and cleared her throat. "But that's not why I came to see you. My dream didn't save Pedí. I made him fall into the chasm and killed him."

The sages said nothing, but each placed a soft hand on her back and helped her go forward.

Why wouldn't they at least tell Adací how evil she was?

When they reached the bench, they sat on each side of her as usual. Gabro was the first to speak. "Jurana and I have been thinking more about these stones and your dreams. This new one you had while wearing the jade is . . ."

Another hesitation, just like the time they talked about the dream of the evil man she'd seen following Pedí. Adací glanced at Gabro. He looked straight ahead and rubbed his beard as if in a dream himself. She turned toward Jurana, who also looked straight ahead, not at Adací.

"You think it's going to happen, don't you? Pedí's going to—"

Jurana grabbed Adací's hand to stop her. "No, Adací! We don't think what happens in your dreams is inevitable. And for certain, you are not the cause."

"No, I am the cause. I put on the jade. I went to sleep in the glow of the moon. My nightmares are all about bad things. I'm not even sure the visions that helped me rescue Larada from the falling Juvia nut and Niala from Chando were meant for that end. Perhaps I was trying to harm them."

Adací stood up and turned to face the sages. "I tried to warn Pedí about the skeletal-faced man, but I failed. Yet, somehow, Pedí must have escaped from that man on his own. But instead of leaving him alone, I sent him new harm. This new dream will kill him, and I can't even try to warn him about it."

Jurana got up and put her arm around Adací. "You nearly lost your life the time you rode after him. Don't you think that was enough?"

"But now he's going to die because of me."

Jurana guided Adací back to her seat on the sandstone bench. Gabro took her hand. "You're certain this dream is going to happen?"

Adací squeezed her eyes tight as if trying to force the dream away, but it didn't help. She opened them and looked first at Jurana, then at Gabro. "This nightmare was too real. The jade and my hair in the moonlight brought on a vision even more distinct than the jade alone. I seemed to be able to direct myself to where Pedí was. I didn't want to kill him, but that's what I did. I could feel the sadness inside him and even some of the pain when his body slammed against the rocks."

Gabro stroked his beard. "There's a reason for this dream and all your visions, but it's not what you think. Maybe it's to help you find a way to save him from what might happen."

"Yes, that's it," Jurana exclaimed. "Someone is sending you these visions. Whoever it is can help you know what to do about them."

"But they're just torturing me. I want to do something to prevent the visions from coming true, but I—"

Adací stopped, touched the front of her blouse right over her moon tattoo, then reached for her braid. She held onto it like someone had thrown her a rescue rope.

"What do you think you should do?" Jurana asked.

"When I think of my birth mama, it's like she's there, wanting to tell me something. But then her image fades."

"Those who go before us still watch out for us. Pedí believes that."

"I want to believe that, too," Adací said. "But I don't know how to talk to my mama or others who might be watching over me."

"I wonder if the jade stones might help you," Gabro said. "The key to fully using your powers may be hidden in these gems. May we see them?"

She nodded and gave him the sack. Gabro opened it and took out the stones. His eyes widened, and he breathed deeply as he touched each stone. He passed them to Jurana.

She also ran her fingers across the stones. "So beautiful! Such exceptional craftsmanship!"

She handed them to Adací. "I sense a great power in this jade. A power that only you can unleash. An essence that will help you know how to save Pedí."

Adací nearly dropped the jade stones as if they would burn her fingers. "Mama told me not to touch them again until I showed them to you."

"Well, now we've seen them, and we give you permission to use them," Jurana said.

"We insist!" Gabro added.

"But—" Adací only got out that one word.

Jurana put her hand over the stones Adací held in her open and trembling palms. The sage closed Adací's fingers tight around them. "Put them on, then you might find the solution you seek."

"I think they only bring the visions at night when I sleep with them."

"Mmm," Gabro murmured. "If Pedí's in trouble, I don't think you should wait. Try now and see what happens."

Adací watched the faces of the two sages as she attached the jade to her braid. Jurana gasped each time Adací used the bone hooks to fasten the green beads. "How ingenious!" the elegant sage said.

When they were all attached, the sages walked her to a quiet place in the orchard. "Now, see if you can get an answer from your ancestors watching over you."

Those were their parting words to her.

They left her alone.

CHAPTER SIXTY-ONE

Mama and the First Adací

Adací surveyed the fruit trees surrounding her and then looked up. The sky was bright blue with only a few thick white clouds. She touched the jade adorning her black braid and wondered how she could communicate with her ancestors. The sages couldn't tell her how to do it. She would need to find out on her own.

In a voice barely above a whisper, she pleaded to her mama and her namesake, the first Adací. "Please, don't let my dream harm Pedí." She whispered again and again, repeating the exact words over and over, but nothing happened. She rocked and wrung her hands.

But still nothing.

In her mind, she created an image of her mama and Queen Adací. She could almost see them, but the vision wavered. "No, don't go," she begged. Adací stared harder into the trees of the orchard, trying with all her might to see and talk to the two women. As she strove, an impression came, at least a vague outline. But it was not her imagination this time.

Adací's eyes widened! Someone was there!

As the form became more apparent, she could see it was not her mama or the ancient Adací. Whoever it was seemed haughty and passionless. It was not a kind ancestor who had come. It was someone evil. Then another dark form appeared, as sinister as the first. And in a moment, four more demonic creatures stood behind them.

They were laughing, laughing at Adací.

Her entire body shook, but she bent down, picked up handfuls of dirt, and flung them at the vision before her. "Go away! Go away! You will not conquer me. You will not keep me from saving Pedí."

The ridicule from the hellish figures grew louder. Then, one of them spoke in an unearthly voice. The words twisted into Adací's core and robbed her of all hope. "You cannot save Pedí because you are the one who will kill him," the eerie voice declared. "You will do our will and ours alone. You are an evil witch under our power."

"No, no! I am not evil! I do not want to harm Pedí."

When she spoke those words, the fiendish six mocked her a final time with an evil laugh and then disappeared. But as they did, the vision she had last night reappeared. Pedí hung over the abyss. The vine he clung to broke, and he spiraled downward and smashed against the rocks.

Adací collapsed face-first to the ground herself. Her body shook, and her hands raked the soft earth. "Mama! Mama! Why is this happening? Can you not help me? I do not want to harm Pedí."

As she continued to dig at the earth with her fingers, she felt something in her hands. It was her braid with the jade. It had swung around into the dirt. She sat up and brushed the soil off the stones and hair.

While holding the jade, a clear thought came to Adací. The Moon Goddess gave the beautiful jade to the first Adací. She wore it, and her birth mama wore it. If this Adací could latch on to the jade and believe enough, Mama and the original Adací would help.

With one hand, she touched the hidden crescent moon on her chest, and with the other, she held even tighter to the green stones wrapped around her black braid. Her heart, which had been pounding in her chest, stood still. An overwhelming sensation passed through. Like a tidal wave, it crested the despair and washed it away.

A new vision came. It was her mama and papa giving her to Marina and Sergol. Adací finally understood why. Her birth parents were dying, even before the wagoners attacked them. Yet, they had held on to life because they believed the ancient Adací had guided them to New Losobon to find new parents for their little girl.

She heard her mama's words when she placed Adací in Marina's arms. "Dear child, we must leave you now in the care of others, not of our race. We could not save our people, and you are all that is left. Our ancestor, who you are named after, brought you to them. We don't know why the great Adací had us bring you here, but she told me in a vision that your new parents would be the ones who rescued you. These are the ones. They will raise you to become what you are destined to be."

The vision of her mama and papa began to fade, but Adací pleaded with them before they were gone. "Mama! Papa! Pedí is in trouble. Evil spirits told me that my dreams would kill him."

Words came to Adací's mind as if her mama had spoken them. "Don't listen to those spirits. The skeletal-masked tribe brought them back from the underworld where your namesake sent them. I am sorry they found you, but ignore them. Close your eyes and go to Pedí."

Adací shut her eyes tight. She floated through time and space until, once again, she stood on the edge of the precipice. She watched Pedí hang from the vine, his hands slipping, ready to fall.

He looked up, and she saw the sadness in his eyes like before. But this time, she followed his gaze to a little Itatu girl high in a tree. The tiny redhead wrapped her arms and legs around a large limb to avoid falling. The girl looked down at Pedí, wanting to rescue him but not knowing how.

A distinct message came to Adací. She knew what to do. "You can save him," Adací called to the girl. "My mama and a powerful queen named Adací will guide you. Listen for their voices."

The little redhead raised her head, looked around as if she had heard something, and then called out to Pedí. "I'm coming to help you."

The vision before Adací shimmered, faded, and then was gone. Adací's heart remained calm, beating slowly, at peace. She knew that Pedí would not die.

A short time later, Jurana and Gabro returned. "The look on your face has changed," Gabro said.

"Pedí is going to live. I was able to see the vision of Pedí hanging from the vine again, but this time, I sent someone to save him—a little

Itatu girl who was there. I learned that I could call on other powers and people. Mama and the ancient Adací are going to help her."

Adací sighed. "I can be a good witch, not a bad one. You were right to say my dreams don't cause the terrible things I see but only alert me to what might happen. Sometimes, but not always, I can stop the dream from happening."

"I am so glad you came to that understanding," Jurana said. "Though, I still sense a deep sadness."

Adací pondered on Jurana's observation. Yes, that was what it was—sadness. Once Adací knew Pedí was safe, another realization came. She no longer needed to think and worry about him, which made her sad.

It was time to end all hopes of a friendship with the young healer. Pedí was in the jungles. It would be like heaven for him with its animals and tropical plants. Not once would he think of her. Even if they could be friends when he returned, he would not seek her out. She would never see him again. The whispering wind that day by the avocado tree had told her the truth.

Adací looked up at the two sages. "I'm no longer going to try to be Pedí's friend. Our relationship is too complicated. My adoptive parents believe that being around him will put my life at risk, and I wonder if I might do the same to him. He's safe now, and I want him to stay that way."

Jurana and Gabro looked at each other and then hugged Adací.

CHAPTER SIXTY-TWO

Leap to the Ledge

"Grab the limb!"

The voice came from below Pedí.

Mirela's voice?

But how could that be?

Pedí had closed his eyes, knowing he had but seconds to live. He opened them and saw the little redhead standing on a ledge on the side of the cliff. She was five feet below him, reaching out with a fallen tree branch. "Uai, hold on to it, and I'll pull you."

Tears streamed down Mirela's face. Her arms and legs were bleeding. Somehow, she'd found a way to slide down from the top of the cliff onto the narrow rock shelf. Still holding out the limb, the little redhead's cries continued. "Grab it, Pedí! Grab it!"

But Pedí couldn't reach the branch. It was too short, and he feared he'd pull Mirela off even if he could. But he spotted another liana hanging along the side of the cliff. It was just a few feet from Mirela. Like the vine he held, it was hanging free, attached to branches high above but not to the ground.

"I can't reach the branch, Mirela, but see that liana vine? See if you can swing it out to me. If I can grab it, I might be able to swing over to the ledge."

Mirela understood his instructions and moved to the liana. But when she pushed the vine toward him, it swung only a few feet before returning to Mirela. She tried again—the same result. Using her small tree branch, she tried to push the liana out toward Pedí. But again, it was too far, her limb too short, and there was no way he could reach it.

"It's not going to work, Mirela," Pedí said, any fragment of hope vanishing. He needed to convince Mirela to leave him, get off the ledge, and back to safety. But he doubted the redhead would listen.

She was not defeated yet. "I'm going to shove the vine out to you. Get ready!" Mirela put a fork of her branch against the vine and then, holding the opposite end, moved back against the cliff face.

When Pedí realized what she was going to do, he told her to stop, but it was too late.

With a lunge, Mirela shoved the vine toward Pedí and let go of the branch. The tiny girl nearly flew off the ledge with the branch, only catching herself at the last moment.

Pedí watched Mirela, fearing for her safety, and ignored the swinging vine. At the last moment, he saw that the liana had swung within a foot of him but was moving back toward the cliff.

He had only this chance and could wait no longer. He grabbed at the swinging liana, caught hold of it, and then let go of the vine he was hanging from. Pedí and the new vine swung toward the cliff, but it loosened from its attachments in the trees and dropped five feet lower. Instead of landing on the ledge, Pedí slammed against the rock just below the narrow shelf. At the last second, Pedí let go of the liana, and his hands caught the lip of the ledge where Mirela stood.

But his hands were slipping. He couldn't hold on.

Tiny hands grasped his. It was Mirela. The added force of her small, freckled hands was minuscule, but through her touch, Pedí felt her indomitable spirit, and it gave him the power to stay suspended, at least for a few moments more.

Yet even so, his strength was gone, and he could not pull himself up. But when he felt Mirela grasp even tighter, he knew that if he fell, she would go with him—she wouldn't let go.

Pedí tried again. Digging his feet against the rock, he found a precarious toe hold and pushed against it. His hands slid forward, with Mirela still grasping at the tops of them. His fingers found a crack in the ledge. Holding it tight, he could lift a knee onto the ledge and roll onto the narrow shelf.

Pedí lay on his back, exhausted, battered, and bleeding. As he strove to catch his breath, his inhalations became more difficult when Mirela, also bruised and bleeding, jumped on top of him and hugged his heaving chest.

"You saved me," he whispered, not having enough air to speak louder.

Mirela responded only by lifting her head, looking into his face, and embracing him again with all her force.

They remained side by side on the narrow ledge, recovering. When they finally sat up, Pedí checked Mirela's injuries and his own. The lacerations and abrasions, although significant, would heal. One of his ribs, which had slammed against the stone, was very painful and made it hard to breathe. He assumed it was fractured.

When he examined his backpack, the tiny frogs were still moving in the sack and had somehow escaped being crushed. He asked Mirela how she'd gotten down to the ledge.

"The voices!" she responded. "Didn't you hear them?"

"No! What voices?"

"I think it was the trees. They told me what to do."

Pedí wondered what the little girl was talking about as she led him along the ledge to a narrow ravine.

"This is where the voices led me," Mirela said.

The tunnel-like ravine rose from the ledge and climbed sharply up to the clifftop. Over the centuries, water rushing off the cliff during storms must have created it. It was the only possible way to the ledge, and Mirela had somehow found it and then slid down it.

"The voices told me to bring the branch, too," the girl added.

Pedí shook his head, wondering what these voices were. Had the Moon Goddess, or the ancient Adací, guided Mirela?

The narrowness of the ravine aided them in the ascent back to the top. Although steep, they could press their hands and feet against the sides to support their weight. He sent Mirela ahead of him to catch her if she slipped, but she ascended much faster than he did. Once on top, they found the path off the cliffs and descended to the moaning valley.

Something was wrong!

When they reached the place where they'd left Elisada and Cashihua, the two women were gone. They had left a message. A hastily drawn arrow was scrawled in the dirt, pointing forward, further into the Rowai-ra Valley, telling the direction they had taken.

But why?

Another discovery explained the reason. Large, fresh boot prints were visible in the soft dirt of the trail. The tracks went in the same direction that Cashihua and Elisada had taken. Whoever made those tracks dragged their right foot with every step.

CHAPTER SIXTY-THREE

Mapondo

Pedí and Mirela walked further into Rowai-ra. The wailing wind blew constantly. It pushed at them, pulled at them, sucked courage, instilled fear. They moved slowly, both hurting—Mirela from her slide down to the ledge, Pedí from slamming into the cliff when he let go of the vine.

Without saying it, they knew who they were following. His boot prints showed on the ground from time to time—the right one, always dragging—the side where Mirela had plunged her sheep shear knife.

Fear told them to go in the opposite direction, to run out of the hellish canyon. But they had no choice, for they were also following the footsteps of Cashihua and Elisada—hoping to find them before the skeletal-faced man did.

But in the confines of the narrow chasm, they had little chance to succeed. The dark vertical walls rose up around them like the sides of a burial pit. They were passing deep into their own sepulcher.

Mirela held her new knife, the smaller one Lucas had given her, in her right hand. Her left hand held onto Pedí. Each of their steps was accompanied by the scratching of the Guasúpe beetle. Mirela had picked up the cage from where she'd left it and carried it in the red sling again. "Uai, we may need it," she had said. Pedí's protests did no good.

He expected to be ambushed at any moment and studied every tree, every rock, every crevice for signs of the man. When they skirted around a massive rockfall, the whoosh of the wind curled with them.

But another sound mixed in with the yowling gusts. Something or someone stirred behind a clump of trees.

Mirela raised her knife. Pedí picked up a rock.

A round, blunt nose poked out from the foliage.

A wild pig.

Pedí dropped the rock, and Mirela lowered her knife. The pig bolted across the trail and went into the small stream that gurgled through the canyon.

The two continued forward, but after passing around the next rockfall, what they saw and heard brought their feet to a stop. The canyon narrowed even more ahead of them, and the sound of the wind pitched higher, more unearthly than before. A waterfall cascaded down the side of the cliffs to their left.

To the right, the mouth of a large cave gaped at them.

Mirela let go of Pedí's hand and ran to the opening.

No, Mirela! The man could be hiding there. Pedí tried to scream the words, but his voice caught, and nothing came out.

He tore off to catch her.

At the entrance, Mirela glanced down, then entered the cavern. Something had caught her attention. Then Pedí saw it himself. Fresh hair—long Mapondo hair—was scattered on the ground.

A new fear seized him, the hollow-eyed man forgotten. The giant sloths would tear Mirela apart. Cashihua said there were babies, and Mirela was headed straight into their den—not afraid, just wanting to see the Mapondos.

Pedí looked to each side of the cavern as he ran into it. There were no Adací glyphs to protect them. He rushed forward and caught up to Mirela after she'd gone in about twenty feet.

"Stop!"

He whispered the command, not wanting to arouse the sloths.

Mirela halted, looked further into the cave, and then turned her head to look back at the opening. Her eyes opened wide, causing Pedí also to look behind.

The shadow of a man was at the mouth of the cavern. The light came from behind him, but his thin face and hollow eyes were visible. It was the skeletal man.

Mirela's sheep shear knife was in his bony hand.

"Now I have you. I'll slash the red hellcat's throat with her own blade."

He dragged his right foot forward, then stepped with the left. He winced when his weight shifted back to the injured side. He hesitated a moment, then repeated the process.

Pedí and Mirela backed away at the same slow pace, going further into the cavern. Their feet clinked through something scattered on the cave floor. Bones. Human bones. Among them were several skulls with masks attached—masks made from the front half of a human skull.

Deathheads wearing deathhead masks.

And twenty feet away, a skeletal man advanced on them. They were in the midst of hell.

A piercing cry filled the cavern from behind as if confirming Pedí's thought. He shook so hard he wondered if his bones would fall out of his flesh. Mirela clasped onto him.

The terrifying cry resounded again, like a human baby cry—but deeper pitched and much louder. Pedí and Mirela turned in unison.

A Mapondo stood thirty feet from them. It was huge—its mass blocking the way. A split in the rock above them let light into this part of the cavern, allowing them to see the three long, curved claws on its forepaws. Behind it, Pedí could make out the movement of two other giant sloths and some baby ones.

The giant Mapondo stretched its claws, ready to react to protect its young. It took one slow step toward them.

Pedí placed his hand over the pocket that held the living Adací's hair and pleaded to the ancient Adací to protect them. He needed her help to talk with this creature. But if he couldn't get a red deer to listen, how would he communicate with a Mapondo?

It advanced another step.

But the black forest cat had listened. Pedí bowed his head and spoke in the Idonata language.

The beast started to take another step but slowed, then stopped.

Pedí continued talking to the sloth but glanced back to the cave opening. The man was twenty-five feet away and dragged his foot forward again. The man or the creature would soon be upon them.

He searched both sides of the cave for options—some way to escape. Where they stood, the roof of the cave was wider than the floor, and the walls sloped gradually to meet the stone roof. At the juncture of wall and ceiling, there was an open space, a narrow shelf they could squeeze into.

Pedí lifted Mirela and put her halfway up the sloping cave wall. He pushed on her feet to assist her, and she scrambled into the narrow shelf.

He followed her up, but his fractured rib twisted and sent a spike of pain through his chest. He slid back down the wall but stopped when he grasped a handhold. He gritted his teeth and pulled himself into the shelf beside Mirela.

A temporary reprieve was all they'd gained. The man and the sloth knew where they were, and one of them would soon have them.

The hollow-eyed man dragged himself the remaining distance, scattering the bones on the ground, cursing with each step. Pedí's eyes had adjusted to the dim light, and he could see why the man walked as he did.

His right thigh was swollen. The trouser leg on that side had been cut off to make room. Pus escaped from the laceration where Mirela had plunged her knife. The thick yellow liquid rolled down his leg. His bony face twisted from the pain.

The man was so intent on catching them that he ignored the Mapondo. He didn't even seem to know it was there. He grimaced, white skeletal teeth showing through his black beard, then waved the sheep shear knife in the air, pointing it at Pedí and Mirela.

"You'll soon be dead."

"You're going to be dead yourself. There's a giant sloth in the cavern."

The man glanced to his left but just shook his head. The sloth was still not moving, standing just twenty feet away. Yet the man seemed unafraid, his only thoughts directed at revenge. Once again, he waved his knife at Pedí and Mirela.

They were trapped with no way to escape.

A click sounded to his side, and Pedí glanced toward Mirela. She had opened the beetle cage and pulled the giant insect out. Its six legs churned, and the sharp mandibles opened and closed. The beetle flapped its wing covers and slipped out of her hand. It flew to a spot on the sloping wall five feet below. Mirela reached down to grab it.

"Stop, Mirela." Pedí tried to catch her but was too late.

She lost her balance and slid face-first down the cave wall, stopping at the side of the beetle. She grabbed its middle section with her right hand and held it tight. The huge insect opened and closed its jaws but could not bite her.

Mirela's left hand and arm stretched below her and had found a projection to halt her descent. But that hand was now within reach of their pursuer. The worst possible scenarios flashed through Pedí's mind. Mirela would be cut in pieces. He reached for her, but the man was quicker.

"Now you die, red cur." The evil man grabbed and then jerked Mirela's hand, pulling her toward him.

Instead of resisting, the girl pushed off with her feet and used the force of his pull to fling herself directly at him. It caught him by surprise as Mirela landed on the man's chest and shoved the snapping beetle into his face. He screamed and stepped back, hurling Mirela to the cave floor. Her knees cracked against its hard surface. The sheep shear knife fell from the man's hand and clattered on the ground near her.

The beetle was fastened with one mandible piercing the bridge of his nose, the other sinking deep into his left eye. The skeleton-like man cursed as he grabbed the insect with both hands and wrenched it off.

The jaws did not open and tore out a large chunk of tissue from his eye and nose. Blood flowed, blinding the man.

He threw the beetle at Mirela. It struck the ground and rolled along the cave floor.

Pedí slid feet first down the slope. When he hit the ground, he heard a new sound, a piercing, more enraged cry from the Mapondo. The sloth was on the move again. Although it came at a shuffling pace, it was several feet closer and was not going to stop.

Mirela picked up her sheep shear knife from the ground and tried to get up, but her scraped and bleeding knees buckled under her. Pedí gathered her in his arms and fled toward the cave opening. They burst into the light at the end of the cavern.

Cashihua's raised voice called out to them from the opposite side of the canyon. She and Elisada were against the cliff wall near the waterfall. Somehow, they had stayed safe.

Pedí raced across with Mirela. "We have to get out of the canyon now! The Mapondo is coming!"

They all glanced back at the cave as the bony man stumbled out of it, blood dripping down his face. The sloth was six feet behind, moving at the same speed as the injured wretch, who still dragged his foot. Instead of continuing, the man picked up a large rock. He threw it at the oncoming sloth. It bounced off its chest but did not slow it down. The creature was now right by him.

The Mapondo swiped its long, curved claws at the man. It cut him in half, right through the middle.

Pedí and the others stood wide-eyed and motionless before fleeing. Pedí carried Mirela, and they went down and out of the valley as fast as their injured bodies would let them.

CHAPTER SIXTY-FOUR

Celebration at the Santol Mansion

Adací sat next to her father in their carriage. They were on their way to the Santol family mansion. Father had insisted on escorting her. The suit coat he wore was her favorite, the one with the largest lapels. He could be a sharp dresser, though most of the time, Father preferred to be in his work clothes. It was the same with Adací.

Tavi drove them and stopped the horses in front of the elegant house. Father helped Adací out and walked with her to the entry. "I'll return with your mother to join the celebration in an hour or so."

Adací nodded and smiled. She had made her adoptive parents happy with her decision to come to Tatena Santol's birthday party. She was trying hard to honor their wishes.

Even so, getting invited to a rich girl's Coming of Age had been a big surprise. Weren't they all afraid she'd throw another glass of wine into somebody's face? Adací had assumed that she would never be a part of New Losobon's high society—that she would continue to disappoint her parents.

But now, their hopes for her had never been greater.

The Santol family owned one of the largest sugar cane plantations in the valley. All the wealthy and prominent would be here. And because Adací had been invited, Marina and Sergol were included. By tradition, at a Coming of Age, the young people would gather first for their festivities, and then the parents would join them later.

The invitation had to be because of Larada. Her best friend must have begged Tatena to include Adací. That assumption was confirmed when she received a second message by courier on the same day the invitation arrived. This one was from Bertol, begging her to attend and to let him be her friend. He wouldn't have known that Adací had been invited unless it was his sister's doing.

Bertol's letter had made Marina and Sergol the most excited. "This is your big chance," they had said. "We knew Bertol still liked you, even though you wouldn't believe us."

Despite Adací's past confrontations with Larada's twin, Bertol had always been her parents' first choice for her. Adací guessed their reasons. Bertol's parents already knew that Adací was adopted, and Bertol was familiar with Adací's strange behaviors and unusual dreams. He and his parents would be more likely to accept the silver hair and moon tattoo when they found out about them.

But her parent's excitement only increased Adací's worries. It was her first public outing since her accident. What would Bertol and the others think and say about her?

But if she was accepted into New Losobon's high society, she might finally get over her thoughts about Pedí. Despite her determination to end any hopes of a friendship with Pedí, the young healer remained her greatest obstacle to finding lasting happiness. On her last visit to the Sanctuary, she talked to Gabro and Jurana about it.

"If you're worried about Pedí and what he thinks of you," Gabro said, "we'll tell him everything when he returns. He'll understand that you didn't want to hurt him, that you wanted to be his friend, but that it's no longer possible."

"Would that help?" Jurana asked.

"Would you be able to be at peace?" Gabro added.

"I think so," Adací had responded.

She didn't really think so, but wasn't it time for her to quit being selfish? Pedí would come back famous. She needed to free him from herself and all her faults, and let him move ahead without her getting in the way. And most important, she needed to keep him safe. Her parents were correct in wanting to keep the two of them apart.

Adací had only hurt Pedí and brought him sadness. Her obsession with him, her worries, had done the same to her. It was only sadness he had brought her. It was time to end all thoughts of Pedí and remember that she existed without him. Adací would start a new life, and going to this party with Bertol and other young people would bring the happiness back.

Adací glanced a final time at her father, who was climbing into their carriage, and then she turned to face the Santol house—to face her new future. A servant swung open the front door, and Adací was admitted to the festivities. Music of stringed instruments, faint from the outside, now greeted her ears in full splendor. She hesitated in the anteroom when she sensed the bustle inside the house. Guests were already dancing in the spacious reception hall, and voices, all talking at once, mixed with the music and created a bee-like hum.

Adací stepped forward, her blue dress swishing across the polished marble tile. Heila had somehow managed to get the black pond mud out of it.

Inside the hall, the first person she recognized was Bertol. He stood on the other side of the room. She looked for Larada and saw her talking with Chando near the musician's stand. When she glanced back at Bertol, his eyes were locked on hers, and he took a step in her direction.

Just then, a girl Adací had met at one of the parties Larada had taken her to came toward her. She hugged Adací on both sides and kissed her cheeks. "Welcome back, friend," the girl said. "I'm glad to see you looking so well." Another girl took her place with the same formal hugs, kisses, and welcome. Then another. A line formed with all the young women greeting Adací. She had never received so many embraces.

All the while, Bertol was weaving his way toward her, past groups of people talking, past those dancing in the middle of the room, and around the last few giving her hugs. The black jacket he wore accentuated his dark, handsome face.

"Will you dance with me?" he asked with an extended hand. Adací looked into his eyes and nodded. It was time to end her battle with this good-looking boy.

"I worried you wouldn't come," Bertol said as they swirled among the other dancers. "But now I couldn't be happier." His voice was calm and sincere.

Adací struggled to answer. Bertol seemed transformed, not the proud Bertol she had once doubted. She also remembered that he had gone with Larada to Niala's house and personally offered to help the Mattaçores girl and her family. Larada said he had been there several times.

"Thank you for being so nice to Niala." Adací smiled at Bertol as she said it. "Larada said you've made her very happy."

"I like her, but I especially like you. You're the most beautiful girl at this party."

Adací's cheeks must be bright red. Bertol did excel at making compliments, and this time, there was no added reproach to undo the flattery.

When the musicians paused, and her first dance with Bertol ended, Larada found them. She had temporarily escaped from Chando. She pulled Adací aside and nodded toward her brother. "I'll give her back to you in a minute."

After giving Adací a giant hug, Larada whispered in her ear. "It makes me happy to see you and Bertol together and not fighting."

"It is nice," Adací whispered back.

Larada smiled but then furrowed her brow. "Any dreams about Chando?"

Adací shook her head and lied. "No, nothing."

"Don't quit trying. Edero and I still believe you're going to save us. He was invited to come today, but he chose not to. He didn't want a confrontation with Chando so close to my Coming of Age."

Adací wondered if she should tell Larada the truth, that she'd had a dream about Chando—a nightmare she prayed would never come true.

But that vision had nothing to do with rescuing Larada and Edero. She couldn't take away their last hope.

The celebration continued, and despite her sadness over Larada's predicament, each dance with Bertol or reunion with her friends and acquaintances was a pleasant one.

Adací was back—back to the society where her real life was supposed to be. She wasn't meant to be a jungle girl or to work with the healer, after all. No one mentioned the crazy things she'd done, and her friends complimented her and even told her how incredible she looked.

One girl asked about her skin. "How do you make your face look so radiant? You have no blemishes. Your skin is perfect."

Instead of being pleased, Adací could only see the scrum on her face. If it hadn't been for Pedí, she would be a deformed witch and wouldn't even be at this celebration. No one would want her.

A tear escaped and rolled down her cheek.

"Are you okay?" the girl asked.

Adací brushed the tear off. "It's nothing."

Stupid Adací. You brushed Pedí away. Don't let him make you sad again.

Adací went outside and sat by herself. The night would have been ruined if Bertol hadn't saved it. He found her, talked with her, danced with her, and smiled at her. He told her she was his favorite girlfriend.

Maybe one day soon, she could tell him he was her favorite as well.

She just wasn't quite ready to say those words.

CHAPTER SIXTY-FIVE

Leaving the Jungle

The dugout canoe cut through the black waters of the Ipixuna River. Pedí's broken rib stung with each stroke of the paddle. He and his companions were nearly back to the village. Despite his injuries, he had carried Mirela most of the way out of Rowai-ra Valley.

She had insisted on walking the last mile. Her knees, although bruised and swollen, were not fractured. She had limped along, holding onto Pedí's hand.

Darkness was setting in when the canoe scraped onto the shore. A fire burned on the bank. A wind spirit effigy was stuck to a post by the side of the flames. Orange light reflected off the figure's wooden mask, and the arms and legs fashioned from bark. Jabuti and Payaku sat by the fire, feeding it small sticks.

They rushed to the boat. Payaku gathered Cashihua in his arms.

"We thought you were dead," Jabuti said. "Now, we celebrate!"

The entire village welcomed the travelers inside a large communal hut. Using their native tongue, Cashihua told the story of their adventures. Mirela became an instant heroine when the villagers heard how she'd rescued Pedí from falling into the chasm and then again when she stuck the Guasúpe beetle in the skeletal man's face.

Mirela had to show every cut, scrape, and bruise. She even had to lift up the back of her blouse so they could see the injuries on her back from sliding down the cliff. The men, women, and children shouted approval with each wound she demonstrated.

They gave her a new name, Guasúpe Girl.

When the stories were finished, Jabuti shouted, "Time for the warana dance."

Pedí covered his ears with his hands. He was exhausted and in pain, and it was the last thing he wanted to hear. Warana seeds were a powerful stimulant. Jungle villages held annual warana festivals where men and women would take enough of the drug to stay awake dancing for three straight days and nights. Jabuti said they'd use a smaller amount for today's celebration, just enough to keep them awake and dancing till morning.

In a large wooden bowl, Jabuti crushed the warana seeds into a paste using a club-like stick as a pestle. Each man and woman of the village came to the bowl and took a measured amount of the mashed seeds using the same small spoon. Each child did the same, using a smaller spoon. Only the youngest toddlers were exempt.

"Now it's your turn," Jabuti said to Pedí.

Pedí hesitated but felt he could not refuse to celebrate with Jabuti and the villagers who had been so good to them. He took a spoonful.

Mirela was right behind him and reached for the smaller spoon.

Pedí caught her wrist. "Maybe you shouldn't. You're injured, and it will keep you awake all night."

The children of Kuloduru began chanting, "Guasúpe Girl must dance with us. Guasúpe Girl must dance with us."

Mirela looked up at Pedí, and he knew he couldn't refuse her. He released her hand, and she took a dose of the paste.

Anton chose not to take the warana because of his ankle injury, knowing he couldn't dance. Elisada also refused but said she and Anton would stay up and watch all night.

Hollow log drums were brought to the open space between the village huts. Men pounded out rhythmic music. A bonfire shone onto the faces of the men, women, and children as they formed dancing lines, then circles, then lines again. Pedí kept making the wrong moves, but Mirela learned the steps and performed each dance despite her injured knees.

The children had wrapped tufts of grass into small wreaths and tied them onto their hair. Mirela did the same. Instead of tiring, the wiry seven-year-old became more energetic and jumped higher and higher as the night wore on. The warana masked her pain. She turned cartwheels and made up dance moves. With each new antic, the villagers cheered.

Pedí had never felt more fatigued, and his broken rib stung whenever he took a deep breath, but the effect of the warana worked inside him and prevented any sleep. He hated the feeling.

Two pretty teenage girls took Pedí's hands and began dancing on each side of him. Sweat poured from his forehead into his eyes and dripped off his face to the ground. The girls giggled and smiled at him, worsening his distress.

Just as the morning was breaking, the effects of the drug wore off. Pedí felt a drain open, and the last of his energy poured onto the hard-packed earth.

Mirela still danced in her wild fashion until she fell after leaping over a log drum. She got back on her feet, looked at Pedí with a strange stare, then collapsed to the ground, fast asleep.

That ended the warana party. After a drum roll, the villagers shouted out a final hurrah. They all stumbled to their thatched huts. Pedí gathered up Mirela and carried her to a hammock, then rolled into the one strung next to hers and slept.

They stayed in the hammocks all that day and through that night, getting up only briefly to drink water and eat a little food.

The following morning, Jabuti extracted the toxin from the orange frogs. He secured the tiny creatures between soft leaves and rubbed the ends of little flat sticks into the secretions on the frog's backs. The toxin dried and adhered to the wood.

Jabuti held up his index finger. "It will stay good for one year."

Pedí put the sticks in a glass jar to transport them home. Jabuti let the frogs go free into a tree with lots of air plants near the village. He hoped they would multiply so Pedí could return for more of their toxin in the future.

New rowers with a balsa raft were hired for the downriver trip to Ipixuna. Pedí inspected the tightly bound cotton bags that were loaded onto the raft. They were filled with medicinal roots and herbs he and Anton had collected with Jabuti. He thought they had everything ready, but Jabuti came to the boat with another bundle.

"Warana seeds," he said, pointing to the bag. "You can have a big party when you get back home."

Never again would Pedí touch or use warana. But he couldn't offend Jabuti, so he put the bag on the raft with the others. He'd keep it but never use it.

They said their difficult goodbyes to Cashihua, Payaku, and Jabuti. They got onto the raft and began the long journey home— first down river to Ipixuna, then up the trail into the mountains toward Itatu.

One night, around the campfire, Pedí and Mirela sat opposite. Her usual spot was at his side. It gave Elisada a chance to lean and whisper to Pedí. "Does Mirela know you're going back to New Losobon? What will she do when you go without her?"

Pedí glanced at Mirela. Her jaw had dropped. She must have heard.

The redhead looked at Pedí, then Elisada, then Anton, then back at Pedí. Her lower lip quivered. "I'm going with you, aren't I?"

Pedí had no words to express the heartache he would feel when separated from Mirela. What could he say to soften the blow to her? "I love you, Mirela. My heart will break to leave you, but I'm a young man. I have no—"

"I'll run away after you!" Mirela screamed across the campfire and interrupted him. She pulled out her sheep shear knife and waved it in the air. "Nobody can stop me!"

Elisada got up, went to Mirela, and hugged her despite the waving knife. "I'm sorry you heard me. But we need to talk about this."

"No! No talk!" Mirela said. Tears were now streaming down her face. "I'm going with Pedí."

Pedí began crying himself. He didn't know what to tell her.

Anton cleared his throat. "Is there anyone in New Losobon who could take her in? Perhaps someone that would allow you to see each other often?"

My mama! Pedí thought, then said it out loud. "Mama will adopt her!"

Mirela broke free from Elisada's hug and leaped across the small fire into Pedí's arms. "Take me with you to live with you and your mama. Don't leave me."

Pedí was afraid to believe it. Was this miracle possible? "Will Luco allow this?" Pedí asked. "I couldn't do it without his permission."

"Of course he will," Anton said.

"This is perfect." Elisada was beaming. "Mirela needs to be with you."

Anton and Elisada had stood and gone to each other. They whispered back and forth, then both nodded.

"It's agreed," Anton said. "We're taking you back to New Losobon in our wagon. The little cart you brought will hardly hold all these roots and herbs you collected."

"But you've already done so much to help," Pedí protested.

"Please let us do this last thank you," Elisada said. "We've always wanted to see New Losobon, and this will be our chance."

"This way, we can make sure Mirela is settled in with your mama before we return to Itatu," Anton said. "If there's any problem, she can come back with—"

"I won't come back!" Mirela interrupted and frowned.

"Adoption is a big thing, Mirela," Pedí said. "Anton and Elisada are making it possible. We'll work it out, but you need to be patient."

"I will try." Mirela's frown remained. "But you can't leave me."

"I won't."

Mirela clung tighter than ever to Pedí for the rest of the trip. As they rode together in the saddle, they made plans. "I'll no longer live at the

Sanctuary, and I'll come home every night after work to be with you and Mama."

Mirela rode in front and tilted her head back. "Can I go to work with you?"

"Not at first."

Pedí wanted to keep Mirela a secret. He was unsure what to expect from the captain and those after his nanimoha. If they knew about Mirela, they might kidnap her and use her as leverage to force him to surrender his new cure, just as the skeletal-faced man had tried to do.

"In New Losobon, some people are unkind," he told her. "They're not always nice to people with red hair or Idonata boys like me."

Mirela reached down to her boot and pulled out the sheep shear knife. "Uai, I'll scare them off with this."

Pedí just learned another reason to keep Mirela hidden for a while. He and his mama would have some training to do. "Maybe we can learn other ways besides knives to deal with bad people and bullies."

When they reached Itatu, all the arrangements were made. Luco seemed relieved to have someone taking care of Mirela. Anton and Elisada's wagon was loaded with the herbs and roots collected in the jungles, and they were off to New Losobon.

CHAPTER SIXTY-SIX

Pedí is Back

Adací and Larada sat on each side of Pitrassa Mendin, Larada's mother. Bertol was on a chair across from them. They were at the long dining room table inside the beautiful Mendin home. Even without settings, the table was elegant with its inlaid wood. Three chandeliers hung from the domed ceiling, spaced evenly along its length.

Adací was there to help finalize plans for Larada and Bertol's Coming of Age celebration. Their eighteenth birthday was tomorrow, and the Mendins wanted this party to be even more magnificent than the one held for Tatena Santol the previous month. They had decided to start the activities in the early afternoon with a luncheon, followed by games for all the younger guests. Then, when the parents arrived at night, they'd have a huge banquet followed by a dance.

Larada's mother suggested games for the young men and women. "Triumph is fun, and four can play. We've borrowed extra tables and chairs, but most will just seat four people. What other games will work with that arrangement?"

"How about Sapo?" Larada asked. "It's a silly game, yet everybody likes it."

"But we only have one Sapo board, and it's damaged," Bertol added.

"I'll have a carpenter make some new ones," Pitrassa said.

"How about First is Last?" Adací asked.

"That would be a good one," Larada agreed.

Bertol nodded. "It's interesting when the winner actually loses."

"Our stable hands taught me how to play a new game with playing cards," Adací said, making dealing motions with her hands. "It's exciting. We bet coins, but they end up with all of mine every time."

"I'm not sure any gambling game is a good idea," Pitrassa said. "Whatever you do, don't let the young men start arm wrestling. It will deteriorate into a betting frenzy and take all afternoon."

The girls nodded in agreement.

At that point, Pitrassa excused herself to check on Larada's younger sisters.

"We need time for some girl talk," Larada told her brother. "Come back in a few minutes."

Bertol frowned but left the room.

Larada scooted closer to Adací. "Edero is coming. I insisted, and my parents agreed."

"That's wonderful!" Adací tried to smile when she said those words, but since she'd failed to find a way to stop Larada's marriage to Chando, what difference did it make if Edero came or not? Larada's father would still announce her engagement to the captain's son at the end of the celebration.

"Edero knows how awkward it will be with Chando lording over me. But he has not given up and believes you'll dream something to drive the beast away."

"I'm trying," Adací said. "I put the jade on every night. Mother let me keep the stones after I showed them to Jurana and Gabro."

"So, you must be dreaming a lot. Aren't some of the visions about how to rescue me from Chando?"

Adací shook her head. The only vision of Chando was him chasing Adací through the forest. It repeated itself every night. But no dream came that would help Larada escape from the promised marriage.

One night, the Blue Dragonfly showed up in that nightmare. It was curious. In the vision, the dragonfly flew ahead of Adací on the trail as she tried to escape from Chando. She hoped the beautiful creature would save her, but it disappeared, and she fled alone from Chando.

Adací wondered how to interpret the appearance of the Blue Dragonfly. She still assumed no real ones were left, so what could the dream mean?

Adací had considered putting the jade away and never using the stones again so the Chando nightmare would end. But she couldn't stop trying to save her best friend. So, the green stones went onto her braid each night.

Larada must have been watching Adací's face and guessed at her thoughts. "I think you already dreamed something about Chando and are waiting to surprise us."

Adací shook her head again but knew she was a lousy liar. Larada always saw right through it. But Adací was not going to tell Larada about the Chando dream. It would not be the rescue Larada wanted and would destroy the last of her hopes.

"I'll be patient," her trusting friend said. "You can tell me about your dreams when you're ready. I know you will find a way to save us."

That persistent faith only made Adací's failure more troubling.

After that, the two girls sat in silence, each deep in their thoughts. Larada surprised Adací when she leaned toward her and said something she hadn't expected.

"Did you know that Pedí is back?"

Those were words Adací had waited to hear, pleaded to hear, but now the words seemed too late and not so important anymore. Her decision to no longer seek his friendship protected him. Her thinking and worrying about Pedí had stopped.

But if that were true, why were her breaths so deep and fast—much too fast? It was making her dizzy.

"Are you all right?" Larada grasped Adací's arm.

Adací put her hand over her mouth to try to slow her breathing. "I have to see him."

Larada shook her head.

"But I need to tell him—"

"No. You said you were not going to worry about him anymore."

"I know, but—"

"Jurana and Gabro will tell him everything that happened, even your fall from the horse."

"Yes, but will they—"

"They'll say that you will always consider him a friend, but why you can't see him anymore. They'll even tell him about Bertol."

Adací could not think of any more excuses. Larada had covered them all. Of course, Jurana and Gabro would explain it to Pedí much better than she would. Her regular visits to the Sanctuary still took place every seven days.

Except for last week.

Mother needed her that day, so Adací sent the sages a message that she wouldn't be there. Strangely, they never wrote back, but they're awfully busy.

She pictured the two of them talking to Pedí, showing him where Adací had sat on the same bench he used to sit on. They'd tell him everything as they'd promised.

Would he forgive her for hurting him?

Maybe he could still teach her how to be a healer, and she could work with him.

No, stupid girl.

She couldn't be around Pedí anymore.

She was Bertol's girlfriend now. Since Tatena's party, they had seen each other regularly. Her parents, his parents, and all their friends expected them to marry one day. Although not formally planned yet, she expected her parents would announce their engagement at her Coming of Age in six months.

She was finally happy, and at least once a day, Adací made sure to tell herself that she was. Her breathing slowed enough to get a whole sentence out. "I get confused just hearing Pedí's name."

"This is what I feared—that you'd be tempted to run to Pedí and throw away your future with my brother the minute the healer returned."

"I won't!" Adací pounded her fist on the table as she said it.

CHAPTER SIXTY-SEVEN

Walking Home

Pedí had been back from the jungles for over a week. Pedí's mother had welcomed Mirela into her home, and Anton and Elisada had already returned to Itatu. Pedí's night and evening duties at the infirmary were much less now, so he moved back home to be with Mirela and his mother almost every night. No one questioned his reasons. No one knew about the little redhead.

Today, after finishing with his patients, he went to the laboratory to experiment again with the herbs and roots he'd brought home from the jungles. He wanted to make a better pain elixir to help Doctor Arias with his arthritis. He'd given his mentor all of the orange frog sticks as soon as he returned. But the doctor took just one, then returned the rest to Pedí.

"I want you to use them for others in severe pain," the doctor had said. "There are many patients who need them more than me."

Doctor Arias had held up his one little stick. "I'll save this for a bad day."

Pedí went to the storage room and retrieved the willow bark he'd brought home from Kuloduru. Jabuti said it worked well for joint pain. Pedí boiled the bark and strained the batch. He'd take some himself when it cooled to make sure it didn't cause any side effects. Then he could let Doctor Arias try it tomorrow.

He picked up the bag of leftover willow bark and returned it to storage. When he got back to the laboratory, he sampled his new concoction, sealed the lid so it would stay good until tomorrow, and then peeked out the back door. His shoulders tightened but then relaxed. No one was there for once.

Crina and Misha had been unbearable since he got back. The two girls finished their work before him, then hovered outside the back of the lab, waiting to pester him the minute he stepped out the door.

Today, he'd escape before they showed up.

Calling on his forest boy skills, he opened, went out, and closed the door behind him without a sound. He scanned the orchard. No one moved. He was safe.

But two steps from the door, the girls jumped out of the bushes that grew up against the rear of the building. He fell over backward.

Crina and Misha couldn't stop laughing. They each took an arm and helped him up.

"We're walking you home today." Crina's eyelashes flashed up and down with each word.

"We need a longer talk." Misha squeezed his arm.

The walk to his house was as painful as he imagined. The girls competed to dominate the conversation. He only stammered out a few disjointed responses. He thought his stuttering had stopped when he returned from Itatu and the jungles.

It hadn't.

Crina and Misha brought out the worst in him.

At least it confirmed he'd been correct in refusing to speak at the sage's schools and in the assembly hall. Everyone wanted to hear his story of stopping the epidemic in Itatu. But the praise and accolades he'd received on arriving home had embarrassed him. He didn't want the attention, and now he knew that not a single word would have made it out of his mouth if he had tried to speak in front of so many people. Doctor Arias had gone to the schools and had spoken to a gathering at the assembly hall in his place.

As they walked, the two girls continued to badger him. They took great pleasure in pretending to like him.

He ignored their words as much as he could, but when they talked about Adací, the stabs to the heart started. It was as if they'd stolen Mirela's sheep shear knife and plunged it repeatedly into his chest. Fortunately, his heart was mostly gone, his insides hollow, or they might have done some real damage. But just the same, each new revelation about Adací struck another blow to him. He thought he was over her.

"We met Adací," Crina said. "She might have liked you a little but promptly forgot you when you left."

"After her accident," Misha waved her arms as she talked, "Adací became the close friend of one of the richest boys in New Losobon. You were never important to her."

"Accident?" It was one of the few words Pedí got out without a stutter. "Is she—"

"She's fine now. She fell off a horse and hit her head."

"Oh."

He was going to ask for more details but decided to say no more. At least Adací was better, they said. The rich boy they mentioned had to be none other than Bertol Mendin.

"Adací didn't care about you." Misha still waved her arms. "But we do."

"We've made a decision." Crina twisted her head in front of him so he was forced to see her blinking eyelashes. "You're seventeen and a half and still not dating anyone. It's time to get serious about a girl."

Pedí shook his head, but it didn't stop them.

"We want you to pick one of us as your sweetheart." Misha stopped waving her hands and grabbed his arm again. "Then we'll quit fighting over you."

Crina grabbed his other arm. Pedí wondered if they were going to pull him apart.

"We both turn eighteen in less than a year. So, whoever you pick will help you learn not to be so shy. Then you'll be ready to get engaged when we have our Coming of Age."

Please leave me alone, he wanted to shout, but when he opened his mouth, nothing came out.

Both girls giggled. "You can take some time. We'll talk to you each day until you decide."

They had arrived at his mother's little shack, and he was able to break away. He was gasping for air by the time he climbed the wooden steps to his home.

He needed someone to talk with besides these girls.

Mirela met him at the door. "Let's go frog hunting in the forest. Mama wants to come, too."

Pedí's mother was right behind Mirela, smiling. The little redhead had called her mama the moment the two of them met. It had instantly bonded them.

Going into the forest was just what Pedí needed to try and forget Crina and Misha, and even more so, Adací. His Itatu friend was a natural at catching frogs and snakes. She soaked in everything Pedí taught her about wild things. She was even more intent than him on finding a giant Blue Dragonfly. Mirela thrilled at every dragonfly they saw, only to hang her head in disappointment when it wasn't a giant blue one.

Before they left for the forest, Pedí thought of his good friends, Jurana and Gabro. He missed them. When he returned from the jungles, they were not home. They had gone to visit their children in the west of New Losobon Valley and would not be back for some time.

CHAPTER SIXTY-EIGHT

Sara is Sick

It was the morning of Larada and Bertol's celebration. Adací had been invited to eat breakfast with the Mendin family. She would stay after the meal and help get everything ready before guests arrived for the opening luncheon.

Larada met her at the main door, and the two girls talked as they went toward the dining room. When they passed through the reception hall, they had to dodge servants running this way and that with decorations and flowers.

Larada leaned close. The tone of her plea was like the last word of a prisoner sentenced to the gallows.

"Any dream about Chando?"

Adací shook her head.

It was another lie. The Chando nightmare kept recurring. Adací wanted it to stop but understood now that she couldn't force her dreams to do her will. They showed what might happen, allowing her to try and change the outcome in some cases but not others. But what was she supposed to do to alter the Chando nightmare? She didn't know. And that horrible vision had nothing to do with rescuing Larada.

Adací had failed her best friend. "I'm so sorry."

Larada made a fist. That was usually Adací's role. Her gentle friend was trying to find courage. "Your vision about Pedí in the jungles came while you were awake. You may still be inspired today to show us what to do."

Adací didn't know what to say. She couldn't even find a comforting word. She had no courage and no hope left.

Larada must have seen the look of defeat on Adací's face. "Oh, I see you've given up. I guess I'll make a marriage to Chando work somehow."

"No, no, no." The thought of Larada having to live with that fiend was too much for Adací. "I'll find a way!"

Larada smiled as if she'd planned her words to make Adací believe in herself. "I know you will. Edero believes it, too."

Adací wanted to fly away like a bird, as far and as fast as she could. She had said the confident words but was ashamed to lie to her best friend.

The young women joined Larada's parents and two younger sisters at the dining table. Susana was thirteen, and Sara was ten. The girls already had their hair curled and styled for the party. They were going to get to watch the celebration.

Bertol came into the room and helped Adací take a seat. He sat next to her with a big smile on his face.

As they ate, Susana, not Sara, dominated the conversation. This was odd as Sara was the noisy one. The youngest sister often followed closely behind Larada and Adací when they were together, and she never stopped talking.

"Our Little Dimples is quiet today," Pitrassa Mendin said. "Did you run out of things to say?"

Sara looked up. Her constant smile and the dimples that gave her the nickname were gone. Her posture was rigid, like a statue, as if any movement caused pain.

"What's the matter, dear?"

Sara didn't respond.

"You can't tell us?"

"I don't want to tell you," Sara said through gritted teeth. "You might not let me watch the party."

"Why wouldn't I let you watch?"

Sara gagged and grabbed her side. Alstir and Pitrassa Mendin got out of their seats and went to her.

"My tummy hurts, Mama. Bad!"

Her father picked her up and carried her to a sofa at the side of the dining hall. Her mother knelt beside her and asked where it hurt.

Sara pointed to her left side. "And it burns when I pee-pee, like last time."

Alstir Mendin motioned to a servant. "Take our fastest carriage and bring Doctor Arias."

Adací watched Sara moan and writhe on the sofa. Bertol stood next to Adací and held her hand. It was a long wait having to watch Little Dimples suffer so much.

The dining hall door finally opened and closed. But it was not Doctor Arias.

Pedí walked in.

Adací gasped. She tried to pull her hand out of Bertol's, but he tightened his grasp. Pedí glanced her way, winced, and then clutched at a bulging pocket on the front of his shirt. He turned his head to avoid looking at her. Obviously, she was the last person on earth he wanted to see.

Adací feared she might get this type of reaction from Pedí when he finally returned. But she had trusted that once he visited with Jurana and Gabro, he would at least be kind to her, maybe even thank her for going after him on the horse. She had hoped he would understand why she couldn't be his friend, hoped that he would still like her a little.

She wanted to rush to his side and ask his forgiveness, but this was not the time. Pedí was not here for her. He needed to attend to Sara and not be bothered by a hysterical girl.

Adací held back tears as she listened to Larada's father question Pedí.

"Why are you here and not Doctor Arias?"

"He sent me with the nanimoha, the potion I took to Itatu. We still have one bottle left. Doctor Arias remembered your little girl being ill last year with a fever and pain in her kidneys and bladder. He could only treat her with extra fluids and wait to see if the illness resolved. Fortunately, Sara got better last time, but that doesn't always happen. Illness with a fever is what we call infection. I believe that infections are caused by invisible creatures that attack our bodies. My nanimoha sometimes kills the creatures. At least, that's what I think happens."

Pedí whispered to Sara as he examined her. When he pushed on the left side of her abdomen, she jerked and cried out.

"Please don't let him hurt me, Mama."

"I'm sorry," Pedí said. "I'll not have to push again."

He put his hand on her forehead. "She has a fever."

"She said it burns to pee-pee," Pitrassa said.

Pedí asked Pitrassa Mendin to help Sara urinate into a bowl. Servants carried the child to a dressing room. Adací saw the blood mixed with urine in the basin when Pitrassa came out and handed it to Pedí.

"There's blood," Pitrassa said.

"From her fever and these signs, it's likely your little one has another infection, but she may also have a kidney stone. The pain and the blood suggest it. People who have had past infections in the kidneys sometimes get them."

"Is there danger?" Pitrassa asked.

"Kidney stones and kidney infections don't combine well. Sometimes, the infection spreads to the whole body."

"And then?" she asked.

Pedí didn't answer. Adací guessed it must be bad.

Sara cried out as they brought her back and placed her on the sofa. "Oh, Mama, it hurts so bad, so bad." She bent over and vomited. Servants rushed forward to help. Pedí gently supported and patted her back while the mess was cleaned.

Adací remembered the same kindness Pedí showed at Poor Man's Field with the Itatu girl. Working side by side with him that day had been an experience she'd never forget. She had dreamed of working with him in the future. Now, that prospect was a splintered, cracked, and worthless illusion.

"I suggest we give Sara my nanimoha," Pedí said.

"We heard what your potion did for the people of Itatu," Pitrassa Mendin said. "Will it work the same for Sara's illness?"

"I've never used it for kidney infections, but I think it will work. However, I feel obligated to tell you that the nanimoha potion is made from a poisonous mushroom."

"Is it safe?" Alstir Mendin asked.

"I've given it to hundreds of people, including many children. It has been safe as long as it is mixed right and given in the correct dosage."

"Then do it quickly!" Sara's father pleaded.

"I'll need to prepare it over a stove."

Alstir Mendin directed his servants, and they led Pedí to the kitchens.

Adscí wanted to go with him. She remembered how carefully Pedí had prepared the potion at Poor Man's Field. She could help him now.

But Bertol was still at her side. He would be angry if she followed Pedí.

When Pedí returned, he poured his potion back and forth between two cups to cool it. He placed the cups on the table and then searched through his pack.

He probably needed her assistance. Adscí stepped toward him. Bertol was no longer holding her hand, but he reached for it to stop her. Adscí twisted away from him and went to the healer.

"Hello, Pedí. It's so good to see you. May I help?"

He had taken a glass container out of his pack. It was filled with short, flat sticks. He hesitated when Adscí spoke, put one hand over the pocket on his chest again, and then closed his eyes. He shook his head and said not a word. He didn't even turn to look at her.

Pedí picked up and swirled the cup of nanimoha potion, checking to see if it had cooled. He acted as if Adscí wasn't even there.

She felt a hand on her arm and glanced to see Bertol. He gently pulled her away, and she followed him, her feet dragging. If there had not been a sick girl in the room, someone who needed everyone's strength, Adscí would have collapsed on the floor. She never imagined rejection could hurt so much. She bit her lip to hold in the emotions and not start crying.

With Pitrassa Mendin helping, Pedí sat Sara up and got her to take his nanimoha drop by drop every five minutes. Twice, Adscí started toward him again. Maybe he'd still let her help? But Bertol's tight grip on her arm only allowed her to shift her feet. She stayed where she was.

Sara cried out in pain several times but didn't vomit again. When the potion was all in, Pedí told Pitrassa Mendin to keep giving her small sips of water every few minutes.

"Is there anything you can give her to relieve her pain?" Sara's mother asked.

Pedí's response surprised Adací.

"I brought some orange frog toxin we collected in the jungles in case Sara needed it. But these are the first orange frogs found in years. I hesitate to use it on a child without first testing it on myself."

"What do you mean to do?" Alstir Mendin asked.

"If I take it first, I can find out if its side effects are the same as before and not more dangerous. Children in severe pain tolerated the previous orange frog toxin and got relief. Once I know it's safe, I can give it to Sara. The toxin will relieve her pain and may even help her pass the stone."

Pedí seemed so confident now. He spoke without any stammer. Adací wished she'd been with him in the jungles to see the change. He'd come back a doctor, not a young apprentice any longer.

Pedí went to the table where he'd left the glass container. He took out two small sticks. "I will put one under my tongue and probably fall asleep shortly after. That's normal. Wake me in half an hour. I should be able to arouse sufficiently to help you give Sara the second frog stick. If so, then I'll know the toxin is safe for her. I may have some strange dreams and even hallucinations, but that's also normal. But if you can't wake me, get Doctor Arias, and don't give Sara the frog toxin."

"Try the frog toxin on me," Adací blurted. "Then you'll be awake to help with Sara."

"No," Pedí spoke without looking at her. "Not you. I have to be the one to try it first."

He held one of the small sticks, ready to put it under his tongue. "I'm sorry I couldn't give Sara something for pain at first, but she would have been too sleepy to take the nanimoha."

The stick went into his mouth.

Fifteen minutes later, Pedí closed his eyes and then stumbled. He nearly fell to the floor.

Adací broke free from Bertol and ran to him. "Are you all right?" She placed her hand on his arm to steady him.

Pedí grabbed her fingers and tore them off. "I don't want your help." He staggered to a chair at the dining table. "I just need to sit down."

Servants carried in another sofa, and they had him lie on it.

Adací stayed near Pedí even though he had just spurned her. Bertol grabbed her arm, not so gently this time, and pulled her back again. He whispered in her ear. "What's wrong with you? Don't you get the message? He doesn't like you."

"Leave me alone," Adací wanted to shout at Bertol, but she held it inside and instead covered her eyes with her hands so no one could see her grief. Pedí did hate her. Even her touch was offensive to him. What happened to that touch under the avocado tree? It was gone forever.

Bertol tried to get Adací to leave the room. "You'd be better off somewhere else. Go wait in the entryway, and I'll come and get you if things change with Sara."

Adací shook her head. "Why don't you go?"

Bertol frowned, instructed a servant to come and get him if needed, and left the dining hall.

Adací remained by the sofa where Sara was propped up. Larada and her mother were on each side of the sick girl, giving her sips of water. Sara cried out every few minutes.

Pedí slept on the other sofa without moving. Half an hour later, he stirred and cried, "Adací, Adací, where are you?"

She rushed to his side. "I'm here, right here." She knelt, grasped his hands, and caressed them.

His eyes were still closed, but he smiled.

Pitrassa Mendin came over. "He's dreaming. It's time to wake him." She shook him.

Pedí's eyelids fluttered.

Adací waited for him to focus, to see her, acknowledge her, thank her. But his hands jerked back. "Don't touch me."

Adací fell over backward. Larada gasped and came to help her get up. Adací cupped her hand over her mouth to keep from crying out. Pedí's words, asking where she was, were nothing but a dream. Awake, he hated her.

She retreated with Larada and buried her head in her friend's shoulder. She glanced back at Pedí. His eyes were closed again but opened when Larada's mother shook him a second time.

He acted surprised, as if he were waking just now—as if he hadn't even seen Adací, hadn't said the cruel words, didn't know she'd fallen to the floor. She meant less than nothing to him.

"Have I been asleep?" Pedí pronounced each word slowly, drowsily. "I feel peaceful."

How could he be peaceful when he'd just torn her apart? What happened to the Pedí she knew before? After talking to Jurana and Gabro, he should understand that she hadn't meant to hurt him.

But he didn't even look her way. Instead, he checked his pulse. "You were able to wake me, and I'll feel fine. The frog stick is safe for Sara."

Pedí helped Pitrassa Mendin place the stick under Sara's tongue. "Leave it there for ten minutes, then take it out so she doesn't choke on it when she falls asleep. "I'm still drowsy, so I'm going to lie down.

In minutes, Pedí was asleep again.

Little Dimples continued to writhe in pain for ten minutes, but not long after her mother took the stick out of her mouth, Sara stopped writhing. She smiled and said, "Mama, I'm better." She rolled over and was asleep.

Adací had no strength left. She found a seat and watched Pedí and Sara sleep. She glanced at her hands, hands that repulsed Pedí. Fortunately, Bertol was out of the dining hall when Adací rushed to Pedí's side after he said her name. She could only imagine how furious Bertol would have been.

Pedí Wakes Up

Pedí opened his eyes and blinked.

Where was he?

Across the room, little Sara was sleeping on a couch.

The Mendin house!

He had taken the orange frog toxin. He remembered waking just enough to instruct Pitrassa Mendin to place the frog stick under Sara's tongue.

But there was something else. Before he gave those instructions, he'd had a dream—probably caused by the frog toxin. The dream had troubled him. He shook his head. It was gone from memory.

Pedí glanced at the clock on the wall. He'd been asleep for two hours.

He stretched, crossed the room, and knelt on the floor to check on Sara. Her mother was sitting at her side on the couch. Nearby, her older sister, Larada, was in another chair.

And . . .

Pedí clasped his hand over his chest to feel for the pouch with the black and silver hair. Adací was still in the room, sitting next to Larada. He jerked back his hand, embarrassed and angry that this girl who had tricked him into thinking she liked him still held him captive—that she had replaced the lost statuette of the real Adací.

The counterfeit Adací was watching him. He turned away from her and back toward Sara, ready to examine her. It was best to ignore the pretend Adací and act as if she didn't exist.

Sara's forehead was not as hot as before, and she was sweating—her fever had broken. Her eyes popped open as he checked her. She smiled.

He tapped on her left flank.

"It doesn't hurt, Mama." The girl giggled.

Pedí spoke to her mother. "She must have passed the stone while sleeping, and the nanimoha worked. Her fever's down. It's fighting the infection."

Pitrassa Mendin hugged Sara, then leaned and hugged Pedí.

He stood up when Alstir Mendin approached.

He shook Pedí's hand. "Thank you for saving our little girl."

Larada hugged Pedí and added a kiss on his cheek. "Adací said your potion's a miracle, and she's right."

Pedí chanced a look in the black-haired girl's direction. Adací had stood up from her chair and was ten feet away—a half-smile on her face. She took a step in his direction.

Pedí pivoted away from her, shaking his head as he did so.

Adací whimpered.

Pedí clasped his hand over his mouth to keep from whimpering himself. He gritted his teeth and refocused on Sara. He knelt and examined her tummy and flank again. She was in no pain. He stood up and addressed the Mendins. "I'll come each day to check on Sara and give her another dose of the potion. Please send for me if she worsens."

Pedí returned to the dining table where he'd left his pack and supplies. Soft footsteps approached from behind as he put the potion bottle and glass vial back into his pack. He knew who it was without looking and once again shook his head.

This time, it didn't stop her. There was another whimper, but the footsteps continued. Adací was right behind him.

"Thank you for saving Sara." Her voice trembled.

There was something in that voice that seemed sincere. And although she didn't say it, he knew Adací was pleading for him to talk to her. But it was best to continue his silence. If he said anything to Adací, he'd only stutter and stammer or, worse, start crying.

The black-haired girl said more. "I missed you while you were gone to Itatu and the jungles. I'm so happy you're back and safe."

Pedí continued to fiddle with his pack and kept his mouth shut.

"Will you not speak to me?"

Sure, then you'll laugh at my stuttering.

"I'm so proud of what you did to save the people of Itatu."

Quit acting like I mean something to you.

It was then that the dream he had while sleeping came back to him. He was in a forest searching and calling for Adací. When he found her, she came and took his hand. He remembered smiling—hoping that Adací still liked him.

But no, she had just been mocking. His peaceful dream turned into a nightmare. Bertol appeared at her side, and she hugged and kissed the man she really loved. When Pedí bowed his head in sadness, she had patted his hands. "Poor baby Pedí. Is our little Idonata boy jealous?"

He remembered shouting for her not to touch him, but then the dream had ended.

Adací's words to him now must be just like the dream—she was trying to deceive him into thinking she was sincere, then she'd tell him that he meant nothing to her.

But when she spoke again, her voice cracked even more. She was sure good at faking it.

"Did they not tell you at the Sanctuary what I did and the truth about—"

Pedí had heard enough. He turned and stopped her mid-sentence.

"I-I know all about you and Bertol. I-I wish you both—" Pedí quit speaking when he saw Bertol Mendin himself. He had come back into the room and walked rapidly toward them with a frown on his face. He was not happy that his girlfriend was talking to Pedí. He wouldn't know that her purpose was to make fun of him.

But Adací's countenance was not a mocking one. The eyes that used to mesmerize him were like those of a lost baby monkey.

Pedí was breaking her heart, like she'd done to him.

How could that be? She never wanted to see him again—at least, her father had said that to Doctor Arias.

What if Ileana had been right, and it was not Adací who had sent that message? It would make sense that her parents would not want their girl to associate with an Idonata boy. He would only drag her down.

Pedí didn't dare face Adací another second. If he stayed any longer, he'd beg her forgiveness for ever doubting her. And if she did really like him, he'd interfere with her chance to marry someone of wealth and status.

He grabbed his pack and ran out of the dining room.

As he went through the doors, he looked over his shoulder. Adací had taken steps as if to follow, but Bertol grabbed her and stopped her.

When Pedí passed out of the doors, he heard Bertol's scolding voice. "For the last time, let him go."

CHAPTER SEVENTY

Arm Wrestling

With a cry, Jaimel gave up, and his hand smashed against the table. He had lasted the longest against Chando but was no match for the captain's son.

Adací was sick of watching—sad for what she had started. The arm wrestling competition had disrupted all the other games planned for Larada and Bertol's celebration.

It was Adací's fault.

She wished now that she had left the party and not stayed to try and find a way to rescue Larada. Of course, Adací would also fail at that.

Earlier, the joint Coming of Age celebration began as planned with the opening luncheon. It started an hour late because of Sara's illness, but everyone seemed to be having a good time—except Adací and Larada.

For Larada, it was having to be constantly with Chando despite loathing him.

For Adací, things worsened after Pedí ran out of the dining room.

She went mute. She was supposed to be helping Bertol and Larada with the final preparations, but her mind was floating free, touching here and there like a butterfly in a flower-filled meadow, never resting on a single thought.

Bertol had stayed at her side and kept talking to her. Adací thought she had answered him from time to time.

Maybe she hadn't.

Part of her brain knew he was saying nice things to her, but she never acknowledged it.

Bertol's patience and tolerance suddenly ended. "You're impossible!" he said to her. "You promised not to seek that Idonata boy's friendship. And though it's obvious that he doesn't like you, you can't give him up."

Bertol left the room, shaking his head. "I'm done with you," were his parting words.

Adací had lost both Pedí and Bertol. They both hated her.

At least Bertol seemed happy about it. Her former boyfriend found another girl to be with at the celebration. During the luncheon, Adací noticed him sitting at the side of Niala and talking with her, a smile on his face—not the frown he'd given Adací as he walked away from her.

Niala had come to the celebration despite her status as a servant girl. Larada had begged her parents to invite her, and Alstir Mendin had given in, just like he did with the invitation to Edero Custal. Larada assumed his acquiescence was because he was not going to let Larada change his mind about the thing that mattered most to him— her engagement to Chando.

Adací noticed that Niala wore the beautiful new earrings Bertol had given her on one of his visits to her house. And as Adací watched the two of them converse, Bertol glanced back. The tenderness in his eyes for Adací was gone, replaced with lowered eyebrows and a scowl. But his kind look returned when he gave his attention back to Niala.

Adací excused herself and got up from the table. She was next to Larada and didn't want her best friend to see the tears pooling in her eyes. Adací went outside into the Mendin courtyard and stared into the greenery. Part of her was happy for Niala and glad that Bertol was not too proud to sit by the side of the servant girl. Yet even so, Adací wished the scrum had eaten her face away. Then, she'd have an excuse for pushing everyone out of her life.

While in the courtyard, Adací sensed someone behind her. It was Niala who had followed her out. It was like the day Adací had followed Niala into the Big House, trying to offer comfort. Now it was reversed, Niala being the one trying to console Adací.

"Are you okay?" the servant girl asked.

Adací swiped the tears from her eyes.

Niala handed her an embroidered handkerchief, like the one she'd given to Adací before. "I asked Bertol why he was not sitting by you. He said you like someone else, even though that person doesn't want anything to do with you. Is that true?"

Adací nodded.

"Is it Pedí?"

Adací looked away but gave a short nod. "I hurt Pedí, just like I now hurt Bertol."

Niala hugged her tight. "I'm going to tell Bertol to come back to you—that you need him."

"No, Niala. I don't think he ever really loved me, and I don't love him. It's better this way. But he needs some comfort, too. Will you be his friend? I know he likes you."

"His parents would never let him be with me."

Adací reached and squeezed Niala's hand. "Maybe they will. I'll talk to Larada about it, and she'll talk to her parents. I know she'll do it for me."

"Oh, Adací! Are you sure you want to help me with Bertol?"

Adací nodded. "I'm sure."

Niala hugged her again, even tighter than before. "But what about you?"

"I'll be okay. Go back inside and sit by Bertol. I'll return in a few minutes."

And though she had wanted to run away, Adací returned to the luncheon table. She sat next to Larada again. Of course, Chando was at Larada's other side, bragging about something as usual.

Edero had come, yet he was never allowed a moment alone with Larada. Chando made sure of that. When he first arrived, Edero had asked Adací if she'd had a vision to save him and Larada. Edero said he was embarrassed to keep bothering her about it but that she was their last hope. They had not succeeded in getting Larada's parents to change their plans for her and Chando.

Sadly, Adací could only shake her head at his plea.

What he asked for was impossible!

Chando was a hero. All of New Losobon thought Larada was the most fortunate of girls. Adací's past efforts to confront the man had all turned around on her, and he only looked better. If her nightmares about him did have any truth in them, the only thing she was going to accomplish was to earn herself the opportunity to be chased and then beaten to death. She tried to push that vision out of her head. She wanted to believe it was just her imagination. But the image was burned into the back of her skull and wouldn't go away.

Adací hadn't feared Chando before, despite his savagery. But now, she worried she'd cower if she had to confront him. And what if the dream was a warning—a message to stay away from the evil beast and not get involved? Perhaps that was what the dragonfly was trying to tell her when it appeared in the vision.

Despite that disturbing thought, Adací couldn't leave Larada to her awful destiny without trying something. If she had brought the jade stones to the celebration, maybe she could put them on, and they would tell her what to do. But she had no jade, no ideas, just her crazy self to try and stop this marriage. She watched for opportunities to intervene but without success.

About an hour ago, Adací caused the arm wrestling fiasco. The luncheon had ended, and everyone was playing games at the tables set up in the reception hall.

Chando had been sitting next to Larada in a group of four, playing Triumph. Edero was with another group playing Sapo. When a long table with desserts was brought into the spacious hall, Chando got up to get one for himself and one for Larada.

Edero took advantage of the moment. He pulled Larada from her table and had her join him on a sofa at the side of the room. It was their only chance to talk.

Chando noticed and started toward them.

Adací cut him off.

"Hey, big guy, let them visit for a minute. Come to our table, and I'll show you how to play a new betting game with cards."

"Look, witchy girl. Don't tell me what to do."

The hair rose on the back of Adací's neck like the ruffled feathers of a hawk watching its prey. No matter how much she feared her nightmare, she would not shrink before this man. She was ready to peck his eye out but decided it was not a good time to lose control.

She subdued her response. "Give them some time alone."

Chando's following words didn't help. "I don't know what she sees in that skinny runt. He's as gutless as they come, and he has no right talking alone to my future bride."

Adací's hands tightened, talons ready to strike, but she sucked in a breath, letting it out in increments. She grabbed Chando's arm—but not too hard, the talons had relaxed—and pulled him toward her table. She'd flatter this lout away from them. "I see how strong you are. You must be great at arm wrestling."

Someone heard. "Ah, he's not so strong. Felix could beat him."

That's what started it.

Chando accepted the challenge. Felix was to be first, but Chando insisted that every young man there had to face him. A few wagers were made, and a small table with two chairs was set up for the matches. The beast then proceeded to twist and smash one after another of his opponents. Chando's boasting and bravado grew with each victory.

Finally, Jaimel, one of the Mendin's butlers, got involved. "May I try?" he had asked. He'd been watching from his post at the door.

"Jaimel can beat him," several guests cried out. "Chando has met his match."

"Come ahead." Chando motioned for the butler to approach.

Jaimel took off his coat and vest and flexed his muscles. His biceps appeared nearly as big as Chando's. Adací was ready to see the monster defeated.

The men were positioned opposite each other. The starter held his palm over their joined hands and then released it to a loud cheer from the guests.

At first, it appeared that neither man was trying. Their hands and arms did not move. But from the red faces, Adací knew they were giving it their all. Chando faltered a bit, and his arm moved back—one inch, then two, then three. Jaimel was winning.

But Chando gritted his teeth and pushed harder. Jaimel also gritted his teeth, but he could not stop the renewed force from the behemoth. It took much longer than anyone else, but Chando forced Jaimel's hand nearly to the tabletop. The butler held out for what seemed an eternity, just one inch from defeat. But with a scream, he had given up, and Chando slammed the back of Jaimel's hand against the wooden table.

The brute had arm-wrestled nineteen others before defeating the butler. His legendary strength was real, and it was frightening.

CHAPTER SEVENTY-ONE

The Hawk Swoops Down

Adací was ashamed for having started the arm wrestling. She shook her head as she looked around the room. Like her, the other young men and women were also shocked at witnessing Chando's feat of strength.

The parents of the younger guests could be heard arriving in an adjoining room. They had missed the contest.

Chando and Jaimel still sat at the small table, but Chando stood up, stretched, and pulled the butler to his feet. "Where's that coward, Edero? Is he too afraid? I'll even wrestle him with my left hand."

Edero stood by Larada. He had been the last to come forward. His face was colorless. Larada whispered to him, probably telling him he didn't have to do it. Adací could see that he was trying to be stoic.

"Come on, Custal," one of the men said. "We all lost and showed our weakness. You may as well join the party."

Edero walked forward, already sweating. Chando bowed and motioned with an open palm, inviting him to sit down.

It was like a vulture inviting a baby lamb to join him for dinner.

Edero took his seat. They locked hands. The young man supervising the fights adjusted their positions. Edero's arm, compared to Chando's, was like a toothpick next to a swollen sausage.

Larada's face was ashen. Adací worried for her friend's feelings.

"Surprise the beast," someone yelled. "You can do it, Edero."

The man refereeing told them to begin.

Edero's face went from pale to dark red. He pushed and pulled with all he had. The sweat beads turned to droplets that rolled down his face. Yet, the two men's arms stayed in a neutral position.

Chando blinked his eyes as if bored. "My, what strength. I'm scared."

His arm bent backward. It looked like Edero was winning, but Adací knew differently, that Chando was toying with him.

Chando's hand descended until it almost touched. Edero raised his elbow off the table in a last-chance effort to finish the fight.

The referee jumped in and pushed Edero's elbow back to the tabletop.

Chando wagged the finger of his free hand in Edero's face. "Cheater, cheater! Time to teach you a lesson."

In one move, Chando snapped his opponent's hand to the other side and smashed it against the table. He didn't let go and slid Edero's hand off the edge, bending it backward until it looked ready to break off.

Edero's face contorted. His mouth was open as if screaming, but nothing came out. With his other hand, he swiped his fingers across Chando's eyes, temporarily blinding him.

Chando swore and brought both hands to his face. It freed Edero, but with a second curse, the captain's son tipped the table over.

It pushed Edero and his chair backward to the floor, but he scrambled to his feet.

Chando stood up, blinking and rubbing his eyes. "You tried to blind me, you little weasel."

He advanced toward Edero, skirting the upended table.

Edero stood motionless.

The two men were just feet apart, and the young people cleared a circle around them. Larada clutched at her throat. Adací was frozen, unable to move. Something terrible was going to happen, and she was the cause.

"You wanna play rough?" Chando dropped his hands and jerked his chin toward Edero. "Show me your stuff. I'll give you a free shot."

Edero's hands stayed at his sides.

"Afraid?" Chando poked him in the chest with his index finger. Edero took a step back.

"Come on, boy." Chando slapped the side of Edero's face with the ends of his fingers. When the captain's son tried to slap him again, Edero raised his hands and deflected the blow. That seemed to be the resistance Chando was waiting for. With his left fist, he punched Edero in the abdomen. With his right, he struck him full force in the face.

Edero flew through the air and landed on his side. Larada rushed to him.

Silence reigned. Adací hadn't moved. No one moved except for Larada, who leaned over Edero.

Chando looked around the circle. "It was a fair fight. He's the one who broke the rules—poking my eye."

The words *fair fight* released Adací's dormancy. The hawk could not sit stuck to a limb while a beast tore into her friends. This brutish man had to be stopped.

However, when Adací took a step forward, the vision of Chando chasing her and ready to beat her to death repeated itself in her head as if it were going to happen that very instant. Adací shook her head to clear it. To make the image go away.

I'm not going to believe it.

She glanced first to see if Edero was all right. Larada knelt by him. He hadn't been knocked out and was testing his jaw. Although badly beaten, he would recover.

Adací marched up to Chando, her long braid swinging back and forth. "Fair fight, was it? How about fighting me? Is that a fair fight?"

She held her fingers together and poked him in the chest. It did nothing except hurt her fingers. But she did it again. And a third time.

Tension buzzed around them. Everything seemed suspended except for Adací and Chando. Outrage blocked out all her common sense.

"Afraid? Too yellow-bellied to fight a little girl?"

"Look here, witch. This is not your fight, and I don't take nicely to anyone calling me names."

He turned away from her. Adací poked him repeatedly in his broad back with her fingers.

The double doors opened behind Adací. Someone had come into the room, but neither she nor Chando turned to look.

"You're nothing but a big cowardly ox. No, you're actually a pig, a giant fat one."

Chando's massive shoulders hunched. His fists alternately clenched and released. His muscles visibly trembled.

"A spineless swine, that's what you are."

Chando swung around with all his power. His right arm moved toward her. The back of his hand struck Adací's face just to the side of her eye. She flew sideways and would have landed hard on the floor, but a boy caught her and lowered her down.

It was like she'd been transported to another world as the room swirled around her. Then the pain, delayed at first, came full on, sudden and sharp. Her right eye flashed orange, and she couldn't hear from her right ear. Adací shook her head, trying to clear her thinking. That worsened the pain, and she retched.

Girls cried around her. Larada called Adací's name.

Then it was quiet.

She tried to see, repeatedly blinking her eyes. The right side still flashed colors, but with the left, she could see Chando standing motionless. He looked straight ahead at the double doors. Everyone was looking that way.

Adací blinked again. It was Alstir and Pitrassa Mendin. That's who had entered just before Chando struck her. They had seen everything.

Pitrassa Mendin shook her finger at Chando. "My husband may have promised you my daughter's hand in marriage, but you never would have won her heart. Everyone can finally understand why. No one who hits a woman or abuses a defenseless man may be a part of our family. You are not going to marry my daughter."

Chando smirked at Pitrassa Mendin. "You're not the head of this house."

With his jaw sticking out and a victory smile on his face, he nodded and winked toward Alstir Mendin. "All that happened here was caused by that black-haired witch over there. You probably don't know that she's an enchantress. I've seen what her strange powers can do. She's just like the old Idonata witch queen and probably has a moon tattoo on her chest, just like she did. That little sorceress deserves what she got."

Alstir Mendin opened his mouth as if to speak, then hesitated. The captain had entered the room, along with the parents of the other young men and women. Durgo Borgesso came forward and stood next to Alstir Mendin.

Chando grinned. "Father knows my true and good character." Then, pointing at Adací, he added, "Father also knows how meddlesome that witch is. This is all her fault."

The captain began a speech full of slippery and convincing words. Adací tried to see him through her one eye that still functioned. His face was blurred, but his sarcastic smile was there.

Suddenly, the big man choked on his words. Alstir Mendin had cut him off.

"You have no say in my house. My wife rules at my side, and what she said stands."

He waved his hand at the captain. "Take your son away. He's no longer welcome at this celebration, and my promise to let him marry my daughter is rescinded. If I lose your business, I don't care. I'm tired of being a part of your filthy regime."

Durgo Borgesso's jaw dropped, his arrogant face not looking quite so grand. "You will lose my business," he said to Alstir Mendin, "and much more. You'll be sorry for your insolence." The captain took his son's arm to walk him out of the hall.

Chando glared at Adací as he moved away. "You'll pay, witch. Just wait and see."

Adací trembled, still lying on the ground. The pain on the side of her face worsened.

Alstir Mendin had knelt to assist her but looked up at Chando and Durgo Borgesso. "Get out of my house, both of you."

<hr>

Adací lay on a sofa in a guest room, and Edero was on another nearby. They each held a cold compress against their face and compared injuries. Adací's ear was starting to work again. The flashing in her eye was less, but the throbbing in her head continued.

Larada went back and forth between the sofas.

She knelt by Adací.

"I knew you'd find a way to save me. But I didn't mean you to take a beating to do it."

Edero rubbed his swollen jaw and tested it before speaking. "Did you have a dream about Chando and not tell us?"

Adací hesitated, then nodded. She was not going to tell them what actually happened in the dream.

Larada squealed. "See, I told you all your dreams come true."

Fortunately, this one hadn't. The nightmare had overplayed what happened in reality. There was no chase through the forest, just one blow and nothing more. And she'd saved Larada from the evil Chando.

"You were like a mother hawk defending her family," Larada said.

"I pretended to be one to give me courage."

Larada hugged Adací tight. "I'll love you forever."

"Me, too. Ouch." Edero put his hand on his jaw.

"No, you can't!" Larada released arms that hugged Adací and turned to hug Edero. "You can love me. You can only like her."

Edero laughed, then rubbed his jaw again.

CHAPTER SEVENTY-TWO

In the Forest

Adací crossed the stream by stepping from stone to stone. The trail petered out on the far side, but she found it again, leading her back into the woods.

Leaves crunched in the trees behind her.

Footsteps?

She turned around. Twice, she thought someone was following her, but each time she waited, it stayed quiet.

It's just a deer.

No one knew she had come here. She had seen a man on horseback far behind her on the road, but he turned and went another way when she tied up her horse.

Adací was in the forest near Pedí's childhood home, looking for the stream he'd described where he caught his first frog.

The one she crossed was too swift—too many rapids for frogs.

Maybe it slowed and meandered further down. She decided to circle back and follow it a little further. She wanted a quiet place to reflect, to think about Pedí.

It had been two days since Larada and Bertol's Coming of Age celebration had come to a glorious conclusion. Once Chando and the captain left, everything went perfectly. Unshackled from his promises to Durgo Borgesso, Alstir Mendin's heart had changed. He witnessed firsthand the love between Larada and Edero. He and his wife Pitrassa gave them permission to see one another, and everyone expected their engagement to be announced shortly.

Adací's joy for her best friend helped her try and forget the mess she had made of her own life.

But that was not so easy.

She had gone to see Jurana and Gabro this morning, but they weren't there. They had left two weeks ago to visit their children in the western part of the valley. Something had come up, and they departed in a hurry. The sages left a message for Adací, but she hadn't seen it since she missed her last appointment with them.

The sages were already gone when Pedí returned from the jungles, which meant they hadn't talked to him. He didn't know about her horse ride to warn him or about her injury, and he knew nothing about what she had done to try and protect him. He didn't know that she wanted to be his friend, but why that was no longer possible.

Instead, Pedí hated her and must think Adací had been mocking him. Even when he learns the truth from Jurana and Gabor, he might still hate her.

Bertol was also gone from her life. The day after Larada's party, the Mendin and Custal families met together for the first time in years. Larada told Adací that this happened not just because of her and Edero but also because of Bertol and Niala. At Adací's request, Larada had talked to her parents about Bertol and Niala. To Larada's surprise, her parents welcomed their son's relationship with the Mattaçores girl, who still worked for the Custal family. But Larada cried for Adací, that she was no longer her brother's special girl. Larada said her parents were also sad that the relationship between Bertol and Adací had not worked out.

However, Adací was happy for Niala and anticipated a joyous future for her and her family. In cutting contrast, all Adací had left was a remembrance of Pedí. And that memory was nothing but a mirage, an illusion that was shimmering, shifting shape and form, soon to vanish.

Pedí would have nothing to do with her, yet Adací hoped to find a way to talk with him. She wanted to say how sorry she was for what had happened and to let him know that she did like him, even though they could never have a normal friendship. She still worried that being with her might endanger Pedí, just like her parents feared she would be threatened by being with him.

Yet, talking with him for a few minutes should be safe. Adací needed Pedí's help to interpret a new dream she'd had. Though she no longer needed to have a vision for Larada, she had worn the jade once again. It was more out of habit. In the dream that came last night, the Blue Dragonfly reappeared. Fortunately, the dream had nothing to do with Chando. The nightmare with that beast chasing her and ready to end her life had just been a warning. There was never any chase and just a single blow to her head, nothing more.

Her Dream Dragonfly—as she liked to call it since it was just mythical—had come bearing a new message. The blue creature had landed on her chest right over her hidden moon tattoo, and then it lifted off and went to her braid. Last, it buzzed its wings, moved ahead on a trail, and kept going back and forth as if telling Adací to follow. She saw in her mind the place the dragonfly wanted her to go. It was a narrow canyon with high cliff walls on either side, like the canyon her birth parents traveled through when escaping from the masked warriors. Was it the same place—the same canyon that frightened Adací?

If only he would talk to her, Pedí might know what the dream meant and what she should do.

The footsteps again! It was louder this time.

She turned.

Thirty feet behind her stood Chando. He was grinning.

Adací fled.

CHAPTER SEVENTY-THREE

Chando Wins

Pedí wandered the forest paths not far from his home. He had told Mirela he needed to go alone. She complained at first but quit when his mother said she'd teach her how to bake a chocolate cake.

Pedí needed time to think about his recent encounter with Adací. He was troubled by the sadness in her face when he finally turned to look at her. Her look had been that of someone carrying an unbearable burden. He sensed that she desperately wanted him to acknowledge her, but he had ignored Adací and been unkind.

Pedí was mistaken in thinking she didn't care for him. It must have been Adací's parents, and not her, who didn't want him to be her friend. He wished Doctor Arias had told him the truth, but maybe the doctor didn't know, depending on what Adací's father had said. If Doctor Arias thought it was Adací's wish never to see Pedí again, his mentor would have remained faithful to that request. That would also explain why the doctor had said nothing about Adací since Pedí returned, including her head injury that Misha and Crina had mentioned. Doctor Arias probably treated her after the accident, but he did not want to tell Pedí about it.

She fell from a horse, they had said.

Could Adací have been the silhouetted figure on horseback he saw on the way to Itatu?

He remembered the fleeting thought that it might be her, but he had dismissed it as foolish. If she had indeed followed him, then his forebodings about her might have been for real.

"Wait for me, Pedí. I'm coming."

The cry he heard! The voice that called to him when they were camped on the hill.

Her voice!

It seemed so impossible at the time; he didn't believe it.

And the lone horse that wandered out of the trees along the road— her horse!

She must have fallen off and been injured. If so, then the impression that he had abandoned her was true.

Pedí slumped against the side of a tree. He had failed Adací—the fearless girl whose name was being talked about all over New Losobon.

The news had reached the Sanctuary. At the Mendin twins Coming of Age, Adací confronted the famous Chando Borgesso and exposed him as an unfit groom for Larada Mendin. The captain's son had struck Adací in the face. No one was known for greater physical strength than Chando, yet Adací had courageously defied him.

Her bravery was the opposite of Pedí's cowardice. He had been too afraid to even talk with her. He wasn't worthy of Adací, and even if she did want him as a friend, it would be better for her if he went away. He would only disrupt her future with Bertol Mendin—with someone of high standing in New Losobon. Adací deserved that honor and privilege.

Pedí would take Mirela and his mother and go to the jungles. It was best if the last Idonata left New Losobon forever.

"Ow!" A wasp stung him on the arm.

Pedí twisted to look at the other side of the tree trunk he'd been leaning against. A giant wasp nest hung from a fallen dead limb, which lay horizontally about four feet off the ground. One end of the branch had caught in the crotch of the tree, and bushes held up the other.

It was a nest of vicious butcher wasps—Kawayutu, as his ancestors called them. Regular paper wasps made round nests, while the Kawayutu made large irregular paper shelters. This nest was like an upside-down triangle—its base stuck to the branch.

Once, he had disturbed a Kawayutu nest and remembered the halo of wasps that circled him before attacking. Talking to them had not helped—wasps never listen. He had to jump into a stream to escape.

Pedí backed away from the paper wasp shelter, step by slow step. As he did, a sound echoed through the trees. Someone was running through the forest. Whoever it was seemed to be coming in his direction.

He walked into the adjacent clearing to hear better.

A voice called out for help. Adací's voice?

What was she doing here?

The black-haired girl burst out of the trees and into the open space forty feet from Pedí. She looked left and right, absolute panic on her face.

Immediately behind her was a man, a huge man. It was Chando, the captain's son. He grabbed Adací's long braid, jerked her to a stop, and then threw her to the ground. Chando struck her over and over with his fists while she kicked and screamed with no effect.

Every muscle in Pedí's body sprang to life. He raced across the clearing and called out for any nearby animal friends to come and help. If there were just one forest cat in the vicinity who would listen and fight on his side, he might have a chance against this giant man. But he sensed no animals in the area and doubted they would listen anyway.

He would have to find a way to defeat Chando by himself. He had to save Adací.

When he neared the captain's son, Pedí reached down, grabbed a stick, and jumped onto Chando's back. He beat him with the stick and tried to pry him off Adací, but the man was immovable. Chando jerked, and the back of his head smote Pedí in the face. He couldn't see for a moment, but he hung on and scratched and struck at the huge man.

In one motion, Chando stood up, wrenched Pedí off his back, then tossed him to the ground. Pedí's left foot doubled back as it struck the earth. Something crunched, and pain tore through him. His ankle had fractured.

He jumped up anyway and hopped on his right foot toward the beast. He swung at Chando's face with the stick, but the big man caught Pedí's arm and twisted it backward. It snapped when Chando forced him back to the ground. Stabbing pain shot through Pedí's arm, but he got up once again.

Chando punched him in the gut, then picked him up like he was a lifeless sack of grain. Held high in the air, Pedí could see Adací flat on the ground, bruised and bloodied. The monster stomped across the clearing toward a large tree and threw Pedí against it.

Pedí held out his one good arm to protect himself, but it shattered against the trunk, allowing his body to slam against the tree in full force. His ribs cracked. He slid down the trunk to a sitting position on the ground, his entire body splintered and in pieces. He couldn't move, couldn't get up. Each weak breath caused piercing pain, like multiple skewers were impaling him.

Chando knelt, facing him. Pedí blinked, trying to clear his eyes. Adací had gotten up. He could see her stumbling toward them.

"Run, Adací," he wanted to scream. *"Get away."* But there was no air in his lungs to produce a sound.

She held something in her hand and advanced toward Chando.

"Save yourself," Pedí's heart pleaded to Adací since his vocal cords could produce no words.

Chando pulled back his fist to pound it into Pedí's face. "Now you die."

At that moment, Adací struck the back of Chando's head with a rock.

He yelled and turned on her, leaving Pedí crumpled against the tree. Adací tried to hobble away, but Chando caught her and lifted her off the ground. He flung her hard against a nearby tree trunk, just like he'd done to Pedí.

For Pedí, it was like watching the thing he most valued being cast into oblivion, and he could do nothing to stop it.

There was a dull thump as Adací's body slammed into the tree. Her battered body slid to the ground. Her head remained upright and leaned back against the bark. She moaned, struggled for a moment, then quit moving.

Chando towered above her. He laughed out an evil chortle, finding glory in what he'd done. "Now, you'll pay for ruining my engagement to Larada." The vicious brute glanced back at Pedí. "The tattooed boy will get to watch what I do to the witch, and then I'll do the same to him."

Adací's eyes were open. It tortured Pedí all the more to know that she was conscious enough to understand what was going to happen to her. He was like a quivering, smashed insect whose last moments of life would be filled with the vision of Adací being destroyed. And he could do nothing.

Chando had won.

CHAPTER SEVENTY-FOUR

Blue Dragonfly

From the moment Adací fled from Chando, she'd silently called for her birth mama and the ancient Queen Adací to save her. She asked them to send the Blue Dragonfly. She didn't know why she asked for the mystical dragonfly but sensed the need to do it. Yet how could an insect, even a giant dragonfly, possibly help? It was just a myth anyway—a dream creature, nothing more. And despite her pleas, the Blue Dragonfly hadn't come, in vision or otherwise.

Now, she lay mangled against a tree, and Pedí was the same. She had hoped that he could escape after she struck Chando with the rock on the back of his head. But Pedí had not moved. Like her, his injuries were too severe. He was going to die! They both were going to die! Chando had just declared it!

So why did the Blue Dragonfly dominate her thoughts again just before death? She could see the creature in her mind and suddenly realized it wasn't mythical but real. Her mama and the ancient Adací had sent her those dreams to prepare her and help her understand, but until now, her mind had not allowed them in.

But they were here now. Adací could sense her mama on one side of her, the ancient queen on the other. They spoke to her mind, and Adací loudly and boldly declared the words she heard. "I am Adací, queen of the Idonata, daughter of a queen, and descendent of the ancient Adací."

Chando laughed. "You're no queen."

"You foul beast. You will not harm us any further," Adací cried. "My Shushuhador, Pedí, and the Blue Dragonfly will save us."

Adací took a deep breath, though it caused her ribs to sting with pain, and called to Pedí. "Summon the Blue Dragonfly. Only a Shushuhador can call for it, but it must be in my name. I am Adací, queen of the Idonata."

Pedí raised his head, and his eyes opened wide. Adací knew he heard and understood.

And though he spoke in barely a whisper, the words were distinct, and Adací could hear them. "Come, Blue Dragonfly!" Pedí said. "I call for you in the name of my queen, Adací, the leader of all the Idonata."

Chando, who had stood watching and listening, laughed in scorn. "What spell are you and that boy trying to weave? You're nothing but a foul witch. I'll silence you so you'll never speak again, then do the same to him."

But as he drew back his fist, there was a loud buzzing, and he hesitated.

The Blue Dragonfly appeared!

It descended from the sky and flew between Adací and Chando, causing him to step back. Then it went and hovered in front of Pedí. The majestic creature was huge, the size of three of four regular dragonflies. Its body glowed with an iridescent blue, just like in her dreams. Adací and Chando watched—even her tormentor was mesmerized.

Pedí talked to the dragonfly, but Adací could not hear what he said. The Blue Dragonfly quickly left Pedí and swooped back between Adací and Chando. It dived at the evil man's face. Chando cried out in surprise and backed further away from Adací. With incredible agility, the striking creature buzzed around his face. The man swung his fists in a wild frenzy, but his blows never came close to the elegant aerialist, which effortlessly moved in and out of his reach.

"What magic have you and that scum conjured," Chando yelled at Adací while swinging his arms at the dragonfly. "I'll crush this insect, then crush you both."

The Blue Dragonfly buzzed Chando a final time, then circled back to Adací. It landed on her chest right over her moon tattoo. The marvelous blue creature stayed still for a moment, and Adací perceived it was gaining power from her. Then it rose into the air above Adací and hovered, facing Chando.

The evil man strode toward Adací, seemingly no longer afraid of the Blue Dragonfly.

She heard Pedí's faint voice call out to the dragonfly. "Now!" he said. "Bring them now!"

Out of the woods, the Blue Dragonfly's compatriots came in a horde. There were green dragonflies, red dragonflies, and small black ones with stripes on their wings. Unlike the Blue Dragonfly, these dragonflies were normal size, but there were a hundred or more.

Like a flying army controlled by the Blue Dragonfly, they descended on the captain's son. They weaved in and out, darting together in formation, their tiny legs and feet scratching at his face and eyes. Chando batted at them but never connected. His brute force was ineffective against the speed and ability of the dragonflies to move in any direction. Chando shrieked as he backed away from the clearing and into the trees—trying to escape from the hordes of flying insects.

For the moment, at least, he was gone.

***

"I am Adací, queen of the Idonata."

When Pedí heard those words, he finally understood. He was a Shushuhador. Adací had called him that. He had the power to call for the Blue Dragonfly in the name of their queen. And Adací was that queen.

Pedí had felt a moment of relief when the dragonfly multitude attacked Chando and drove him into the forest. However, he suspected the horrible man would soon return, intent on killing them both. He needed more help from the Blue Dragonfly, which hovered above Adací. And, as if it had understood his thoughts, the blue marvel left Adací and returned to Pedí. It landed on the pocket with the pouch containing Adací's hair.

Something surged inside Pedí. Strength came from out of the black and silver locks, from the Blue Dragonfly, from the tree he leaned against, and from all the insects and birds flying nearby. The dragonfly had brought a gift from all of nature, from the ancient Adací, and at the same time, unlocked power from the hair of the living Adací.

Pedí's arms, legs, ribs, and head were battered and broken.

Nothing worked.

He got up anyway.

He pushed off the ground with his hands, turned, and grabbed the tree trunk to force himself up. Every part of him screamed, but he had to protect his queen. Yet, in his mangled condition, what could he possibly do?

And he had little time left. Chando was coming back. His voice echoed out of the trees, cursing Adací and Pedí's names and boasting that he no longer feared the dragonflies. "These flying bugs you magically sent may slow me down, but they won't stop me from killing you both."

"Please help me save Queen Adací," Pedí said to the Blue Dragonfly, which had remained over his pocket with the pouch. The incredible blue creature buzzed its wings, left the pocket, and flew twice around the tree Pedí had been thrown against. The second time it circled the tree, a few Kawayutu wasps came with it and flew across Pedí's face. Their nest was right behind the tree where he stood. The Blue Dragonfly had brought him a weapon.

But was it too late? Chando's voice rang across the clearing, cursing Adací and Pedí again. Pedí turned to watch the big man stagger out of the forest, the dragonfly army still circling and diving at his face. But Chando had both his hands open and in front of his face, protecting himself from the insects. He moved forward despite their attacks.

It was up to Pedí now. He hopped around the tree on his one good foot and, ignoring his injured arms, grabbed the end of the dead branch from which the Kawayutu nest hung. With one jerk, he tore it out of its moorings. Incomprehensible pain surged through him, but instead of passing out, it woke up every fiber of his body.

The force of ripping out the limb moved him backward. He stumbled in reverse across the clearing, walking as best he could on his injured ankle, holding the branch with the nest above him. Wasps were already circling, trying to find him. The Blue Dragonfly hovered between the wasps and Pedí, fanning them back and away from him.

Pedí whispered to the wasps in Idonata. "I am your brother. Please don't attack me. The Blue Dragonfly will tell you what to do." The circle of wasps grew thicker, but they seemed to hesitate as if they'd heard him, and not a single one stung him. The Blue Dragonfly moved above the wasps as if he were now their commander.

Every step Pedí took, every motion, brought stabs and stabs of pain from his injuries, but it only gave him more determination. He swung the limb with its nest around, and its weight helped him stagger toward Adací.

Despite the dragonfly horde still buzzing him, Chando had made it across the clearing. He was just a few feet from Adací. When Pedí approached, the flying army suddenly left Chando and spiraled upward into the sky.

The big man laughed. "There's nothing to protect you now, witch."

But the captain's son did not realize who and what was behind him, having been distracted by the dragonflies. He knelt before Adací and drew back his fist. Adací's eyes blinked. She was fully awake, watching her doom.

But the captain's son stopped and stood up when he heard Pedí's movements.

When Chando turned, Pedí yelled "Attack" to the wasps and swung the nest into the man's face.

Enraged wasps burst out of the shredded shelter, and the halo of their circling companions descended and covered the captain's son. They were in his eyes, nose, and mouth and clung to every part of his body—stinging him right through his clothes. Chando screamed and took off running. The swarm followed.

Pedí fell to the ground next to Adací. A few of the wasps had remained and flew around her. Despite the pain, he sat up partway and gently waved them away, expressing gratitude to them as his grandpa had taught him.

When Pedí sat up, the pouch with Adací's hair fell out of his pocket and landed on the ground. The Blue Dragonfly, hovering nearby, landed on the small cloth bag. The shining insect turned its head right and left as if looking at each of them. Then it flew to Adací's chest, and Pedí saw the crescent moon tattoo inscribed into her skin. It was exposed, the top of her dress having torn in the scuffle. He startled, and a tremor passed through him. Adací even had the symbol of the ancient Adací!

The dragonfly looked back and forth at each of them before flying off and disappearing into the trees.

"That creature is so beautiful," Adací whispered the words.

Pedí nodded in agreement.

"Thank you for saving me," Adací said to Pedí.

With the last bit of his strength—and despite every motion causing extreme pain—Pedí touched and traced Adací's moon tattoo, then gently caressed her face. With his other hand, he picked up and squeezed tight the tiny sack that held her hair.

"It was the Blue Dragonfly that saved you and saved me. You told me what to do and how to call for it. You are my queen, the Adací of my people. You may not know it, but your powers protected me many times while on my journey."

Pedí choked out his final words. "Thank you for rescuing me over and over again."

Then he passed out.

⎯⬥⎯

Pedí had touched Adací's tattoo and then caressed her face. That tender motion caused the pain, the previous terror, and the visage of Chando, ready to kill her, to vanish.

After Pedí passed out, Adací's pain returned, but not the terror. She was safe at his side. She watched him breathe and knew he was alive.

Each of her breaths caused sharp stabbings from where her chest had struck the tree.

She looked at Pedí's hand that still gripped the little cloth pouch that had rolled out of his shirt pocket—the pouch that the beautiful Blue Dragonfly had landed on. She remembered his shirt pocket bulging, most likely from the pouch, when Pedí treated Sara at the Mendin's house. He kept covering it with his hand that day. Something very important to Pedí was inside that pouch.

With her one good arm, Adací reached and unwrapped his fingers from the pouch. Her other arm she couldn't move—like Pedí's, it was swollen and deformed. Adací fingered the little bag. It was difficult to open the lacing with just one hand and with the pain of each breath and movement, but she succeeded. Then, with her finger, she pulled out a coil of hair. It was her hair! There were a few black strands, but most of the hair was silver, with the black dye partially rubbed off. It must be the hair he'd picked up from the ground that day by her bird feeder. He had saved it, carried it, and cherished it.

Adací spoke to the unconscious Pedí in a whispered voice. "You are my friend, my best friend. And you are my Shushuhador."

With the last of her strength, Adací tucked the hair back into the pouch and put the cloth bag into Pedí's hand. She wrapped his fingers around it, then put her hand over his.

She rolled off the tree and lay next to him. Then, all went dark when she passed out.

CHAPTER SEVENTY-FIVE

Alive

Adací opened her eyes. A beam of morning sunlight brightened the room. She turned her head just enough to see without causing too much pain. Pedí was sleeping a short distance away in the bed next to hers.

It had not been a dream. She hadn't imagined it.

The Blue Dragonfly had come.

The beautiful creature protected her and then helped Pedí talk to the wasps and carry their nest. The stinging insects chased the evil Chando away.

She and Pedí had survived.

Adací remembered waking on the forest ground when the healers from the infirmary arrived. She learned that Mirela had come looking for Pedí and found them lying side by side. Mirela ran home to get help, and Pedí's mother had sent for Doctor Arias.

He had come with many helpers who carried Adací and Pedí to the infirmary. The rest of yesterday was a painful blur as Doctor Arias and the other healers treated each injury.

Adací's ribs were fractured, her right arm was broken, and dark bruises were everywhere. She had a huge bump on her head but no new skull fracture. Doctor Arias said he was grateful for that.

Pedí's injuries were similar but worse. No one could understand how he'd been able to dislodge the branch that held the wasp nest, walk over to Chando, and smash it into him. Even more astonishing to everyone was how the wasps had left them alone—not one sting.

Yet it had happened.

Adací breathed in through her nose. It was hard to get much air into her lungs with the tight wraps around her ribs. The smell of chalky plaster, which held her injured limb in place, was not a pleasant one. She lay quiet in the infirmary bed, not wanting to move because of the pain, but she turned a little more to look down at the petite redhead sleeping on a mat on the floor between their two beds. Mirela had insisted on staying with Pedí. Until yesterday, no one but Pedí's mother had known about the Itatu orphan he had brought home with him.

Adací had watched the devotion the freckled-faced girl had shown to Pedí. Mirela seemed to experience herself every wince, every grimace of pain that Pedí had shown when his fractures were set and cast.

The room brightened a little more from the sun as Adací waited for Pedí to wake. He stirred, then opened his eyes.

"Hi," she said.

"Hi," he replied. His smile was huge, and he didn't turn away as he had in the past. He didn't act shy or embarrassed.

"Do you hurt?" she asked.

"A lot."

"Me, too."

She reached with the hand of her unbroken arm as far as she could, but her grasping fingers were still short of his bed.

Pedí could not lift his arms as both were in casts and slings, but he waved the fingers of the hand closest to her as if trying to reach her. "Thank you for telling me how to call for the Blue Dragonfly."

"Thank you for saving me with the wasp nest," she said.

"It was nothing," he answered.

Adací opened her eyes wide and glanced at her casted arm and then at Pedí's casted arms and legs. "Nothing, huh?" She started laughing, and Pedí joined her.

Then she groaned; the pain was so bad in her ribs.

Soon, they were both laughing and groaning at the same time. But it was a joyous pain, and the little redhead on the floor jumped up and joined in the laughter.

CHAPTER SEVENTY-SIX

A New Witch Queen

When Doctor Arias and the other healers rescued Adací and Pedí in the forest, they searched for Chando Borgesso. They found him a hundred yards away—unconscious and barely alive. Stung by hundreds of wasps, his body was swollen and bloated, his face deformed almost past recognition. He was taken to the infirmary at the Sanctuary, where Doctor Arias and the other healers tried to help him. When Chando woke up, his first words were curses against Pedí and Adací for what had happened to him.

In addition to his distended and weakened body, the captain's son lost the function of his right eye. The wasps had stung it multiple times, right through the lid. The tissue around the eye was puckered, the eyelid drooped, and the pupil grayed over. The left eye had also been stung, but he could still see out of it a little. Chando looked more like a hideous monster than a man.

But despite all that, his proud and domineering spirit only worsened and transformed into that of a ruthless demon whose only purpose was revenge. For two days, the healers at the infirmary had to tolerate his multiple threats against Adací and Pedí. The Sanctuary was finally spared the ordeal of listening to his rage when Chando's father had him moved to The Big House, where Breno Torred took over his care.

Though Chando's verbal threats were no longer heard at the infirmary, it wasn't long before forewarnings of a gathering storm reached the Sanctuary. Rumors circulated throughout New Losobon, generated by the now grotesque Chando and his father. In their version of the incident in the forest, Chando was lured there by Pedí and Adací, who used their powers over the wild creatures to send dragonflies and murderous wasps to try and kill him.

The old fears about the Idonata helped make the false narrative seem authentic. Adací was a new witch queen, and Pedí was her Shushuhador. The captain and Chando's account stated that Adací and Pedí used the same evil magic the old stories told about in the battles between the Idonata and the first captain's soldiers. How else would thousands of wasps attack only his son and leave Adací and Pedí untouched? Their story claimed that the injuries Pedí and Adací suffered were only from his innocent son fighting back, trying to save his life.

Everyone at the Sanctuary feared for Adací and Pedí. Doctor Arias recommended they stay at the infirmary for their protection. He already wanted them there to help them heal. "Fortunately, not everyone believes our lying leader's story," Doctor Arias said. "And we have shared the true story with our family and friends. I hope most people in New Losobon will believe our version, not the captain's. Anyone who sees your injuries will realize that Chando's claim of simple self-defense does not make sense."

The doctor twisted his gnarly hands together. "I'm not sure what the captain and Chando hope to gain with their false story. But something must be in the works. The fear of the Idonata queen and the Shushuhadors still rings loud in many people's hearts. These stories about your powers will stoke that fear."

"Do you think the captain will send the police or soldiers to arrest me and Adací?" Pedí questioned the doctor.

"It's possible," Doctor Arias said. "But if he arrests you for what you did to Chando, he has to have a way to prove your guilt before the Municipal Council. Though it sometimes seems as if the captain controls them, the Council will be just in a trial. I think the captain's got something else planned."

"And he's waiting for Chando to get better so he can be a part of whatever they try and do to us," Adací predicted.

"I'll stab that man if he comes after you!" Mirela said. She pulled her knife from her boot and waved it in the air.

Pedí went to the little redhead and gave her a squeeze. "Thanks for watching out for us. But please be careful. I don't want you to get hurt too."

"I won't let that monster do something to you and Adací again," the little girl said, still brandishing her blade, with tears now streaming down her face.

CHAPTER SEVENTY-SEVEN

Rowai-ra

Despite the worry over what Chando and the captain might be planning, two glorious months began. Pedí got to see and talk with Adací every day. Doctor Arias found separate rooms for them, but they were next door to each other. Adací, Pedí, and Mirela got together whenever they weren't sleeping or getting treatments.

While recovering from their injuries, the trio became best friends and got along as if they'd known each other for ages. They talked about everything, primarily birds, frogs, dragonflies, and all the wild things. They laughed and joked. Adací teased Pedí over his shyness and funny behaviors. She taught Mirela to do it, too. But that teasing endeared them all the more to him. It was a strange but delightful companionship between the shy tattooed healer, the silver-haired clairvoyant, and the feisty redheaded girl.

At mealtimes, Mirela helped Pedí to a wheelchair, and they ate together in Adací's room. Mirela helped feed both of them at first, but Adací learned to eat left-handed, so Mirela just helped Pedí since both his arms were in casts.

After clearing the meal trays, Mirela's routine was to pull a chair over and sit beside Pedí while they all talked. Often, she would lean her head against him. One day after supper, instead of sitting by the wheelchair, Mirela got in bed by Adací and snuggled beside her.

"Hey, what's going on?" Pedí said.

Adací put her uncasted arm around Mirela, who stuck her tongue out at Pedí.

"Uai, I love you, but I love Mama . . ." she giggled, "I mean Adací, as much as I love you."

Adací squeezed Mirela even tighter when the little girl called her Mama.

Pedí laughed. "I'm so happy you love Adací. And it's okay if you love her even more than you love me."

<hr>

Adací heard detailed accounts from Pedí and Mirela about their adventures in Itatu and the jungles. She shared some of what had happened to her but left out many details, including the complete account of the vision in the orchard. That dream was pivotal for her. Yet, the beginning of the vision was a nightmare—when the six evil spirits appeared. She hated to recall that part of the dream.

Adací did finally tell Pedí more about her fall from the horse and that she had nearly died trying to warn him of her dream of the skeletal-faced man. When she told him about it, Pedí stopped talking. Adací waited, watching his face. He looked down like he used to, not like he'd been since saving her in the forest. He seemed afraid once again to look at her.

"You shouldn't have worried about me," he said. "If I had died, then everyone would have been better off."

"If you had died, you wouldn't have saved the people of Itatu. If you had died, you wouldn't have been there to rescue me from Chando. Is that what you wish had happened?"

Pedí shook his head, but he still would not look at her. "Why did you risk your life for me? I'm not worth anything."

"You're the opposite of worthless," Adací said. "No one is smarter or has done something as wonderful as you. Like I said before, your special cure is a miracle."

<hr>

The invalids had many visitors. Jurana and Gabro returned from visiting their children and came by every day. When the sages brought jellied guava for Pedí, Mirela ate more than he did. Larada came often, Edero at her side. And Pedí's mother was there every day. She began teaching Adací the history and culture of the Idonata people, including their language. Mirela sat in on every learning session.

Adací's parents were also frequent visitors. They thanked Pedí over and over for saving their daughter.

"But it was Adací who saved me," Pedí kept telling them.

Marina and Sergol asked his forgiveness for telling him that Adací did not want to be his friend. "We were wrong," Sergol said. "But we thought we were protecting her by hiding her identity."

"You were right to keep her away from me," Pedí responded.

"No, Pedí!" Marina shook her head. "When we met you, we should have welcomed the opportunity for Adací to become friends with another Idonata. And now that the captain has let everyone know that she is like the Idonata queens, you're the one who is in danger by being around our daughter."

"Not true," Pedí said.

"Some might say we endanger each other," Adací interjected. "But I say we protect each other and are powerful together."

"That is true," Doctor Arias said. He'd been listening to the conversation. "But that very power, though you use it for good alone, could still cause the wrong person to fear you and seek your death. The captain will incite that kind of behavior. We know the captain hired someone to kill Pedí when he went to Itatu, proving that he will stop at nothing. And now, since Chando's injuries, revenge is all he and his son want. I'm afraid that no amount of goodwill on your part will be able to change that."

"So what are they going to do? And what can we do?" Pedí and Adací asked at the same time.

No one had an answer.

The day the casts came off all the fractures, a crowd gathered at the infirmary to celebrate the occasion. The sages, Pedí's mother, Larada, Edero, Adací's parents, and even Pito had come. Heila and Niala were there, too. And, of course, Doctor Arias was there as he was the one who inspected each healed fracture. It was a happy day, but yet a fearful one. The captain's rumors about Adací and Pedí had only worsened, and Adací reminded them that Chando must also have recovered from his injuries—and thus be ready for revenge. Everyone seemed to sense an impending disaster.

Also, now that Adací and Pedí had recovered, they were ready to leave the Sanctuary, which offered some protection. But they could not hide there forever. Where could they go to be safe?

As they visited and tried to celebrate, Gabro asked Adací to tell them what happened that day in the orchard. "You haven't even told Pedí all of it. Everyone needs to know how you saved Pedí and what you learned about your dreams."

Adací consented and told of her struggle that day. "I thought my vision was the cause of Pedí falling into the chasm. I believed it was my fault—that I was going to kill him. But Jurana and Gabro convinced me that the vision was a chance for me to save Pedí, not harm him. They said the bad things in my dreams were not my fault and were only warnings of what may happen. I believe that now. The sages suggested I try and talk to my ancestors and get their help to save Pedí."

Adací described the rest of her experience in the Sanctuary orchard. When she told the part about seeing Mirela in the tree and telling her to rescue Pedí, Mirela smiled.

"I heard your words," the redhead said. "I thought it was the tree talking to me." The Itatu girl's eyes widened. "It was your voice at first, but then I heard other voices. They helped me find the way to the ledge."

"It was my mama and the ancient Adací. I asked them to guide you."

"So, that was the voices you heard and how you saved me," Pedí said. "You both saved me." Tears flowed down his cheeks. "Thank you, Adací. Thank you, Mirela. I owe my life to you both, not just once, but many times."

When Adací finished the rest of the story, Sergol spoke to her. "Your dreams are wonderful."

"I thought you didn't believe in my dreams. You used to scoff at them."

"I was wrong. But I have a question for you. No one seems to know what you and Pedí should do. But I see something in your face. You've had another dream, haven't you? You know what you're supposed to do but are afraid to tell us because it will make us sad."

"I thought so!" Larada exclaimed. "I saw that look on her face, too. You're leaving us, aren't you?"

Adací bowed her head but gave a short nod.

"Please tell us what you saw," Marina asked. "We will try to bear it."

Adací asked for Pedí, Mirela, and Pedí's mother to come close to her. "These three already know my vision. They are going with me."

Adací paused to wipe a tear from her eye. "I'm starting to dream all the time again like I used to do before my head injury. I don't even need the jade stones, though they help my visions be clearer. Lately, the Blue Dragonfly has been coming in a dream every night. I see him leading four people—a young woman, a young man, a redheaded girl, and a beautiful lady on a long journey. The dragonfly comes from time to time to show them the way, but they will face many difficulties and obstacles. They are on their way to Rowai-ra. A people in need waits for them and prays for them to come."

"Then you have to go there," Marina said, her voice choking.

"I agree," Sergol said.

Adací had never seen her father cry, but tears began flowing down Sergol's cheeks.

"But Papa! But Mama! You have given so much to me. You planned all your lives for me to be married in the nobility, where I could continue to be a part of your lives. I don't know what will happen to us in Rowai-ra and if we will ever return."

"It will break our hearts," Marina choked out the words, "but it is the right thing. Your birth mama and papa brought you to us to raise you for them. They would want you to follow your dreams. But would they be happy with how we've brought you up? I know we've made many mistakes."

"No, you haven't! No one could have had better parents," Adací was now in tears herself, joining her father in his sobs. The adopted daughter and adoptive parents hugged each other in a tight circle.

When the embrace finally broke up, Pito came to Adací and squeezed her. "What am I going to do without my swearing companion?" He covered his eyes and left the room.

Larada, Edero, Niala, Heila, and the two sages were next. They each hugged Adací and then all of the other future travelers.

Doctor Arias watched from the side. "When are you going?" he asked.

"We waited for our casts to come off," Pedí said, "and will leave in a week or two, as soon as we get supplies ready."

Pedí picked up an empty medicine container left in the room where they were meeting. It was one that used to contain his pulverized mushrooms. "Before we go, I need to review the nanimoha with the healers using it. They keep coming to me with questions, but when I'm not here, they'll have to make the correct decisions on their own."

After Pedí returned from the jungles, Doctor Arias selected a few of the healers to be taught by Pedí how to use his special mushroom. Also, two young healers were chosen to be the only ones to know where the secret meadow was located and were taught how to collect and prepare the little toadstools for use.

Pedí continued. "I'll try to review everything about the nanimoha with those using it before we leave. And I hope you don't mind if I take a good supply of it with us. I suspect we may need it."

Doctor Arias nodded. "Please! Take as much as you wish. It's all yours anyway. And thank you for helping us use it. Because of your mushroom, we've cured quite a few people with infections."

After saying that, the doctor removed his glasses, rubbed his eyes, and looked out the window.

"What is it?" Pedí asked him.

"The captain's spies are watching the Sanctuary. How will you get away without them seeing you?"

"We'll go at night. I know a secret way through the orchard. I think we can get away without being discovered."

"Tell me the day you'll be leaving," Sergol said, trying hard to choke back his tears, "and I'll have four horses ready for you. They'll be saddled and supplied with food and travel gear."

He paused to look at Adací. "One of the horses will be Suza. But don't come to our house to get them, as the captain could also be watching for you to come home. Pito and I will take the horses to the south fields and hide them in the wind shelter."

"Thank you, Papa," Adací got the words out despite her continued sobbing. "But we may never be able to return the horses."

"That's okay. This is the most significant thing my horses have ever done."

When all the visitors were gone, Adací asked Pedí, his mother, and Mirela to come to her room. She shut the door. "There's something I haven't told you about in my new dream. The six evil spirits from my nightmare in the orchard come during part of the vision. They summon the warriors who wear the skull masks over their faces. Those warriors begin hunting for us. It's a terrible part of the dream, and though I hope it doesn't come true, I suspect we may have to face those same masked warriors who tried to kill my birth mama and papa. I wanted you to know and to be prepared for the worst."

CHAPTER SEVENTY-EIGHT

Orange Thrushes

The following day, Davi Gonço came early to the Sanctuary seeking Doctor Arias. "Have you seen the signs?" the captain's butler asked the doctor. "They're all over town."

Davi told Doctor Arias that during the night, the captain's men had placed signs with drawings of Adací's face and Pedí's face on trees and walls throughout the city. Beneath their likenesses was written: *The new Idonata witch queen and her Shushuhador are a danger to everyone in New Losobon. They should be judged and executed not just for attacking Chando Borgesso but for the safety of the entire community.*

"I found out what they have planned," Davi said, "The captain has been secretly gathering agitators who have no fear of storming the Sanctuary if it means they can capture and kill the new Idonata witch and her Shushuhador."

Davi shook his head before continuing. "The captain will deny he had anything to do with these crazy signs. He wants an excuse for what's about to happen and will blame the attack on those who put the pictures on the walls and trees."

"We've been expecting something like this to happen," Doctor Arias said. "Why have they waited until now?"

"That's the strange thing," Davi answered. "They waited for Chando to recover enough to go with the angry mob. He insisted on it. I'm not sure what excuse they'll make if he's seen as a part of the crime. But I suspect they'll all wear masks."

"When are they coming?" the doctor asked.

"I'm guessing tomorrow!" Davi said it loudly. "That's when the captain is sending most of the police and soldiers to Victory Harbor on some feigned errand. There will be no one around to stop the rabble from attacking the Sanctuary and killing Adací and Pedí. The perpetrators will escape to their homes without anyone knowing who did it."

When Pedí and Adací learned of the impending attack on the Sanctuary, they decided they would need to leave that very night. Pedí met with the healers a final time to discuss using the nanimoha correctly. He also gathered a supply of mushrooms to take with him. Adací sent a runner to tell her father that they would need the four horses and the supplies brought to the wind shelter in the south fields by nightfall so they'd be there for their escape.

That afternoon, Pedí, Adací, Mirela, and Pedí's mother crowded onto the sandstone bench in the courtyard to make their final plans. They would leave for Rowai-ra when all was dark. Pedí explained how they would steal through the Sanctuary orchard and then go into the west fields and plantations to escape detection. They would then circle the city by going south and east through the farmer's fields and groves of trees until they reached the wind shelter in the fields belonging to Adací's parents. Once on the horses, they would find the old trail to Itatu that Adací had followed when she went after Pedí.

While talking, a bird's song interrupted. In a tree nearby, a pair of orange thrushes sang to each other. They all took a deep breath, the melodious sounds relieving, at least for a moment, the tension and worry they were facing.

Adací picked Mirela up, and they both sang and mimicked the music of the thrushes. Adací had taught Mirela how to do it. The little Itatu girl's red hair rested against Adací's chest as they followed the singing thrushes to the other side of the tree. Pedí watched the two girls. His family consisted of himself, his mother, and now Mirela. Would Adací one day be a part of it too?

Pedí wondered if his grandpa was observing them from the other world. *"You were right, Grandpa,"* Pedí would say to him. *"I'm a Shushuhador, after all! And Adací is our new queen, the leader of all the Idonata. Together, we'll escape from New Losobon and find our lost people."*

Pedí thought about how the Moon Goddess had given each of them something special, a gift to share with others. Pedí's gift was being a healer and communicating with wild things. Mama's was her kind spirit and knowledge of the Idonata ways. Adací's gift was her fierce courage, tenacity, and dreams that guided her to help others. She would be the perfect queen of his people. And even little girls with sheep shear knives had something unique and special to offer the world.

Acknowledgments

I want to thank my wonderful wife for her support and patience in this ten year writing process. Despite her suffering from difficult illnesses, she is always there for me. She says in jest—but I'm not sure she's really joking—that my best friends are the fantasy ones I write about. She also claims I'm too much like my male protagonist—strange, nerdy, and more comfortable talking to the gopher snake I found while biking today, than I am to people.

My manuscript was written and rewritten a hundred times. I got help at writing conferences and from several different editors with early drafts. Of those who helped, I want to single out Sarah Newcomb. She was my last editor, and is Native American—a member of the Tsimshian tribe. Sarah did sensitivity reads and had many excellent suggestions for my writing. She was the greatest! *Blue Dragonfly* is so much better because of her edits and comments.

I also want to thank the insects, frogs, and snakes that have been a part of my life. I'm not sure I should thank the parasites and infectious diseases which I included in this book, but I have to acknowledge my fascination with all of nature, good and bad, in our complex and beautiful world.

Author Page

Joseph Bingham grew up near an irrigation ditch full of frogs and snakes. He began catching and studying them at a young age. An old cabinet in his basement study was filled with cigar boxes that housed his pinned insect collection. That's also where he kept a cheap microscope with which he studied protozoa—one celled animals which he grew in bottles full of stinky pond water. The top of his desk was decorated with an empty peanut butter jar which held his pet black widow spider. He fed the spider on hornets which regularly found their way into the makeshift study through a gap in the window.

Joseph's reading included any book he could find on nature, but especially reptiles, amphibians, insects, and dinosaurs. As a young teenager, he read *White Waters and Black*, the story of a scientific team who explored the Amazon basin in the early 1920's, and he fell in love with South America. He lived in Brazil for several years and speaks Portuguese. In his medical practice as a family physician in Sioux City, Iowa, he organized a program to help with prenatal care and do all the baby deliveries for the Winnebago and Omaha Indian Reservations which were just over the border in Nebraska. He was later able to get additional training in tropical medicine. He went on five different medical trips to the Amazon and to Ethiopia. *Blue Dragonfly* gave him the opportunity to use all of his interests within the story of Pedí and Adací.

Joseph began his writing journey ten years ago after retirement, and lives now with his wife on the central coast of California. There, in his own yard, he is able to find fence lizards, striped racer snakes, and many insect friends. He shares his stories and love for nature with his three sons and his grandchildren.

www.ingramcontent.com/pod-product-compliance
Lightning Source LLC
Chambersburg PA
CBHW051254130726
47987CB00004B/1528